PRAISE FOR CHRISTI CALDWELL

"Christi Caldwell writes a gorgeous book!"
—*New York Times* bestselling author Sarah MacLean

"A Christi Caldwell book never fails to touch the heart!"
—*New York Times* bestselling author Tessa Dare

"Sizzling, witty, passionate . . . perfect!"
—*New York Times* bestselling author Eloisa James

"Christi Caldwell is a must read!"
—*New York Times* bestselling author Mary Balogh

"Romance worth swooning over!"
—*New York Times* bestselling author Grace Burrowes

Along Came a Lady

CHRISTI CALDWELL

JOVE
New York

A JOVE BOOK
Published by Berkley
An imprint of Penguin Random House LLC
penguinrandomhouse.com

Copyright © 2021 by Christi Caldwell

ISBN: 9780593334911

First Edition: August 2021

Printed in the United States of America
1 3 5 7 9 10 8 6 4 2

Book design by George Towne

For Doug,
who reminded me all the best heroes
enjoy time in the kitchen.

Prologue

Rafe Audley hated the Duke of Bentley.

It was a particularly strong sentiment, given that Rafe had never met the powerful peer, even once, in his thirteen years on this earth.

Rafe, however, didn't need to meet the man who'd given him life to know that death was too good for the ruthless lord.

Screams rent the tiny cottage, and Rafe's fingers twitched from the need to clamp them over his ears. To drown out the sounds of that misery and suffering.

Except that would be the coward's way, and Rafe was many things: a bastard, a fighter, when he needed to be. But he was no coward.

Nay, a coward was the manner of man who'd get a woman with child again and again and again . . . and know nothing of it. It didn't matter that Mama had defended the duke's ignorance, explaining she'd not wanted him to know. A real man knew where he was spreading his seed, and took ownership of his responsibilities, as the duke had failed to do for his three—about to be four—children.

Rafe's lips twisted in a bitter smile. But then, would an

all-powerful duke truly see his bastards as children? He would actually have to pay a visit and be part of his children's lives. Otherwise, he was nothing more than a stranger.

Another piercing cry split the otherwise quiet night.

Moisture dotted Rafe's brow and slicked his palms.

"*Jesssssusss.*"

Did that high-pitched plea belong to Rafe, or his mother on the other side of that door panel? Since she'd begun laboring ten hours earlier, everything had been jumbled in his mind.

Rafe began to pace.

This wasn't the first time his mother had given birth. Nor, given the state of her relationship with Bentley, would it be her last. Off she'd go, spending months on end in London with the duke, while Rafe looked after his brothers; eventually she returned. Whenever she had a babe in her belly, that was when she sought to hide from her cherished protector.

And yet, with Rafe waiting outside, as he'd done before, this night felt altogether different than the previous times.

This time, the thick summer air hung heavy and ominous. Even from where he waited, the stench of sweat permeated the room and spilled out into the narrow hall where Rafe stood.

So why did it *feel* different?

For all the similarities, something in this moment . . . felt a sea apart from the last times she'd gone into labor.

"Stop it," he whispered to himself, needing to hear any voice other than the weak one—growing increasingly weaker—on the other side of the oak slab.

She will be fine. She had to be. Why . . . she always was. She'd scream and cry and plead with God, as she'd done struggling to bring his younger brother Hunter into the world. And then there'd come the cry of a newborn. And after that, she'd smile tiredly up at Rafe when he stormed into the room to verify with his own eyes that she was alive and well—still.

Then . . . then, they'd resume their lives. Until Mother left, and Rafe had three siblings to look after.

And then what happened? They began this same hellish process—*again*.

A burning rage coursed through Rafe, a volatile force that sent his hands curling into fists. Had the Duke of Bentley walked through this modest cottage the monster paid for, Rafe would have gleefully and viciously beat him to death for what he'd done.

"Rafe . . . is everything all right?"

He spun about. "Wesley," he said blankly, "you are awake." But then, could anyone sleep through what their mother now endured?

His younger brother tugged at his sleeve. "What is happening?"

He strangled a sob, needing to give it life, but even more, determined to be the person his brother needed him to be. "Nothing." Which wasn't far from the truth. Mother's inability to birth the babe was what accounted for her suffering even now.

And where there was usually a challenge in the stubborn boy's gaze . . . indecision, the likes of which Rafe had never before seen from him, radiated from his brother's eyes. "Is she going to be a-all right?" There was the faintest of quivers to that whisper.

"Wasn't she fine with me? And you, and Hunter?" Rafe hedged. "Why should this time be any different?" *Why? Whyyyyy?* That silent scream pealed around his mind, a mantra born of agony and fear.

Wesley smiled. "You are right." His grin instantly faded to a scowl. "Don't let it go to your head."

Rafe inclined his head. "You wouldn't let me." He softened that with a wink.

"You're right, big brother," he said, and yet, still Wesley lingered.

Rafe firmed his mouth, knowing what was coming.

"Perhaps we should write him?" Wesley suggested.

"No."

"I know Mama would not wish it, but if he knew, then he might—"

"I said 'no,'" Rafe growled, his voice harsh, and he immediately regretted that outburst, as his younger brother's shoulders sagged.

"Fine," Wesley mumbled, and then quit Rafe's side, returning to the room he and Hunter shared.

The moment Wesley had gone, his mother's sobs renewed with force, sparing Rafe from guilt and plunging him headfirst into terror. "I cannnnnnn't. I *cannnnnn't.*"

And where, in the past, there'd been a steady assurance from the same midwife who'd delivered Rafe, Wesley, and Hunter, a confidence-infused voice from the sturdy old woman . . . now, there was none. There was nothing beyond Mama's cries.

I cannot take it.

Rafe clamped his hands over his ears, muting everything. He focused on that ringing behind his palms, not unlike those times he and his brothers competed to see who could stay submerged the longest.

And then he registered it—silence. Lowering his arms, Rafe said a silent prayer of thanks.

Only . . . this quiet wasn't like the two times prior. Nay, it was thick and heavy and hung in the air, twining with the echo in his mind of Mama's shouts.

Please. Please, say something.

Someone—

The door opened a fraction, and Rafe surged forward.

The midwife, Hazel, who'd delivered Rafe and his siblings after him, stepped out, and Rafe froze in his tracks.

Because he knew.

He knew even with no words spoken, from an innate understanding that could only come from deep inside life and death—that this moment was born of the latter.

The old woman pushed the door open a smidge more, allowing him a greater look into those small chambers. If he wanted that look. Which he didn't. He didn't want any part of that room.

Rafe gave his head a shake. "I'm not going in there," he

snarled. Ever. Because the moment he stepped across the threshold, all of this became real. And he wasn't ready for it. Mayhap he'd never be.

The midwife nodded.

"No," he clipped that word out past his clenched teeth.

She dusted her hands together. "Your mother would have wanted that."

Wanted. As in, a moment from the past. Two little letters that confirmed his every fear and first suspicion.

Emotion wadded in his throat, and he choked on it.

"Come," she urged, and put a hand out.

If she'd been weeping, he'd have turned on his heel and taken off down the corridor. But she wasn't. She was steady and sure in ways Rafe wasn't, and never would be again, and it gave him the strength to follow her.

The pungent odor of sweat and blood permeated the air; it stung his nostrils and turned his stomach. And somehow, he found himself moving forward, following Midwife Hazel.

They reached the side of Mama's bed.

Not bringing himself to look at her, Rafe stared down at the tips of his scuffed boots. Tears pricked his eyes, and he dashed a hand angrily at them.

"Do you know the last thing your mother said before . . ."

"She didn't do anything but cry," he spat angrily. How dare she? How dare she have chosen *him*. She'd abandoned Rafe, Wesley, and Hunter . . . and for what . . . ? So that she might bring another babe that they couldn't afford into this world?

"That isn't true. Her voice was weak. You likely wouldn't have heard it," the midwife murmured.

And certainly not with your ears covered, a voice silently jibed. *And you were covering your ears through it.*

The old white-haired woman looked to the young maid across the room, a girl cradling a babe.

The babe who'd claimed Mama's life.

Hatred singed his veins.

"Don't look at her like that," the midwife said tersely.

Her.

A girl.

What the hell were he and Wesley and Hunter going to do with a damned girl, without a mother?

"I'm not looking at her," he spat. And he resented that he'd have to ever look at her . . . or after her . . . again.

"You had your mama thirteen years. Your sister's never known her even a minute," the same woman who'd birthed him and his siblings after him chided.

Rafe's chest constricted, and he stared with stricken eyes at his newest sibling.

"The babe is going to need you," Hazel said in a low voice. "She's going to need l-love." It was the first crack in the woman's composure. She glanced away, and when she looked back, she was once more collected. "Your resentment is misplaced. You know where it belongs . . . and it ain't on that babe."

The Duke of Bentley.

"Aye, that is right. The man who got her with child is the one deserving of your hatred, but you can't have two equally powerful emotions. They cancel one another out."

Confused, he shook his head. "I don't understand."

"Someday you will," she said, and gave no further explanation. "Your mother asked that you look after your siblings. That you be the parent they won't have." A muscle rippled in his jaw, and feeling the midwife's eyes on him, he glanced away from his mother's dead body, and down at the old woman as she asked, "Are you able to do that? It is a tremendous responsibility for a young man."

"There isn't any other choice, though, is there," he said, bitterness twisting around his words.

"You always have a choice, my boy."

And with that, she called the maid over. The young woman placed the tiny babe in his arms.

Her body was so slight, and yet, there was something steadying in the feel of her against him.

He wanted to hate her . . . and yet . . .

Rafe swallowed.

He could not.

And in that moment, holding his sister close, Rafe made a vow—he'd never become his mother, putting love before those he was responsible for.

And as sure as his mother lay lifeless before him, the duke was dead to Rafe now and forever.

Chapter 1

In the many years she'd been working as an instructor in etiquette, Miss Edwina Dalrymple had advised everyone from the daughters of powerful members of the gentry to the daughters of obscenely wealthy merchants.

She'd taught women who'd not so much as attempted a curtsy in their life the intricate and essential motions they required among the previously unfamiliar Polite Society.

She'd written articles offering advice to young women new to the *ton*.

She'd even written—although not sold so very many copies of—a manual with her instructions and advice meticulously laid out.

In all the time she'd worked in her respective positions, however, she'd never entertained . . . a duke and duchess.

Though, in fairness, there wasn't an overabundance of those highest of peers below a prince.

Even if there had been, however, they'd certainly never sought to enlist her services.

Or they hadn't before now.

At that very moment, the Duke and Duchess of Bentley stared across Edwina's modest chestnut table. Etched upon their faces were matched expressions of austere confidence and regal power. It was a skill they'd likely perfected in their respective nurseries, and one Edwina had schooled countless students on. And the duke and duchess also represented the closest Edwina had ever found herself to the dream she'd long carried of working among their vaunted ranks.

Ten years. It had been ten years, nearly to the date, that she'd secured herself references that would set her on a course to be the most sought-after and, more importantly, most respected governess.

Folding her hands neatly before her, Edwina opted to train her focus on the Duke of Bentley. "You would like me to instruct your child." Because, really, the matter of that out-of-the-blue request required clarification. A duke and duchess seeking her services. Such an outrageous impossibility, one she'd only ever carried in her dreams. She discreetly pinched her thigh.

No, she was most definitely awake.

The duke nodded. "That is correct. However, he is not a . . . child in the traditional . . . sense."

Edwina sat up straighter on the upholstered armchair and waited for him to say more. "Your Grace?" she asked, seeking clarification.

The duchess silenced her husband with a single look, the manner of which Edwina had used sparingly, and only with her most recalcitrant charges, in order to preserve its effectiveness.

And wonder of wonders, it appeared even dukes could be tamed.

The just-graying gentleman adjusted his cravat and sat back in the sofa he occupied alongside his wife.

For the first time since they'd arrived and the duke had stated his intentions to hire Edwina, the duchess took command of the meeting. "We've come to enlist your services, Miss Dalrymple," Her Grace intoned. "And I gather, from your . . . response, you are wondering *why* we've requested you specifically." The gentleness in the duchess's tone kept that question from being an insult.

The duke frowned at his wife. "We do not mean to offend you . . ."

His wife gave him another look, this one a wry smile that proved just as effective in silencing him. "By everything I've read to you about her, the woman is clever enough to know. She knows that we're aware she's never had a patron among the peerage."

"That is correct," Edwina murmured, appreciating that directness and honesty. People of their station did not solicit her help. Unless they had to. "I have never had a client who was born to the peerage." Once that truth had stung. Edwina, however, in time, and with her work, had come to appreciate her lot for what it was—outside the sphere of the ruling elite. Despite the fact she'd been working her way to establish a place among them from the start. "As such, I must confess to . . . some surprise." And elation. Under her hem, Edwina danced her slippered feet about in a quiet, unseen celebration.

"We may not have had much success with previous instructors," the duke volunteered, and by the chastising look shot his way by his wife, too honestly this time.

Ah, he was desperate, then, and the duchess was determined to reveal no vulnerability. It mattered not. This represented her chance to prove to her father that she was completely capable of moving among his equals. And perhaps . . . even then, earn, if not his love, respect.

"She is going to have to know something of it," the duke said.

Edwina's intrigue redoubled.

And the older woman might have whispered something that sounded very much like, "You're the one responsible for your actions, dear heart."

Had they been attempting to rouse her intrigue, they couldn't have done any better than they were with their sotto voce exchange.

The duke slumped in his chair, giving him the look of a naughty charge. "Get on with it, then."

They were a fascinating, if peculiar, pair. One that fit not at all with the image society pedaled of dukes and duchesses, and yet, mayhap it was that elevated rank that allowed them that freedom of expression.

Her Grace looked to Edwina. "Until recently . . . *very* recently, His Grace had something of a . . . reputation."

"Most gentlemen do," Edwina said pragmatically. It didn't make it right, or anything she wished for her charges' future, but it *did* make it accepted by Polite Society.

"Not like this, Miss Dalrymple. Not. Like. This," the Duchess of Bentley said.

"She hardly requires all the details," the duke muttered.

His wife cupped a palm around her mouth, concealing it from her husband. "He was quite the rogue, really."

Again, most men were.

"I hear you, dear," he groused.

His wife, however, wasn't done with him. "In your mind you have likely conjured rogues and rakes and scoundrels, Miss Dalrymple. My husband would have put them all to shame with the depth of his depravity."

Edwina's mouth moved, but no words came out.

"How many other governesses have you come to before approaching me?" she asked, curious.

"Does it matter either way for our discussion?" the duchess returned.

Edwina considered that question a moment. "No," she allowed. "I suppose it does not." Only in the sense that it would provide her an indication of just how difficult an assignment she was taking on. Nor could there be any doubting or disputing that she was taking it regardless. This represented her first, and perhaps only, chance to gain entry into a clientele previously beyond her grasp.

"As I was saying, we've attempted to enlist the services of others. But governess after governess has refused us. First for the reason of my husband's past as a rogue"—and his not-too-distant one, at that—"and then, there is, of course, the matter of his children."

"She doesn't require details, dear heart," the duke mumbled, a blush on his cheeks. He wrestled with his cravat.

His Grace needn't have even bothered wasting his breath. The duchess would not be silenced. "Until our marriage, just six months ago." The stunningly regal woman leaned forward. "I assure you, my dear, had we been married some years earlier, the duke would not find himself in the very predicament he does now." And in a very unduchesslike way, she winked.

And perhaps it was that unexpected realness from the woman that compelled Edwina to ask her next question. "What exactly is the predicament you speak of?"

"His reputation has been so terribly damaged that the governesses most highly recommended by our peers, well—"

"Won't work for me," the duke said, the color deepening on his cheeks. "I'm not nearly as bad as society has made me out to be."

His wife lifted an eyebrow in his direction.

"Anymore," he allowed. "It was my youth. My distant youth," he added. "Alas, the reputation . . . stuck."

At last, all the pieces of the puzzle were in their proper place, and the reason a duke and duchess wished to hire *Edwina* made sense. They'd not sought her out because they wished for her services. They'd sought her out because there was no one else who'd take on the assignment. Either way, her pride wasn't fragile; her determination to work among the peerage was far stronger.

His wife nodded. "Precisely. My husband has been making an attempt at a new beginning. He wants to . . ." She paused, and glanced at the duke. "Tell her."

"I want to make right my past, where I can." He made that avowal as if it was rote, committed to memory, and mayhap with the commanding woman he'd made his duchess, he'd been required to do so.

Edwina puzzled her brow. The Duke and Duchess of Bentley were only recently married. Which meant . . . Edwina went still.

"They are all bastards," the duke said quietly.

"Illegitimate," the duchess admonished. "They are illegitimate."

His Grace frowned. "They mean the same thing."

"Ah," the Duchess of Bentley said, putting up a single finger, "but one is vastly more polite than the other, and therefore, that is the descriptor we shall go with."

Aye, bastard . . . or illegitimate . . . They both meant the same. Edwina's stomach muscles clenched. Bastard-born herself, a secret that would have destroyed all hope of an honorable existence if revealed, she knew all too well society's opinion of people born outside wedlock. It was the very reason she'd crafted a new identity for herself and lived a life and lie of respectability. She'd carved out a respectable life. Yes, whichever polite word one wished to dress it up with, a child born out of wedlock was nothing more than a bastard, always searching for and never finding society's approval.

But if I can groom a young woman, the daughter of a duke, to take her place among Polite Society . . . What that would do for her business. This represented her entry to the *ton*—that sphere that had previously been closed to her. One she'd sought so very hard to infiltrate.

"There is just one more detail I might mention . . ." The duke's pronouncement went unfinished.

"It is my husband's eldest son."

A son?

And just like that, those eager musings were popped. Oh, blast and damn on Tuesday. "I do not have male charges."

"Correction, Miss Dalrymple." The duchess tipped her lips up in a perfectly measured little smile. "You didn't have them. It is our expectation that after today . . . you will."

How very confident they were that Edwina would simply accept the assignment, no matter how unconventional and outrageous it was. But then, to those of the peerage, the word "no" meant nothing. It was why they weren't incorrect in their assumption that she'd not reject the assignment they put to her outright.

"Oh, and there is just one more thing, Miss Dalrymple."

What else could it possibly be? "Yes, Your Grace?"

"My husband's son? He's no interest in the title, or . . . receiving our company. We've sent our man of affairs . . ."

"Solicitors," the duke put in.

"Investigators. All of them have had little success in securing a meeting."

Edwina puzzled her brow. "Are they unable to locate him?" she asked, perplexed. And how was she supposed to find the gentleman if others had not?

Husband and wife exchanged a glance.

"Oh, no. We currently know where he and his siblings reside. We'll need you to convince the eldest of the lot to join you in London and begin instruction," the duke said.

They were mad. "Me?" A small laugh escaped her. "You expect me, a stranger and a woman at that, one who has never met him, to not only convince him but bring him back to London."

The duchess beamed. "You've stated it all quite clearly."

"And just what makes you believe I shall succeed when you have both failed?"

It was a bold, if accidental, challenge to two of London's most influential peers, and by the like frowns marring their mouths, they chafed at it.

"The fact that you and he both stand to benefit, Miss Dalrymple. That is why I expect you to not only accept the undertaking, but convince him that returning to London and claiming his rightful place as a duke's son is an opportunity neither of you can afford to pass up. If you take on this endeavor and succeed? You'll be richly compensated," the duke vowed. "Five hundred pounds if you manage to convince him to return to London." Her heart jolted, and she choked on her swallow. "And another two thousand upon your completion of his . . . transformation."

Edwina choked again, hurriedly covering her mouth with a fist.

It was a veritable fortune for a woman reliant upon her own skills and work in order to survive. And yet, neither was it enough to see her set. Nay, ultimately, her reputation and her skill set were what Edwina relied upon and would continue to rely upon, regardless of what decision she made this day.

"But I can also promise you far more than that, Miss Dalrymple," the duchess murmured.

Edwina straightened and retrained her focus on the elegant woman across from her.

"Once you transform His Grace's son, Polite Society will see there is no charge you cannot transform." The older and very astute peeress had been wise enough, then, to grasp just how much Edwina's business . . . and reputation meant.

As such, they'd offered all they might to bring her 'round to accepting, and yet she'd not succeeded as she had in the world by not analyzing every situation from every possible angle. She eyed them carefully. "Given the importance of the undertaking, why do you not pay a visit to the gentleman yourself?" she asked, removing all inflection.

"My children don't wish to see me."

Was it merely a trick of the room's shadows responsible for the glint of sadness she detected in his eyes?

Pulling off her gloves, the duchess proceeded to slap those fine leather articles together. "And with good reason," the duchess muttered. "We trust you might be more capable of conveying the benefits of his stepping forward into his rightful role."

They'd cracked open a door, allowing her a peek inside a life that, even with her successes as an instructor, she'd been without—entry to Polite Society and their daughters . . . and the respectability that would elevate her business . . . and set her on a path to independence, the likes of which she'd never known. And that had only existed as a fanciful musing she'd stopped allowing herself. "Very well," she said, forcing calm, while inside giddiness threatened to overwhelm that weak facade. "I shall accept your assignment." Edwina silently tapped her toes about, once more in a private celebration.

"Splendid." The duchess took to her feet, and Edwina

quickly followed suit. Her Grace fished a small stack from within her cloak and placed a heavy packet atop Edwina's desk. "The details we've been able to gather about his sons, Miss Dalrymple, are in there."

Edwina picked up the packet and studied it a moment, as her newly acquired employers started for the door. "Staffordshire?" she asked, picking her head up.

The pair paused briefly. "Oh, we might not have mentioned before . . . Rafe . . . ? He is a coalfield miner." With that, the couple let themselves out.

A coalfield . . . miner?

She choked. That was why the most elite instructors had declined the duke and duchess's request: not because of His Grace's wicked past, but because of his son's rough existence.

She'd agreed to the task of teaching a thirty-one-year-old coal miner how to conduct himself among Polite Society. That is, after she convinced him to accompany her back to London so he might claim a place among the *ton*.

"How difficult can it be to convince a miner to accept the wealth and lands awaiting him?" she murmured.

Nay, the greater difficulty lay in transforming a piece of coal into a diamond that sparkled.

Chapter 2

Greed and arrogance made men do and say stupid things. Nor could there be any doubting that the small-pit owner, W. M. Sparrow, possessed both in spades.

Rafe Audley, however, hadn't survived as long as he had in the Staffordshire mines by taking the bait of the more powerful colliers.

"I'll tell you what I told him, Audley. It's poor quality. You know that. And I won't give him a pence more." The greedy old bastard who owned the Cheadle coalfields dipped his pen in a crystal inkwell and made several annotations in his ledger. "I suggest you advise he take it before I pay him what it's really worth." With his spare hand, the collier pushed the small bag of coin across the desk. "Pfft. With the amount of slack in his latest delivery, it's a wonder I didn't fine him."

Behind him, Rafe felt Hunter, his youngest brother, surge forward. "You bastard," Hunter hissed between his teeth.

Shooting him a hard look, Rafe held up a staying hand.

Rage flashed in the younger man's eyes. Irate since the moment he'd come screaming into the world, in matters of business and in life, Hunter only knew varying degrees of recklessness. This time, however, Rafe's sibling managed to restrain himself.

Rafe refocused all his attention on Sparrow. "There is nothing wrong with that coal, and you know it," he said coolly.

And those crisp tones managed to penetrate the other man's previous indifference. The collier finally glanced up. The man, who'd gone fat on the efforts of the men, women, and children who sacrificed themselves underground in the name of their survival and his fortune, went pale. His heavy jowls jiggled under the force of his swallow.

Aye, Sparrow might be a man of power in these parts, but he was also nothing without Audley's efforts . . . and he knew that, too.

"Now, Audley," the other man began in placating tones. "You know I'm fair. You know I've only been fair."

Rafe flashed a hard, mirth-free grin. "Ah, but I don't know any such thing, Sparrow. I know you don't hesitate to withhold a man's rightful earnings." He'd tried it once when Rafe had been more boy than man. It was a mistake the collier hadn't made again where Rafe was concerned. "I know you falsify reports on the quality of the coal."

Sparrow adjusted his cravat. "But I haven't done it with your family."

"No," Rafe allowed, "you haven't in the past." Because skilled as he'd been as a miner, Rafe had climbed up the ranks to the role of Butty—the one who found and employed the workers who provided Sparrow with his coal. And in turn, all miners involved enjoyed fine wages under Rafe's supervision. Pressing his coal-stained palms on the surface of the collier's desk, Rafe leaned in. "You have now, though."

"Damned right he has." Hunter spat on the collier's floor. "The bloody bastard."

Sparrow slammed a meaty fist down hard on the desk, rattling the crystal inkwell. "Get him out. I've been patient enough, not turning him out the moment he stepped through the door with you, Audley." He pointed a finger Rafe's way. "I deal with you so I don't have to deal with those uncouth others."

"'Uncouth others' am I." Hunter spat once more; this time the wad landed at the foot of old Sparrow's desk.

"That is precisely what you are." Sparrow tugged at his lapels.

"Wait outside, Hunter," Rafe said, his gaze trained on Sparrow's.

His brother tensed, but he knew better. Everyone—his family included—knew better than to challenge Rafe . . . and certainly never before an audience.

The moment Hunter had gone, Sparrow came out from behind his desk. "You need to do something about that one," he said, as he made his way to the sideboard filled with crystal bottles. "He could stand to learn a thing from your other brother. Where Hunter's concerned, I've put up with more than I should because of our work together, Audley, but my patience and goodwill only go so far," he warned, selecting a decanter of brandy.

Rafe scoffed. "Let us not pretend you're capable of either patience or goodwill, Sparrow. The only exceptions you make are when you stand to profit, and you know as well as I . . . you've profited mightily from Hunter's work. And Wesley's." He leveled a look at him. "And mine."

"There's always other workers—miners stronger, younger, and less damaged—who might take their places."

Their places. Not "your" place.

Rafe remained deliberately silent while the other man returned to his desk with his drink in hand.

Sparrow wasn't so much a fool that he didn't realize the greatness he'd attained in the mines of Staffordshire was due to Rafe and the team of men, women, and children he'd assembled. Mayhap that would be enough for another man. But Rafe's loyalty to Wesley, Hunter, and Cailin was the same as it had been when they'd been babes and he was their surrogate father. Even with Wesley having left, and quit their family as he had, in search of a greater life.

"Returning to Hunter's coal," he said as Sparrow took another swallow of that amber brew. "I'm not going to debate you on the quality. I can haul a bucket full and pour it on your desk and lecture you on just why it's good. You're not going to find any slack in there. Not Hunter's. Not any of my men."

Sparrow compressed his fleshy lips into a line. "Fine," the collier snapped. Yanking out the middle desk drawer, he drew out two purses and tossed them down. "One coin. One token."

They hit the surface with a noisy clink.

Tokens to be used in Sparrow's shop. That compromise in coal payment was just another way colliers stuffed their pockets at the expense of the people who worked for them. "He doesn't want—"

"He's getting tokens," Sparrow said, and gave Rafe a warning look.

A man in the mines needed to become an expert at assessing a situation and knowing when to retreat, or stay and fight. As such, Rafe knew he'd already secured far more than Sparrow had anticipated or intended to give.

He grabbed the bags up. "Don't let this happen with my brother again. Are we clear?"

Sparrow gave a jerky nod. "Audley."

Stalking from the collier's offices, he found his brother pacing a path on the graveled drive.

The moment he caught sight of Rafe, he abruptly stopped and shifted course, kicking up dirt and rock as he went. "What—?"

"Here." Rafe tossed the coins and tokens at his brother.

Catching them, the younger man weighed them in his palm. "Damned tokens?" he hissed, not needing to check. But then, one with his skill in measurements wouldn't need a visual confirmation to know he'd been given two different forms of *currency*.

"It's a compromise," Rafe said out the corner of his mouth as they started back toward the cottage they kept, halfway between the mines and Sparrow's offices.

"A bloody compromise?" His brother unleashed a stream of vitriolic curses. But he did pocket his earnings. The Audleys were proud, but they weren't fools when it came to surviving. Hunter managed to keep pace with Rafe despite the injury he'd sustained ten years ago in an old mine collapse. "One-hundred and fifty fucking feet he has us going down," Rafe's younger brother muttered. "He's got more damned roof collapses and explosions and he's still the most blasted profitable and he's going to cheat me."

They reached the modest quarters afforded to Rafe because of his role as Butty. Rafe stopped at the small walkway leading into the cottage. Mindful of his sister inside, he lowered his voice. "The wages are still higher than you're going to earn from any other collier."

"And you think that makes it all right?" Hunter demanded, slashing a hand angrily through the air as he spoke.

"I think it's the best you or any other miner could hope for." Rafe spoke with a matter-of-fact understanding of the way the world worked, and the way it would always work. His brother had simply failed to accept that just because something was unfair didn't mean anyone would ever make it right.

"He's becoming increasingly greedy, and the conditions are worsening."

"The conditions have always been bad," Rafe shot back, unable to keep the defensive thread from underscoring his retort. Ultimately, as Butty, Rafe was the one who supplied the miners and tools, and had ownership of what happened to the people he employed. His work was about more than the coin he earned or the rank he enjoyed; it was about the people who earned their livelihoods because of him.

Hunter ground his feet to a stop; his boot kicked up dirt and gravel. "You're making excuses for Sparrow and you know it."

"I'm not. I know precisely what the situation is down there."

Hunter stuck his face in Rafe's. "But you don't go down there," he snarled. "Not daily," he corrected. "And not the way the rest of us do."

Almost ten years in his current role had prepared Rafe to deal with agitated workers. There was no exception in how he handled those outbursts from Wesley and Hunter simply because they were his brothers. They shared blood, but they also shared a craft. As such, Rafe kept his face a careful mask, refusing to give in to the fight his brother was spoiling for. "I spent more than fifteen years belowground," he said quietly. "Don't you talk to me about not knowing what it's like down there."

His brother wouldn't be deterred. "The ventilation isn't what it was when you were down there daily. We're going deeper and the quality of the air isn't the same, and certainly not for the pittance Sparrow would give us." Angrily yanking one of the bags from inside his jacket, he shook it, and this time, as he railed, his voice climbed in volume. "And certainly not for goddamned tokens to be used at a store that bastard owns, and charges us exorbitant prices in."

Their sister appeared in the window; pressing her nose against the lead pane, she shifted her gaze between the quarreling brothers. With her golden curls and rounded cheeks, she was a vision of their mother from years ago . . . and the look of disapproval she cast their way may as well have been a trait passed down along with her coloring and form.

"I've heard you and your concerns," Rafe said, using those even tones and the words he reserved for the surliest miner.

Hunter glared at him. "Fuck you with your foreman-talk. I'm your damned brother, not any miner collecting tools from you." With that, Hunter stalked off. But then, he abruptly stopped and whipped about to face Rafe. "I don't mind hard work. I enjoy what I do. But I'll be damned if you don't at least acknowledge the conditions have changed and hold Sparrow to higher wages for it."

"Hunter?" he called when his youngest brother made to go.

Hunter stiffened.

"If you've tired of mining, there are other roles I can assign you."

Because ultimately, Rafe knew, despite whatever grievances his brother had, and despite the frustration and anger he carried about the wages or the conditions, he reveled in the work he did. That pride had only magnified after the accident that had nearly cost Hunter his leg.

Fury filled the younger man's flinty gaze. Without another word, Hunter left.

From the corner of his eye, Rafe caught the flutter of curtains as Cailin let them fall back into place. She'd always been rubbish when it came to eavesdropping, and now, at almost eighteen years of age, she never really made much of an effort to hide whenever she listened in.

Bold as the English day was wet and cold, she didn't allow anyone their secrets.

Cailin greeted him at the door as he entered. "He's not wrong, Rafe."

"I didn't say he was." Bloody hell, the debate was to continue then, this time with his sister . . . who'd always had a greater bond with his youngest, angriest brother.

"You all but did."

Of all his stubborn siblings, she'd always gone toe to toe with him the most. Which was saying a good deal, given the obstinate blighters their brothers were. "Times are not what they were." He struggled out of his boots and cast them onto the floor. "We all have to be mindful of that."

"Do you think I need to be reminded of that?" Cailin's eyes formed narrow slits upon him.

There was a warning there. A familiar one.

Rafe was careful to keep his features even. "I wouldn't dream of it." At the very least he knew when not to prod her.

His sister snorted. And fortunately, this time, this Audley let the matter go—for now.

"Another note arrived." Cailin plucked a note from inside her apron.

"Wesley?" he asked. His brother who'd gone off to fight a damned war because he thought he was better than the mines, because he wanted a future different than theirs. And whose letters had ceased to come with any real frequency.

"No."

Not Wesley. He stilled. Which meant it could only be the other person who'd made a habit of sending 'round *missives*.

"Burn it." He hung up first his hat and then his jacket on the hooks fastened near the entryway.

"I burned the others," she said.

"Then you should already know what to do without asking," he muttered, and headed to the kitchen. "Nothing more we need it for than kindling."

Tenacious as the Staffordshire day was long, Cailin followed close at his heels. "Oh, let us be clear. I *wasn't* asking what to do with it. Rather, I was telling you he'd sent another, and this one is different than the previous ones."

He paused briefly, and looked her squarely in the eye, with a directness that had made many a man tremble. But then, most men didn't have the gumption of his sister. "You suggested we burn the others," he pointed out.

"Yes, that is true. But I've . . . had some time to consider what he's asking."

"Don't give two damns what he's asking," he said, eager to let the matter rest. The "he" in question was none other than their *father* . . . or if one wished, the man who'd sired them. The Duke of Bentley had been no father to them. And Rafe had little interest—none, at all, to be exact—in appeasing some old lord who was trying to atone for sins that could never be forgiven.

He pushed the kitchen door open.

The scent of burned bread filled the room, and he made for the loaves set out on a white clay plate.

The moment his fingers touched one of the almost completely charred loaves, Cailin slapped at his fingers with that missive. "I'm trying to talk to you, and given you'd rather eat my burned bread, I know you're just trying to avoid it."

He perched his hip on the table. "Fine." Of all their siblings, Cailin had been most fascinated by the belated emergence of the duke in their lives and open to having him there. Nay, that wasn't altogether true. There had been Wesley, after all, who'd made contact first, informing Bentley of their existence and requesting a commission because of it. One that he'd granted. It was just one more reason to despise the man who'd sired them—for thrusting Wesley into a damned war, and driving a wedge between them. "Out with it." With his teeth, Rafe wrestled free a bite of bread, and attempted to chew his way through.

"I want to go to London."

Rafe promptly choked. And for the first time in all the years Cailin had taken on the baking and cooking, his inability to swallow the bread had nothing to do with it being inedible, and everything to do with—"Youuu?" he strangled out, when he could at last get a proper breath.

She nodded.

"The same sister who insisted he could go hang."

"I didn't say it in *quite* those terms," she said under her breath.

"'The only place I'd be happy to see him was in Tyburn, hanging from a gibbet'?" He reminded her of the time when they'd learned Wesley had gone and appealed to the duke for a commission. Back when he and Cailin had been on the same page. "Is that familiar?"

She wrinkled her nose. "Fair enough."

"Now, all of a sudden, you're of a different mindset?" He gave her a look.

"I know what you're thinking, Rafe."

They spoke at the same time.

"That you want to meet him."

"That I want to have him in my life. I don't. I don't," she repeated, a more strident quality to that denial. "It isn't about him. Not really. Staffordshire is small," she began in what was an all-too familiar argument.

"Small is safe."

"Do you really intend to tell me to my face that you believe I need protecting?"

No, she'd had a tendency to beat up the village boys

who'd been bullying some of the smaller, unkindly treated children in Cheadle.

"So you're willing to forget a lifetime of hatred for the man who sired us because you wish to explore London's culture?" he asked flatly.

"I've come to appreciate his tenacity, and he did help Wesley with his commission." She continued quickly, speaking over him when he would have interrupted with his own opinions on the duke's *generosity.* "And if I can explore some world away from this, then by God, I want to do it."

With his teeth, Rafe ripped off a corner of the loaf, or attempted to. "You've a sudden and inordinate fascination with the duke."

"With his methods," she countered, throwing a finger up. "*With his methods.* Fine fancy gentlemen, out of their element, coming here to implore you to grant a meeting."

Aye, because of course, a beast like Bentley couldn't be bothered to come out this way. Not that Rafe wanted him to. Not when he couldn't himself be sure that he could face the old duke without taking him apart with his hands. And it was certain that such a beating would be met with imprisonment . . . or worse, for a bastard like Rafe Audley.

Cailin set the note down in favor of a piece of bread, breaking her own rules for evening meals. "I must confess, after the last man you ran off, I thought that would put an end to the duke's efforts." Only if it had. Because then he wouldn't be dealing with the latest Audley who'd faltered, and now considered meeting the duke and the life he offered.

"I didn't kill him," he said. The duke's man of affairs had managed to walk off with his life. There was that.

His sister raised an eyebrow.

"I barely beat him." She crossed her arms. Oh, very well. "Not badly, anyway." And only because the fancy gent had, in his attempts to cajole Rafe, put an appeal to Cailin . . . and then attempted more.

"It was just an almost kiss," his sister said, exasperated

and perfectly following the path his thoughts had gone down.

Rafe gnashed his teeth. "There's no such thing as an 'almost kiss.'"

"Of course there is. There are the ones—"

He held up the blackened bread imploringly. "No. Absolutely not. I'm not discussing *that* with you."

She smiled widely; a dimple appeared in both her full cheeks. "Then we shall carry on with Bentley."

Cailin was the only one of the remaining Audley siblings still in Staffordshire to speak that title aloud. And it seemed as though she'd begun doing so with an increased frequency. "He sent his apologies."

"I don't care if he bends a knee and wants to put a damned knighthood to my name."

"And he promises he won't send any more gentlemen around."

That gave Rafe pause. After almost a year of turning out the unwanted visitors sent by that old scoundrel, he'd taken the damned hint.

Rafe managed his first smile that day.

His sister slapped the duke's latest missive against his arm. "You're biting off your nose to spite all our faces."

Rafe reached over and pinched the tip of her nose, much the way he'd done when she'd been a small girl. "Well, that doesn't make much sense," he said. "That, however, is a letter I'll take from the old duke."

No more missives. No more requests or unwanted gents paying calls and taking up time Rafe didn't have.

At last, he was done with the damned libertine who'd sired him.

It was done.

Chapter 3

Edwina despised the country.

Years earlier, as a young woman who'd left the village of Leeds, where the people had known precisely what she was and the circumstances of her residing there, she'd set out to build a new life for herself. That day, as she'd climbed aboard the mail coach, Edwina had vowed to never step foot outside London.

Nor had she looked back.

There'd been clients enough in London. Particularly because the gentry and men made into lords overnight had sought to shed their bucolic ways and clamored to be close to Town. From that moment on, she'd never set foot in any English countryside—until now.

All it had taken were the exorbitant funds dangled before her . . . and because there was, at last, the chance of proving herself before Polite Society, and expanding her name and reputation in ways that had previously eluded her.

Drawing back the curtain, Edwina peered out . . .

Though, in fairness, Leeds was nothing like Staffordshire. The land was a blend of two worlds; between green rolling hills and then industry marring the landscape, Staffordshire was a place that didn't know whether it wished to be countrified living or an industrial center. Having arrived in the small market town two days prior, with funds supplied by her employer, Edwina had set herself up at the local inn . . . and prepared for her first meeting with the duke's son . . . the same way she went into all meetings with her charges.

In that time, she'd also discreetly quizzed one of the innkeeper's daughters, who had proven most elucidating over many cups of tea. From her, Edwina had gathered the hours Rafe Audley kept: twelve-hour days that began at six o'clock. Where exactly in the mining village one might find him. And when to avoid him, too . . .

Because the gentleman was always working. Because his life was the mine.

And it had been that former revelation that had given Edwina the proverbial carrot she needed. For what she'd present to him, on behalf of the duke, was a way out.

As such, there was only one place that made sense to meet him.

With a frown, Edwina let the curtain slip from her fingers.

The duke's carriage rattled along; the road grew bumpier and the ride more uneven.

With one hand, Edwina caught and braced herself as she'd done so many times along the never-ending journey. In her other hand, she reread the already memorized notes His Grace had provided.

And then, the carriage rolled to a slow stop.

Her heart knocked hard against her chest.

They'd arrived.

She'd been so very focused on convincing the duke's son that she'd not allowed herself to think of actually meeting the gentleman. Or . . . being in this place. A coalfield village filled with people who would never take well to an interloper in their midst. It wouldn't be the first time she was treated as an outsider . . . and as such, she should be

immune to the rudeness invariably shown her. Even so, all
the muscles of her stomach knotted.

"Meet them with a smile." She spoke that motto aloud,
as a much-needed reminder to herself. "Meet them with a
smile."

The driver knocked once, and then opened the door. "I
cannot get closer than this, ma'am," he explained. Doffing his
hat, he wiped at a slightly damp brow. "The road ends here."

Edwina glanced past the crimson-clad servant. In the near
distance, people bustled about . . . men, women, and children,
all pushing equipment. Frantically rushing about. Noise filled
the countryside; shouting that all melded together, so that it
was a wonder any person might hear anything.

And worse, it would be a wonder if anyone managed to
find a person in that crowd.

Her heart dropped.

"Ma'am?" the driver urged.

Accepting his hand, she allowed him to help her down.
"I will return shortly."

Or so she hoped.

Gathering up her wool skirts, Edwina started forward.

At first, as engrossed as they were in their tasks, no one
paid her so much as a glance. The slight heels of her leather
slippers sank into the moist earth, and she struggled across
the uneven ground.

The closer she drew to the heart of activity, the more
notice she earned.

People paused in their work to gawk openly, their eyes
filled with suspicion.

That nauseated feeling in her stomach returned in full
force. *Meet them with a smile* . . .

Or . . . mayhap, this time, just focus on her assignment.
Edwina pushed her bonnet back. She kept her chin up and
continued her forward march.

All the while she scoured the area for Rafe Audley, foreman. Where was he? She'd imagined just one man above-
ground, while his workers toiled below. And certainly not

this veritable army of people at work. Children pushing carts filled with coal that a grown man should have struggled to move. Women, in dark-stained garments, physically operating the equipment above the mine shafts. And men preparing for their climb below.

People stared as she passed; however, no one bothered to question Edwina's presence. They all went about the tasks driving them.

And never had she been more grateful for the career she'd fashioned for herself. For all her reservations in coming here, it had been the right decision . . . to spring the duke's sons from such a fate.

Lifting her sealed parasol, she waved it at a small boy pushing a wheelbarrow. "Excuse me," Edwina called over the noise. "Little bo—" The child looked up, and Edwina missed a step.

It was a girl.

A very small one, at that.

Edwina quickly collected herself. She offered a gentle smile that had always managed to have a calming effect on her charges and their parents. This child proved no exception. She wheeled her cart to a stop before Edwina.

"Ma'am?" the little girl asked.

And that returned warmth proved . . . different than what had usually greeted her from the villagers in her own county. Or the others she'd visited along the way, in her work as a governess.

Edwina dropped to a knee. "Hullo," she murmured.

The whites of the young girl's eyes stood out stark against her soot-stained cheeks. "Are you a princess?"

Edwina caught that awe-infused whisper even over the cacophony of the miners' shouts.

She laughed softly. "Hardly." In fact, she couldn't be further from it. Edwina, as the bastard-born daughter of a marquess and a woman who'd loved far beyond her reach, would never wear the title of lady. In fact, if the world knew the truth about the origins of her birth, there'd not even be the secure, respectable life she'd created for herself.

The little girl touched the puffed sleeve of Edwina's ice-blue muslin cloak, and in her exploration of the fabric, she left little smudges upon the previously unsullied fabric. "It is realllll," the girl said softly.

"Indeed. Very soft, isn't it?" she asked in gentle tones.

The wide-eyed girl nodded.

Edwina sank back on her haunches. "I was wondering if you might help me, I'm looking for—"

"Who in hell are you?" a deep baritone boomed behind her, slashing across the unexpectedly sweet exchange she'd shared with the child. "What is going on here?"

And as the girl hurried to grab the handles of her filled wheelbarrow and scurried off, Edwina knew. She knew without receiving a name, or having so much as a glance, that the peremptory voice could only belong to one who commanded this noisy, filthy place. One who also apparently thought nothing of scaring off children.

Annoyance snapped through her.

Mayhap that high-handedness was a trait all the children of dukes—even illegitimate ones—were born with.

Edwina struggled to get herself upright in the thick mire, and turned. "I beg . . ." Her breath caught, and words left her as her gaze landed on the heavily muscled stranger stalking toward her. His long legs easily ate away the distance, bringing him closer.

She'd thought about much where Rafe Audley was concerned—who he was, how she'd convince him to join her on the journey back to London. The work he did.

But she'd never thought of him . . . *the man.*

Broad of shoulders and narrow of waist, he'd drawn his dark hair back in a queue. Some slightly curled strands had pulled loose and hung about his shoulders, giving him the look of Apollo.

And shameful though it was, for it marked her very much her mother's daughter . . . one with a head easily swayed by a handsome form—Edwina found herself riveted by the mere sight of the approaching miner. He was . . . nothing short of magnificent. The manner of man that pushed all rational thought from a woman's head and filled it, instead, with thoughts of him in all his glorious male beauty.

The barrel-chested mountain of a man stopped before her and stole her breath in the process. Every last bit of air, gone from her lungs and trapped somewhere in her throat.

In a bid to break this quixotic spell, Edwina pointed her parasol toward the slick mud and made a show of adjusting the umbrella. Only it proved to be the wrong action, for it brought her gaze into direct line with his beautifully contoured, muscular thighs.

Edwina swallowed spasmodically.

"What the hell are you doing at my mines?" he barked, effectively shattering the moment of madness that had held her in its grip.

With his mouth and manners, she was going to have her work cut out for her. "I'm looking for Rafe Audley."

The sharply chiseled contours of his face, from the bold slash of his cheekbones to the perfectly squared jaw, were a mask that may as well have been etched in stone.

Nearly eight inches past five feet, Edwina had enjoyed the luxury of looking down at most people, or in the eyes of most men. The surly stranger glaring darkly at her must be a foot taller, and she was required to tip her head back to meet his gaze.

Then she wished she hadn't.

Those dark blue depths pierced into her, driving every last single thought she'd managed to hold on to until then straight out of Edwina's mind, but for one question: "Are you him? Are you Rafe Audley?"

He sharpened that penetrating gaze on her face. "Who is asking?"

She wetted her lips. "Well, *I* am." This was a first for her—all of it. Being unsettled. Being the one without proper words. Struggling to find her footing. Those responses were generally reserved for her charges. And there'd been so many that she shouldn't be reduced to this hesitant mess, and all because of a man's physique.

His thick, dark lashes swept down. "Are you wasting my time with some damned jest?"

Was she . . . ?

She shook her head. She'd never been one to jest, and she'd only been a straight talker. "I'm afraid I do not follow."

"Who are you?" he snapped. "And why in hell are you on my grounds and talking to my staff?"

And with that, she'd confirmation of what she already suspected. "You are Rafe Audley, then." Edwina stretched out a palm. "How do you do?"

He stared at her fingers but made no move to take them, and that icy disdain was enough to snap her out of whatever momentary muddleheaded state she was in where he was concerned. Edwina let her arm fall to her side. Shouts went up around the grounds, and she raised her voice to ensure she could be heard over it. "My name is Miss Edwina Dalrymple."

All the gentleman's focus remained beyond her. For one sought after by countless clients, who even fawned in a bid to secure her work, it was a humbling moment to find herself—invisible.

"Stabilize the headframes," Mr. Audley thundered, and she followed his gaze over to the miners scrambling to right a framework that supported some manner of pulley system over the shaft.

The gentleman started for the commotion, but she slipped herself into his path, blocking his escape. "As I was saying, Mr. Audley, my name is Miss Dalrymple—"

"Your name means nothing to me, and I've work to see to." He easily stepped around her, and she gathered up her now muddied hems and started in pursuit.

"No, I don't suppose you would know me." Splendid. As rude as any villager she'd ever known in Leeds. She'd now be saddled with him as her latest charge. "We've never met and . . ."

He hastened on ahead, so that she was left slightly out of breath and staring after him.

With a little huff, Edwina pushed her bonnet back and

followed his fast-retreating frame. "Mr. Audley?" she called, waving her parasol in the air and attracting even more curious looks. Alas, she may as well have been invisible to the one person whose attention she sought. All his focus was on—

She stopped walking; the sight ahead of her freezing her square in her tracks. A team of miners worked together to harness a small pony. Edwina widened her eyes. Hefting her heavy hem higher, she bolted after the duke's son, her reason for being here briefly forgotten. "Are you . . . lowering that horse underground?" she demanded. For what end? "Horses don't belong underground, Mr. . . . ." Her words ended on a sharp squeak, as he wheeled abruptly about and faced her.

Narrowing his eyes once more, he started toward her with sleek, quick, and anger-fueled strides that sent her into an automatic retreat.

"Stop," he thundered.

The hell she would.

In her haste to escape him, Edwina tripped over herself.

He was upon her in three long strides.

"Stand back!" she cried. Edwina was lifting her parasol to swat him back when the earth sank under her heels. She shot her arms out to steady herself . . . in vain.

On a rush of movement, she found herself sliding and skating backward on loose, slick mud. She cried out as her parasol and bag went flying free, and she went tumbling back and back.

She was going to die here . . .

That was to be her fate for wanting more for her life . . .

A scream tore from her throat.

But then, the world righted itself.

Or rather, he righted her.

Rafe Audley caught her hard at the waist and hauled her forward. And this time, in a bid to dodge peril, she threw herself at the unforgivably hard wall of his chest.

Her pulse racing, Edwina clung tight to her unlikely savior; curling her fingers in the coarse fabric of his wool coat, she simply hung on to him and survival.

Until, at last, the earth stopped moving under their feet . . . and they skidded to a stop.

Edwina's pulse hammered in her ears and muted all sound of the bustling mine, including whatever words were falling from the hard slash of his angry lips.

She tipped her head and focused on his mouth.

Of a sudden, all sound came whirring back to her ears on a noisy rush.

". . . are you off of your goddamned mind? You don't have a brain in your head . . ." Then, holding her at the wrist the way a nursemaid might a naughty charge, he tugged her along, away from the weakened ground. "You're a long ways from home, princess. A woman like you doesn't have any place here."

Princess.

Slung in that condescending way, his was hardly an endearment. "You are mistaken," she said, struggling to match his stride; otherwise, she'd be dragged down. "I have business here."

That brought him to such a quick stop that Edwina crashed against him.

She grunted.

She may as well have hit whatever mined stone now sat in an enormous heap behind them for the strength of him.

He eyed her up and down, and she felt her skin burning hot under the condescending scrape of his gaze. "Business with who?"

"You."

"Me?"

Edwina nodded.

"What the hell did you say?" he thundered over the din of the work-yard. Or that was, anyway, what Edwina told herself. Because that was safer and eminently more preferable than thinking he was, in fact, yelling *at* her.

Before Edwina could respond, a miner called out. "You're needed, Audley."

Cursing enough to bring a different color to her cheeks, Mr. Audley walked off to meet the young man.

Doing a quick search of the muddied earth, she located her bag and parasol. Holding her already hopelessly muddied hems, Edwina lowered herself to retrieve each article. Her bag had landed atop a boulder, but her parasol had proven less fortunate.

Drip.

Drip—drip.

Mud slipped like a slow stream of teardrops, one after the other, from the lace-trimmed masterpiece. Her heart sank. She could well commiserate with the cherished object. Edwina shook the parasol several times, splattering mud as she did. It didn't help. Alas, there'd be time enough later to lament and clean the piece.

She made her way back to Mr. Audley.

And found the gentleman still conversing. Tapping the tip of her parasol upon a jagged boulder beside her, she waited.

And waited.

And was still waiting several moments later before it hit her: he'd not only *dismissed* her, but he'd returned to . . . to . . . whatever mining business he now saw to.

As Mr. Audley responded to the young miner, Edwina backed up a step, not out of fear this time but, rather, so she might again look at, and not up at, her new charge. For there was no doubting . . . she was not leaving Cheadle without Rafe Audley. She'd come to that determination somewhere between the moment he'd sent a child running and the moment he'd saved her from a nasty fall. Initially, she'd been compelled by the offerings made by the duke and duchess. Now, it was about . . . the challenge he posed.

"Ahem."

The sound of her clearing her throat was overwhelmed by a god-awful grinding sound that went on several moments, at an intermittent pace, before at last stopping. "Ah-hemmm," she repeated, this time louder and clearer.

Mr. Audley turned his attention back to Edwina, and blinked. "You're still here."

She fought the urge to wrinkle her nose. *He's trying to*

get a rise out of you. Only . . . as he wheeled about, it hit her . . . he really had forgotten her. Like hell. And she'd never been the cursing sort, priding herself on being proper and using proper language, but damned—blast, if Mr. Audley hadn't driven her to it. A duke's son, indeed. Gathering up her hopelessly ruined parasol, she waved it in a bid to capture his attention. "It is my hope and expectation that we will have shared business with one another."

That managed to freeze him in his tracks.

Mr. Audley flicked a cool stare over her cloak, and that mocking gaze lingered on the lace that dripped along the rim of her puffed sleeves. "And what kind of business do you think I'd have with you, princess?"

Her ears fired hot. Did she imagine the suggestive meaning to his question there? Nay, she'd not. And by the taunting sneer on his lips, he'd intended for her to read those words precisely as the double entendre they were. "It will take more than uncouth innuendos to unnerve me, Mr. Audley."

"I did call you 'princess,'" he drawled.

And in that moment she appreciated that this assignment would be the greatest challenge of any to have ever proceeded it, and for the first time since she'd agreed to take him on, she found the first real stirrings of eagerness. "Yes, well, that didn't alter the first part of your suggestive words, Mr. Audley. One that hinted at an improper connection between us."

"Do you want to clarify about the improper connection?"

At his side, the forgotten-until-now miner snorted a laugh.

Hmph to him, too. Refusing to give either of them the satisfaction, she went on, "No, I do not want to elucidate for you, Mr. Audley. Instead, your endearment."

"It wasn't an endearment."

She pounced. "Precisely. As such, that word choice only added a layer of insult to—"

"Mission accomplished then."

She let out an indignant huff. "So you are in the habit of going about insulting women."

"Consider yourself the first."

Giving her head an annoyed little shake, she reached inside the small satchel at her wrist and fished out her notepad.

"What in hell are you doing?" he blurted as she jotted down her notes.

"I think it should be fairly obvious," Edwina said, not lifting her focus from her book. "However, I will elucidate *this* part for you: I'm making notes about you and your habits, Mr. Audley." She added several more, before snapping the book closed. And when she looked up, she found she'd managed the seemingly impossible: to completely silence the lout.

Another miner trotted over. The young man hesitated, slanting a glance Edwina's way, and she reflexively tensed under that brief scrutiny. "Audley, do you want the hewers in now?" he asked. "Or do you want us to wait?"

His high brow creased, Rafe Audley looked at the wiry miner shooting questions his way and then back at Edwina. "What are you on about?"

She cleared her throat. "Are you talking to me?" she pointed the end of her parasol past him, to the miner waiting a yard away. "Or were you answering—?"

"Do you think I'm talking to him or you?" he bellowed.

He's a surly, cantankerous one.

Even as the young miner ducked his head in a bid to make himself invisible, Edwina refused to be cowed. She tilted her chin up a notch. "Given my question, I think it should be fairly clear that I have no idea to whom you were framing your question." She didn't allow him to get a word in edgewise. After all, as any good instructor knew, every moment was a teachable one. "And for that matter, neither did *he*." She glanced over at the round-eyed fellow, staring back at her and Mr. Audley. "Isn't that right . . . Mr. . . . . ?"

"Trout," the miner provided, with a little blush on his coal-stained cheeks.

A blush proved safer and warmer than the usual glower she was met with from villagers. Edwina's smile widened.

Mr. Audley, however, leveled a scowl to silence the lad, who immediately directed his stare at the ground.

Hmph. Well, she had no intention of letting Mr. Audley off that easily. Every moment was a teachable moment, and this one had a good deal to learn. "It would generally help for clarity's sake in terms of conversation," she went on to clarify for the uncouth gent, "if you addressed the person to whom you are speaking. In this case, the subject being me. Therefore, other parties needn't be confused as to who is the intended recipient of a particular query." When he continued to stare blankly back, she patted him reassuringly on the forearm, the way she did her young female charges. Alas . . . none of her female charges felt like he did. Shoving off that wicked observation, she drew her palm back and smiled at him. "Worry not. We shall work on that later." She made a mental note to add that detail to her book after they began their journey back. She'd be starting with the very basics with this one and earning every pence of her two thousand pounds.

Wordlessly, the miner backed slowly away.

Her smile dissolved into a frown. "Tsk. Tsk. And here I believe you've gone and scared the young man, Mr. Audley. That's hardly appropriate, either." They would work on that in the future, as well.

Mr. Audley's dark brows came shooting together, and his jaw went slack. "Who the hell are you?" he whispered.

Edwina offered her now mud-stained palm. "As I said, you may call me Miss Dalrymple." She flashed her most winning smile. "And I've come at the behest of His Grace, the Duke of Bentley."

Chapter 4

~~~~~

There'd been, in total, five men sent to retrieve him.

And that was only counting the ones who'd secured a face-to-face meeting with him. There'd been an additional four who'd not persisted beyond a knock at his door, before scurrying off with their tails tucked in terror between their legs at the threats he'd hurled.

Three of those who had persisted hadn't needed anything more than an inventive threat to also be sent scurrying off with their tails drooping below their cowardly arses.

Two, he'd planted a facer on.

All five had been males.

This . . . this was a first, a damned female showing up here.

And though there'd be no violence for the tiny thing, the answer would also remain the same: "Get the hell out," he said, clipping that utterance past clenched teeth. He started past her.

Beaming brighter than the Cornwall sun, the lady stepped in front of him, blocking his escape. "Ah, but we're already outside. Might I suggest we meet somewhere more—"

"No." Rafe took a wide step around her, and headed back to his work.

"Private," she called, her incessantly bell-like voice managing to rise above the machinery.

He took longer strides, hoping that increasing the space between them would serve as both an answer and the deterrent that had until now failed.

Alas, she proved bolder and braver—or mayhap stupider—than her predecessors. "Yoo-Hoo! Mr. Audley! Mr. Audddley."

He briefly closed his eyes and turned to face her.

Some five paces back, eyeing the ground as she went, the lady moved at a decidedly more cautious pace than when she'd gone hurtling toward an open mine hole moments ago. When she reached him, she was slightly out of breath, her painfully pale cheeks splotched with color from her exertions. And through it, she wore that same noxious grin.

"What?" he snapped.

"Our meeting," she began.

"We don't have a meeting." He had work, and he'd already allowed her more time than all the other duke's lackeys who'd come before her, combined.

"Precisely." The lady proceeded to dig around that garish golden valise on her arm. She immediately produced her tiny nub of a charcoal pencil and notebook. "I was thinking we might agree upon a time—"

"Audley," Tabbot called, "are you still intending to check the bell pits?"

"Damn it, Tabbot. Yes." He lifted a hand. "I'll be there."

"A time that is agreeable for both of us." Miss Dalrymple spoke loud enough to be heard over that interruption.

This had gone on long enough. All the patience he'd shown her, he'd done so because she was a female and he wasn't a bully. Because he hated bullies. But as much as he hated bullies, he equally hated presumptuous people who thought they could command him. Rafe removed his hat and used the top of it to wipe the sweat off his brow. "How about high noon."

Those dimples and slightly crooked smile were firmly back in place. "Splendid. As the duke is currently my only client, I've wide availability within my schedule. If you can tell me which day you've in mind. The sooner, rather than the later, would be immensely preferable . . . As we will need to begin the journey on to London." She proceeded to rattle off a megrim-inducing explanation as to why it would be better to leave sooner.

Wait. She . . . Even with all this . . . she thought he was leaving with her? It was decided. The lady wasn't brave. She was damned stupid. There was no else accounting for this . . . this . . . cheerful optimism and confidence.

". . . of course the sooner we meet to go over the terms of . . ." she was saying.

That was really enough. Rafe stuck his face close to hers. "How about high noon on never."

That managed to silence the garrulous chatterbox. The lady's plump mouth tensed with her displeasure. Any quiet, however, proved short-lived. "That is rude." Almost instantly, the lady's usual smile chased off the frown. "We shall just add that to your lessons."

"My . . ."

"Lessons. We can talk about that more later."

He stood there, his brain blank.

The young lady sighed. "Le-ss-ons." Miss Dalrymple used the tip of her parasol to punctuate each of those elongated syllables. "As in a section into which a course of study is divided, especially a single, continuous session of formal instruction in a subject . . . something that is to be learned or studied . . . a useful piece of practical wisdom acquired by experience or—"

"I know what a damned lesson is," he thundered when it appeared there was no end in sight to her laundry list of definitions.

"Audley!" Tabbot called for a second time.

Rafe shot a hand up. "Goddamn it, I said I'm coming."

The chit jumped several inches in the air.

Her wariness proved as short as her common sense. She patted her notebook. "I'll also add a session on 'proper tone and not yelling' and taking the Lord's name in vain," she said, in that nauseating cheer-filled voice. All the while, she continued to scribble away at that little leather book; her hand flew across the page as she wrote with a grand flourish.

After she finished, she read through her notes and gave a pleased nod. She packed them away, then looked up at Rafe.

She smiled. "You were saying?"

It was deliberate. There was nothing else to explain . . . any of this. His patience snapped. "I wasn't saying anything," he bellowed. Whatever this was? It was officially at an end. He marched toward her, and she backed away as he did. "I do not know who you are."

"I told you, my name is—"

"And I care even less about *who* you are. All I know is you were sent by the duke, and that's reason enough to have no dealings with you. So I suggest you take your pretty self off before you find yourself hurt."

As if on cue, the lady's foot snagged on an uneven patch, and for the second time in their very short acquaintance, she lost her footing. Dropping that parasol once more, she emitted a birdlike chirp and grabbed for Rafe. Even as he wrapped an arm about her painfully thin frame to keep her upright, her fingers were already curling in his shirt front.

Pressed against him as she was, he felt all of her. What there was to feel . . .

Her hips trim, her waist even trimmer, and her breasts small. She was also narrower, gaunter, and sharper than anything he preferred in a woman.

The young lady gripped him tight, her flawless, manicured nails leaving little crescents upon his chest. Her round eyes grew impossibly rounder, and instead of pulling away her palms clenched and unclenched.

He flashed a wolfish smile, and for the first time since she'd arrived, he began enjoying himself. "Now, *that* I might oblige, princess."

She gasped and pushed herself away from him. "Mr. Audley! I'll not tolerate your boorishness."

"And you don't have to," he whispered against her ear, and immediately went stock-still. For the scent of her also wasn't like anything of the women he knew or kept company with. She had the sweet smell of different flowers he couldn't place, all melded into that untamed, fragrant garden he walked past every day on his way to and from the mines. The scent of her as pure and cleansing, and— He quickly set her away. "We're done here. You can go back and tell your duke I'd sooner spend a summer's day in hell than join you or him. Now get the hell out so I can go back to my work."

"I'm not leaving, Mr. Audley," she insisted, hurrying to keep up. There was a resolute set to her faintly sharp jaw. "I will sit here as long as I must."

His second-in-command looked Rafe's way, and Rafe lifted his hand in acknowledgment. "Find yourself a good seat, then, princess. I'll not be around a third time to save you from getting yourself killed." And with that warning, she was free to take her leave, and he rejoined his crew.

"What the hell was that about?" Tabbot asked the moment Rafe finally reached him. They'd begun working together in these very mines when they were boys, and there wasn't a person he trusted more. But neither did Rafe intend to get into an irrelevant discussion about his latest unwanted visitor.

"London nonsense," he said, with the shortness meant to discourage any further questioning. That's really all it was, anyway. Some old lord with regrets about how he'd lived— or not lived—his life wasn't Rafe's problem. And neither were the fools who took on the duke's assignments. "Are we in position for the inspection?" he asked, immediately putting the young woman from his mind.

"Everyone is set."

They'd just been waiting on Rafe. It was how mines were run, with all the men, women, and children deferring to the foreman. As he hastened to join the assembled inspection crew, he set his jaw with annoyance. Rafe hadn't been and wasn't one who took advantage of his authority. He respected his workers, and more, he respected their time. Because every miner knew how precious each moment was. And how perilous it was, wasting any of it. The princess showing up today didn't have respect for any of that. All she knew was whatever assignments had brought her here and her allegiance to a cold-hearted duke. And Rafe had permitted her entirely too much time. They'd both put his crew at risk.

Rafe and Tabbot reached the six men at the vertical shaft.

He nodded to Austel, who stood at the ready. "I want any deficiencies noted. Any weaknesses . . . no matter how slight," he instructed.

"Aye."

With that, Austel, with the help of the crew in position, began his descent.

"Sparrow know about this?" Tabbot asked quietly for Rafe's ears alone.

He frowned, all his attention tunneled on the operation. That shaft allowed them to mine for the coal in the most shallow seam. The bell pit could only be used as long as the roof was secure and proper ventilation ensured. Hell no, Sparrow didn't know. As much had been evidenced that morning, when he'd squabbled with Rafe's brother over payment, and then had ended up issuing it in tokens. Paid Hunter in tokens. Rafe hedged for the other man. "Sparrow doesn't need to know about the details that go into day-to-day operations. He gets his money. And that's all that matters."

"Aye. To him. That's why I trust he wouldn't approve of another inspection."

No, he certainly wouldn't. Most owners and foremen didn't bother with regular inspections. They were content to let those structures collapse and lose whatever workers were unlucky enough to be mining on those days. But when Sparrow wasn't counting his coins, he was drinking, and by the slurring of his speech earlier that day, Rafe could squeeze in another inspection without answering for it.

Tabbot snorted. "You're going to get yourself sacked one day."

The hell he would. Rafe was too good at what he did. "I bring Sparrow too much money for him to replace me, and he knows it," he said, folding his arms and watching as the levers continued to roll, indicating Austel's ten-meter descent continued.

Nearly thirty minutes later, Rafe stood with his arms folded beside his second-in-command, waited while the operation was carried out.

"Who is your fancy guest?"

His fancy guest?

"The bird," Tabbot clarified.

"The what?" Rafe asked, not taking his focus off the ground. From the corner of his eye, he caught Tabbot nudge his chin. He followed his stare over and blanched. "You've got to be kidding me."

Not only had the *bird* remained but she'd perched herself right in the thicket of the mining activity. All around her, children and women pushed wheelbarrows. Men hefted equipment from one place to the next. Through it, she sat with her umbrella perched against her left shoulder, a perfect shield above her, while she wrote in that notebook with her right hand.

"Not your usual type," Tabbot jibed.

"Go to hell," he muttered. But then, maybe the duke's emissary having cornered him and refusing to leave was hell. "She's not my concern."

"She's going to get herself killed, there. Or break something."

Neither of which would be his fault; that chit had taken it into her stubborn head to gainsay the orders and warnings he'd already given her numerous times. "She's not my responsibility." Ironically, she would have it so that he was hers.

As he worked, Rafe refused to look the lady's way.

Tabbot continued stealing glances at the princess. "It still would be a shame if something happened to a pretty thing like her."

He frowned. A pretty thing like her . . . ? "Be quiet, and do your damned—"

A god-awful screech went up, and his gaze immediately went flying across the muddy, open space toward her. Of course it was toward her. At some point she'd abandoned her place on the makeshift bench, and she went sprawling face forward, landing on her stomach in an enormous puddle of mud.

"Goddamn it. Finish up here," he ordered, not even waiting for Tabbot's acknowledgment, and took off flying toward the damned princess.

Ten-year-old Abby stood beside Miss Dalrymple. "Think she drowned, sir," the girl whispered, her eyes huge circles.

Reaching forward, Rafe fished the young woman out.

She emerged sputtering and spitting mud from her mouth as she did. The puddle had caked her face in black soil. The lady frantically swatted the equally damp, dark strands of auburn hair that blocked her vision.

He expected one such as her to dissolve into a watering pot. If the stubborn minx hadn't been driven off before, this would surely do it.

She rubbed her fists against her eyes in a futile bid to clean them.

Rafe had mercy on her. Reaching inside his pocket, he pulled out a kerchief and jammed it into her fist. "Here."

"Thank you," she said with all the aplomb of one who was accepting tea from the queen . . . an impressive feat, given the fact she was covered from her "pretty little head," as Tabbot had referred to it . . . to the bottom of her toes. Her slipper-encased toes. What a damned fool.

"What in hell were you doing?" he bellowed, cursing and then promptly catching the lady, still fully engrossed in wiping her face, as she walked, nearly falling over the same log that had taken her down in the first place.

When she lowered his kerchief, instead of the expected and requisite fear in her expressive hazel eyes, there was a horrifying amount of awe and appreciation. Rafe found himself squirming under that unwanted attention. The lady turned a blindingly bright, even white smile on him. "You saved me yet again, Mr. Audley."

Why was he destined to be wrong where this woman was concerned?

Her already impossibly wide smile grew wider. "There is hope for you yet. Not that I ever doubted it. You are after all a—"

"Do not say it." He let that whisper hiss from between his teeth.

The concession she made was a whisper. "A duke's son."

A loud whisper.

He swiped a hand over his face.

Around them, a crowd had begun to form. "She's fine," he barked. "As you were." The miners immediately dispelled, bustling about with whatever work they'd temporarily put on hold because of *her* . . .

He swiveled his gaze back to her. Sharpening a glower on her. The lady didn't have a lick of proper fear. She continued to look up at him, still with that puppy dog expression. "On your feet, now," he clipped out. Rafe gripped her painfully trim waist and saw to the task himself. "In my office."

Curiosity chased away the earlier adoration. "Indeed? You have an office here?" Recovering her parasol, she popped it open; the edge of that silly scrap caught his nose. The lady proceeded to search the mining yard.

"That way, Miss Dalrymple," he jammed his finger toward the crude path, and at last, she began to move in the direction he had wanted her to be moving since she arrived. Away.

"I'll have you know I'm not usually so clumsy. Just the opposite, in fact," she prattled on. "I've had some of the finest instructors."

Thank God for small miracles; the din of the courtyard swelled.

Miss Dalrymple raised her voice to be heard over it, confirming the Lord was otherwise dead or previously engaged helping some more worthwhile fellow than Rafe. "I've had endless lessons on the art of walking," she said.

The art of . . . ?

As if to provide an illustration for his silently unspoken question, the lady held her arms out and proceeded in a graceful glide across the muddied, rock-cluttered ground. And . . . as she did, his gaze, of its own volition, slipped lower.

Her eyes collided with his, and she smiled widely. "After all, what manner of instructor *would* I be if I were incapable of carrying out the same feats of ladylikeness that I was expecting my students to follow?"

There was only one certainty in this moment . . . the little bird had no idea the path his thoughts had wandered down. She'd not be smiling so innocently if she did. Though, likely if . . . The lady tossed a glance over her shoulder, with her head at a jaunty angle, and flashed a smile. "Do you see?"

It was then that he tuned in to her gait: a slight sashay of those narrow hips that lent them a false curve . . . but drew a man's gaze lower, to her buttocks, which were surprisingly lush for one of her slenderness. "Aye, I see," he said, his voice guttural. And he did. There was a grace to her movement that made a man—

From out of the corner of his eye, he caught the miners all lined up, staring.

Rafe glared at their audience, and those young men tripped and stumbled over one another in their haste to get back to their respective jobs.

Seemingly oblivious to both his brief lapse into insanity and the lewd stares she'd been the recipient of, the young woman did a little pirouette . . . and curtsied, with her mud-drenched parasol in hand.

He opened his mouth to deliver another blistering rebuke . . . when he honed in on another detail. She'd had her weight balanced over her left foot, which indicated, despite her sheer and surprising lack of complaint, she'd in fact been injured.

"You're hurt," he said, the charge accusatory.

"A lady never shows—eep!" Whatever latest deportment lesson she intended to launch was thankfully, effectively cut off by the little bird's perfectly birdlike squeak as he swept her into his arms and marched onward.

The sooner he got her out of here, the sooner he could be done with Miss Dalrymple and her pleasantly plump arse.

"You injured your ankle, princess. You're hurt. Do you know what I risk every day?" He didn't wait for her to answer. Nay, he didn't allow her to answer. "Do you know what all the men and women and children here risk every day? Cave-ins. Fume poisoning that leaves a person spitting up blood. Explosions that separate a person from their limbs." The more he spoke, the rounder her eyes got. A gentlemen, the one she took him for, would have felt some compunction at speaking so to a lady—to any woman— with the shocking candor Rafe now did. But he wasn't done with her or his list.

Chapter 5

Clinging to Mr. Rafe Audley as he marched onward through the mining courtyard, Edwina saw two possible fates awaiting her.

One, Mr. Rafe Audley intended to deposit her somewhere far, far away, so she might not ever be a bother to him—or anyone—ever again.

Or two, he intended to help her.

She wasn't one given to wagering, as it was a cardinal sin no lady should commit, but if she were of the gambling persuasion, she would have placed all the coins she'd accumulated over the years on Rafe, with all his gruff bellowing and bellicose temperament, being set on outcome one.

She peered up at him; his features were as harshly beautiful as those stone statues of the Greek gods . . . equally chiseled . . . and cold. His eyes, a dark brown that leaned toward black, even colder. And even with all his blustery annoyance from before, this was the first she'd ever felt the stirrings of real unease where her new charge was concerned.

Oh, dear. Yes, it appeared with every long stride he took,

away from the crowd, and onward to . . . wherever they now went, that he was going to dispose of her.

It was the silence that made him seem more like a statue and less . . . human. As such, Edwina opted for the most tried and true course of disarming volatile individuals and situations—*Do not allow a person to simmer in silence. Get to the heart of it, Edwina.* "You are angry." Or, perhaps, he was not? Perhaps she was needlessly worrying because he was a foreign-to-her gentleman, and she was in the middle of the even more foreign English countryside and—

"I'm not happy," he said curtly. That was it. Three words, confirming his displeasure.

"One might say that is a contrary way of saying, 'I am angry.' I prefer plain-speaking, in most situations. This being one of them. Of course, all situations should be considered separate from the other, and we will also add that to—"

Mr. Audley glared her into silence, and this time she allowed him to do it.

His lessons. She made a mental note to add this latest discovery to her journal. Alas, it appeared with every turn, she learned more and more just how much dire help her charge needed.

He quickened his stride, and took a narrow path that led away from his courtyard, and even farther away from the crowd of workers assembled there.

She peeked over his shoulder, to where the men, women, and children grew to distant and then invisible specks . . . and the noise of those grounds faded altogether. Unease traipsed along her spine. Mr. Audley had been menacing enough amid a crowd of onlookers, but to be alone with him and his displeasure?

Suddenly, it felt very, very important that she be set down on her own two feet.

Feet were, after all, for running. Even hobbled feet allowed a person a chance to escape. Hers had served her on such occasions requiring flight. And she'd feel a good deal better having them under her. "I am more than happy to walk," she said, forcing a dose of cheer and optimism into her voice that she decidedly did not feel.

He grunted, adjusting her in his arms so that for a moment she thought he intended to honor her request.

Alas, he merely shifted her weight and drew her closer, startling a squeak past Edwina's lips.

Blast. "In fact, I much prefer it," she continued on when it became apparent he'd not put her down. "Walking, when done with measured steps, is good for one's constitution."

"Do you know what else is good for one's constitution, princess?"

"Of course I do," she scoffed. "Dancing. Needlework. Shell-work. Paperwork. Quilling. Feather-work."

He cast her an odd look. "Anything else?"

"Watercolors." She paused. "And sketching." That wasn't really inclusive enough. "All forms of art, really. Also, knotting. Though, I'm likely leaving a number of other suitable ones off my list."

"Silence," he snapped. "Silence is good for one's constitution."

Her cheeks warmed. "You were *not*, then, looking for an enumeration."

"I was not." And brusque and rude as he always was, there was a trace of sarcasm to his deep baritone that suggested amusement. Which she would gladly accept, as humor was humor and, well, *not* dangerous.

"Hmph." Edwina found herself preferring the silence after all, too.

That was until they reached a small rise, and a small, dilapidated stone cottage appeared. She frantically searched about for hint of any persons . . . and found none.

Double-dee blast.

She swallowed around an enormous lump of nervousness and fear that had formed in her throat.

So this is where he intended to leave her. When she'd set out with her directives from the duke, she'd not considered that her assignment might be altogether difficult. Mr. Audley might be bastard-born, but he was a duke's son. Challenging. Rewarding, even. What she'd not thought he would be was perilous.

"If you would?" she said, her voice creeping up an octave, along with her panic, as she wiggled, attempting to free herself.

"Would you stop moving?" he snapped, as they reached the wooden door. Reaching around her, Mr. Audley let them in. He paused only long enough to kick the door shut with the heel of his leather boot. She peeked over his broad shoulder, eyeing the panel as it shook, the resounding boom echoing in the narrow, untidy space.

Her eyes struggled to adjust to the dimly lit one-room house. Cluttered with desks and books and papers, it gave no indication that it was a place anyone actually resided in.

Except . . . for the bed.

Fear pitted her belly.

Then, he stopped beside that small cot. Her entire body tensed in preparation of being tossed upon that light, small bed. But with a surprising gentleness, he rested her atop the mattress.

There was a tenderness to his efforts that under *most* any other circumstances would have awed her, but given that she was alone with him, a strange man . . . and everything she knew about being alone with any man sent her back up in tensed preparedness.

Mr. Audley straightened, and headed back across the cottage . . . and hope flared in her breast. Perhaps, he was going to leave her here alone, after all. Which now seemed the decidedly safer—

He stopped at a desk, and grabbed a vicious-looking pair of scissors.

Not safer.

It was not at all safer.

Her heart knocked erratically against her ribcage.

While he searched through that cluttered desk for . . . something else, Edwina frantically looked about with only one intent in mind: escape.

Yes, the gentleman was a duke's son, but he was also one

who'd expressed no interest in joining his respectable father. And who'd expressed even more annoyance in her presence.

Edwina's gaze took in all the ways in and out of this place. Three windows. One door. The largest ones a person could fit most easily through required passing him.

Arching her neck back, she stared at the narrow little window overhead. Edwina assessed the space. Climbing was generally forbidden for all ladies, allowed under only the very most extreme of circumstances. Her current one, however, she'd place firmly in the peril column.

Never. She would never be able to climb that high, and open it, and squeeze herself through before—

The wide-plank wood floors groaned, and she immediately jerked her attention forward . . . to the gentleman approaching with a strip of long, white fabric between his coal-stained fingers . . . and scissors. The metal gleamed, mocking her with their brightness and size.

Mr. Audley stopped before her, and she stiffened.

Wordlessly, he sank to a knee, and grabbed the hem of her skirt. With a little squeak, Edwina kicked him with her uninjured foot . . . which didn't even move him.

In fact, he gave no indication that he'd even noticed the gesture, let alone felt it.

And this time, she gave another attempt at shoving him, kicking him with all her might. She gasped as her foot promptly throbbed.

"What the hell do you think you are doing?" he demanded with such indignant outrage, it would have been laughable had she not been rattled with fear.

"Kicking you." When she'd been a small girl, she'd been running exuberantly up the cottage lane to meet her father when he was visiting, and in her haste, she'd drifted slightly off course and collided with the uneven stone wall that ended at the entrance to the drive. She'd been knocked square on her buttocks and had all the thoughts rattled in her head for days. In small part because it had been like running into a wall. And in larger part, because he had the most dizzying effect on her senses. Even having put all the force she could manage into that kick, the only things she ended up with were hurt toes, and an immobile Mr. Audley. "I was kicking you."

"Well, that is certainly not going to secure my cooperation." His cooperation, he'd speak about? "You are—?"

Edwina scrabbled for her parasol, and brought it down over his head.

Mr. Audley cursed and gripped his temple. All the while he singed her with a black look that sent her inching backward on the mattress. "What the hell was *that* for?" he barked.

"Defending myself?"

"From *what*?"

There was such a healthy dose of bafflement to that question, it cut through the panic that had been gripping her since they'd entered his cottage. "You weren't . . . you . . . I thought . . ." Her face went hot once more.

His eyes went wide. "You thought . . . I left my mines in the middle of the day, and carried *you* all this way with the intention of forcing myself upon you?" And this time a different bark escaped him, one of laughter.

She bristled and bit her tongue to keep from pointing out the fact that he'd brought her to a bed and had come at her with bindings, and of course, the fact that they were very much alone. "I am glad you find this situation amusing."

After his mirth had faded to a small chuckle, Mr. Audley gave his head a rueful shake. "I assure you, I've no intention of taking advantage of you, or any woman. Even if you were the manner of woman to tempt me." He paused. "Which you decidedly aren't." He muttered that last part to himself.

Relief. It *should* be the dominant emotion. Expressed in the form of an audible sigh.

Indignation should be the absolute last of what she felt. And yet, there it was. She chafed at the sarcastic-once-more insult.

This time, however, he hesitated with his fingertips at her hem. "Do I have permission to check your ankle?"

"My ankle?" she asked, breathless, as it finally dawned on her just what he'd intended.

"As in the one you injured." There was a heavy dose of sarcasm in that droll response as well . . . but his tone did nothing to erase the daze cast by his request.

He'd . . . not only asked permission but insisted on . . . caring for her?

Edwina sat there, motionless. Breathless. And both captivated and confused.

Over the years, Edwina had had any number of dealings with men. Most had been merchants. Others gentry. There'd been heads of household and their sons.

And, as she had come to find out, there were two ways in which a woman without the benefit of marriage or even legitimacy to her name was treated:

One, she found herself fending off unwanted or improper attentions.

Or two, she remained invisible, being instead left to the women of the household.

Not a single man had ever helped her. And certainly none had ever saved her. And in the most literal sense of being saved.

And several times at that. Three to be specific. All in the span of one meeting. It was why she knew, even though Mr. Rafe Audley didn't want her here and had been crude and rude at every turn, that he was still a true gentleman. And that gave her hope for her assignment.

Still, she remembered the years of instruction she'd received on deportment and propriety and uttered the requisite, expected response. "That wouldn't be proper," she murmured.

He snorted. "And how proper is it for a young lady to be gallivanting around a mine by herself?"

Edwina wrinkled her nose. "Yes, well, that is a fair point." But she wasn't a lady in the traditional sense of the word. Instead, she was one who instructed those young women, and it was, therefore, expected that Edwina conduct herself in a like way . . . When she could. "Alas, it would have been a good deal easier and I would've been spared my gallivanting as you called it, if you had simply returned for your lessons." As such, nothing about being sent to fetch her latest charge, however, was traditional.

"Listen, princess, I am of half a mind to let you go traipsing about on your injured leg . . ."

But he wouldn't . . .

"Let me look at your damned foot. You've my word I won't attempt anything more than that."

And this time, she who was never without a word, reply, or retort found herself nodding her head, over and over, even after he'd directed his focus to her hemline.

All those butterfly sensations low in her belly were effectively doused as he haphazardly pushed her skirts unceremoniously up, exposing her legs from the knee down, and a blush burned up the whole of her body from the roots of her hair to the tips of the toes he now handled. She needn't, however, have worried; he gave no indication that he noticed anything beyond the foot cradled in his palm. Lightly wiggling her slipper loose, he drew it off and tossed the article aside. "You know these are ridiculous, don't you?"

She glanced about before realizing what it was he spoke of. "My slippers?" she gasped with indignation. "I know no such thing."

"No, you don't know anything. Which is why you went and nearly got yourself killed, and hurt your ankle," he shot back. "Slippers have no place in these parts."

"There's no wrong day for slippers," she said calmly. "Slippers brighten every day, in every way. They are colorful and bright, and easy to dance in and glide in. They—"

He laughed, the sound of it unexpectedly rich and full and boisterous . . . and also at her expense. "Tell me, princess, does the 'brightening of a day, in every way' also include sprained, swollen ankles? Because if I put on the footwear favored by the gents, I'd have shredded soles and shredded feet."

She lifted her chin up. "I beg your pardon?"

"As you should," he said between his mirth. "What rot is *that*?"

She bristled. That rot, as he referred to it, also happened to be the oft-uttered words of her mother whenever her love had arrived with a new pair of silk slippers.

"Tell me, have you ever donned quality shoes, Mr. Audley?" She looked pointedly down at the tattered, mud-stained articles he wore on his feet. "For, if you did, you'd know there was nothing more glorious than sliding your foot into an expertly crafted article, made of the highest quality."

Mr. Audley glanced up her way, a wry grin on his hard lips. "Then you don't know what glory is, princess." He winked, and with that scoundrel's flutter to his black lashes, there could be absolutely no doubting the double meaning to his words.

She gasped, her hand coming up to cover her mouth. "*Mr. Audley!*"

She opened her mouth to school him on the importance of proper dress but thought better of it. With his reticence, he'd already revealed his nervousness about claiming his rightful place among the *ton*. She didn't wish to spook him any more than she already had.

As such, she remained quiet as he returned his attention to her injury. "You've my assurance that the only thing less enticing than a right foot is the left one." Edwina leaned over and stared at her feet. Yes, he was correct on that score. There was hardly anything less interesting or appealing . . . than a foot. "Well?" he asked impatiently.

She gave a reluctant nod.

Ever so delicately he prodded the inseam of her arch up to the overly sensitive sole of her foot, earning a breathless laugh; she had to bite her lip to keep it in.

The silk stockings she wore were no barrier. Instead, that soft, thin fabric only heightened the most delicious tingles that left her nerve endings confused as to whether to elicit a sigh or giggle from her.

And then, ever so slowly, he curled his fingers around her foot, enveloping it in a gentle, almost reflexive caress.

The hum of the quiet thundered in her ears; that sound of silence only added to a heightened awareness of the slightly harsh quality of his breathing, and hers.

Hers as it came in little, uneven spurts.

Which was . . . of course . . . impossible. Because he'd been abundantly clear that feet were not seductive or tempting, and yet if that was the case, why was his thumb even now stroking that slight indentation where her foot met her ankle? And why was her heart racing all the harder for it?

It's simply because he is a stranger holding your foot in his hand. Not because she liked the feel of it. At all. That wouldn't be proper.

Conversation, as she taught her charges, was the great equalizer of tumultuous emotion. "Do you have some training as a doctor, then?" she asked, as he continued his examination of her leg.

"Not a day," he said gruffly, directing his words to the place where her ankle met her foot. "Rotate your ankle. Slowly," he cautioned.

Edwina carefully turned her foot, to the right, so that her toes pointed at the door. Then she rolled it back the other way. Tingles raced up from where he touched her, and she bit her lip to keep from sighing.

"Any pain?"

It was hard to turn her focus away from the pleasure. She shook her head. Before recalling that he couldn't see her, that he was firmly focused on her foot. "None."

"Does it hurt?"

"Some." Also, when he held it as he did, in that strong, calloused grip, it was hard to concentrate on anything beyond his touch.

Someday . . . someday you shall find a man whose touch makes you forget your name . . .

She recoiled as that long-ago warning her mother had given her came roaring into her ears.

Mr. Audley looked up. "That hurt?"

"Yes," she blurted out. It hadn't. Not really. Her mind, however, was all muddled recalling her late mother's teasing, a mother who had insisted that Edwina would fall as hard and fast and as deeply and completely as she herself had for the Marquess of Rochester. "Some. Not a lot." Guilt at lying made her rush to reassure him. "Just the teeniest bit." To demonstrate her point, she lifted her thumb and forefinger, and held them apart the tiniest fraction.

Mr. Audley eyed her as though she had gone mad.

And perhaps she had, because Edwina had been so very convinced she wouldn't ever be so aware of any man. "It is just when you touch it," she finished weakly, the closest thing to the truth. When he extended his search, higher up her leg, Edwina's heart raced faster, and she directed her eyes at the ceiling. "You've had no training, and yet you know so very much about breaks and sprains, Mr. Audley?"

"I do."

That was it.

Goodness, he was brusque. That would hardly serve him well when he was attending dinner parties and other formal affairs. There was always room for a lesson. This moment proved no exception. "The discourse in which you engage is helpful in diffusing tension other people may feel in your presence."

"I don't much care if people feel *tense in my presence*," he said coolly.

"Why?"

"Why?" Even with his head bent, she caught the lines that creased his high brow before several loose strands tumbled across it, concealing them.

"It is just that I cannot see the benefits of relishing another person's discomfort." *And if he carries that mentality with him to a London Season, the only resulting outcome would be cold shoulders and gossip.*

At last, he finally shifted all his attention away from her leg and up so that his eyes met hers. "It has nothing to do with relishing a person's discomfort. And it has everything to do with not caring what other people think, because I don't have the time for it." He nudged his chin pointedly at her throbbing foot. His meaning was clear.

He wanted to get back to tending her, and did not care much either way whether she was comfortable or uncomfortable.

This time, when he went to collect her foot, she angled it to the right and just out of his reach. "But I'm not at ease," she said.

"And that matters?"

"Yes, I rather think it does. It certainly matters to me, and you should be gent—" She abruptly stopped herself from completing that word. Because for whatever reason, he delighted in thinking of himself as anything but. "—generally one who doesn't wish to make people uncomfortable."

Mr. Audley growled, not unlike that enormous black bear her mother had once taken her to visit at the Royal Menagerie. Strange, how that ruthless, ferocious-looking creature should have scared her less than the living, breathing human before her.

"If I answer you, will you let me get back to it?" he demanded.

Edwina nodded sagely. "Oh, absolutely. You have my word."

"Anything I know comes from helping any miners who've been hurt working."

And then as he returned to tending her injured foot, Edwina's heart did somersaults all over again, for altogether different reasons. "You take care of them, then," she said softly, as with that curt explanation he revealed so much . . . about himself and more, his character.

Ruddy color splotched his cheeks. Near as he was, she felt his entire body tense and stiffen as he turned a dark scowl on her. "You're not one for keeping your word, are you?"

She smiled widely. "Ah, just the opposite. I am very much one who honors my word. *You* asked if I would allow you to 'get back to it,' and *I* assured you I would. Which I have. Which you were, until you stopped this time to quiz me."

Chapter 6

In his years working deep under the grounds of Mr. Spar-row's mines, Rafe had found himself caught in a cave-in. Twice.

He'd had the rungs of his ladder collapse, which had sent him tumbling deeper into the mine, requiring an entire team to extract him. And then, only days later, there'd been the explosion when such a thick, black cloud of smoke had filled the air, making it impossible for a man to see his hand held directly in front of his face.

Never, in any and all of those circumstances, had Rafe ever been as turned around as he was just then by the always-smiling Miss Dalrymple.

Miss Edwina Dalrymple with her dimple-cheeked bird given to laughs and giggles and smiles.

Which was just *one* of the reasons she'd turned him up-side down.

Her endless stream of chatter.

Her nauseatingly cheerful disposition.

And then, there was also . . . her foot. A part of the la-dy's body that he'd been absolutely certain, before her, was neither enticing nor seductive. In fact, he'd been so confident of it, he'd given her assurances that had previously been true about that appendage.

Only to be proven wrong.

In fairness, he'd never felt a foot like hers. One clad in silk and soft against his coal-stained palms.

Suddenly, it seemed essential to get this over and done with so he could send her away, and never again think about the chatterbox and her sexy foot.

"Yea, I take care of them," Rafe finally said when she continued to stare at him with those wide, hazel doe-eyes.

Resting her elbow atop her knee, she dropped her chin in her hand . . . and sighed. "That is very heroic of you. And gentlemanly," she added softly.

And in another show of firsts that day, his cheeks went hot. My God, he was . . . *blushing*? It was fortunate not a single other miner was about, because all of Rafe's authority would be lost, and for just cause—showing any weakness because of some lady from Town was grounds for dismissal. "You're wrong." Rafe kept his tone curt and cold to dissuade and discourage any further nonsense. "In fact, you're making more of it than it is, princess." Which was no doubt an attempt on the lady's part to lessen the unease she'd spoken of feeling around him a short while ago. And that strategy appeared to be working.

"I don't think I am." Straightening, Miss Dalrymple beamed. "Quite the opposite. In fact, one might say I am very rarely wrong. *Very* rarely."

He snorted. He'd known her just under an hour, and would stake his future as foreman that nothing could be further from the truth.

"I shall ignore that, Mr. Audley, as I suspect you are less than comfortable with any praise directed your way. Furthermore, I also suspect that you would prefer it if myself and others took you as an unfeeling beast. But you're not. I'm quite certain of it."

And by the steady conviction in that pronouncement, the ninny believed it.

"Do you want to know the truth?" When she went to answer that rhetorical question, he glared her into silence. And miracle of miracles, she didn't continue with her prattling. "Injured men, women, and children are unproductive men, women, and children. Miners who aren't working aren't pulling their load. Which means money isn't being earned. Which means my role as foreman is in jeopardy. So do not go making more out of anything I've said."

Her smile deepened. *Deepened.* So that her eyes positively sparkled.

"Ah, but if that were true, then why would you care for me even now? Certainly my injured ankle has nothing to do with your productivity. In fact, some might also argue that you spent an inordinate amount of time looking after my injury at the expense of a day's work."

Well, hell . . . if she wasn't right on that score.

Miss Dalrymple leaned close, placing her lips close to his ear, and whispered, "As I said, Mr. Audley, I am very rarely wrong, and there is something else you should know about me . . . I'm a determined woman and I'll neither fail nor take 'no' for an answer where you are concerned."

It was her insolence he should be focusing on. And annoyance he should be feeling.

Not the hint of rosewater that whispered about him, filling his senses with that sweet, fragrant scent. And damn, if those garden smells weren't more intoxicating than the too-strong ale Old Mr. Ward served at the inn. And as close as they were, unbidden his gaze slipped lower, as he noted a detail that had previously escaped him about Miss Edwina Dalrymple: that slightly more lush upper lip that lent an interesting pout to her mouth, and conjured all manner of wicked delights to be enjoyed with and by such a mouth.

Just then her lips parted ever so slightly, giving the illusion of surprise.

Aye—he swallowed hard—that made two of them.

Salvation came in the click of the door opening. "You summoned . . ." Hunter's words trailed off. "My apologies. I didn't know you had company."

Miss Dalrymple's clear-eyed gaze slid past his shoulder. Only the pretty blush that filled her cheeks gave a hint to the brief, charged moment they'd shared.

Rafe hurriedly lowered her skirts back into place. "I don't suspect you have any tears in your ligaments. Nothing is fractured. Probably currently have nothing more than a light sprain." With brusque movements, he grabbed for her ruined slipper. All the while he slid the previously ivory satin scrap onto her foot, he was aware of his brother taking it all in.

"I was told there was an emergency?" his brother drawled, and with his usual boldness, he sauntered over.

"Oh, hello," Miss Dalrymple greeted him. Extending her gloved palm, she gave Rafe a pointed look. "This is where you help me to my feet," she said in a ridiculously loud whisper that would be a secret to no one.

Quickly standing, he grabbed her hand and hauled her to her feet.

"Many thanks, Mr. Audley." She continued to stare pointedly at him.

He shook his head in abject confusion. Why was she looking at him like that?

The lady emitted a soft sigh and, also not discreetly, cupped her fingers around her mouth and spoke in those hushed tones. "And now for the introductions."

Introductions? Where in the hell did she think they were? But then, it only reminded him why she was here. Who had sent her. And what both of those unwanted people were expecting of him. "This isn't a goddamn London ballroom," he snapped, and it was the first time those always-uptilted lips turned down at the corners. And damned if he didn't feel like the village bully who had delighted in sharpening his insults on Rafe's younger brother, until Rafe had put a quick end to it.

His brother cleared his throat. "I brought the wagon."

Good. Now, he could be done with her. "Miss Dalrymple, this is my assistant, Hunter." Rafe placed the very slightest emphasis on that name, as the only concession he was willing to make in terms of her *introductions*. "He will see you back. These mines are no place for you. I trust you've learned as much."

"Oh, dear. I would never be so bold as to refer to you by your Christian name, Mr. . . . ?"

"Hunter," his brother said bluntly.

"Very well, then." The young lady shifted her weight over her uninjured leg, and with those same graceful movements she'd displayed while conducting lessons on walking in the middle of the mine, she whirled about, and dipped ever so gingerly, and collected her parasol. Using the tip of it, as if it were some prop on a Vauxhall stage, she brought herself back so she faced them. "I must decline the offer, as I've already a carriage waiting for me. Though it was a pleasure to meet you, *Mr.* Hunter."

And reflected back in Hunter's own eyes was Rafe's very real horror.

"What the hell?" his brother silently mouthed over the top of the young woman's head.

Rafe made a slashing motion across his throat once. "Don't ask," he returned, in an equally wordless response. Alas, it was the wrong response. The befuddlement was replaced by curiosity, which meant this was decidedly not the end of his brother's questioning. *Splendid.* Rafe turned his ire back where it belonged . . . on Miss Dalrymple. "He'll escort you to make sure you find your way back." And Rafe was sure she was gone.

"I must in—"

"You're going with my . . . Hunter, here," he said cutting her off.

The lady wrinkled her nose. "Very well. If you can send word for the duke's serv—"

"Get her out."

Hunter jabbed a finger in Rafe's direction. "You. Owe. Me." He impressively clipped out each word without making a sound.

Rafe lifted his head in acknowledgment. Saddling anyone, let alone his beloved brother, with Edwina Dalrymple was the height of cruelty.

"It has been a pleasure making your acquaintance," the young lady said once more, while making an elegant curtsy better suited for a presentation with the queen and not a rushed introduction made by two miners. "I thank you very much for your rescue, Mr. Audley. But alas, I have to take my leave."

She had to take her leave? Or he'd ordered her gone? Either way, to debate was to prolong her stay. "Then, do that," he said bluntly when she made no attempt to do so.

Behind Miss Dalrymple's shoulder, Hunter snorted another laugh.

Giving no indication she heard that amusement at her expense, Miss Dalrymple extended her right hand, and tilted her four middle fingers down toward the floor. As if she expected him to collect those fingertips. As if she expected him to drop a kiss atop them. As if she were nicked in the damned bob. Once again, she flashed one of those silly, encouraging smiles and waggled her palm. "Yes, well, then," she said when he made no move to take it. She turned to Hunter, facing him instead. "I shall be waiting outside."

His brother took a hasty step back, as he eyed the door behind them.

And Rafe proved a completely disloyal brother for preferring that attention be fixed Hunter's way, instead.

He offered a crooked grin as his dumbfounded brother collected Miss Dalrymple's palm and escorted her toward the door. Hunter had a hopeless look to him.

When the unlikely pair reached the door, she made a delicate clearing sound with her throat, and with enough effort to be clear about what she intended but not enough to be completely noticeable, she discreetly pointed the tip of her parasol at the door. "This is where you open the door, Mr. Hunter."

Hunter immediately grabbed the handle and drew the panel wide. With a flourish, Miss Dalrymple gathered her skirts, swept forward . . . and thankfully out.

Until, at last, there was silence.

Blessed silence.

After her incessant chattering, Rafe would never, ever take that state for granted again.

The minute she'd gone, Hunter drew the panel shut a fraction, and looked to Rafe. "Who the hell is she?"

"The duke's latest."

"As in, he sent that pretty little thing to fetch you?" And that managed to bring his usually humorless brother to a laugh. Giving his head a shake, Hunter glanced over his shoulder and then back to Rafe. "That still doesn't explain why you're here playing nursemaid to her."

No, it didn't. And what was worse . . . Rafe had no good reason to explain it. For there was none. "Will you just get her out of here?" he snapped.

And this time, his brother must have heard something in Rafe's tone, for Hunter hurriedly backed out of the cottage. Of course, his brother hadn't been wrong in puzzling as to why Rafe, who had run off every other man the duke had sent his way, had personally escorted the young lady away from the mines and himself seen to her injury.

Perhaps that had been the game the duke played this time. Perhaps His Grace had expected he could send an innocent young miss and yield different results. Rafe tightened his jaw. He may have helped care for the injured woman, but that was a load different than agreeing to accompany her back to London and taking his place among Polite Society.

Whatever it was didn't matter. She was gone and he could get back to his work at the mines, free of interruption.

Hopefully, this had been one last, desperate attempt on the duke's part, and Rafe would now be left alone.

For good.

It took a complete and total stony silence of approximately eight minutes per the timepiece affixed to the bodice of her dress for Edwina to determine her chaperone back to the inn, "Mr. Hunter," was in fact Rafe Audley's brother.

Of course, that determination had *nothing* to do with the gentleman's physical appearance. In fact, the two men could not be any more different from each other. Though both were tall, each man approximately several inches past six feet, that was where all similarities ended. Mr. Rafe Audley was broad and heavily muscled, with hair blacker than sin and several days of equally dark growth upon his stubbled cheeks. The man beside her now may as well have been an archangel counter figure on a shelf, with not a scrap of growth upon his sun-bronzed cheeks, and a halo of tightly cropped golden curls.

Equally brusque, and from what she had been able to ascertain in the brief exchange of moments ago, possessed of the same droll sense of humor as Mr. Audley.

And the same flinty stare. They both had that, too.

Edwina favored him with a smile. As Mr. *Hunter* Audley's hard gaze was fixed firmly ahead, she needn't have bothered, if not for one indefatigable truth she'd carried all these years in her work: always be smiling. Invariably it improved something, even if it did not seem as such at the time one offered said smile. "I wanted to thank you," she said, breaking the stony impasse. After all, it really was something of a waste to have her charge's brother at her side, and not gather up something useful to help her along with her lessons and plans for him. And not using every moment on her charge's edification was decidedly not a sin she'd ever be charged with. "It really was most gracious of you to offer to bring me to my abode."

"I didn't offer," he said, with what she was coming to recognize as the Audley bluntness. "It was a directive. I followed it . . . ma'am." The gentleman did not take his focus off the graveled path when he addressed her.

Hmph. Very well, then. That taciturn reply, with that reluctantly tacked on "ma'am," was still a shade more polite than Mr. Audley's early ordering of her to silence, and as such, she knew bringing around this gentleman would be a good deal easier than bringing around his older, colder counterpart.

Gathering her parasol, she popped the article open, and dangled it artfully over her left shoulder, so that it shielded her from the bright Staffordshire sun, and also allowed her to look freely, if she so chose, at Mr. Hunter Audley. "You must be very important for Mr. Audley to summon you."

Still nothing.

So he didn't respond to false flattery, and he'd be cautious of confirming his identity as Rafe Audley's brother.

Tapping a fingertip along the ivory handle of her parasol, she searched the catalogue in her mind for ways to deal with one such as he.

Edwina sighed and lowered her parasol. Snapping it closed, she let her favorite—and now ruined—piece hang over the side of the wagon, as they went. "I must apologize. It is hardly fair for a skilled miner such as you to be saddled with the task of bringing me to my inn. You hardly want to go about playing nursemaid, to me . . . or anyone. Regardless, I am grateful."

From the corner of her eye, she detected the faintest easing of tension in his broad shoulders. Not that he released it so easily, or entirely. But enough to know she was on the right track.

"Wasn't working today anyway." It was a gruff admission, but also confirmed that, one, she had taken the correct approach with him.

And two, he would reveal far more than his brother ever would.

Success.

Tapping the muddied parasol at her side, Edwina kept back a smile. "Your brother also proved inordinately generous in his assistance, though I know he was put out at having to see to the task," she ventured, keeping her tone disinterested and conversational.

"He's put out when he has to deal with anyone and anything that isn't the mines."

This time, she couldn't keep her lips from curling in their corners. Success. He'd confirmed his identity . . . whether intentionally or not, she could not say, but it was just further evidence that the information she needed to glean about her charge might be best served from . . . his brother. "I confess to not understanding how such work should inspire such devotion." And why a duke's son, whose father wished to include him in his life, and give him every opportunity, should prefer to stay here. If her own father had acknowledged her in such a way . . .

Edwina pushed back that wishful musing that had been with her since she was a girl.

"I don't expect you would. Only a miner understands the miner's ways . . ."

"And it is something you and Mr. Audley know a good deal about?" she murmured.

"We've been miners since we each reached the age of eight, older than most." Older than most . . . Every part of Edwina's heart squeezed at that matter-of-fact revelation from Rafe Audley's brother. "And yet, early on, Rafe proved himself, and did the work that men two decades his senior weren't doing. He rose up to what he is now. We both did," he added, as if he himself were an afterthought to his brother's accomplishments, and it spoke volumes of the respect he carried for Mr. Audley.

Mr. Rafe Audley truly had no desire to return with her, and reclaim his rightful place. He would rather toil in mines that any sane person would leap at the opportunity to escape. It was . . . nothing short of madness. With the backbreaking work he was responsible for, and the peril he faced, why should he ever, ever wish to hold on to it?

And the irony of that wasn't lost on her . . . she'd spent the whole of her life in search of being accepted as he so was. And he'd just . . . throw away that gift the duke held out? It was . . . unfathomable. And also something she'd not accept.

Unfortunately, any further hopes of gathering information from the gentleman before her were at an end.

They crested the small rise and proceeded the remaining twenty paces that led to the inn she temporarily called home.

The moment the horses stopped, Mr. Hunter Audley jumped down. He came around the makeshift carriage, and then reaching up, he gripped her by the waist and set her down.

She sank into a curtsy. "Many thanks to you, Mr. Audley." For everything he'd shared.

As if her silent thoughts had given her away, he scowled. "I told you what I did so you know it is an absolute waste of your time coming here to attempt to sway him into giving this up," he said bluntly, revealing that she'd been less subtle and he more aware than she'd believed. "He'll never do that. Ever. More persuasive men tried to convince him to go to London. They all failed. And that isn't because of them, just as it isn't because of you. It's because of who Rafe is and what he wants."

"I . . . see," she said slowly, filing away everything he'd revealed. Proud. He was too proud to give up his work as foreman, overseeing those in his care.

"The mail coach comes at four o'clock every day."

It took a moment to register that abrupt shift away from talk of Mr. Rafe Audley. The mail coach. The mail coach. What reason did she have to care about . . . ? And then it hit her. "I thank you for that. However, I have the benefit of His Grace's carriage." Even as she said it, it registered belatedly that the man before her, was, in fact, that same duke's other son. Perhaps . . . he could be persuaded? As soon as the idea came to her, she squashed it. It was abundantly clear that he deferred to his older brother. "And I'm not leaving."

"You're not?" he asked flatly.

"Not at all. That is, of course, not until your brother, the other Mr. Audley, is prepared to make the journey on to London."

Mr. Audley's younger brother strangled on something that sounded very much like a laugh. With nothing more than a wry shake of his head, he cracked the driving reins and urged his mounts on, riding off.

For a long while, Edwina squinted against the bright Staffordshire sky and peered after that departing crude conveyance. Yes, he might laugh at her as his brother had. But that was fine. They still had yet to realize they had greatly underestimated their opponent—Edwina. That was invariably the case. People formed one immediate opinion of her and then inevitably found out . . . invariably she triumphed—over her charges and assignments. And over any negative opinions that were held of her.

The one person whose opinion she'd been unable to alter had been her father. But this? Venturing into his world and proving herself capable of assisting a duke? It filled her both with hope and an even greater resolve to succeed.

Nay, before she'd been motivated by the prospect of venturing into the world of Polite Society and establishing herself there. Now, it was about something else, as well. As unlikely as it was, a kindred bond had been forged between her and Mr. Rafe Audley—both of them bastards. Both of them self-made people who'd risen up, despite the circumstances of their birth. But only one of them was too afraid to take his proper place when granted that opportunity. Using the tip of her parasol as an improvised cane, she limped onward to the inn.

Nay, over the course of her carriage ride with Mr. Hunter Audley and the consideration of her charge, something had shifted. It was about helping the stubborn lummox see the gift for what it was.

Whether he liked it . . . or not.

Chapter 7

He was amused. And Hunter, since he'd come scowling and silent into the world as a babe, had never been smiling.

Ever.

That, coupled with the fact that Hunter now stood in wait, was enough to send warning bells chiming loud in Rafe's ears as he entered his family's cottage.

What in hell was happening here?

Judging by that crooked half grin, however, Hunter was enjoying this, and just waiting for that question to be put to him.

Still wearing the apron from the work she'd done to prepare the evening meal, Cailin swept out of the kitchen, her thin cotton dress stained and bearing marks of the day's work, and the previous ones before it. "You're late," she said with the stern disapproval likely more impressive than the military generals barking orders at their brother Wesley. "Later than usual." Her threadbare garments stood in stark contrast to the finer ones worn by the lady who'd been intent on getting him to accompany her to London. Cailin's dress also highlighted just how much his sister toiled. Details he never really paid much attention to given how most people in Staffordshire lived. Until today, when Miss Edwina Dalrymple had arrived . . . a woman who'd served as a visible reminder of how the other half lived. That, coupled with the earlier requests Cailin had put to him, forced Rafe to think about . . . things he'd not allowed himself to think about—his sister's existence here in Staffordshire.

Vastly different than the one their mother had enjoyed and not the one he'd have hoped to give his siblings. And he alternately hated himself for not having focused on that overmuch before now, and for questioning the existence he'd provided his family with.

"Where have you been?" She reached past him and pushed the door shut. As she did, he followed her fingers, callused and rubbed red and raw.

Over the years he'd regretted that Cailin didn't have more, but he'd also been mindful of the fact that neither did she have to live the life that most women did in Staffordshire, working the coalfields.

"There were problems at the coalfields, today, that put Rafe behind with his work. Or should I say 'one problem'?" his brother supplied, with a teeth-grating level of humor.

Cailin instantly paled, and the cloth she held sailed through her fingers and fluttered to the floor, forgotten at her feet. "Another fire," she whispered.

Rafe cast a warning glare their brother's way. "There was *no* fire," he said, and stalking over, he retrieved the cloth and handed it back to her. "Everything is fine." This time. That wasn't always the case in the coalfields. Inevitably, some tragedy struck. Two years earlier, Cailin's sweetheart had been trapped in one—on Rafe's watch. Severely hurt and burned, Alfie Carter had severed all connections with Cailin . . . and the living world, and Cailin wore the sadness of that still.

Some of the tension left his sister, but the worry remained etched in the corners of her mouth and eyes. "A cave-in? Was someone injured? What—?"

"Rafe had company from London," Hunter interjected, and this time, he ignored Rafe's glower. Nay, he wore that same pleased, entirely too amused expression, and perched a hip on the arm of the upholstered sofa that had once belonged to their mother.

When neither man said anything more than that, Cailin glanced confusedly between them. "And?"

"*And*," his brother said with apparent relish, "it was a lady."

Cailin shook her head slowly, revealing the same level of confusion Rafe had felt throughout the day where Miss Edwina Dalrymple was concerned.

And, having had enough of his brother's games, he denied him the remaining satisfaction of sharing more than he already had. "The duke sent another in the hopes of retrieving me. This time . . . it was a woman." A fancily dressed, bright-cheeked lady with impressively luscious buttocks. That latter detail, he'd really had no place noting. Considering the matter at an end, Rafe started for the kitchen.

Alas, it appeared both of his siblings were determined to deny him any peace that day.

"What did she want?" Cailin pressed, hurrying into the kitchen, close at his heels.

The evening meal had been set out. Three bowls filled with—he peered at a mashed concoction with a potato-like texture, and some charred bits that had traces of orange within, marking them as possibly once carrots. "What is this?"

Cailin swatted at his arm with her kitchen rag. "Do not go about attempting to change the topic."

"Yes," Hunter said as he seated himself. "Let us not change the topic away from the pretty thing who visited you at the coalfields."

Her eyes forming slow, round circles, Cailin claimed her usual chair, drawing it out and seating herself. "She . . . paid you a visit at the coalfields?" Yes, because everyone knew you didn't disturb a miner in the coalfields. And you never did it to Rafe Audley, foreman.

"Indeed she did," Hunter answered for him, ripping a

piece of bread off with his hands, and adding it to whatever monstrosity their sister had cooked this time. "The lady is hoping to bring him back to London."

"And you are still determined not to go," she said, exasperation rich in her tones. Yes, because just like Wesley, she'd been the only other one of the Audleys who'd actually entertained the possibility of them venturing to Town.

Rafe grabbed the hard breadloaf his brother had already torn into. "And I'm determined none of us will ever go." Without another word, he ripped off a piece with his teeth and chewed. Or attempted to. His jaw ached from the effort it required of him. Abandoning his efforts, he reached for his spoon, but Cailin slid it out of his reach, seeming determined to keep this unwanted conversation going.

He scowled at his brother. Damn Hunter. Hunter, however, sat there, happily eating away, watching as Cailin debated Rafe.

"You are no coward, Rafe."

"Thank you," he cut into his sister's latest lecture.

"I'm not done," she went on. "Or you haven't been one, before now. But you've never really heard any of them out. You have not listened to what the duke has to say."

"Because it doesn't matter." There was nothing the old nobleman could say now that would undo the misery he'd brought to their mother. Or undo the years of neglect. "I already know what he wants. He wants us to come to London. And we collectively don't want to go." Rafe made another attempt to collect his spoon. To no avail.

Cailin grabbed the wooden utensil, moving it out of his reach. "Collectively *was*," and she jabbed the spoon at him, swirling it in a circle, and overemphasizing that word, "the three of us . . ."

Was.

Implying—nay, stating clearly—she was no longer of the same opinion. He scrubbed a hand down his jaw. Bloody hell.

"And then there were two," Hunter murmured.

Rafe sluiced a glare at his younger brother, and then

shifted his attention to the latest Audley defector. "I said it's done. I sent her on her way, and that is the end of her and Bentley."

She dropped his spoon, and with her jaw set at the familiar obstinate Audley angle, proceeded to eat, glaring at Rafe all the while.

"Except that isn't quite true," Hunter said as he wiped the back of his sleeve across his mouth.

Both Rafe and Cailin whipped their attention his way. Rafe narrowed his eyes. "What are you saying?"

"I'm saying you may have sent the lady away and think she left, but she has no intention of doing so. Has every intention of escorting you back." Hunter grinned. "Her words."

Miss Dalrymple . . . was still here? And sudden traitor that she'd become, Cailin laughed.

It was the first time in longer than he could remember that he recalled her finding amusement in anything, and under any other circumstances he'd have been only glad for it. Ignoring his sister's amusement, Rafe focused on what Hunter had revealed. Despite his directives to leave, and his insistence that he'd never make that trip to London, she had stayed here in Staffordshire? The bloody insolence of her. Believing that what he wanted and the decisions he made mattered less than what she wanted. It was the way of all highbrow elites. Making demands and having expectations, without caring or even listening to those whom they took as their inferiors. And the bit of baggage could dress it up with a smile and her fancy, fine words, but that veneer of innocence didn't erase what her intentions were. Over his cold, lifeless body . . . and he'd no intention of kicking up his heels anytime soon.

Growling, he shoved back his chair quickly and quit the kitchen, heading for the front door.

Cailin gasped and flew to her feet. "Do not be a boor, Rafe," she called after him. "*Go* with him, Hunter."

"Not my business," their brother replied.

"But it was yours when you were baiting . . ."

That debate faded as Rafe headed for the stables to ready

his mount. As he did, his fury and annoyance swelled: at the duke for being unrelenting . . . thirty-one years too late. At his perverse brother for having found amusement in any of this. And at Miss Dalrymple herself. The one who'd not quit. A short while later, he found his way to the Old Crow . . . determined to end this nonsense with Miss Dalrymple once and for all.

He entered the inn. Laughter and conversation swelled around the room, with the mining occupants who came here to drink at the end of the day raising their voices to be heard over the others gathered, which only increased the cacophony. Tankards clanged. Men bellowed with laughter. Always busy at this hour, with miners having retired from the coalfields to partake in an ale, the taproom had not a scrap of space to be spared at any table or anywhere else.

Smoke from the many pipes being puffed upon hung like a hazy curtain over the room. Rafe passed a gaze quickly over the patrons . . . and even crowded as it was, he instantly found her.

Seated at a table square in the middle of the taproom, the young lady stood out like a lone flower that had managed to bloom in a coalfield, and given the pale pink gown stitched with roses all over it, she had the look of one, too.

And through the chaos around them, there she sat . . . *working*: papers and notebooks stacked in neat little rows she'd made with her belongings. And a crystal inkwell set out near her fingertips. Periodically, she would dip the most ridiculously long feather quill into that pot, the remnants of ink along the side, before dashing whatever notes she did on her page. All around her, people streamed past her table, nearly brushing her shoulder, while she worked, none of which fazed her.

The proprietor, Old Mr. Ward, joined Rafe. "You be wanting a glass, do you, Mr. Audley?" he yelled, barely loud enough to be heard over the din. The stocky man held a pitcher aloft.

Rafe waved off that offer. "That won't be necessary. I've come for different reasons." His focus went back to the young lady now chewing away at the end of her feather, engrossed. The entire establishment could have been ablaze, and Rafe would wager she would've went right up with it and her papers.

Mr. Ward followed his gaze. "Interesting one, she is." He scratched at his balding pate. "Been here four days, she has. Every day, she comes down and does the same thing. Seems like a right fancy lady, a right fancy lady, indeed, but there's no gentleman about. No servants. None of us know quite what to make of her."

That made the lot of them, then.

Mr. Ward leaned in. "Do you have a problem with the miss?"

The meaning behind that inquiry from Mr. Ward was clear: all Rafe needed to do was say the word, and Miss Edwina Dalrymple's time here was done. That manner of loyalty wasn't just afforded Rafe because he was foreman at the mines where nearly every person had a family member employed. Rather, it came from the close-knit nature of the mining community in general. "No problem." Or rather, soon, he wouldn't, after he was done with this exchange.

Just then Mr. Ward's daughter, gruff, always-scowling Maryam, approached Miss Dalrymple's table with a plate of hotchpotch and bread. This . . . should be interesting. No-nonsense, and with little time spent on pleasantries, the eldest Ward daughter couldn't be more different than the effervescent woman whom she now served.

Unnoticed as he was by the lady, Rafe watched her as she at last looked up. Miss Dalrymple smiled that wide smile she seemed to be in perpetual possession of; her lips moved quickly as she chattered in what he'd learned in no time was her also-familiar way, and made to clear a place on her crowded table. Once she'd made proper space, she patted the spot, her lips moving in the motion of a "thank you."

Maryam returned that smile. Or . . . the closest thing to it that Rafe had ever observed from her. More a half twist, and a grimace at that, but still a smile. Rafe narrowed his eyes. Mayhap, he had better be more wary than he had been where the duke's latest servant was concerned.

"Was hoping you weren't going to say she was a problem. Because my Maryam has taken a liking to her," Mr. Ward said loudly. And, by his tone, the old proprietor had little interest in gainsaying the daughter who really ran this place. "Not that I wouldn't be rid of her if she was a problem," he hurried to assure Rafe. "Just that I'd rather not be the one to toss her out." As if he were afraid Rafe might change his mind, the proprietor hurried off to fill another patron's tankard, and Rafe was left to freely observe Miss Dalrymple once more.

Having worked for a man who delighted in bullying about all those in his employ, the last thing he'd ever sought to do was be a bully back to someone else. But neither would he tolerate the insolent busybodies who thought they were better than him, seeking to drag him back to London, all at the whim of a duke who'd decided he wanted to finally play at father.

Thirty-one years too late.

In fairness, this latest to show up on his doorstep wasn't like the others. Not just because she was female. Rather for the simple truth that he really didn't know what to make of Miss Edwina Dalrymple, which was perhaps even more reason to fear her. The resolve she had displayed hunting him down at the coalfields and then refusing to leave Staffordshire altogether made her more fearless then all the men who'd come before her, combined.

As such, he wanted her out as soon as yesterday.

That sprang him into movement, and he started to weave through the crowded taproom, winding his way past the patrons milling about. As he walked, he returned the greetings of fellow miners but didn't break his stride. All the while, he kept his focus on her.

Miss Dalrymple.

She continued chatting amicably with Maryam, moving the tip of her fork, with the same gracefulness she exuded when she walked, gliding it over the top layer of her hotchpotch. ". . . never had anything quite like it. Rather a splendid dish," she was saying.

And damned if the always-unimpressed Maryam Ward didn't blush under that praise. Oh yes, with this one's sway, there was only one resolution Rafe was walking away with this day—her immediate departure.

Stopping directly across from her, he gripped the back of the empty chair and tugged it out.

The lady looked up, her shock and startlement giving way to such pleasure, he thought she must have taken him for a friend whom she was excited to see. "Mr. Audley!" she exclaimed, confirming he was, in fact, that someone after all. Miss Dalrymple immediately sailed to her feet, and sank into a curtsy better suited for the king and queen themselves than a duke's by-blow coalminer son. "How lovely it is to meet again! Won't you please sit?" she invited him, motioning to the chair he'd already had every intention of claiming. "And perhaps a hotchpot, as well?" He opened his mouth to disabuse her of the idea that this was a social meeting, but she had already turned to Maryam Ward. "If you would be so good as to fetch Mr. Audley a plate of this splendid dish, when you are able."

"Aye." The gruff woman dropped what may or may not have been a curtsy. And that would be the first time he'd ever witnessed a single person in these parts attempt that formality. "Mr. Audley," Miss Ward said as if it were an afterthought. Because of a lady, and a stranger at that.

"Miss Ward." As she scurried off, he gave his head a wry shake. Displaced by a highbrow London lady in Staffordshire? The world had gone insane. Perhaps Miss Dalrymple was, in fact, one of those mythical witches or fairies his mother used to tell him tales of at bedtime.

Miss Edwina Dalrymple held her arms aloft and floated back into her seat. "I am so happy you came," she said. Collecting the white napkin she'd discarded, she quickly picked it up and dabbed at the corner of her immaculate lips. It was a dainty dusting of imagined crumbs, while all around them, men and women belched and scrubbed the backs of their sleeves across food-stained faces. Much the way his brother had a short while ago. It was just one more unnecessary reminder of how far apart she was from his world . . . and steadying for it.

After she returned that article to her lap, she proceeded to clean up her makeshift work station. "Forgive me, I wasn't expecting company."

Though he would give credit where credit was due: she didn't meet the coarse crudeness of the villagers around her with the horror and disdain he would have expected from an uppity one such as her. It was the first time since she had crashed into his life, and made a nuisance of herself, that he wondered about the woman. One who conducted herself with the deportment and mannerisms of a highborn lady, but who was also apparently wholly at ease wandering around the coalfields, and keeping company with the rough-and-tough men and women of Staffordshire.

However, he had neither the time nor any reason to care. "Listen, Miss Dalrymple," he began, when moments later she was still clearing a space for him. "As I said, I'm not here for—"

"Oh, splendid!" She lifted a finger, silencing him, as Maryam returned with another dish.

The moment Miss Ward had gone, Rafe pushed the plate aside. "I'm not here for dinner."

"You really should try it, though. It's really quite splendid," she said as she used her knife and fork to dice up a piece of mutton and take a little bite. Her eyes slid closed, her dark lashes drifting down as if in complete and total rapture. And amid all the bustle that was the taproom, Rafe went absolutely motionless. It was . . . her lashes. Dark ginger, thick, and long . . . and the way she fluttered them held him briefly captivated.

Rafe yanked at his collar. Captivated? What in hell was this madness? And it was then that his suspicions came roaring back to life. No one, no one was this innocent. Everything about her was affected. It had to be. Grabbing the sides of his chair, he moved himself closer to the table, lightly shaking the surface enough that her inkwell rattled, and her eyes flew open. "I said, I'm not here to join you for food." As he spoke, Rafe jammed a fingertip into an old stain on the old oak table. "Nor is this a social visit."

"I . . . see." Ever so slowly, she put her fork and knife down, so they were perfectly aligned and facing up toward him. "I assured you earlier I didn't require looking after. My ankle is quite fine. It hardly even hurts anymore."

Rafe scrubbed his hands over his face. That was her take-away? That he'd come to verify she was unhurt? "I want to know what you're doing here."

She glanced about, looking briefly down at her pretty pink leather journal, as elegant and out of place as the lady herself. "I'm . . . working. Just completing a review of my notes and planning my lessons to come."

Me, his mind registered dumbly. She was speaking about . . . him?

She favored him with another of those bright smiles. "Or, I should say, our lessons."

"There are no lessons," he bellowed, that shout cutting across even the noise of the busy establishment. "Not today. Not tomorrow, and not one hundred tomorrows from forever." Everyone fell briefly quiet, turning all their attention his way. And he resisted the urge to squirm under that scrutiny. That interest lasted the fraction of a moment, before everyone went back to their own business. There was nothing he hated more than being the recipient of anyone's interest. In fact, even if he didn't hate the man who'd sired him, the prospect of facing all of Polite Society would have been reason enough for him to avoid journeying to London.

When he turned back, he found Miss Dalrymple more serious than he'd ever seen her in these past hours of knowing her. In fact, before this instant, he'd have wagered his role as foreman she wasn't capable of anything but bright, cheerful optimism. And he should not be the one to put out that light. It was just one more reason to send her on her way, as quick as he could. To protect her from becoming jaded by someone as cynical as himself. This time, when he spoke, he tempered his response. "I understand you're just attempting to do the role that you signed on to do." And he respected a woman of such strength, one who'd go toe to toe with him. "However, my frustration comes from the fact that I've given you my answer. I will not return to London. With you, or with anyone." And certainly not because the Duke of Bentley had summoned him.

"I . . . see," she said quietly. Then ever so meticulously, she pushed aside her dinner that she'd been previously enjoying, and set to work folding her napkin. That stained and aged cotton fabric that no doubt bore the marks of wear from all the hands that had previously used the rag, she now folded first in half, and then over into a square, and then over once more, into an even smaller square. When she'd finished her folding, she studied her work, smoothing her manicured fingertips along its perimeter.

For a moment, he wondered if she had dismissed him, and he'd simply missed the cue. Until, at last, she looked up. "I understand a lot of what you are feeling."

"I highly doubt that." She couldn't know a thing about the resentment and hatred Rafe carried for the man who served as her employer . . . and how Rafe's past had shaped who he had become.

"You don't care to have people looking at you or any real attention being paid you." He frowned. She couldn't know that. That was, the lady wasn't wrong, but how could she have gathered that in just a pair of short exchanges? Grasping her chair, as he had moments ago, she drew her seat closer and dropped her elbows atop the table, so that she mirrored him. "How do I know?" she asked in answer to the silent questions he'd carried. "Color filled your cheeks when your men came and found you speaking with me. Because you didn't like them being observers to any business we had together. And when the other patrons looked our way a bit ago, you had that same look of discomfort to you."

Flummoxed, he was incapable of a response.

And unfortunately, Miss Dalrymple had words enough for the both of them.

"You don't like being challenged, and you feel my presence here, and my intention to escort you to London, does just that."

Unnerved, he made a concerted effort to conceal it.

She was insightful in ways that he'd previously taken for flighty. She was keenly sharp when he had thought her embarrassingly innocent and naïve. And she saw too much. Entirely too much. And those smiling, twinkling eyes glimmered with a knowing sparkle.

Yes, it was official. He needed to get rid of her . . . now.

"May I escort you to your room?" Rafe was already pushing back his chair.

"That won't be necessary."

"I'm not asking you," he said bluntly.

She wrinkled her nose. "Then, you shouldn't have added a question to your tone, because that implied it was a question, Mr. Audley. Now, if you had said, 'I am escorting you to your rooms', that would have been a clear statement that required no answering on my part." She must have seen something in his eyes, for she abruptly stopped talking, and coming to her feet, began to meticulously gather up her papers. Filing them into neat, clean piles, and then depositing them into a floral valise that, until now, he'd failed to see.

He grabbed her bag and headed for the stairs.

"I assure you, I am more than capable of seeing to my own things, Mr. Audley," she called after him, hurrying close. "Though that is quite gentlemanly of you."

Gentlemanly? He took the stairs quickly, and she kept an impressive pace, nearly matching his stride.

"Door?" he asked when they reached the main hall.

When she didn't speak, he glanced back.

She shook her head.

"Which door is yours?" he snapped.

"See, that is vastly better. One-word utterances only beget confusion and—" He growled. "The second on the right," she said hastily.

Rafe was already striding over. He gave her a pointed look.

The young lady shook her head. "I don't know what you are—?"

"The key."

"It is not locked."

He briefly closed his eyes. "You don't lock your door."

"It did not seem important to do so."

It was a damned wonder she'd survived to . . . the twenty-something years she had.

Grabbing the handle, he pushed the panel open, and stormed inside.

And promptly fell into a fit of choking, as he took in the monstrosity before him with horrified eyes. A floral embroidered coverlet of silk had replaced the serviceable wool blanket that always covered the beddings of the Old Crow Inn. A pillow encased in a matching fabric had been set in the middle, and artfully arranged atop that were a pair of pale green and pink silk pillows adorned with gold tassels. As if the designer feared they might not be garish enough, they'd stitched a child gardening into the center of that already busy design. Dumbstruck, he picked up from the nightstand a small crystal-cut vase that contained a lone pink flower. "What in the hell is this?"

"A peony."

He closed his eyes and prayed for patience. "I mean, *all* of this," and he slashed a hand around the room.

She glanced about. "My rooms?" It was a question.

At least, he wasn't the only one of them confused this time. "I've seen these rooms. Every room in this inn," he said, awe and horror comingled as he spoke to himself. "Not a one of them looks like this." As if the sun had been swallowed and thrown back up all over the tiny quarters.

"Thank you," she said, bowing her head.

"It wasn't a compliment."

"I know that."

She had? He highly doubted—

"However, kind words do not cost much. Yet they accomplish much."

He puzzled his brow. It was irrelevant and yet— "Who the hell said *that*?"

"Blaise Pascal. He was a French writer. And mathematician." She paused. "And physicist . . ."

And . . . the lady who'd been sent to retrieve him proved more and more of a peculiarity. Who was she that she spoke like a lady and recited French mathematicians and charmed gruff villagers in Staffordshire? "And you know so much about . . . French physicists?" And . . . oddly, that question came out not as a taunt, but out of genuine curiosity that demanded asking.

The young lady gave a toss of her artfully arranged reddish-brown tresses. "As I told you before, I know a good deal about everything. It serves a young lady well to be accomplished in many, *many* domains, Mr. Audley."

He stalked over to the frothy curtains hanging over her windows, and gave them a light tug. "Such as prettily decorating temporary lodgings?"

"Precisely," she said with an enthusiastic nod.

And this time, he couldn't help it, and didn't even bother trying to stop it—he smiled.

The first real and true one that wasn't inspired by sarcasm or an attempt to unsettle her.

Miss Dalrymple folded her arms at her chest. "You are being sarcastic, this time."

"And you are catching on," he murmured, more to himself, as he strolled about her rooms, inspecting the fripperies she'd crammed into each corner and wall space. My God, she even had sketches hung. Colorful watercolors of flowers and angels and—

"It is important to make one's home where one is."

Rafe shifted his focus from the pair of cherubs frolicking back to Miss Dalrymple. "And where is your home, Edwina?"

"That isn't appropriate," she immediately replied.

"Which? My using your Christian name, or probing too deeply?" he asked, dropping a shoulder against the wall.

A pink blush filled her pale cheeks, and that rosy hue did her features a favor, making her more pretty than he cared to notice. "Both. Either. Just as . . . it is inappropriate for you to be here, in my chambers. Alone." She coughed artfully into her fist. "That is . . . alone *with* me or any young woman, really."

"This isn't London," he said, eyeing her anew. How . . . interesting. He'd managed what had otherwise until now seemed impossible—he'd unsettled her.

Rafe shoved away from the wall and started a slow stroll across the room. Another might have met that approach with wariness. The woman before him could teach a thing or two to commanders about facing down charging forces. He stopped before her, and she angled her head enough so that their gazes met. "And yet, you who don't believe I should call you by your Christian name, and who doesn't wish to share anything remotely personal, expect that I should happily welcome your interference in my life, *Edwina*?" he asked, adding a mocking edge to that overemphasized use of her name. And yet, what had set out as an attempt to run her off and shame her for refusing to consider his wishes . . . shifted, and changed in that moment. As close as they were heightened the intimacy . . . of their bodies' nearness, and a different tension hummed to life in these rooms.

His gaze slid lower, to the mouth that continued to fascinate, those lips a shade that didn't know whether it wished to be red or pink, and had settled into a hue in between, like the neighbors' raspberries he'd snuck off to pluck before they'd fully ripened, as a boy. And oddly, this was a like hungering for this taste of an altogether different, and even more forbidden, fruit.

"Are you . . . attempting to scare me, *Rafe*?" she whispered, laying a deliberate command of his name, in what was clearly a challenge, a stubborn response that left it clear that fear was the last thing she felt.

He wished he was. Because then she wouldn't be standing there, her chest heaving and her lips parted, and he was the one who suddenly found himself on the defensive. His senses jumbled as desire stirred to life within him. He brought his mouth lower, closer to hers, and she sucked in a shuddery little breath just as he shifted course and placed his lips beside her ear, that delicate, curved, perfectly formed shell. Another part of a woman he'd never truly noted, but now would never stop noticing. "And what if I said I was, Edwina? What would you say then?"

"I would say your efforts are in vain."

Aye, he rather suspected those to be the truest words ever uttered. The king himself couldn't go toe to toe with a warrior such as her. And that only fueled the ever-growing desire that seared through his veins. "And what if I said I was going to kiss you?" he asked hoarsely, in what should have been a taunt, but was really a request. And it took all his efforts to fight the hungering to take her mouth under his, as he wished.

Her eyes flared . . . and then darkened a shade, before those lashes so red they were nearly black swept low, lying like a blanket upon her skin. "I should say that it isn't proper to kiss one's charge," her voice emerged breathless, "and that I've never allowed it." He silently cried out at the frustration of that rejection. "Until now—"

Until now . . .

It was all the permission he required.

He covered her mouth with his.

The lady stiffened for one span of a heartbeat, before her hands climbed about his neck, twining like ivy, and she clung to him. Clung to him as he kissed her, and she kissed him in return.

He brought his mouth down over hers again and again, tasting that overly full upper lip that had so fascinated him, and he suckled the flesh, he licked the seam of her lips, and she moaned, that little hum reverberating inside Rafe.

There would be time enough later to recoil at the horror of having surrendered in any way to Edwina Dalrymple, but in this moment, there was only this aching need to have her in his arms.

Chapter 8

Edwina had been kissed a total of eight times in her life. All lecherous attempts she'd ultimately managed to escape.

Four of the kisses she'd received had landed on her cheek, a product of her quick reflexes and the drunken attempts of the men who'd employed her.

Four had landed on her mouth.

All of which had been sloppy and wet and gross enough to make her stomach churn.

None of which had moved her . . . in any way, beyond that horror and revulsion.

And none had ever dared ask permission of her, a mere servant to them. None had showed restraint, allowing that decision to be hers.

That was, until now.

And that recognition of her right and her choice was a heady aphrodisiac.

Nor had any of those shameful bounders dared kiss like Rafe Audley. As if he were possessing her and asking to be possessed *by* her, all at the same time. He teased and tasted the seam of her lips, licking those contours she'd spent years practicing ways to conceal for the sinful attention paid them . . . only to at last learn the glory she was capable of feeling . . . and giving because of them. She relaxed, softening her mouth, surrendering herself completely to him and this moment.

And then he touched his tongue, a fiery brand that burned her from the inside out, to hers.

Whimpering, her fingers curled reflexively, clenching and unclenching against his nape, sinking into his skin and leaving her marks upon him. So this was the manner of madness that possessed women to forget their names and reputations.

"Th-this is really quite informative," she rasped, as he drew her hands up, collecting her wrists, and bringing them above her head. He used them to drive her gently back against the door.

It rattled behind her, a naughty little knock created by the wicked game they now played. "Is it?" he panted, dragging a trail of kisses down her jawline, and lower, to her neck.

Had she spoken aloud? Or were their thoughts moving as one, as their bodies now did?

She moaned, a long, keening, desperate little sound, and her legs sagged under her. The only thing keeping her upright were his hands and body, anchoring her there to this moment and her pleasure. "Undoubtedly so." And that was the only reason, the only reason at all, she was allowing herself this. All of this delicious wickedness in his arms.

"You must tell me how, princess." Then, he lightly suckled and nipped at the sensitive skin of her throat. An area of skin she'd never before known was sensitive.

He'd asked something. He wanted something. What was it? It was all confused in her mind. "Are you teasing me?"

"Oddly, this time I am not," he said, taking her lips in another kiss, before returning his attention back to the tender skin of her neck he'd abandoned. "This time, you have me intrigued about your lessons, princess."

And then, through the fog of passion, she recalled her mission. "I-It is an important lesson," she panted lightly, as he lifted his head, to take her lips once more.

"Is it?" That question came hoarse and graveled between one kiss and the next.

"O-oh, yes." Perhaps, the most important one she might have ever learned. "Because it i-is essential to kn-know the reasons a young l-lady might be s-so tempted to throwwww . . ." That word ended on a moan, as he kissed a path along the bodice of her dress. ". . . away her reputation."

"Never much cared for anyone's opinion," he whispered harshly against her mouth.

"We will address more on that later," she said, and tipped her head back to take his kiss once more. And he proved obliging, at least in this. Yes, this was no doubt shameful. And wicked. And all things bad. And she who had so closely guarded her virtue should only be scandalized with herself for having allowed Rafe Audley's embrace. What was worse, not only had she allowed it, but she wanted it, desperately.

Edwina closed her eyes. At last, she understood that which she never had before. Her mother. The fears raised about young ladies everywhere. Why women had a lapse and forgot all the important lessons on morality. For what was morality, when put against this?

With a gasp, reality came rushing up to meet her. Lowering both hands to the sculpted wall of his chest, Edwina shoved, and shoved hard.

And this time, unlike earlier that day, she managed to move the mountain of a man.

Rafe Audley stumbled back, and nearly tripped over his feet . . . before righting himself.

Struggling to get a proper breath in through her lungs, Edwina collapsed against the wall, horror and the lingering effects of his touch a shared culprit.

If he was smug, she was going to wallop him. She was going to gather up her parasol for a second time that day and bring it down atop his head.

And yet . . . as passion receded from his gaze, there was

a brief moment of horror—good. So they were of a like opinion on some things, after all.

"That was—"

"An important lesson?" he drawled.

She blanched. She'd spoken aloud—*again*. All her thoughts had been clouded . . . because of him and his masterful touch. By the mischievous twinkle in his usually cynical eyes, she feared just that. "A mistake," she managed a calm that she did not feel inside. "It was, of course, a mistake, given that we are, one," she struck a finger up, "strangers to one another." Edwina lifted another digit. "Two, I am in your employ."

"You aren't any employee I'd hire, princess."

She bristled. He needn't be so rude. Refusing to let him sidetrack her, she raised a third finger. "Very well, I am in your father's employ, which means you and I are working together. As such, it is inappropriate for a tutor to have relations of such sort with one's charge." It was the wrong thing to say. Reminding him who had sent her, and why she was here.

That ghost of a smile on his hard lips vanished as quick as haunting specters might. "We are not working together, in any capacity. Today or ever."

He'd returned to his surly self. And it was a regrettable transformation as she'd found she so very much appreciated the glimpse of a gently teasing and smiling Rafe Audley, to this . . . angrier version he presented with an even greater ease to the world.

Edwina rested her hands on her hips. "You are being obstinate about this." And here, when she'd give anything to be so accepted as he was by his father. Nay, not accepted . . . wanted. His father truly wished to have Rafe in his life. She smiled. "But fortunately for you," she went on, wagging her finger, "I am even more so."

He matched her movement. "You think you're more obstinate than me, Edwina?"

Well, this certainly didn't seem like a battle she wished to wage. Neither fighting him about the use of her name, nor debating who was more stubborn. Not when she desperately needed to convince him to return with her.

In a bid to take back the gauntlet she'd inadvertently thrown, she forced her lips up another fraction and batted her lashes, in that trick she trained all her students to do.

He peered at her. "Is there something in your eye?"

She immediately stopped that artful flutter. "No, there is not something in my eye, you great lummox," she snapped, and then promptly gasped, stifling that sound of her horror with her palm. First an embrace with Rafe Audley . . . and now *this*? Never in the course of her career had she so lost control of her temperament. She'd always been in complete command of every part of herself. And by the smug, cocksure grin he wore, he knew it, and was relishing it. Refusing to rise to that silent bait, she angled her chin a fraction. "Forgive me. I . . ." *Don't know what overtook me?* Nor did she have a good and proper response.

"Not one who loses your temper, princess?" With his voice a husky, silken purr, he both teased and taunted at the same time.

Edwina bit her tongue to keep back the sharp retort that sprang to life. Blast and damn this man. What was it about him that made Edwina forget herself around him? She, who was never shaken by anyone, at any time?

Well, it was time that she asserted herself as she'd been forced to do with only the most vexing charges. "*Mr. Audley*," she began, resurrecting that formal divide. "Be assured, I have both listened to you and heard you. You do not wish to return to London." Because he preferred the godforsaken country, which was something she'd never, ever understand. "You've blustered and bullied everyone before me, but I am not going anywhere." She shook her head. "Do you hear me? I. Am. Not. Leaving." She clipped out each syllable, over-enunciating each as she spoke. "So you can pout and stomp, and resist all you want, but this is happening. Whether you like it or not. Have I made myself clear?"

He slowly lowered his arms to his sides, and took a slow, languid step toward her, something subtly predatory in his approach that sent Edwina's toes curling into the soles of her slippers to keep from abandoning the spot she stood. She would be damned ten times to Sunday if she ceded an inch to him. And then he stopped that prowl, just beyond her shoulder, so that she had to angle her neck a fraction to see him. Those hard lips that had been on her just moments ago, responsible for more pleasure than she'd known was possible in a mere kiss, curved up in a slow, dangerous grin. Little shivers trickled along her back. Nervousness is what it was. Surely not desire. Not again. Not when she'd already recognized the temporary lapse, and sworn she'd not let herself do it again.

Even so, as he brought his mouth close to the shell of her ear, her lashes fluttered, and she angled her head away from him, in a bid to conceal her weakening.

"You've made yourself perfectly clear, *Edwina*," he whispered. "This is war, then."

That brought her eyes flying open.

And with that promise of a threat, Rafe turned on his heel and stalked off.

He closed the door, not with a bang but with the faintest of clicks, so eerie in its silence it proved more powerful than had he slammed the door in its frame.

The moment he was gone, her legs sagged, and she caught the slightly curved back of the Welsh stick chair.

This is war, then . . .

Gadzooks, what had she gone and done now?

Chapter 9

The following morning, seated in the nearly empty tap-room, Edwina found her legs firmly under her, once more, and not only braced for the war Rafe had spoken of, but eager for it.

And as sleep had eluded her, she'd spent the night thinking of the battle to come because between travel, and instructing the gentleman, and having him ready to take part in the Season, she had little time left with which to convince him.

You harebrain. It hadn't been the coming war he'd spoken of that had kept her up—as it should have. But rather, their embrace. Magical. Dizzying. The memory of it had been so strong that sleep had eluded her, and left her attempting to think about her reason for being here in Staffordshire.

Enough.

It was just one kiss.

And she was a woman of twenty-seven, and as such, certainly old enough to take part in . . . in . . . those activities if she wished to. Not that she *did*, but if she did, she was an independent woman who didn't need to rely upon a man, as her mother had.

No, but you do need to rely upon your reputation.
That reminder proved the most sobering one.
Grabbing her pale pink leather notebook, she flipped it open.

Biography of Mr. Rafe Audley

She tapped the edge of her feather quill back and forth from the table to the book, in a deliberate rhythm, while she thought. All her assignments began with a description of her charges. She would ask each mother or guardian to complete their own cataloging, and then she would complete one after an initial meeting to compare assessments. In the case of Rafe Audley, however, there had been no father or mother or guardian or . . . anyone from whom to elicit details. There'd been Hunter who'd told her but a few things. According to everything that had been revealed to her by His Grace, Rafe was even more a stranger to his father than she was to her own. Therefore, anything and everything she gleaned about Rafe was a product of her own observation and work.

Biography of Mr. Rafe Audley

She reread the same incomplete list she'd begun last night.
Edwina dipped her pen into the crystal inkpot, and tapping the excess from the tip, she set to work.

Biography of Mr. Rafe Audley

She stared at the line she'd just drawn.
Yes, well, that was something. And as she'd always said, doing something was better than nothing. Even if was just a little something. And in this case, it was very, very little.

Rafe Audley . . . has a sense of humor.

There, it wasn't entirely a lie. She chewed at the feather,

studying what she'd written. Neither, however, was it at all the truth. Just as it wasn't helpful to not be completely honest with oneself in terms of her charge.

1. Rafe Audley . . . has a sense of humor . . . that lends itself to dry and sarcastic wit, that falls to either borderline or completely rude.

With that, Edwina found her rhythm.

2. Rafe Audley revealed himself capable of smiling. It is a perfectly captivating and interesting smile.

Nor was this particular detail about Rafe Audley an insignificant one. Smiles served both ladies and gentlemen alike. The perfect smile had the ability to ease awkward or tense exchanges. It had the ability to earn the attentions and affections of a potential spouse. And there was no doubting that Rafe Audley's real smile would have the ability and power to captivate . . .

He might not be nobility by the rules laid out in Debrett's Peerage, but he very much had hundreds of years of powerful, commanding, austere blood pumping coldly through his veins.

A figure stopped beside her table, jerking her out of her musings, and she looked up. "Miss . . . oh," she said; Maryam Ward, the one who usually greeted Edwina as she broke her fast, had been replaced by her father. "Mr. Ward," she substituted. "How are you this morn—?"

"What do you want?" he demanded sharply.

From what she'd discovered in her short time here, scowls ran in the Ward family, as distinct as their hooked noses and high foreheads. This one, however, was a good deal darker and grimmer than any that had ever been turned her way. "Tea, if you would." She offered him another smile, and made to return to her work.

"Tea? You think you are the bloody queen of England?"

"No, just a tea-loving Englishwoman."

"I've got ale," the taproom owner snapped.

Another who was untrained in dealing with people of all temperaments might have been shaken by the dour fellow. "Water will suffice, Mr. Ward."

He grunted, and shuffled off, returning a moment later. He heaved the pitcher onto the table, spraying droplets everywhere, splattering the notes she'd begun.

She gasped. Her papers. Her precious papers. Edwina skidded her chair back, and jumping to her feet, she searched with her hands for something to blot the damage that had been done. "A cloth, if you please?"

"Don't have one."

There came a hiccoughing chuckle from the old drunken patron set up at the corner table.

Hmph. She wiped her damp palms along the front of her skirts. Well, everyone here had turned rather rude, rather quickly. Why . . . it was as though, after four days here, those who'd been entirely pleasant were quite put out with her and by her. Edwina narrowed her eyes upon her damp documents . . .

And then all the pieces of the puzzle slid into their proper place:

The suddenly unfriendly owner.

The lack of tea when everyone, everywhere knew that people of every station and all castes in England drank the comforting brew. This time, when she looked to Mr. Ward, she kept her features even and her smile serene. "I . . . see . . ." And . . . she did. "That will be all, Mr. Ward."

Nor did she imagine the flash of remorse in the old fellow's rheumy eyes, right before he rushed off. No. Undoubtedly, she did not.

. . . *war has been declared* . . .

Why, Mr. Audley was trying to run her off.

And he'd enlisted help.

She drummed her fingertips. Well, that was fine . . . two could play at this game. Of course, it required two to play and . . .

She stopped abruptly.

Gathering up the folio she'd received from her employer, the duke, she searched through the documents until she landed on the one she sought.

Edwina tugged the page out.

You have at your discretion and disposal an unlimited sum by which to secure my son's cooperation. Anything within your power to see that he complies, please, see to it . . .

See to it.
Unlimited funds.
Her discretion.

Drumming her fingertips on the top of the folder, she read those already memorized words over and over.

And then, Edwina's gaze locked on those last two words.

Her discretion said he wasn't going to come easily. Nay, it said he wasn't going to come at all. He was, for reasons she'd never understand, determined to remain at the Cheadle coalfields, risking life and limb, when he could be pursuing a future that was safe and secure. She'd already ascertained that she couldn't make him give up his work here . . . for any sum. Why, she rather thought he'd set the fortune his father would give to him ablaze than use those funds. Which was unlike any person she'd ever known. Because well, frankly, it was mad. People needed money. And most people could be bought . . .

Edwina immediately stopped her drumming.

Of course. Why had she not thought of it before now?

Why had not the duke, for that matter?

Rafe Audley couldn't be bought . . . but his employer . . . well, he likely could.

Edwina snapped her book shut. Quickly gathering up her things, she stuffed them into the embroidered satchel at her feet.

She had *two* visits to see to this day.

Chapter 10

There was little rest to be had for miners. They worked twelve-hour days, and had but one day to call their own.

The miner's day was one of the longest days a man, woman, or child could work. One filled with back-breaking labor that left a body sore, and eager for rest.

The last thing a person employed at a coalfield wished was for an end-of-workday summons from the coal master.

For Rafe, however, it was not an unfamiliar call to receive. As the foreman, he was often summoned to give reports on the day's haul and provide updates on any injuries or problems at the coalfield.

In fact, for him, these calls to discuss his work were welcome. And they were a good deal more welcome than dealing with the bothersome chit who'd been pestering him yesterday.

Rafe ducked under the slight doorjamb, and doffed his hat. "You called for me," he said, by way of greeting.

He and Sparrow didn't bother with pleasantries. They weren't friends. They weren't friendly. They didn't even like each other. But they got on well enough in this arrangement in which Rafe had freedom and control over the coal-fields.

"Aye. Sit. Sit," Sparrow said distractedly. Puffing away on the pipe clamped between his teeth, the coal master held a magnifying glass close to the page of his books, and attended those numbers there.

Rafe slid into the seat across from the older man. And waited.

This was also a familiar game. Sparrow possessed a fragile ego, and though he needed Rafe, he didn't like the fact that he did, and welcomed any opportunity to exert his power where he could.

That, however, was win enough for Rafe . . . that these waiting games no longer bothered him. Because it was a sign of his influence over the one who owned most of the village. Propping his mud-stained boot across his opposite knee, Rafe leaned back in his chair. And waited.

"I'm letting you go for a bit."

Well, this was a new game. Calling him here for no reason, and then dismissing him. Rafe came to his feet. "Don't waste my time, Sparrow. I have a coalfield to run. Your coalfield."

"No. No. No. You misunderstand me," Sparrow exhaled a perfect ring out the side of his mouth, and then waved the residual smoke away. "I am relieving you of your responsibilities."

And for the first time in all the years he'd worked for Sparrow, the coal master managed to knock Rafe off-balance, cutting his feet out from under him, and he reseated himself, claiming that previously released spot in an attempt not to fall down. All the while, through Rafe's tumult, Sparrow continued that relaxed survey of his profits.

Because surely Sparrow had not just said what he'd said.

As if he'd not stated his intentions to upend Rafe's world.

Surely Rafe had heard him wrong.

Because nothing about this summons, and the words being spoken, made sense.

"You're sacking me," Rafe said blankly, in dumbfounded confusion.

"Didn't say that." The old coalfield owner didn't even bother to lift his head. He just continued to move that glass against his eye, back and forth, skimming those numbers, his profits, profits he wouldn't have come close to having without Rafe working for him as he had.

The ticking of the bracket clock at the back center of Sparrow's desk grated, that incessant beat more pronounced in the otherwise heavy silence of the room.

And it took seven of those passing moments for Rafe to realize . . . why the old bastard had no intention of saying anything else. Surging out of his chair, he leaned across the desk and slammed his coal-stained hand upon those neat, meticulous columns, leaving a black palm mark upon it.

Sparrow jumped. "Hey! Have a care, Audley." The coal master swallowed wildly, his cheeks pale and his gaze uneasy, rendering that warning empty.

"What the hell game are you playing?" Rafe snarled.

Sparrow adjusted his snowy white cravat. "N-No game. I'm merely . . . testing out some changes."

Testing out some changes? Why in hell would he even think of, let alone do such a thing? Ridding Rafe of his role threatened his profits. "I bring you a fortune. No one could make you even consider—"

He narrowed his eyes. Of course, now it made sense. It had been inevitable.

"By God . . . the duke got to you." That was all there was to it. He'd come here, to his place of work, and robbed him of what mattered most: his work in the coalfields, that role he'd risen to and took pride in.

"Nobody gets to me," Sparrow scowled. "But . . . I do see the benefits to your improving yourself in London. You'll serve me better when you come back."

Rafe inhaled through his nose and exhaled slowly through his clenched lips, the breath leaving him on a quiet exhale.

Dead. He was going to kill Sparrow dead.

And yet . . . neither was that rage properly placed. It belonged squarely with the one who'd set to work interrupting Rafe's life these past months.

"I am asking you to reconsider."

The coal master took another pull of his pipe, holding that smoke in his mouth for several moments, before letting it out. "I'm a man driven by money. You know that better than anyone. You can't make me more than I'm being offered to just give you up for a bit."

Give him up for a bit . . .

His father had coordinated and his employer had agreed to what Rafe would do. Robbing him of choice, as if he weren't a man free to make his decisions. "How much?" What was the going rate to control one's son?

"One thousand pounds." Rafe choked. "Enough to cover the salary of you and the next five foremen after you." Sparrow shrugged his wide shoulders. "Can't expect a man would turn those monies down."

No. He didn't. And certainly not this man before him. Not for Rafe. And yet, it also did all come down to how much stood to be made. Rafe ground his finger into the desk as he spoke. "My work earns you much more than one thousand pounds a year. You'd never go about thinking to replace me with someone inferior for that amount." He'd be a damned fool, and a poor businessman, and Rafe had worked with him long enough to know he was neither.

Sparrow leaned back in his chair and settled one hand over his enormous belly. With the other, he clasped his pipe. He took another puff from that nauseant scrap. "I'm far too clever with my profits and the running of my mine to hire an inferior."

Rafe narrowed his eyes. "There's no one better than me."

"Yes, but there is . . . someone close. Someone you've trained, and whom you respect, and as such"—Sparrow's spine grew, as with each word spoken strength returned to those nasal tones—"you would be hard-pressed to fault your temporary replacement."

"Who?" Rafe asked bluntly.

"Quite skilled. Efficient."

"I said *who*?" he thundered.

The other man jumped a meter in his seat. "Hunter."

Rafe rocked back on the balls of his feet. "Hunter?" he echoed dumbly. As in . . .

"Your brother," Sparrow clarified that confused question Rafe still attempted to sort through. "Hunter Audley."

"Have you—?"

"I shared the news of his changing role with the coal-fields earlier today."

Rafe reeled under this revelation . . . and betrayal. It felt very much like that, too. Rafe glanced about. This didn't make sense. None of it did. "You despise Hunter."

"Yes, I do." Sparrow gave another shrug. "But I don't much like you, either."

Fair enough.

He tried again, fighting for his place here. "You don't want to do this, Sparrow."

The old coal master lifted a bushy white brow. "Are you challenging your brother's ability to oversee your role, Audley?"

As a boy, his often-sad mother only found a smile when she was either preparing to journey to London to visit the duke . . . or sitting down to play chess with Rafe. Even though she'd been rubbish at it, and he'd invariably won.

This, however, was a first: another person had declared checkmate against him. For Sparrow, in this, was correct. To gainsay these changes would mark him as disloyal to the last person he'd be disloyal to. The brother he loved and sought to protect and had . . . and the brother who would now also fill Rafe's role.

The same brother who'd apparently thought nothing of stepping in to fill Rafe's role here.

Resentment soured in his belly and filled his mouth. "How much of my time here did he buy from you?"

"The London Season. See . . . just a few months and then you can resume your work. Really convenient for the both of us. I couldn't agree more with you. It is ridiculous imagining *you* going to Town, but . . ." He shrugged. Again. Just that and nothing more.

To keep from storming around the desk and burying his fist

in the other man's face or, worse, saying something he might regret about his brother, Rafe grabbed his cap, jammed it onto his head, and stormed out, slamming the door hard behind him. With fury fueling his strides, he made the march home.

First, Bentley had sent a steady parade of his minions.

Then, he'd sent the always-ebullient Miss Dalrymple.

And here he'd been so very convinced that no one could be worse than her. Yes, Rafe had been beyond certain that it couldn't get any worse than having his peace and work disturbed by the Duke of Bentley's latest lackey, Miss Edwina Dalrymple.

Only to be proven wrong.

So very wrong.

For when Edwina and the lackeys before her had failed, the duke had persisted. When nothing else had worked, he had come for Rafe's job. It was an infuriating reminder of how the duke thought nothing of manipulating Rafe and his siblings. To the Duke of Bentley, they were mere strings that he was pulling on; Rafe was being forced to dance to whatever tune he played.

And apparently, in order to secure his role as foreman, Rafe would have to journey to London. Or, at least, that was what the duke expected. He no doubt thought he'd tied Rafe's hands.

Over my dead body.

Stalking quickly down the gravel path that led to the front door of his cottage, he pressed the handle and let himself in.

Rafe knew by the absolute absence of the familiar charred scent that greeted him at the end of every long workday that something was decidedly amiss.

That, coupled with the absence of the sister who always rushed to greet him. Not even bothering to look as he tossed his cap at the crude nail that served as a hook behind the door, he did a sweep of the still room. Perfectly tidied as it always was, nothing outwardly out of place.

"Where's Hunter?"

"He's not here," Cailin called back from the kitchen.

"Yes, I see that," he muttered to that obvious answer from the sister who'd always taken an unholy glee in goading him.

Nor did he find it a coincidence that Hunter was conveniently missing. His brother hadn't even had the decency to prepare Rafe for the news of his post. Instead, he'd let that bastard Sparrow be the one to tell him? No wonder he'd not returned after that particular meeting. Heading for the kitchen, Rafe gave his head a disgusted shake. This had been the duke's latest gift to their family—turning brother against brother.

No, that wasn't true. He might envy Hunter; he might be jealous of the role he'd snagged from Rafe. But he would never resent his brother. Particularly in this. Hunter had been fighting for the opportunity to prove himself capable of a leadership role at the Cheadle coalfields. And it appeared he now had it.

Rafe pushed the kitchen door open, speaking as he went. "Did he come home after . . . ?" Shock cut off the remainder of that question. His gaze landed not on his sister seated at the table, but on the woman beside her. The two of them, sipping tea and chatting like they were the oldest of friends.

Suddenly, she stopped and looked up.

Edwina's eyes brightened. "Mr. Audley!" she greeted him, as if they were, in fact, old friends, *too.* "How wonderful it is to see you again!" And she said that last part as if it were the greatest of surprises that she found him in his own home. Which he didn't take for any kind of coincidence.

With the day he'd had, the last thing he cared to do or the last person he cared to see was the duke's latest emissary.

This goddamned day.

"What the hell are you doing here?"

The young lady froze with a teacup halfway to her lips. Those lips did not deviate from their usual smile. Smiling as she always was. And on this day, with what he was facing, it grated all the more.

"Rafe," Cailin scolded; shoving her chair back, she came to her feet. "Forgive my brother's rudeness, Miss Dalrymple. He's not usually *this* boorish." His sister favored him with a glare . . . that he completely ignored. "Actually, I'm lying. He's usually about this boorish." Cailin winked at this interloper.

Edwina laughed, the sound effervescent and bright against the dreariness that was his Staffordshire cottage, and he found himself . . . sucked into whatever spell she cast. Their eyes caught, hers twinkling and bright with her merriment . . . a merriment that came at his expense . . . and because of his sister's jesting.

Rafe growled. "Boorish?" he directed his question at the one responsible for letting the interloper in. "I'm boorish? This from the sister who'd let this . . . this . . . *woman* in my home?"

Cailin gasped, and coming around the table, she punched him hard enough in the arm to earn a grunt. "Behave. Furthermore, it is *our* home, and she is *my* guest." She looked to Edwina. "Despite my earlier teasing, he's not usually this rude. I do not know what has come over him."

"Betrayal," he mumbled under his breath. It had that effect on a man.

With slower, more graceful movements, Edwina sailed to her feet. "Please, there is no need to apologize for Mr. Audley," she assured. "You should hardly be held to blame for his rudeness." She reached for the opened notebook and pencil, and picking them up, she directed a question at Cailin. "How would you describe his general disposition, if not boorish?"

"Oh, well, certainly blunt to the point of near rudeness," his traitorous sister happily supplied. As if Rafe were not even there. As if they both spoke about a naughty little boy whom they had removed from the discussion.

Rafe was promptly forgotten by the two women, who proceeded to discuss his character.

What in hell was happening here? It was as though the world had all gone mad, and he was left the only one sane of the lot.

He narrowed his eyes upon the source of his misery and woe—Miss Edwina Dalrymple.

And suddenly, it felt very good to have a proper place to direct his rage. This latest person who sought to manipulate and influence his life. One who'd become a wedge between him and Cailin. Well, if that was what Edwina Dalrymple and the duke wanted, they were both bound to be disappointed. Because his father may have cost Rafe his work, thinking that in tying his hands he'd secured his cooperation, but he had every intention of digging all the way in on this one.

"I. Asked. What. You. Are. Doing. Here." He iced out each syllable.

This time, his sister remained silent.

Edwina showed no such compunction. "Well, at present, your sister and I are having a discussion about your general demeanor and personality."

He searched for some hint that she was teasing, but found only her usual guilelessness.

"Before. That." Fury darkened his vision, briefly blinding him. When the curtain of rage lifted, he registered the patient smile she still wore.

She blinked innocently. "Oh." Had she been any other woman, any other person, he would have taken that innocent doe-eyed look as affected. "I think it should be clear. I was speaking with your sister about the offer from the duke."

That was it. The thin thread of control he maintained since his meeting with Sparrow snapped.

Anger whipped through him, and if he wasn't so outraged by that unapologetic admission, he'd have been impressed with her blunt directness. It was entirely one thing for her to challenge him. Her staking out his sister and involving Cailin? That was altogether different, and was a grievance he'd neither forgive nor tolerate. It was enough the duke had interfered with Wesley. "Get out," he seethed. He was already marching for the kitchen door, and grabbed the handle.

"Rafe," his sister repeated, again forceful and sharp in her tones. "*Enough.*"

"You are angry," Edwina murmured, her calm, dulcet tones a contrast to his sister's barely suppressed rage.

"Damned straight I—"

"I was not finished, Mr. Audley," she said politely but firmly, knocking him briefly off the scathing tirade he'd planned to deliver. Beside them, Cailin's eyes grew huge. Yes, because neither of them, nor anyone for that matter, was accustomed to Rafe being blatantly challenged. "You are angry, but as I see it, your sister has even more reason to be so."

And just like that he was knocked off balance. "My . . ."

"Sister," Edwina finished for him when he remained unable to get the rest of his words out. "Yes. Your sister. You have made your feelings entirely clear about coming to London. But those are *your* feelings. And your wishes and your opinions. What of Cailin's?"

It was the first time in the whole of this thirty-one years that anyone had dared question the manner of brother he was. What was worse, it was the very question he'd silently asked himself just yesterday. And with every fiber of his being he resented this stranger for putting the same one to him. Rage swirled in his gut. "You would call me out as a brother?" A smarter, wiser, more aware woman would have heard the warning in that whisper.

Yet again, Edwina proved unlike anyone he'd ever known. "I cannot speak of matters before this, however, in this instance? Yes, I would."

A growl worked its way from deep in his chest and rolled up his throat and past his lips. "Leave us."

The insolent baggage raised her chin. "I've already stated my intention to remain."

"I wasn't talking to you," Rafe said flatly.

"Oh."

Cailin firmed her mouth. "I'm not leaving."

Goddamn it.

The always-smiling Miss Edwina Dalrymple looked to his sister. "I promise, I shall be quite fine. I've come to learn his bark is worse than his bite."

"Undoubtedly. Most don't know that. Most fear him. Not me." His sister's grin was firmly back in place. "And now I see, not you, Miss Dalrymple."

"Oh, not at all."

Not at all? He growled. Of course, either of the stubborn

pair would have to be listening to hear that animalistic grumble. The minx had no idea. None at all. Between her meddling and the duke's? It was too much.

"Who the hell do you think you are?" he shouted, and Edwina and his sister finally stopped talking. "Do not go reassuring my sister. *I* will be the one to do so."

"If 'reassuring' is the air you intend to convey, with all that blustering and bellowing, you are not doing a very convincing job of it, Mr. Audley," Edwina chided, disapproval rich in her dulcet tones.

Cailin's eyes grew round in her face, as she looked first to Rafe, then to Edwina, and back to Rafe once more. And for the first time in her life, without a word, his sister stayed silent, headed for the kitchen door, and hastily quit the room until he and Edwina were . . . alone.

The moment she'd gone, Rafe launched into his insolent *guest*. "You, a stranger, coming into my household and my village, thinking you know what's best for any of us. Except that's not really the case, is it. This is a job for you. You do not care about me or my siblings." Nor did he expect her to, as they were strangers. "But I'll be damned if I'll let you come here trying to exert your influence and presume to control my family to get what you want."

"And I'll ask again: is it what *they* want?"

It hadn't been what Wesley wished for, a voice taunted. He tamped it down. "It's what Hunter wants," he said flatly.

"What of Cailin?" she persisted.

Cailin, whose heart had been broken by this village. Cailin, who was likely never to marry a miner because of the loss she had suffered. And in a mining village, there were few other options; nay, there were no other options, in terms of sweethearts or husbands. He took an angry step toward her, but she did not back down. "What of *my* sister?" He lowered his head, and she angled hers back at the same time. A different tension danced in the air, a dangerous awareness lent heat by the fury that burned between them. "I'd advise you to have a care, Edwina," he whispered, his breath mingling with hers.

The lady wasn't done. "But have you thought about what she wants? Truly wants."

"You know nothing," he snarled, sticking his nose near hers. "*Nothing.*"

"Actually, I do, Mr. Audley." Edwina edged her chin up. "And I suspect you know it, and you despise that I do," she said, her voice emerging as a slightly husked whisper, one that bespoke . . . an awareness. One that he shared.

His gaze locked with hers, a volatile energy thrummed in the air.

Of their own volition, Rafe's eyes slipped to her mouth.

Their chests rose and fell, fast and hard.

He trailed a taunting finger from the line of her jaw up to the high, graceful curve of her cheekbone. Except . . . it was intended to be a mocking touch. And yet, if it was, he'd no place luxuriating in the creamy softness of her skin. He immediately stopped that inadvertent caress. "And you think you know what she wants? You who have met her once and for one afternoon?" he asked coolly, logic once more restored.

"I know her hardly at all, and in just an afternoon's visit I've learned she has an interest in seeing museums and the theater and attending an opera." She managed to speak with both a calm and quickness that didn't allow him an opportunity to respond. Or mayhap it was that the chit didn't want or need to hear from him.

She'd gathered all that?

Except she wasn't done.

"Do you know what else I believe?"

"I don't c—"

"I believe your prejudice against Polite Society and even your father, and everything associated with that gentleman, might have impacted your ability to make a decision free and clear of your own feelings, yes," she said with such assuredness and control of her voice and her opinions that outrage burned his neck and face hot with fury.

His lip peeled back in an involuntary sneer. "This from a woman who thinks it is so very important to pluck me out of Staffordshire and see me placed in a part of society and England she approves of?"

That brought the young woman back on her heels, and her mouth slackened a bit.

Good. He'd knocked the insolent baggage off balance.

The moment proved fleeting. "I know taking your rightful place among Polite Society would open doors for you that would see you spared from risking your life in a coalfield. I know that you'd have warmer winters and more comfortable summers. And I know your sister wouldn't be toiling over kitchens, which she hates, because all women hate that manner of work and only ever see to it out of necessity."

And oddly, she spoke as one who did know. And what was worse, she'd again raised such specific thoughts about his sister.

It wasn't lost on him that it had been he who'd declared war upon her, and yet she'd cut a path through his household, dragging onto their makeshift battlefield Rafe's sister, the one whom he'd sought to protect at any and every cost.

She was ruthless.

And Rafe hated this woman before him, in this moment, for forcing him to think about that. Even as he should probably be grateful.

Yet, the truth remained, Cailin might have had her heart broken in Staffordshire, but that same exact fate awaited her if they joined High Society. Nay, worse. There, he and Cailin would both find themselves the recipients of scorn and scandal and mockery. And while Rafe didn't doubt that any insult would roll off him, he couldn't say the same for his sister. And that was why he would not expose her to life in London.

"You know what I'm saying is right," she said quietly, into the void of their silence, filling it with her convictions and seeking to weaken his. "You know this has the potential to be about improving more than your life, and that is why you still haven't thrown me out as you want to."

"As I should," he sneered. Rafe scraped a condescending glance up and down her lace-ruffled, pale pink satin gown, as out of place here as he would be if he set foot in her fine end of London. "You think you know anything about what I feel? You think you have some preternatural insight into my thinking? You insist you know and speak of how easily it would be for me to forsake my life, my career for the whims of a duke." This time, when she attempted to speak, he cut across her interruption. "But if the roles were reversed, princess. And I asked you to give up everything you knew, everything you did, and start anew here, you'd turn tail and run."

Edwina wrinkled that pert little nose. "Why would I—" She immediately closed her lips, but he thinned his eyes, as that unuttered meaning filtered into the air.

"Why would you give up your fancy lifestyle for my lesser one?" he whispered, starting a path around her.

The young lady stiffened, angling her head and fearlessly following his movements. "I did not say that." There was a wariness in her hazel eyes.

"Ah, dishonest once more," he jeered.

She sputtered, "I have *not* been dishonest once about my identity or my intentions or my feelings about your refusal to speak with His Grace. How *dare* you suggest I've behaved in any way other than honorable and forthright?"

"I dare because it's true, princess," he said, against the shell of her ear, and Edwina's breath caught. Near as he was, he felt the little tremble that shook her long, willowy frame. Was it fear? Desire? He could no longer tell where she was concerned, and even more disconcerting was the masculine hungering for it to be the latter. "Just because you didn't bring yourself to speak it aloud, Edwina, doesn't mean it wasn't what you were thinking, and your failure to own that makes you a liar."

"Very well! I was going to say as much. The country is unforgiving and harsh." As she spoke, she whipped a hand about, punctuating every point she made. "Why, you yourself spoke of fires and cave-ins and there was my injured foot, and why should anyone, man or woman, prefer such a dangerous, disagreeable existence?" She tossed her arms up and didn't allow him a word edgewise. "They *wouldn't*."

"It's not dangerous and it's not disagreeable to me," he

seethed. And it was that there which divided them; they were two people from two very different worlds. It was why she could never, ever understand the reasons that compelled him. All of them. "Now, I want you to leave."

Her face fell. "But . . ."

W ell, *this* hadn't gone as she'd expected.

He was supposed to have temporarily lost his position at the coalfields and, therefore, be free to accompany her back to London.

Free of excuses and with nothing else keeping him here.

He was proving even more stubborn than she'd anticipated.

His eyes sharpened on her face. "What is that, Edwina?"

What it was, she would certainly not say. Not when she had sense enough to know he'd be livid at the reminder of the change in his circumstances.

And he'd be even more enraged if he knew the hand you had in it.

Unable to meet his probing eyes, Edwina took a hurried step away from him, and made a show of drawing on her gloves. She put an inordinate amount of attention and effort into drawing each digit through each hole of the lacy articles, all the while regaining her composure. "Thank you for your time." She dipped a curtsy, and gathering up her bag, headed for the door. "I . . . was going to say I had such a lovely time speaking with your sister." Which wasn't a lie. It had been so . . . wonderful to simply speak with another young woman . . . one who wasn't a charge, and who Edwina didn't feel she had to instruct. "She and I can meet again some other—"

"You'll do no such thing," he said, cutting her off. Heading for the front of the room, he reached past her to open the door, allowing her to exit.

Edwina started. "Why, thank you, Mr. Audley."

He grinned, and it was a smug, cocksure turn of his lips, and the sheer cynical nature of it certainly shouldn't be responsible for the butterflies that fluttered in her belly. "Surprised that I've got some manners, princess?" It was a taunt that didn't know whether it wished to jest or jeer, and settled for something in between.

"Not at all," she lied. "You are, after all, the son of a duke." Bringing her chin up a notch, she exited the kitchen . . . and found Cailin Audley standing near the front door, as if she'd been debating escape.

And Edwina well knew how the young woman felt.

Rafe's sister collected Edwina's cloak, and then rushed over with it.

"Many thanks," Edwina murmured as she shrugged into the article. Accepting the bonnet next, she drew it on and neatly tied the pink satin bow at her chin.

"I also had a most wonderful time speaking," Miss Audley said quietly; her gaze caught Edwina's, and within the younger woman's eyes was a resolve.

One that Edwina recognized all too well. A kindred partner who well knew this wasn't their last meeting.

They shared the very briefest of smiles.

"As did I." Collecting Cailin's hands, she squeezed lightly. "Until our next meeting," she whispered.

The young woman's smile widened. "I look forward to it."

"What was that?" Rafe snapped.

Edwina stole a peek at the surly gentleman. By the hard glint in his eyes, he knew precisely the nature of Edwina and Cailin's exchange. "I was merely saying how very much I enjoyed my meeting with your sister." She dropped a curtsy for the duke's daughter. "Good evening, Miss Audley."

Yet again, Rafe held the door open, and folding his arms at his chest, he glared at her.

Hmph. It was hardly his fault he didn't know how to be a proper gentleman. Silently tacking on additional areas to be worked upon, she favored brother and sister with a smile and one last curtsy, and then took her leave.

Edwina was just making her way down the overgrown pathway from the cottage when she registered the figure falling into step beside her. Slowing her steps, she cast him a wary glance. "Are you . . . following me, Rafe?" This did not bode well. He likely sought to berate her away from his—

"I'm escorting you back."

Her heart leaped in her breast, and she missed a step.

Rafe instantly caught her by the forearm, steadying her before she fell flat on her shocked face.

"You are escorting me?" She could not suppress the breathless quality of that question.

Color filled his cheeks. "Don't get to thinking that this makes me some manner of gentleman," he said gruffly, effectively dousing that warmth in her chest. "I'm not going to allow you to pay anyone else any more visits on your way."

Of course. That was what he would worry about. It had been nothing but foolish to believe anything else motivated him. Unable to quell the unexpected rush of disappointment, she tossed the strings of her bonnet over her shoulder. "So you think I might glean something of value from the other villagers that might prove helpful . . . ?" She caught the flinty look of those eyes, and immediately stopped. "Either way, I shan't require their assistance."

While they walked down the path toward the inn, Edwina adjusted the bag on her arm, and reaching inside, she pulled out her notebook and pencil.

He slanted a look her way. "What the hell are you doing?"

"I think it should be clear," she said, as she flipped through to find an empty page. "I'm beginning our lesson. Your first lesson, that is."

"*We* are doing no such thing," he told her in his usual taciturn way.

"There is nothing worse than wasted time. Now, if I might suggest we begin by—"

Rafe snorted. "What does that even mean?"

Annoyance lent an increased pace to her step, until she realized what she was doing and slowed her stride once more. "It means that if a person has time, it is to be filled, and to not make the most of every moment of every day is a sad waste of that gift."

"That's utter horse shite."

"And as we've begun your lessons, it is essential that I point out that particular choice of language is not at all appropria—"

He stopped abruptly, and she slowed, looking back to where she'd left him. More than half-fearing she'd pushed too hard, too fast, and he'd decided to return home. Until she caught the dark scowl he wore . . . and thought perhaps his retreat home might be the safer, better option for her in this instance. "Let us be clear about several things," he began in a chilly tone, as he started for her.

No, stalked her. The steps he took were calculated and ominous, and it was all she could do to dig her feet into the ground and remain rooted there to face him.

"First," he began when he reached her, "your maxim? It is, as I said, horse shite. You speak about making the most of time, and time being a gift." The sneer on his lips told her even more clearly all she needed to know about his opinion of her maxim. "Most people don't have time for anything but work, rest, and if they aren't bone-weary from toiling all day, food."

It was a world she didn't know about. Not truly. From everything she'd gleaned, they were both bastard-born, but their lives had been . . . different.

They resumed their walk in silence, their boots grinding and crunching the gravel and rock under their steps as they went, along with the errant chirp of the birds who'd not yet sought their day's rest. He didn't want to speak any further. He'd been inordinately clear on that. And she'd likely be wise to leave him to the silence he requested. Rafe Audley was like a skittish colt. It was, better, after all, not to push too hard, too fast.

When they reached the tavern, the raucous din from inside the taproom spilled out into the empty courtyard. The patrons had already gathered for their ales, and by the swell of their laughter and song, they had been at their merriment for some time.

Climbing the lone step, she paused on the little patio, and dropped a curtsy. "I thank you again for your escort."

Rafe reached past her and opened the door. The cacophony immediately spilled out, near deafening. "To your rooms," he said, loud enough to be heard over the ruckus.

It took a moment to register not only what he was saying, but what he was suggesting. Why, he thought to escort her to her rooms again? After her lapse the last time she'd allowed him inside her temporary chambers, she'd not be so careless again. Cupping her hands around her mouth, and in a bid to make herself heard over the cacophony, she yelled up at him, "That will not be necessary, Mr. Audley. I am entirely capable of—"

A pair of unsteady patrons stumbled out of the taproom, and square into Edwina's back. She gasped and went flying into Rafe's waiting arms. She shot her hands out, curling her fingers in the rough fabric of his cotton shirt. Her palms burned at the heat of him, even through the barrier of his garments and her gloves.

"Caught yourself a pretty bird, did you, Mr. Auuudley?" the taller, grayer fellow slurred.

"Wilson. Brown," he greeted them, and then winked for the two coalfield miners swaying as they stood. "I've caught myself a noisy one."

That pronouncement was met with roars of laughter.

Setting her back on her feet, at his side, was a clear statement that their perceptions of interest on his part, for Edwina, were nonexistent. And also, unexpectedly a sign of his support and protection. And a mark of his honor, that he was so determined to distance himself from.

Tipping their caps, the men continued on their way.

The moment they reached the middle of the trail, they broke into song.

"Go," Rafe said tersely, and this time, when he followed, she allowed him that role he was determined to serve as escort.

"You may rest assured that I'm a grown woman quite capable of looking after myself." She cast a glance back, and found him directly at her heels. "I've stayed in all manner of inns and taverns, and usually on my own." Her feet touched the landing, and she headed for her door. "I've never run into any trouble, and never have I encountered a situation I was incapable of handling."

"You've never found any trouble?" When she reached her rooms, he folded his arms and leaned against the wall, indicating what he thought of her assertion of independence. "Now, *that* I find hard to believe."

Hmph.

Edwina tugged off her gloves and stuffed them into her bag. Well, then.

Having never had a father about, or a brother, or any relative who truly looked after her, she'd become all too accustomed to her independence. This . . . hovering presence, though considerate, was also wholly unfamiliar to her. "It is quite true," she said, letting herself into her rooms. "I am quite adept at avoiding . . . my rooms." Her breath caught, and shock gave way to horror as she ran her gaze over her temporary chambers.

Her thoroughly destroyed chambers.

All the bed coverings had been ripped off the mattress and strewn about. Her coveted porcelain pieces had been upended. Her portraits and paintings ripped from the wall.

The bag slipped from her fingers and sailed to the floor with a quiet thump. "I have been . . . robbed," she whispered, venturing into the mess around her. "But . . . I locked my door this time." She'd taken his advice from the day before, and made sure to not leave her rooms unlocked.

Except . . .

She cocked her head.

"They have not . . . taken anything." Surely she was wrong. Edwina picked her way over the dresses that had been ripped from the armoire and thrown haphazardly about. Her gaze caught upon the gold locket her father had given her as a girl. Releasing the hold she had on her dresses, she sprinted across the room, and scrabbled to gather up that precious necklace. The moment the cool metal touched her palm, she glanced about in abject confusion. "They've just destroyed my rooms. Why would anyone . . . ?" Her question trailed off, and she slowly returned her focus to the figure who'd been silent and stoic. Understanding lit her eyes. "You did this," she whispered.

Had he destroyed her rooms?
The immediate and literal answer was: no. He'd not. Not personally, that is.

Technically, however, he was very much responsible. Though he'd not himself had a hand in the actual destruction, nor had he even given the command that someone do this. But his message had been clear, and the words received by Ward: "I'm not looking for her to be comfortable."

He'd thought she'd find herself with charred food or loud neighbors. He'd never expected . . . this.

He briefly closed his eyes.

When he opened them, he found her kneeling amid that swath of pastel fabrics, silent as he'd ever known her in their exchanges.

And worse . . . stricken. Her eyes reflecting such hurt, and a wealth of pain and shock, hit Rafe like a fist to the gut.

When he didn't immediately respond, she pushed slowly to her feet, staring there, amid the clutter of her many garments and gowns. "Did you . . . do this?" she asked again, a pained hesitancy in that question. As if she so desperately wanted his answer to be different than what it was.

Her anger would have been preferred to . . . this.

"I . . ." He scrabbled with his jacket collar. ". . . not intentionally."

He welcomed the inevitable explosion of her fury and rage. Perhaps even the lecture and lessons she was so often doling out. That would certainly be a fitting punishment.

But it didn't come.

Instead, there came the faintest little sniffling.

Oh, God.

He blanched.

Tears filled her eyes, leaving them hazel pools of her grief. And what was worse, she whipped away from him, presenting her back, and discreetly wiping at the corners of her eyes. It was a proud attempt from a proud woman to hide her misery.

The ache in his chest, an uncomfortable blend of guilt and pain, sharpened.

And he found he didn't much like himself in that moment. In fact, he quite regretted who and what he was. And more . . . what he'd done.

The young lady drew in a slow and slightly shaky breath. Then, she faced him, her features perfectly composed, her lips even . . . and for once, unsmiling. He'd been annoyed by her smile. So why did he suddenly find himself craving that sunny smile? "You may leave now."

That would be the wisest and safest course. She'd ordered him gone and he could steal himself a reprieve from the guilt of watching her in all her heartbrokenness. And yet . . .

With a sigh, Rafe started for the mound of pink and white fabric in the middle of the room and picked up the pair of porcelain shepherds. Carrying the baubles to the upended nightstand, he eyed it a moment. Then, using the tip of his boot, he shoved the oak furniture back up into place.

"What are you doing, Mr. Audley?" she whispered.

He was Mr. Audley again. Given the circumstances, that certainly seemed appropriate. Strangely, he found himself missing the familiarity of his name on her lips.

Unnerved by that inexplicability, Rafe deposited the collection of sheep and shepherds in . . . some attempt at a proper arrangement. "I think it should be clear, Edwina." He eyed the glassware a moment, and then shifted the little figurines so they were front and center.

"It is not," she said, following him with a confused gaze as he moved on to the bedding littered about.

"I'm . . . putting it to rights." As best as he was able. "Your room." No, he didn't want any part of her or her intentions for him. But neither was he a bully who'd see her or any person hurt . . . not even in an attempt to have his wishes honored. Bending over, he gathered up the sheets and coverlets and pillowcases and pillows, more bedding than all of his siblings collectively owned. Rafe deposited that armful at the side of the bed, and then sifting through the bedding, he fished out a sheet. Snapping it several times, he let it float onto the lumpy mattress.

The floorboards groaned as Edwina hurried to the opposite side of the bed. And gathering each end, she quickly set to work, tucking the ends under the mattress. She made quick work of her side, perfectly folding and smoothing her edges. She attended that task with an ease he'd have never expected from a fine lady with manners and mannerisms like hers.

When she glanced up, there was a pretty flush upon her cheeks from her work, and several auburn tresses hung over her brow. "You're surprised that I know how to make my own bed?" That sparkle was back in her eyes, the glimmer having replaced the sadness, restoring their relationship to . . . whatever it had been before this . . . and it left the oddest . . . lightness in his chest. "Who do you think arranged my belongings? Hmm? Decorated my room?"

"I would have expected you'd have enlisted one of Mr. Ward's daughters."

She leaned across the mattress and said on a loud, exaggerated whisper, "Then you would have been wrong. I told you. I'm capable of a great many things, Mr. Audley."

Yes, he would have. And yes, she had. And it also left the question . . . just how much else had he been wrong about where Edwina Dalrymple was concerned? As discomfited as he was with that question niggling at his brain, he was grateful when she came around and retrieved the top sheet. Because he didn't want to soften toward this woman who was an emissary of the duke. He didn't want to feel badly about or for, and certainly not any affection toward, one who cared most about the role she served and not what Rafe himself wanted for his life.

She snapped another sheet across the mattress, and Rafe caught the opposite ends. Together, they lay the high-quality fabric over the previous sheet.

"How does a lady who speaks like you and dresses like you also know how to oversee the tasks of a servant?" he asked, despite his resolve not to explore too closely this woman and *her* life.

"Are you a servant?" she countered.

"We're not the same." At all. Either in dress or in speech or in the people they worked for and with.

"We're also more alike than you think," she murmured.

That he didn't believe. Rafe snorted as they finished tucking the corners of the top sheet. "I don't sleep with Witney blankets." It didn't, however, escape his notice that she evaded volunteering any real information about herself, which only further increased the unexplainable intrigue surrounding Miss Edwina Dalrymple. That was the only reason he was interested. Because of her deliberate evasiveness.

As one, they made for the next quality article of her bedding.

Edwina studied him with a thoughtful expression. "You know of Witney blankets, then?"

He immediately shuttered his expression. She, who was hanging on to her secrets more closely than even Rafe, thought nothing of probing him for more. "Aye." Because after giving birth to her babes, his mother would make her trips to London to resume her role of mistress to a faithless nobleman, and then would return with trunks filled with fine baubles and fripperies. "They aren't the types of things a servant or person in the working class possesses."

"But working class is what I am," she said with a gentle insistence.

He strangled on a laugh.

The lady arched a dark brow. "You find that amusing?"

"That you somehow believe you are 'of the working class'? Aye, I find it hilarious." Rafe tossed her pale pink and green satin coverlet onto the bed.

When they finished putting her rooms back together, Rafe reached for the last garment.

Edwina rushed to intercept him. "I have that."

But he proved quicker.

And then he made the mistake of looking down at the item she'd been so determined to relieve him of.

And he had to remind his brain of the movements behind the whole task of swallowing. Finer undergarments he'd never seen on a single woman. Lace so sheer a person could see clear through it. Leaving next to nothing to the imagination but for the pink bows that adorned the top sleeves.

Edwina yanked the article from his hand and shoved it behind her back. As if that might make him somehow unsee what he'd seen . . . and unimagine what he was now imagining.

The least of which was the taste and feel of her mouth. And the most being her resplendent, in that garment—in only that garment—she all but tossed into the armoire, closing the door hard behind it.

She faced him, her cheeks flushed, her usually perfect chignon having come undone, leaving long, loose curls falling about her shoulders.

And his body tensed at the sight of her.

I should go.

I should go for so very many reasons. The least of which was he found himself recalling too clearly the last time he'd been in here with her in his arms. The most of which being that she was employed by the duke.

"Thank you," she said softly.

He grunted and started for the door, but she slid into his path, stopping him. She wore a somber set to her features.

Rafe stared questioningly at her.

"I . . . what you said, on our journey here," she began. "It doesn't have to be that way," she said softly. "Yes, most people are bone-weary from, as you said, toiling all day." Edwina took a step closer to him. "Despite your opinion that I know nothing of it, I've spent a good many years working. Most work from the moment the sun rises until it sets. The majority are at the mercy of employers. Too many who are oftentimes cruel, and too often are given to overworking them." She laid a palm upon his arm, and his muscles bunched under the tenderness of that touch.

He met her gaze.

"But that does not have to be *your* lot, Rafe," she said

imploringly. "You do not have to live the tiring existence most every other person does. You have this opportunity to live a life different than the one you've spoken of." She lightly squeezed his arm, before releasing him. "Not only for you but also for your siblings, and anyone would trade places for that gift."

She was determined. And he wanted to fault her for that, when he already faulted her for so much.

Perhaps it was the guilt of what he'd inadvertently wrought upon her room.

Or mayhap it was the fact that he now found himself unemployed. Albeit, according to Sparrow, temporarily.

Or perhaps it was because she'd raised mention of his siblings . . . particularly Cailin.

But an idea stirred to life. "You are so determined that I accompany you to Town and take part in your London Season."

"Well, it is not my London Season, per se. The London Season is the time of year when all members of the *ton* leave their country estates to take part in their . . ." She caught his look, and had sense enough to stop with this latest lesson. "*Ahem*. Yes, I am determined that you will take your rightful place among Polite Society."

Distaste soured his mouth like the vinegar his sister had a horrifying habit of overusing in too many recipes. Those words, now spoken by Edwina, were the exact same ones that had been written in the one note he'd bothered to open and read from his father. And the same ones uttered by every other man whom Rafe had managed to send packing. "There is nothing I can say to convince you otherwise."

She gave a little flounce of her dark curls. "Nothing at all. I'm quite determined in my course I set, and am not thwarted. Ever." Unblinking, the lady held his gaze. "Ever," she repeated, in such somber tones that didn't fit with Edwina and her cheerful nature, he found himself fighting an unexpected smile.

"Yes, I have come to find that," he allowed. Edwina Dalrymple was a veritable virago. Had she been going toe to toe with any person other than himself, he would have admired her. With the endless stream of words always sprouting from her interestingly shaped mouth, he would admit—at least to himself—that he was never going to win a word match with her. "Very well. I will go with you."

Shock brought her crimson lips apart, and she immediately corrected that gape. "You . . . will?"

"I will."

"Oh, this is quite splendid! Very splendid, indeed." Edwina clapped her hands several times. "There is much to be done. Packing your belongings, and having the carriages readied." And animated as she was, gesturing and speaking rapidly, color filled her cheeks. And as she celebrated, he almost felt bad.

"Of course, there are your lessons, which we really must begin immediately. There is no time to spare . . . etiquette and decorum and . . . proper forms of address, of course," she prattled.

And Rafe heard but two words among that torrent of them:

Your lessons . . .

As if he were a schoolboy in desperate need of tutelage that only she, the great savior of a teacher, might manage.

That did it.

It effectively quashed the very brief, and entirely fleeting guilt.

"I have . . . terms."

That brought an immediate cessation to her rambling. Edwina eyed him warily. "What . . . type of terms, Mr. Audley?"

"You do precisely what you're expecting me to do. You stay here, and fit in," he said, relishing more than he ought teasing her with his *uncouthness*.

Edwina winced. "Very well," she said, bringing her shoulders back. "What exactly does my fitting in Staffordshire entail, Mr. Audley?"

"First, my name is Rafe. You'll call me Rafe because anything else makes you some fine governess, instructing me."

"That is . . . essentially what I am," she said slowly.

He sharpened his gaze on her, and she hastily cleared her throat. "I'll allow that concession."

Given she had already done so, that wasn't much of a *concession*, as she called it. "You'll be part of Staffordshire life, live here. Fit in with the locals. Do what we do. Live how we live." Just as she expected him to live how she lived.

She blanched, and for all the revulsion there, he may as well have suggested she fish her own trout, gut them, cook them, and eat them there, raw. "We don't . . . have the time for that. There are your formal lessons to see to and—"

Rafe cut her off. "Is it that we don't have time for that, or you don't want to take part in quaint village life?"

She sputtered. "Of course not! That is not it, at—"

"Or is it that you don't want to forsake your fine balls and dinner parties? Not fancy enough for you?" All of that fit with the manner of woman who had arrived in her fancy apparel, and who thought so very highly about the peerage, just because of the titles they carried.

Her lips formed a harsh line. "I did not say that," she said tersely. "Any of it."

Rafe smiled coldly back. "You didn't need to. You've been quite clear since you arrived that you presume your way of life is better than mine, and what I'm saying is if you think it's nothing giving up all I know and venturing to Town, then you try it, princess."

Chapter 11

Princess.

What would he say if he knew just how very far off that mark he was? That she wasn't some highbrow lady who happened to be down on her luck and in need of respectable work but, rather, bastard-born like him . . . living a secret and a lie so that she might have that respectable work.

It was a secret she could and would breathe to no one. She'd no choice but to leave him to his erroneously drawn opinions about her, and try and convince him. And yet, convincing him also required that she agree to this outlandish proposal.

"You aren't going to do it," he stated smugly.

"I am . . . thinking. After all, impatient contemplation has the power to destroy clever ideas."

He eyed her as if she'd sprouted a second head. "Who said that?"

Edwina gave a toss of her head. "I did."

"Of course you did," he muttered, and she refused to rise to his bait.

Because that was what he wanted. Just as he didn't truly want . . . or expect her to agree to his terms.

She tapped a finger against her chin.

That was the sole reason he'd capitulated. Because it wasn't really a capitulation. He expected she'd turn tail and run at the prospect of fitting in his world. In fairness, however, the gentleman wasn't off the mark. The last thing she wanted was to remain in any countryside of England, and that he chose to be here? She shuddered. That was a preference she could never understand. After her mother had passed, the moment she'd gotten out of the country and into London had been the only happy thing to come of that loss. The country brought with it memories of the father who rarely visited, and the people who were small-minded and cruel. And yes, she quite abhorred country living. And yes, all her least favorite memories involved places just like this one she now found herself in, but no, she was not incapable of seeing to whatever challenges he thought to throw her way.

And yet . . . taking on this assignment had the power to set her free from ever having to worry about returning to the country and being gossiped about and mocked as she'd been growing up.

Edwina ceased her tapping and let her arm fall to her side. "Very well. We do not have much time. At most, ten days. However, all would not be lost as we would have the opportunity to interact and I can learn more about you."

His jaw slackened. "You're agreeing . . ."

"To become one with your Staffordshire life?" she supplied for him, when he didn't or couldn't finish. "I will. What exactly does this entail?"

Surprise brought his dark eyebrows creeping up. Good. He thought he knew so much about her. He thought he knew why she didn't want to take part in those silly events, and what she would or would not countenance to secure his cooperation. What he didn't know, however, was that she wasn't a woman to back down. She had made her way in this world, and it had always been difficult, and from it, she had developed a resolve that gave her the strength to do anything in order to succeed.

"Helping in the kitchen."

"The kitchen?" Edwina repeated back this latest ridiculous task he'd have her complete.

"Yes, the kitchen." He enunciated each of the two syllables in a grating manner that required she draw on a lifetime's worth of lessons on propriety and decorum to keep from remarking rudely over.

"Fine." She infused a certain amount of boredom into her voice. "Is there a particular favorite you'd like for me to bake?"

"I . . ." His mouth moved several times before he shook his head dumbly. "Uh . . . no?"

Yes, he hadn't been expecting that, had he? It was all she could do to keep from dusting her palms together in gleeful triumph. "Is that all, Rafe?" she asked with false innocence.

His dark brow dipped lower.

"*You* are going to . . . *bake*?"

The gentleman thought he was so clever. He'd no idea of just how removed she was from the world of Polite Society he thought she belonged to. Yes, she educated young ladies. Yes, she conducted herself with a like decorum and properness—outside of kissing him madly and thinking of it in detail and depth afterward, of course. But she was not a woman who attended fine balls and dinner parties . . . not as anything more than a companion or chaperone, that is. "I am going to work in your kitchen and live the life of a Staffordshire village woman. Just as you requested."

She wasn't a woman who enjoyed life in the English countryside. But neither was she unfamiliar with her way around it.

Nay, since she'd been born, the illegitimate issue of a marquess and his well-regarded mistress, Edwina hadn't really fit into any world. Instead, she'd straddled two, striving to belong to one or the other, but finding her place in neither.

And she resented this man before her. He, with his erroneous opinions, and his ill ones at that, about her.

Edwina released a sigh. "Why do you sound so surprised as to your own terms?" she returned with a question of her own, one that she filled with deliberate confusion. "Unless . . ." She made her eyes go round, and slapped a hand against her breast in pretend shock. "Unless . . . never say you are thinking I'll say no, and you'll drive me off, Rafe?"

"No, I don't think you'll say no." A cold smile played at his lips. "I don't think you have the sense God gave a snail to do so. I think you'll say yes, fail, and then I'll drive you off."

Hmph. She bristled. The gentleman was destined to be surprised and disappointed when she succeeded and, in turn, secured his cooperation. "So what else does this entail? Am I to also spend a day at the coalfield? Haul coal buckets?"

And the hard set to his lips softened, giving way to that very real half grin, a lopsided smile, as if even when he was genuinely amused he resisted it with all that he was. "I'm not trying to kill you."

She released a breath she hadn't realized she'd been holding. "Well, that is reassuring."

He chuckled, and she bit the inside of her cheek to keep from pointing out that she'd been speaking in all seriousness.

"The miners meet at the tavern at nine o'clock, for drink and song. I'll have you join in, Edwina."

She swallowed wrong and promptly choked, struggling and gasping for air. Until tears streamed down her eyes, and she hunched over in an attempt to get a proper breath.

Rafe took mercy on her, thumping Edwina hard between her shoulder blades.

"Y-You . . . y-you . . ." She still struggled to get those words out. This time, not because of the paroxysm he'd induced, but because of the scandalous nature of what he suggested.

"I want you to join the men and women who meet at the tavern?" He folded his arms across that broadly muscled chest. "Aye." Rafe winged another eyebrow up. "Is there a problem with that, princess?"

No, there was not *one* problem with what he suggested. Nay, what he *required*. This was, after all, one of the terms that would determine whether or not he accompanied her to London.

Rather, there were a whole host of problems with this latest item on the list of his ultimatums. Every night she took her meal in the taproom, but she was sure to take to her rooms when those raucous revelries began. With the drinking and the bawdy singing, it was the last place a woman with her reputation could afford to be. Furthermore . . . "Those people do not want me there."

He lifted an eyebrow. "Those people?"

She felt her cheeks warm.

"The people in your village. They are . . ." At his questioning look, she searched her mind. "Not welcoming to outsiders."

"Oh, now, that is rich coming from a woman who thinks Polite Society will be welcoming of me and my siblings."

"It is different." Entirely so.

He rested a hip on her makeshift desk. "Enlighten me, princess."

Not correcting that endearment-insult, she clasped her hands before her, and proceeded to elucidate. "I'm not speaking as someone who is unfamiliar with how people new to a village are treated." She knew that firsthand from when she and her mother had moved to Leeds. And she'd witnessed Rafe and his brother's resistance to her being here. "There were Mr. Ward's efforts." This time, it was Rafe whose cheeks went ruddy. Hammering home her point, Edwina gave him an up-and-down look.

"Fair enough."

At that concession, Edwina's eyes widened.

Rafe crossed his arms and continued. "Has my sister been anything but warm to you?"

That gave her pause. The whole of her life she'd simply

taken it for granted that she was a woman without a place in the English countryside . . . because she was an outsider. And yet, his sister had only ever been gracious. "No," she allowed. "She's been welcoming and kind and warm."

He smirked at his triumph, but he was not content with having secured even that agreement. "And what of Mr. Ward's daughter, Maryam?"

Edwina chewed at her lower lip. What of Mr. Ward's daughter, he asked. The young woman who'd been kind and generous and . . . "You are right," she said with a quiet, dawning realization.

Rafe's jaw slipped, and he dropped his arms to his sides.

Edwina patted at her chignon. "My expectation that I would be treated unfairly tainted my views of the people here, and blinded me to the very real kindness I've been shown. As such, having had my eyes opened, I trust if you'd simply accompany me to London, you'd find that your own expectations for how you'll be treated in London are as erroneous as mine have been."

"There is nothing simple about me joining the duke's household."

She resisted the urge to stamp her foot. He couldn't simply make this . . . easy.

Everything with him was a test.

Just as everything was intended as a deterrent to her efforts.

And failure was not an option, for her. Not when this represented entry into a world that had been far beyond her reach . . . first as a child born the bastard of a marquess, and then, as an independent woman building a career for herself.

She bit her lower lip and nodded. "Very well. I'll live in your countryside and bake in your kitchen and drink your ale and sing your songs. Is there anything else, *Rafe*?"

He drifted closer. "Do you want there to be?" There was a husky quality to both his low baritone and the question he asked that awakened the wickedest heat within her.

She'd rather there be none. If she said as much, he would likely have doubled his list.

"N-No. This is sufficient," she whispered.

"Then, as I see it," and he dusted a coal-stained, calloused finger along the curve of her cheek, "we're done here. For now."

They were done.

And yet . . . neither did he leave.

Her breath caught in her chest.

What was worse, she didn't want him to.

She couldn't make herself move after he caressed her that way. She didn't want to break that unexpectedly tender, almost afterthought of a touch. And what did it say, that a throwaway caress should affect her so?

"I'm going to kiss you again," he whispered, even as he lowered his head.

She nodded, and her eyes fluttered shut, as she lifted her mouth to receive that kiss. "I think I should like that. Once . . ." *More.*

His lips consumed hers. Taking and tasting. And she gave, in return. Twining her arms about his neck, she pressed herself against him.

Rafe slanted his lips over hers. And then licked the full contours she vowed to never again hate after this moment. Not when his worship of them brought this heat. This hungering. She dashed her tongue against his, and a raw, primal half growl, half groan rumbled from his chest; that sound she took in her own mouth.

Rafe caught her firmly under the buttocks, and she gasped at the exquisiteness of that unexpected touch. He kneaded and sculpted her with those enormous, callused, and very real hands that had fascinated her from their first meeting. Dragging the fabric of her gown up, he exposed her skin to the night air; that slap of cool should have been sobering. Her body in this moment didn't care about respectability or her post or her reputation. She cared about nothing beyond the throbbing ache between her legs, a cross between pleasure and pain, and then he slid his knee between her legs, and she sank onto him. She moaned, and shamefully rubbed against his oak-hard thigh, the fabric of his trousers rough against the softness of her naked skin, and somehow all the more arousing for it.

Edwina gasped softly as he brought her right leg up around his waist, and then, with his mouth never breaking contact with hers, Rafe backed her the handful of feet until she had the wall behind her.

The thin plaster shook, knocking under the weight of their bodies pressed together.

"You are maddening," he whispered between kisses.

And this was madness.

She knew that.

She knew it with every fiber of the person she was who'd studied the ways of proper ladies.

But no one had ever said that madness could also be magic.

Rafe moved his attentions to her neck, and she let her head fall back on a long, keening moan. "Mmmm." She arched her hips, searching for him, and he answered that wordless plea, sliding his leg back between her legs so that she could rub herself against him. The sensation so delicious, so overwhelming.

He trailed a path of kisses along the swell of her breasts, and then he freed them from the constraints of her gown. Lowering his head, Rafe took a nipple in his mouth and sucked deep and hard.

Biting her lower lip, she buried her face into his shoulder, her shame was strong . . . but not strong enough, for the yearning for him and this, and the wetness pooling at her center, proved even stronger. Perspiration beaded on her brow and streaked a damp path over her cheek. This . . . she had never felt anything like this. The pressure grew, unbearable, the ache sharpening, and Edwina grunted, little animalistic sounds born of lust. She arched her hips harder, faster.

She'd thought herself above such feelings.

Stronger than her mother.

More moral than all the governesses.

All the while, never knowing desire could feel like this.

That it could set every nerve ending afire, and burn her up in a conflagration of desire that she was so very happy to be consumed by.

Switching his attention to her previously neglected breast, he drew that swollen, puckered peak between his lips.

"O-oh, my," she rasped, tangling her fingers in his hair, anchoring him close. "Th-that . . . is . . . *mmm* . . ." Magical.

Alas, words failed her as Rafe cupped the globes of her buttocks, kneading and squeezing, guiding her along, urging her on. Edwina's movements grew more frenzied. Panting wildly against his shoulder, she undulated her hips.

He placed his mouth alongside her ear; his scruff-covered cheek scraped hers. "You're going to come for me." His voice came harsh and graveled, a command.

Edwina bit hard at the fabric covering his shoulder and nodded unevenly against him. She would have offered him anything in this moment had he asked it, including her promise of departure if he just assuaged the unforgiveable ache between her legs.

Cupping her buttocks as he guided her hips, rocking her, at the same time he ground his thigh lightly against her damp thatch of curls.

Panting, Edwina let her head fell back, and she rolled it from side to side as everything in her tunneled to the rising tide of her desire. That pressure grew and grew, as Rafe's ministrations pushed her up, higher and higher.

And then her body stiffened; a scream tore from her, echoing wildly around the tiny chamber, the sounds of her desire bouncing off the walls and reverberating back in her own ears. She ground herself against his oak-hard thigh, over and over again, moaning his name. Keening incoherently. Until the shudders subsided, and her breath came in noisy spurts.

Out of breath, she collapsed against him; her pulse knocked wildly in her ears and blended with her noisy inhalations and exhalations.

Until she could at last draw proper air into her lungs.

And as the haze of her desire ebbed, it ushered reality slowly and uncomfortably back in.

Oh . . . dear. What had she done? Edwina clenched her eyes tight, never wanting to open them again. And certainly not to look at the man still cradling her. A man who was a stranger she'd only just met two days ago, but whom she also had become familiar enough with to understand what awaited her when she at last met his gaze.

Mortified heat burned up her cheeks, and Edwina put her hands upon his chest and pushed him lightly.

He immediately stepped away.

Her hands shaking, Edwina drew the bodice of her dress back into place, and shoved her skirts down. Until she was righted enough, and there were no other distractions afforded her, and she was left with the task of finally facing the taciturn Rafe Audley.

She lifted her head, forcing her eyes to meet his.

And yet . . . those thick lashes hooded his eyes, but there was no hint of mockery there.

What did one say after . . . after . . . what she had just done? Was it a return to casual conversation with no direct mention of what had transpired? Or was some form of acknowledgment necessary? Edwina cleared her throat. "For all the lessons I have received, I must confess no one has instructed me on what to say after . . . after . . ." She waved a hand, gesturing from herself to Rafe. "You know. *This*."

A slight smile danced at the edges of his hard lips. "Are words really necessary, afterward?" he drawled.

She scrunched her brow. "I . . . yes, I suppose you are correct on that score."

He leaned down, so their breaths caressed once more, and Edwina's body immediately went all warm in anticipation of the kiss—that this time did not come. "And today is the day the teacher became the charge." He winked, that enthralling, flirtatious flutter of those dark lashes that wreaked its usual havoc upon her.

Breezy.

That was the lesson she'd advised her students when

dealing with the "masterful wink." Edwina swatted lightly at his arm. "Good night, Mr. Audley. I shall see you tomorrow."

Rafe moved his gaze over her face, and she followed that study. "Six o'clock," he murmured. "You can lend my sister help with the morning meal, and have your first real village experience, then."

And with that, he took his leave.

Edwina remained motionless for several moments, staring at that oak panel. And then springing into movement, she rushed to lock the door. Edwina sagged against it and pressed her eyes closed. All these years, she'd believed herself too strong to ever be tempted by carnal pleasures. Incapable of being distracted from her work by anything, and certainly not the touch of a man.

Only to be proven wrong by her latest charge.

She opened her eyes, and stared absently at the immaculate bed she and Rafe had made moments ago.

In the days to come, she was going to be working closely with the captivating Rafe Audley, and she could not quell the fear swirling in her belly at whatever this weakness was that she held for him.

Chapter 12

When Rafe had named the meeting hour, he'd expected Edwina would be late. In fact, it had never entered his mind that she'd ever be remotely close to being on time.

And in that, he'd not been incorrect. She'd not been remotely close to being on time.

She'd arrived early.

Attired in yet another ruffled lace gown, this one an alternating pattern of pink and then white rows of those ruffles.

But she'd arrived on his doorstep with that parasol raised at her shoulder at that ungodly hour, when the moon hadn't even thought about relinquishing its place in the sky. She'd looked bright-eyed, well rested.

And despite the other expectation that she'd shirk and fuss in a kitchen, there'd only been the sounds of her laughter, mingled with his sister's, as they worked . . . and talked.

It was a welcome distraction from the fact that he himself was, in fact, not working. And it was also . . . enlightening.

". . . Oh, if you enjoy fossils, you would greatly love the British Museum," Edwina was saying.

"I found several once, near the coalfields. I don't know anything about them," Cailin remarked, sadness tinging her voice. "Not really. Not as much as I would like."

And not as much as she could if Rafe just conceded and let her have the experience she could by going to London with Edwina. When had his sister been anything other than melancholy? After the loss of her sweetheart, when had she smiled or spoken about her interests? Nay, she'd been despondent and had simply gone through the motions of living. Until Edwina's arrival.

Why did the thought of going not inspire the same horror and fury as it had when Edwina had first arrived?

"You've been staring at that door for the better part of fifteen minutes. Any plans on actually passing through?"

Rafe jumped, and faced his brother. The candlelight shadows played over Hunter's face, and in that slight flicker of light, there came a wry, knowing look. That was gone as quick as it had come, so that Hunter was left his usual serious, unsmiling self. He took a sip of his black tea. "I take that as a 'no,' then? So you didn't send this one away, but made her a guest instead."

A guest . . .

His neck went hot. It wasn't . . . the way his brother was trying to make it seem. "She's helping Cailin," he said tersely. All of this boiled down to a battle of wills between him and the one emissary who'd not backed down. But she would.

There came another of Edwina's tinkling laughs.

He winced. Eventually. Soon.

His brother rested a hip on the back of the ancient walnut sofa that had been one of their mother's most cherished pieces, and rightfully showed its age for it. "This is . . . an unexpected turn of events."

He scraped a gaze over his brother. "Yes, but then that could be said about . . . a good many things, couldn't it?" Particularly his brother's betrayal.

Hunter had the good grace to go red in the face. Good, he heard the intended insinuation. Rafe would be forced to remain behind here, sitting around on his arse all day . . . doing what? The duke had stolen his purpose out from under him. "Shouldn't you be at the coalfields?" he snapped, unable to bury the sting of resentment in that question.

There was a flash of regret there in Hunter's eyes, but Rafe would be damned if he felt guilty for it. The only one of them who deserved to feel that sentiment was the one before him. The brother whom he'd taken care of since they'd both been babes, and who didn't have the decency to return last night for the conversation he owed him.

"I'm sorry," Hunter said quietly, setting that clay cup, cracked along the rim, down.

"For what? Stealing my work? Or failing to talk to me about it? Or letting me learn of it from Sparrow?" Rafe clipped out.

Another round of bell-like laughter carried from the kitchen and filtered into the parlor, those light, joyous sounds at odds with the tension enveloping Rafe and this room.

Hunter dragged a hand through his hair. "That is fair. I didn't know what to say, Rafe."

"To the work or to me?"

"To you," his younger brother said quietly. He'd not deny that he'd always wanted Rafe's role at the Cheadle coalfields, and perhaps another time that forthrightness would have earned Rafe's admiration. "What will you do?"

What would he do? A cynical laugh spilled from his lips. That was the question. What the hell would he do now that his work was gone and his brother was overseeing that role he loved? "Does it even matter?" *To you.*

Hunter winced, perceptive enough that he would hear the accusation there.

I will not feel bad. I will not feel bad.

"Of course it matters," Hunter whispered, those four words ripe with hurt. "What would you have had me do? He was determined that you would be replaced and—"

"You were all too happy to do it," Rafe cut in.

"The duke is determined you'll go to Town," his brother hissed. "You know that as well as I. And if you had, then that bizarre bird he sent wouldn't even now be in the kitchen, for some reason baking you breakfast."

That woman was Edwina Dalrymple. "She's not a bizarre bird. And she's not . . . making me . . . oh, go to hell," he snapped. "You could have answered the duke."

"He didn't summon me," his brother pointed out. "He wants you. Because he knows we'll support whatever decision you'll reach."

"Except when it comes to my work, no?"

Ruddy splotches of color filled Hunter's cheeks. "Rafe," He took a step toward him.

Rafe looked away, rejecting that attempt at outreach.

And his brother stopped.

"You should go, Hunter." Before he said something he couldn't take back. "You'll be late, and Sparrow doesn't tolerate that."

Hunter hovered, looking as though he wished to say more, but instead, avoiding Rafe's eyes, he left.

The moment the door closed, he let loose a stream of curses.

Damn Hunter.

And damn their sire.

And Sparrow, and everyone in between who was so determined that Rafe shouldn't have the ultimate control over his life.

Feeling eyes upon him, he glanced back.

Edwina hovered at the door, her cheeks red. "Forgive me," she said quietly. "I didn't mean . . . I . . . had to fetch something from my valise." She remained there, waiting, and it occurred to him that she sought his permission.

"Of course," he said tiredly.

The young lady sprang into movement, hurrying over to those hooks at the back of the door where her fine cloak and valise rested alongside his and his siblings' lesser things. Fishing through that ivory satin bag, Edwina withdrew a pink ribbon.

She lingered there, that pretty scrap between her fingers.

"You were early," he remarked.

"You were awake," she pointed out.

"Yes, but—"

"You live in the country and I'm a Town dweller?" she answered for him. Her eyes twinkled. Like the stars that still dotted the Staffordshire sky. He blanched. Where in hell had that romantic drivel come— "It bears noting, you were late in the time you indicated morning meal preparations began, Rafe."

He paused. And how in hell did she know *that*?

"I told you, there is nothing I do not know," she said on a teasing whisper. And then, the proper, lesson-doling-out governess tasked with his tutelage winked.

Likely all the time she'd lived in one of those elegant households. He watched as she scurried off to rejoin Cailin, and then he was . . . alone.

With his thoughts about his changed circumstances and the relentlessness of the duke.

All he'd been since he was a boy of eight was one who worked in these mines and who cared for his family. And . . . when that was taken away, what was he? Who did he become?

You can go on to London with the lady. You can get on with this . . . get it done . . . fulfill those responsibilities, and then happily leave, free to return to your foreman role, once more . . .

To do so, however, would hand the ultimate victory to the father who'd suddenly taken an interest in his children.

More of Edwina's laughter spilled from the kitchen, distracting Rafe briefly from those bitter musings. And it was only boredom, and the sole fact that he who only knew work had absolutely nothing to do, that accounted for his heading for the kitchen, even now.

It had absolutely nothing to do with her.

The moment he entered the kitchen, both women paused in the middle of their conversation and stared expectantly at him. Edwina stood behind Cailin, and was in the midst of tying that ribbon she'd fetched out of her bag.

She was . . . giving it to his sister.

"What are you doing?" he asked gruffly.

"I'm weaving a ribbon through her plait," Edwina answered, her fingers returning to their task.

Rafe frowned. "*Your* ribbon."

"Yes," she said patiently, as if advising a child. "It is a gift."

Cailin rested a hand on Edwina's, halting her efforts. "As much as it brings me physical discomfort admitting my eldest brother is right," she paused, sliding a droll smile his way, "he is. I've no need for such finery."

Had his sister been forlorn and mournful it would have been easier to take than that matter-of-fact statement. But this reminder of the luxuries he couldn't and hadn't been able to provide his sister hit him like a fist to the gut.

"Absolutely not!" Edwina insisted, gently but firmly disentangling Cailin's grip on that ribbon. "Why, there doesn't *have* be a reason to have articles that one likes or wants to wear.

Still, it was a battle of the wills between his sister and an impressively stubborn Edwina.

"You should take it back," his sister said, trying again to remove that satin scrap.

"I'll do no such thing," Edwina insisted. "I've any number of ribbons."

"Of course you do," he muttered, attracting a glare from Cailin. Edwina, however, gave no indication that she'd heard that petty and bitter rejoinder from him.

And in the end, it wasn't an Audley who proved triumphant but this peculiar stranger who'd stormed their lives.

"There!" Edwina said happily, and assessed the satin ribbon she'd woven through Cailin's hair.

Clearing his throat, he headed for the hot stove, and proceeded to make himself another cup of stiff tea.

Edwina and Cailin resumed working, quietly chatting as they did, their words low enough that he strained to hear.

Not that he wanted to, necessarily.

Of course he didn't.

At all.

It was just—

". . . Pigeon au Poivre . . . it really is quite clever," Edwina was saying.

From where he stood at the stoves, Rafe blew on the hot brew, and used the opportunity to study the duke's latest emissary. As Cailin stoked the fires, Edwina cut up strawberries, handling the knife with surprising ease. His sister set down the poker, and next checked the flame under the small cast-iron stove.

When she'd finished, she gathered up another small bowl of strawberries and carried them over to Edwina. She set them down. "Is this enough?" And equally surprising, that question was directed at . . . Edwina.

Edwina assessed the clay bowl. Using the tip of her blade, she sifted through, her lips silently moving as she counted. "Perhaps a bit more."

Smiling, Cailin rushed off and collected the wicker basket hanging from the wall. Making her way past Rafe, she let herself out into the back gardens.

He narrowed his eyes. What in hell was *happening* here? His sister was taking directives from . . . the high-in-the-instep governess? The same governess who was humming softly to herself and cutting fruit. And all the while, he wasn't for once at the coalfields. Yes, there was nothing else for it. The world had been flipped upside down.

But . . . his sister was smiling again. And it had been Edwina who'd managed to penetrate the numb way in which Cailin had been moving about life since the coalfield accident.

And as Edwina continued slicing the strawberries there, it occurred to him just how very much of the lady was a mystery. And ratcheting up terror was the realization that he, for some strange reason, wanted to discover those secrets.

With a forced calm he did not feel, he set aside his coffee. Strolling over to her, he plucked one of the berries from her bowl. As Edwina made quick work removing the stems and slicing up the strawberries, he picked up a knife, and proceeded to cut the bowl of fruit with her.

From the corner of his eye, he saw Edwina stop, and

watch him several moments, before resuming. They worked that way, in companionable silence.

As she worked, he studied her with the same scrutiny she'd given him. She moved effortlessly, skilled in the kitchen with every tool she'd held, and every task she'd been assigned. "You've got me," he said, placing the berries he'd cut into her bowl. "I'm intrigued."

The lady paused, and with the crook of her elbow, she brushed back the errant dark curl that had fallen across her brow, and alarming him once more was the overwhelming envy to see to that task himself. "And I'm confused as to why—"

"Who are you?" he asked bluntly. He set his knife down.

At that little clatter, she looked up. Confusion filled her eyes. "I've already told you. My name is Edwina Dalrymple and—"

He cut her off. "What is your story?" She continued to look back blankly. No one was this naïve. When it became apparent she needed further clarification, he volunteered the possibility that made most sense. "You were a poor relation taken in by unkind relatives and had no choice but to seek out a lady's work."

She snorted. "My, you can have a prosperous career as a gothic-tale writer with those manners of speculation, Mr. Audley."

Rafe leaned across the table, and Edwina's body stiffened. "You're being deliberately evasive." Grabbing an apple, he took an enormous bite, before holding the partially eaten apple out to her.

Horror paraded across her all-too-revealing features, as she shook her head, rejecting that offering. Or was her response a product of his observation? His curiosity redoubled. With a shrug, he spoke around a mouthful of fruit. "Well? What is it?"

Her expression as she took in the half-eaten apple was pained. "It is impolite to speak with food in your mouth, Mr. Audley."

This was going to be entirely too easy, and shockingly,

even more enjoyable than he could have ever imagined. In an attempt to hide a grin, Rafe took an even larger chomp of his apple.

She licked her lips, and against all better judgment, fueled by illogic and desire, he suddenly had a taste for an altogether different crimson fruit, the same one he'd tasted in her rooms just last night. When she'd been screaming his name to the rafters—and his shaft strained uncomfortably at the wicked memory of her as she'd been. He reminded himself to swallow his latest bite of apple.

Edwina set her knife down, and reaching for the rag left behind by Cailin, she dusted the remnants of the red berries from her palms. "My mother was of the gentry and my father was a nobleman."

That immediately killed his lust. There it was. Confirmation of everything he'd assumed about her birthright.

"And I take it they were in love."

Edwina paused, her unblinking eyes focused on the edge of the discarded knife. And then, she nodded. "Yes," she said softly. "Very much so."

Rafe rested a hip on the side of the table, waiting for her to say something more.

Only to find the chatterbox at last silenced.

As she made an exaggerated show of working, Rafe honed his eyes on her. The lady had secrets.

And against all better judgment and reason—Rafe wanted to know them.

Chapter 13

Edwina had always welcomed the time she spent in the kitchen.

For all the heat, there'd been a calm she'd found there. That this time . . . escaped her.

He was . . . working in the kitchen, alongside her. Handling a knife and slicing strawberries as if he'd done it countless times before.

And what was more . . . he was also asking questions about her.

No one asked questions about her, in short because no one cared about Edwina Dalrymple.

The only information that mattered to the families that hired her were her credentials, her previous clients, and the success she'd had in transforming sow's ears into silk purses.

And not only had Edwina preferred that lack of probing, but she required it.

Because the world didn't take instruction from banished bastard daughters, no matter how lofty those lords were. Illegitimate daughters weren't ones anyone would take any manner of instruction from, let alone hire to tutor cherished daughters, with reputations to be guarded at all costs. No, if the world learned who her father was, she'd never be hired. At least, not for any job that was respectable.

And now, this man should be the one to probe her, questioning her about her past and her origins and everything that was dangerous to her. For he could never understand. He wore his bastardy like a badge of pride, as if he taunted the world with it.

Perhaps that was an advantage afforded him as a male? Perhaps he well knew that Cailin had his and his brothers' protection. Edwina, however, had neither of those luxuries.

As such, her secret was and would forever remain just that—a secret.

"And do you have siblings?"

She jumped. "Siblings?" Her mind raced to formulate a reply. A lie. Anything to keep from thinking of the time four years earlier when her mother died, and she'd gone off to London to meet her father, only to have him send his son—his legitimate child—to meet her. And turn her away, with a request that she not come back. The shame and pain of that ripped at her insides, still.

Rafe stared at her, with a growing question in his eyes.

She shook her head quickly. "Not like you," she settled for, an evasive lie at best. "I always . . . wanted siblings as you have." She made herself go quiet, lest she say anything else revealing.

"Why so quiet of a sudden, Edwina?"

Of course, he'd not let her have that silence. It would have been easier if he had been taunting her again. Not this. Not this somewhat gentle delving.

"I'm working." She hastily grabbed the knife, and a strawberry, and resumed slicing and dicing the piece of fruit.

"Ah, but that has never stopped you from chattering away, little bird."

He knew that detail about her? Her mother had oft called her little bird, because she was chirping away from the moment the sun was climbing to the sky, until it made its final flight, and found its nighttime rest. And she didn't know what to do with a person wondering about her life and her past, because no good could come of it were it to be discovered that she was in fact, a bastard—

The tip of her knife slashed through the soft flesh of her thumb.

Edwina's breath hissed from between her teeth as she hastily dropped the blade. It clattered to the counter, knocking against the clay bowl.

She applied pressure to the bleeding wound, hiding the injury within the apron Rafe's sister had lent her.

Rafe immediately abandoned his relaxed pose and came quickly around the side of the table. "Let me see," he ordered in what she would wager were his foreman's tones, the ones that brooked no tolerance of gainsayers from the people who worked for him.

To what end? So he might confirm exactly what he'd already believed about her being incapable of undertaking tasks? And she didn't know why she should care so much about his low opinion or his ill opinion, anyway. For some reason . . . she did. "It is fine," Edwina said evenly, refusing to yield her hand for his study. She resented that he should treat her with disdain because he believed she was of an elevated station . . . when nothing could be further from the truth. "There is no reason for you to—"

"Let me see it, Edwina." He frowned, and contained within those downturned corners was the hint of not the expected annoyance, but . . . concern. "Please."

She hesitated, caught entirely off guard. People, as a rule, treated her as though she were at their beck and call. They made demands, as even Rafe Audley had done numerous times before this. But no one ever allowed the final decisions over any matter to belong to her, as he did just now with that single-syllable plea.

Edwina released the hold she had on the now-crimson-stained apron and unfurled her tightly twined hands.

He caught her hands in his, raising the injured one close for inspection. Unnerved by both his gentleness and the concern in his scrutiny, she stumbled about for words. "I am so sorry for the state of your sister's apron. I know you believe I don't have experience in the kitchen." But she did. So much of it. And she'd convinced herself she'd not missed moments such as those she'd shared today with Cailin, only to find the lie that she'd told herself. She'd missed this. "Despite how it may now appear, I am, in fact, more capable, and rarely make such a mistake. I just . . ." *Was distracted by you. By the thought of you learning anything about me . . .* "I just . . ."

Rafe touched an index finger to her mouth, silencing that second attempt on Edwina's part. "It is fine. I am not concerned with the apron. Here . . ." He gently guided her over to the oak chair. And as she complied this time, taking the seat he offered, her heart tripped over its beat, as she realized she was, in fact, the one he was concerned about. It was also an unfamiliar way for her to find herself. People didn't care about her. People used her. People needed her. People hired her.

They didn't care about her or for her, as this man was now doing.

As if to accentuate that very point, he dropped on a knee beside her, pulled a faded white kerchief from inside his jacket, and snapped it several times, unfolding the linen. With quick, meticulous purpose to his movements, he wound that fabric about her injured finger.

Her breath caught.

Rafe immediately stopped and raised a concern-filled gaze to hers. "Forgive me. I've hurt you."

"It was . . . just an unexpected . . . feeling," she hedged, which wasn't altogether untrue. All the while, she prayed he mistook the breathless quality of her voice for pain, and not . . . whatever mayhem now affected her senses.

"Apply pressure. Like this." He immediately folded his calloused palm over her knuckles, enveloping them in such warmth, even the sting left by her carelessness receded.

As he strode about the kitchen, quickly and efficiently filling his arms with a bowl, a pitcher, and a rag, she watched him. This riddle of a man, steeped in incongruities, that she didn't know how to solve.

She studied the old kerchief he'd wrapped about her palm. Upon inspection, the embroidered silk was not an ivory or white fabric, but rather contained hints of gold and autumn orange shades that had since faded to a pale yellow, revealing its mark of age.

Edwina peeked up, and finding him still busy hurrying about the kitchen gathering supplies, she swiftly unfurled the kerchief.

In a dark gold silk embroidery, three letters adorned the now-stained fabric:

FH, D of B

She flared her eyes.

A cabinet closed, and she startled, looking up. But Rafe continued moving about with his back to her.

Her heart knocked against her chest at the significance of the revelation.

It was his father's kerchief. And he might be adamant that he despised the man, and had no intention of joining him, but he'd also retained this small scrap that had once belonged to the duke . . . and that said more than all the words of disdain he'd uttered about his sire.

Edwina froze.

It was clearly a cherished piece, as he'd held on to it, and even so, he had thought nothing of giving it over to her. Knowing it would be ruined the moment he wrapped it about her bleeding finger, but he'd done so anyway.

She hastily rewrapped the makeshift bandage as he'd left it.

At so many times, in so many exchanges they'd had, it was as though he'd gone out of his way to be as miserable as possible. It didn't fit with this thoughtful gentleman, worrying after her slight injury. Just as when he'd carried her back after her fall, insisting there wasn't more to his actions.

And then there'd been last evening, when he'd helped her straighten her room.

Yes, he might insist he was cold and heartless. Saying it,

however, didn't make it true. For, at every turn, he revealed through his actions he wasn't the beast he was determined to have her think he was.

All these details were important for her research, and belonged in her notebook, for the purpose of her assignment. And yet, as she recalled each kindness and consideration shown her, it didn't feel very much like she was thinking about her work. At all.

Rafe returned, startling her from those disquieting musings. He reached for the hand that was injured.

Edwina cradled it close to her chest, not knowing how to turn it over to his care. Or his attention. Once more, unfamiliar with anyone wanting to attend her or even noticing her discomforts. And more, uncomfortable with this continued tender look on him.

Collecting the pitcher, he poured enough water to fill half the bowl, and then grabbed a chair. Rafe dragged it closer to Edwina and sat. "May I see it?" As he asked he was already reaching for her, as if it was simply expected and understood that she would allow him those liberties.

"No," she blurted out. Because the last thing that seemed safe or sane at this moment was placing her hand in his, and allowing this intimacy. Or, for that matter, any further intimacy between them.

His coal-black brows came together. "No?"

And by the scowl he wore, he was a man unaccustomed to being told no. Good, that was a familiar, and safer, Rafe Audley whom she knew what to do with. "It really is fine," she insisted, as she held her hand out for his inspection. "See."

They looked as one at her covered hand.

Except blood had already drenched the makeshift bandage made about her left index finger, turning the yellowish material crimson and black, and effectively making a liar of her.

"Yes. Everything looks quite normal there," he said dryly. He leaned in, close enough that their noses nearly kissed and her mouth knew envy. Close enough that their breath mingled. "Let me see," he said abruptly, a harsh quality to his already deep baritone, and when he spoke that way, she couldn't have denied him anything. And was grateful that it was just her finger he requested, or she'd have meandered back along the happy path he'd shown her last evening.

She held her hand out.

He proceeded to unravel the bandage.

"Y-You know, we really are making something of a habit with this. Your tending me, that is." She could no more stop her more-than-usual prattling than she could stop her heart from racing under his attentions. "I know you'll likely not believe it, but I'm generally not so careless. At"—Rafe removed the kerchief, and tossed it onto the table so that her naked fingers rested upon his—"a-all. There have been many times when people have remarked upon my . . ." *grace* . . . He turned her hand over in his, inspecting her injury, and she promptly let the remainder of her thoughts go unspoken.

"Grace?" he supplied for her.

She nodded before recalling he wasn't even looking at her, and was therefore incapable of seeing that gesture. "I-Indeed."

And as he lightly probed the flesh around her injury, she briefly closed her eyes and fought to control the flutters in her belly that came from the gentleness of his touch.

She'd never been angry at her mother for loving where she shouldn't. She'd regretted that her mother hadn't chosen more wisely, and given her heart to someone who was deserving.

But she'd also not understood her mother. For that matter, she'd not understood what madness compelled women to forget themselves and toss away their virtue and reputation and hearts. And yet, here she was, just a handful of days of knowing this gentleman, and she understood those things in ways she hadn't before.

Edwina went absolutely motionless.

Not that she was losing her heart to this man. That was utterly preposterous. They barely knew one another. And he barely liked her.

Except, caring for her as he did now, it didn't quite feel that way, and she was all the more confused.

Guiding her palm over the bowl he'd fetched, Rafe

dunked it under the surface, the clear water instantly going red. "You're not squeamish," he remarked.

"Should I be?"

"Aye. And you shouldn't be able to handle a knife in the kitchen as you do."

She smiled. "Yes, but one might argue, given my current circumstances, that I'm less skilled than you're presently giving credit for."

He glanced up, and that assessing glint, the one that threatened to pierce and penetrate her every secret, pinned her to the spot. "You weren't unskilled; you were distracted by my questions. That is altogether different."

Yet again, he'd seen that, and known that about her.

Edwina tensed in anticipation of those questions he'd put to her before . . . that, this time, didn't come. Instead, he resumed washing her wound. Then lightly, gently squeezing, and then applying pressure. Repeating that pattern with the familiarity of one who'd done this many times before.

Which, by his admission the day they'd first met, was, in fact, truth. He was a man capable of caring for injuries, and himself wasn't put out or nauseated by the sight of a wound. Yet again, so . . . different than all the men in all the households she had worked within.

While he attended her, she studied the top of his bent head, those thick, luxuriant black tresses that she'd wound her fingers through the night before while he showed her body the pleasure it was capable of. Her body heated, burning up with a blush at the reminder of his touch and the peak he'd brought her to. Yet again, that proved to be another incongruity with the cynical, mocking, and rude gentleman who so delighted in teasing her. Not once had he taunted her about what had transpired between them last evening. He had not sought to shame her for it.

And she would be forever grateful to him for it.

Rafe removed her hand from the water. The flow of blood had slowed to a mere trickle, with only the errant drop squeezing from the flesh wound, which he continued to wipe away. He shoved back his chair, the legs scraping along the stone floor. Crossing over to the cupboard, he fetched a rag hanging from the hooks there and returned. "So you don't want to talk about it?" he asked as he wound the cloth about her finger.

Edwina furrowed her brow.

"How you, the daughter of a woman from the gentry and a father who is a lord, are equally capable of curtsying and cutting up berries in a kitchen."

And to earlier accusations he'd leveled at her, it was as he'd pointed out . . . unfair to share nothing when she expected him to freely reveal. Studying her wrappings, Edwina carefully chose her words. "My mother enjoyed baking. She didn't think there was anything untoward about being in the kitchen and . . . I came to find and feel the same."

She held her breath, waiting for him to ask more. Dreading it. Fearing it.

Disassembling hadn't been a chore for her over the years, not because she was skilled in lying, but because people didn't ask the questions of her that this man now did.

Rafe worked his gaze over her face. "You are a mystery, Edwina Dalrymple."

And it needed to stay that way. For the sake of her reputation, which was exhaustingly linked to her employment.

As such, all closeness with this man should be discouraged. It needed to be.

So why, then, as he leaned closer, did her lashes flutter, and she lean up, offering her mouth once more to his?

The door exploded, saving her from temptation when Eve had so been failed.

"Forgive me." Cailin came streaming in, with a basket looped over her arm. "I—" The remainder of whatever she would have said abruptly ended as her focus landed on Rafe kneeling beside Edwina. And then, her hand in his. The young woman's brow dipped.

Rafe immediately surged to his feet. "Miss Dalrymple was injured," he explained to do away with any questions or reasons for his earlier closeness to Edwina.

Cailin gasped. Hastily disentangling the basket from her

arm, she dropped it by the door and raced over. "You've been hurt!"

Edwina stood. "I'm afraid I was clumsy and careless."

"She wasn't," Rafe put in, with a surprising defense that brought her up short. "But given the injury to her hand, perhaps it is best that Miss Dalrymple's time in the kitchen be concluded for the day."

She should be relieved. He had provided Edwina with her second out since his sister had arrived.

So what accounted for this latest irrational disappointment? "It would hardly be fair for me to leave Cailin on her own with the recipe I provided," Edwina said, in an attempt to remain. To learn more about her charge, of course.

Liar.

"I can see to it," Rafe offered.

He'd . . . help his sister in the kitchen? At every turn, she was left with more and more questions. "You cook?" Edwina blurted, before she could recall that stunned exclamation.

He opened his mouth to respond, but his sister beat him to it. "He is ever so wonderful in the kitchen."

And wonder of wonders, a blush filled the sharp planes of his cheeks. Blushing! The gruff, tough, and rude Mr. Audley was blushing? It was alternately intriguing and endearing.

He shifted on his feet. "You are just saying that because you hate cooking."

"That is only one part true." Cailin looked to Edwina. "He is being entirely modest," Rafe's sister said in an exaggerated whisper. "One time, there was a contest in the village for—"

"She doesn't want to hear this," he interrupted. And as one who clung to her secrets, she recognized the effort he now exerted.

Edwina smiled encouragingly at Cailin. "Oh, I most certainly do."

"She's being polite." Rafe looked to Edwina. "Tell her you're being polite."

"As a rule, I am polite." Edwina dipped her voice to a teasing whisper. "This, however, is not one of those times."

Cailin beamed. "See?" the younger woman said for her brother's benefit. "She does. Where was I?"

Rafe and Edwina spoke at the same time.

"You were agreeing to say nothing else."

"You were mentioning the contest," Edwina said, raising her voice so that her response was heard over Rafe's.

"Oh, yes, the contest. The prize was a cameo necklace for the best-made pastry, and Rafe was the only man to enter. All the women were vying for the necklace. And he won!"—The gentleman scrubbed the back of his hand across his eyes, charming once more in his modesty—"He was the envy of all the village women for that prize, but he only entered so that he could give it to me because he knew there was no way I could win."

"That isn't true," he protested, with a telltale devotion that spoke volumes once more about the manner of brother . . . and man he was.

"I love you, but you are a liar!" Cailin clasped the chain at her throat and revealed the small trinket, a paste bauble, and yet, for the story that had been told, which went with that piece, the cameo of the queen herself could not have been finer.

While brother and sister teasingly bickered back and forth, Edwina freely observed Rafe—this new version of Rafe Audley, that was.

Later that day, when he'd escorted her back to the inn, with a neatly wrapped piece of the strawberry tartlet made by the gentleman himself, she found herself thinking that it might prove best after all if she left Staffordshire. Because those intimate moments she had spent with him had no place in her work, and were only dangerous.

The moment she was alone in her room, Edwina shut the door behind her. She headed for her makeshift desk and dropped her reticule on the floor. Sitting down, Edwina proceeded to set out paper, and reaching for the pen, she dipped it into ink, and dashed off the update the duke would be expecting.

This time, however, unlike with all her previous correspondence to Rafe's father, words proved elusive. This time, there wasn't the cataloguing that had come so easily before.

Because at some point, Rafe had become more than . . . her charge. He'd become a man who . . . fascinated her. And tempted her.

Edwina abandoned the pen, and her efforts.

Switching her attention instead to the pastry, she carefully unwrapped the packed treat Rafe had assembled for her.

The sweet scent of strawberries immediately wafted about, filling the air, and she breathed deep of the sweet smell.

Opening her eyes, she stared at the masterful confectionary creation, the gently rounded crust, perfectly formed. The finest London cook could have been responsible for such baking.

Not only did he not scoff at working in the kitchen, and alongside two women . . . he was capable and skilled in ways that men generally weren't.

And the truth of that brought a crushing weight of terror down on her chest.

Because she didn't know what to do with this new version of Rafe Audley. A man who did dangerous things to her heart . . .

Dropping her chin into her palm, she stared forlornly down at the strawberry tart. With her other hand, she raised the pastry, and took a bite.

She stilled, and of their own volition, her eyes slid closed as she savored the ambrosial taste of Rafe's masterful efforts.

Edwina made quick work of the tart, and when she'd finished, with a shamefulness that would have seen her unemployed forevermore, she licked the remnants of sugar from her fingers.

Yes, the sooner her assignment was done, the better off she would be.

Chapter 14

Later that night, the crowd in the taproom was even more raucous and rowdy than usual.

Even at the second floor of the inn, the noise was deafening.

As such, any young lady unfamiliar with the ways of miners and the ways of the country village would have turned tail and run at the prospect of joining that fray.

Rafe, however, should have learned by now the woman who'd been haunting his steps here in Staffordshire was unlike any other woman he'd ever known. Nay, unlike any *person* he'd ever known.

Edwina's door opened, and she stepped out of her room, wearing a smile, a bright yellow ruffled gown, and a ridiculous lacy bonnet. "Hullo, Rafe!" she greeted him, shouting loud enough to be heard over the racket.

And from her outfit on down to her elegant attire, he may as well have been collecting her for a fancy curricle ride about Town than belowstairs to a tavern. "Are you ready?" he called back.

It was a nonsensical question, given the fact that she

clearly was. But something about her left him all twisted and tied.

Her smile widened, dimpling her cheeks. "Indeed." She drew the door shut behind her, and removing a chain about her neck, she inserted the key and locked it. "Never let it be said that I don't learn," she said as she put the makeshift necklace on once more, and tucked the rusty brass key into her dress, in that V between her breasts. And he swallowed hard as his gaze went to the place that now hidden key rested.

Edwina started down the hall with a jaunty little sway to her step, and he remained there several moments, appreciating that subtle glide of her hips. Recalling when they had been shifting, in a similar way, toward him. Desire flared uncomfortably, his shaft stirring.

Edwina stopped and looked back. "Is there a problem?"

There were. Many of them. So very many of them. All of which had to do with the very determined, tenacious Edwina Dalrymple and his unexplainable interest in her.

Rafe followed after her. She waited, and when he reached her side, resumed walking. "I must admit, and you are going to find it truly scandalous, that I am exceedingly intrigued by what happens down there." Excitement filled her voice and colored her cheeks red. And as they descended the stairs to the taproom, apparently no input was required from him. The chatterbox was content and capable of carrying the conversation for the two of them. "I have wanted to see what happens, but it seemed neither proper nor safe. And as such, I was ever so glad when you stated that this was one of your terms."

"How . . . fortunate for you," he drawled. He gave his head a wry shake. Only he would have come up with terms intended to send her away that had done just the opposite.

She nodded enthusiastically, the smile she lifted up to him ever wider. "Oh, yes."

And for all the ways in which she'd proven adroit in so much, sarcasm entirely escaped her. And he'd sooner cut off the arm he used for mining than admit as much, but it was rather endearing.

She baked.

She made her own bed.

She didn't cry over injuries.

And now, she'd join a roomful of coalfield miners.

And he was intrigued. He was done denying it to himself. He had questions that he wanted answered. And they were all about her.

They reached the crowded main floor; smoke from too many pipes hung like a haze over the taproom. Men were crammed into every corner. Every table was occupied, every seat filled.

The excited glimmer in Edwina's eyes dimmed.

Aye, now this was the expected—

"I fear we are too late!" she shouted over the pandemonium too much drink had resulted in. "There are no tables left."

That was her worry? Not the idea of being here, but rather that there wasn't space for her to take part in the revelry?

Mr. Ward shot an arm out and waved at Rafe. "Audley!" he bellowed loud enough to be heard over the din.

"Come," Rafe urged, and motioned Edwina on ahead of him. They cut a path through the crowd, men knocking into one another and splashing drinks on them as they went.

And through it, Edwina remained unwavering.

They reached the back corner table, and Mr. Ward. There was a brief flash of confusion when his gaze landed on the tall woman at Rafe's side, but the man knew better than to probe. He tugged out one of the chairs. "Saved your table, I did. I'll fetch you a drink."

"Two, please," Rafe called after him. He waited until Edwina had seated herself before claiming the chair across from her.

An excited flush stained her cheeks, and her eyes darted about the room, taking in everything and everyone around her.

Leaning back, Rafe folded his hands and rested them on his stomach. "Different than your usual pastimes, no doubt."

"Oh, very much so. There's of course the theater, which gets quite loud, but nothing such as this."

A few days earlier, he would have expected her disdain for the Staffordshire way of life. He would have never anticipated that she would freely immerse herself in this world. And it had been decidedly easier rejecting her request that he join her in London when she'd looked down upon his way of life. Instead, she had done precisely what he asked.

And what did that mean for him . . . and the very reason for her being here—his attempt at fitting in with Polite Society?

Saved by those unnerving thoughts, he looked up as Mr. Ward reappeared. The innkeeper set down two steel tankards, and then raised the pitcher of ale in his other hand and proceeded to pour.

"Thank you very much." Edwina flashed another blindingly bright smile at the older man, earning a blush. And then muttering to himself, Mr. Ward shuffled off.

"He likes you," Rafe remarked.

"Not enough to *not* destroy my rooms," It was the first hint of droll sarcasm he'd heard from the lady, and it roused guilt for his role in enlisting Mr. Ward as he had.

"I am . . . sorry for that," he called over the noise.

Surprise sent the thin dark line of her eyebrows flying up. "Well, war was declared, Rafe."

They shared a brief smile, the moment interrupted by the rolling thunder of men stomping the floor with their feet, and then one of the patrons broke out in song.

> *Oh my name it is Jack Hall,*
> *Chimney sweep, chimney sweep,*
> *Oh my name it is Jack Hall, chimney sweep.*
> *Oh my name it is Jack Hall,*
> *And I've robb'd both great and small,*
> *And my neck shall pay for all*
> *When I die, when I die,*
> *And my neck shall pay for all when I die.*

Edwina widened her eyes. "That is . . . terrible," she called over the ribald song being played.

"Aye," he agreed. Collecting his tankard, he sipped his ale and surveyed the crowd. "This one is more grim than—" He narrowed his eyes, as his focus landed on the leader of the first of the evening's songs.

Usually on the fringe, Hunter had found himself at the very center. Surrounded by merry coalfield workers, his station elevated, Rafe's brother had also found himself the leader of the night's merriment.

Rafe's fingers curled reflexively around his tankard, the handle fitting sharply into his calloused palm. How at home his brother appeared. When always before, he wore a scowl, now he had a smile. And bastard that Rafe was, in every sense of the word, he envied the younger man that happiness.

"Your brother," Edwina began loudly.

Blinking several times slowly in confusion, he looked over, and then followed the slight nudge of her chin, over to Hunter. "Aye?" he said stiffly.

"He has a lovely voice," she remarked.

Rafe hadn't known as much because his brother barely took part in the revelries to the extent that he now did tonight. Now, when he had reason for song and merriment.

And Rafe didn't want to think of his brother. Not this night. Rafe didn't want to think about the fact that he had been displaced from his job, replaced by his younger brother. Or that he was now in the midst of trying to figure out how in hell to spend his days.

"Are you going to drink it or cradle it?" he asked, changing the subject. Rafe lifted his tankard, clarifying his question.

Edwina raised the steel cup to her lips and inhaled. Her pert nose wrinkled, and her face pulled in a grimace, and with that, Rafe managed another smile since he'd caught sight of his brother in all his happiness. "It smells horrid."

Holding his tankard out, he clanged the ring against hers in a mock toast, challenging her.

He thought for a moment she intended to reject that challenge, he should have known better.

Taking in a deep breath, Edwina raised her glass, tipped it back, and chugged.

Deeply.

The long, graceful column of her neck moved rhythmically and quickly as she downed the contents of her drink.

"Whoa, you are not supposed to consume it quite so quickly," he instructed her, hastily reaching across the table, and resting a hand on the fingers cradling her mug.

Edwina set it down with a little splat and then, ever so gingerly, dabbed at the corners of her mouth. "That is . . . rather horrid stuff." Her shoulders and chest lifted as she hiccoughed, and he grinned.

Mr. Ward immediately reappeared and eyed Edwina's empty tankard approvingly. "I knew I was right about this girl," he said proudly. "Knows her spirits, she does."

From over the top of the innkeeper's hand, as he poured, Edwina caught Rafe's eye.

"Do not say anything," she mouthed at him, perfectly forming each syllable.

"I wouldn't dream of it." Rafe mouthed back, following that assurance with a wink.

"What is that, Mr. Audley?"

"I was just saying to the lady I couldn't dream of a more splendid ale," he expertly substituted, and the already tall innkeeper grew several inches under that praise. Bustling off, Mr. Ward went to refill the tankards of the table of nearby patrons.

"You're not horrified."

Her tankard still in her hands, Edwina dropped her elbows on the table and leaned across the small, cylindrical surface. "That was your intention and plan."

Rafe's cheeks went warm.

Edwina's eyes rounded. "Why . . . why . . . you are blushing, Mr. Audley."

"That is p-preposterous," he sputtered. "I would never do anything like . . . Like . . ."

"Blush?" she winged up an eyebrow, and edged forward another fraction so that their elbows touched. "You needn't worry," she whispered. "Your secret is safe with me. The men and women who work for you will never learn about your blushing."

And his brief good humor ended with that reminder, the reminder of his brother's new role. And their father's determination to control Rafe's life. The muscles along his jaw tensed. "They aren't my workers," he said coolly. "Not anymore." Inadvertently, his focus slid over to Hunter, who was just concluding his rousing rendition of Jack Hall.

Edwina followed his stare.

"My brother replaced me."

"And that . . . displeases you?" There was confusion and a question there.

"No. Yes." He scraped a hand through his hair. Picking up his tankard, he took a long swallow. "I don't . . . know. I just know . . ." He stopped.

"What is it?" she asked, as laughter rolled around the taproom from men deciding upon the next ditty to be sung.

"I just know that it's my role. And I want it. It's what I'm comfortable doing. And being. And I resent losing that assignment, even if the one to replace me is my brother." Even as that truth and admission marked him a disloyal brother, there was no freeing Rafe of those sentiments.

Edwina took another drink, this time slower and more tentatively. When she set it down, she was more serious than he'd seen her these past days. "Just because it is comfortable doesn't mean that it is best for you."

A sneer formed on his lips, replacing the earlier grin that had come too easily. "And you think after but a few days, you know what is better for me?" She gave no outward indication of the layer of steel in that mocking question he put to her.

"No," she said calmly, "I don't know that. But I don't know and you don't know that there isn't a better future that you might want, because you've never experienced it. Just as I've never experienced this." She raised her tankard and took another long swallow. "Or this." She motioned to the taproom. This time when she spoke, her cheeks were brightly flushed, likely from both the heat of the room and the amount of spirits she'd consumed . . . and the pace at which she'd consumed them. "In fact, prior to this, I wasss certain I hated the country and never wished to return." There was a slight slur to her words.

Never wished to return.

So she'd spent some time outside London. It was, he'd wager, an accidental admission on her part.

He and Edwina returned to their drinks, settling back into their seats and watching as the lively crowd stomped their feet and raised their voices in song. As the evening wore on, Edwina continued drinking her ale, swaying and tapping her feet in time to the songs.

"Why are you looooking at him like that?" Edwina asked loud enough to be heard over the cacophony.

"Because I envy him," he called, not bothering with a lie. "I know it is wrong," he made himself acknowledge. "He's always wanted this." At her questioningly look, he clarified. "To be foreman, and it's only temporary, but then in the meantime—"

"In the meantime, Rafe, you should be happy for him and look at this as fate's way of telling you to carpe diem!" She threw her arms up. "Seize the day!"

Seize the day.

She dragged her chair closer, until she was seated on the same side of the table as Rafe. So that their knees brushed. "Come with me." He went completely motionless under that sultry whisper, and his eyes went to her mouth. "To London," she finished with her big smile.

Come with her . . . to London.

When she said it as she did . . . in those husky tones, a plea in her voice and her eyes, it was as though she wanted it. And that she didn't speak for and because of the duke. And perhaps it was a product of drink or the celebratory mood of the room, but there was . . . an appeal to Edwina's request.

Then she took his hand in hers. "Do you know, I rather like this." He glanced down at their connected fingers. "Being in the country. And I didn't think I would," she rambled on. "But I do. And if you came to London, you would, too, and you know it." She jabbed him with a finger. "I know it, but you're scared.

He opened his mouth to debate that point. He wasn't afraid . . . of anything.

And yet, a voice whispered, *What if that's what it was? Fear and resentment? Of the mother who'd loved that place, and a determination to have nothing to do with it for how it had weakened her?*

Edwina jumped up, saving him from the tumult of his musings. He stared questioningly, as she wended her way to the makeshift stage and, hefting up her skirts, climbed atop it. She spoke several words to a blushing Alan Meadows on fiddle. The young man nodded, and then raised the instrument to his chin. And when Meadows plied the strings with his bow, Edwina lifted her hands above her head, and clapping in time to the beat, she launched into gusty song.

> *Lord Lovel he stood at his own castle gate,*
> *A-combing his milk-white steed,*
> *When up came Lady Nancy Belle*
> *To wish her lover good speed, good speed.*
> *To wish her lover good speed.*

Cradling his drink in his hands, Rafe sat back bemused and watched as she danced around the small stage, singing and motioning with her arms for the men and women around her to join in.

Which . . . they of course did. Because the same way she'd enthralled Cailin, she'd managed to beguile the whole of the damned village.

And you, too . . .

Rafe took a long drink, hoping liquor might dull that silent realization. Reclining in his seat, he continued to watch.

This was, yet again, another new glimpse of her.

Granted, this present exuberance was a product of strong ale, but that didn't take away from the fact that she knew those old folk songs and moved comfortably among the villagers. Rafe looked on at the engaged crowd . . . including his brother.

Smiling, as Rafe had never seen him, and clapping enthusiastically alongside the other miners. Edwina's surprisingly deep, husky contralto soared throughout the room.

> *He had not been gone but a year and a day,*
> *Strange countries for to see,*
> *When a strange thought came into his head—*

And in that moment the depth of his selfishness and resentment hit him, as he acknowledged that perhaps Edwina had been correct. That Rafe's going to London might be for the best . . . just for reasons he'd not before considered. He could simultaneously free his sister from this place . . . if even just for a short while, and allow his brother to have this opportunity without Rafe here. Rafe, who had gone out of his way to protect his siblings but might have also inadvertently constrained them. And the most unlikely of persons had opened Rafe's eyes to that.

From across the crowded room, Edwina caught his eye, and as she sang, it was as if the lyrics spilling from her lips were reserved for him.

He found himself returning her smile.

He'd only had two tankards, and yet, perhaps it was a stronger-than-usual brew. There was no accounting for . . . *any of this.*

A tall figure stepped between Rafe and Edwina, shattering that connection.

He glanced up to find Hunter's smile gone and his features in their usual serious set. "May I sit?" he shouted over Edwina's rousing rendition of "Lord Lovel."

"Of course."

A tankard in one hand, Hunter slid into the seat previously occupied by Edwina.

Despite the merry revelry of the taproom, there was tension between them. One that had never been there before, and one that Rafe didn't want there. He'd raised his brother and had only wanted happiness for him. Well, now he had it, and it would be wrong not to allow him that moment.

In the meantime, Rafe, you should be happy for him and look at this as fate's way of telling you to carpe diem! Seize the day!

She'd been . . . correct. Which raised the uncomfortable question, what else might she be right about?

"You've been smiling tonight. Am I to take that . . . as hope that you might not be quite so angry as you've been?" Hunter ventured to ask, and in the hesitancy there, in his voice, and in his eyes, he had the look of the small boy whom Rafe himself had cared for.

"I'm not. Not with you," he corrected. "It was never about you," he said, needing Hunter to understand that.

Hunter's wide shoulders sagged, his relief palpable. And just like that, they returned to the companionable way it had always been between them. They sipped their ale, watching the crowd. "She's still here," Hunter remarked.

"Aye."

Just then, the "she" in question kicked up her heels and danced a lively jig that earned a rousing cheer from the crowd.

"Bothersome wench hasn't taken the hint, has she?"

Rafe frowned into his drink. "Bothersome wench" wasn't at all different than how Rafe had thought of the lady, but hearing Hunter speak of Edwina that way grated on him. "I'm going to London," he said quietly.

His brother, in the middle of bobbing his head in time to the music, abruptly stopped. "What?" he blurted out.

"I'm going with her."

Hunter's features darkened. "This is because of me," he said tightly. "I knew you were angry—"

"This isn't about that," Rafe interrupted. Perhaps initially it had been the reason for his capitulation. "I . . . thought it would be beneficial for Cailin to have some time away from Staffordshire and I've never been afforded an opportunity to do so." Not with his work.

His youngest brother eyed him skeptically. "You can't possibly wish to go see him."

"No," he said calmly. That hadn't changed, and never would. "This isn't about him. Not really." It was about the Audley siblings. "The duke is determined to interfere in our lives and will continue to do so." That is, if Rafe didn't agree to this. "It's the surest way to be done with him."

"And so you'll go with her?"

They looked as one to where an increasingly breathless Edwina danced about her stage, singing; Meadows's playing built to a frenzied crescendo. "I will."

Edwina concluded her song, and the entire tavern erupted in cheers. Her heart-shaped cheeks flushed from her exertions, her hair, those strands of auburn that melded every shade of brown and red there was, hung in a tangle about her shoulders. The young lady swept her arms wide and bowed for her besotted audience.

"Good luck with that one," Hunter said, with a wry shake of his head.

Good luck, indeed.

Edwina came crashing and stumbling through the crowd, a tankard supplied by some patron or another in each of her hands, and she alternately drank from them.

"Oh, hell," Rafe muttered. This was not going to be good.

She knocked into the table. "Did you hear me?" she asked breathlessly. "I was *magnificent*, wasn't I?"

"Modest, too," his brother drawled.

"*Other* Mrrr. Audley," she greeted, lifting her drinks in a double salute. "How very good it is to see you again."

Shoving back his chair, Rafe hastily relieved her of those tankards and set them out of her reach. "I think you've had enough of this."

"I am sooo happy to know you are happy with your work," she said, as she seated herself.

Hunter tipped his cap. "Miss." Finishing off his ale,

Hunter came to his feet. He smiled wryly at Rafe. "I'll leave you to your pleasures." His sarcastic tone, however, indicated his words were anything but false.

Again, Rafe had been of a like opinion where Edwina Dalrymple was concerned: she was a bothersome, underfoot busybody. Something, however, had changed.

The moment his brother had gone, Edwina all but flung herself across the top of the table, sprawling over that ale-stained surface. "Did you *seeee* me?" Her eyes glimmered from the depth of her excitement.

"I did," he murmured. He'd been unable to look anywhere but at her.

She grabbed his hands in hers, crushing them against her breasts, and he swallowed hard.

"This isn't so very terrrrible, you know."

Touching her like this, in the middle of a crowded taproom, when she was three sheets to the wind, however, was. And not because he didn't like the feel of her. Nay, not that. It was because she felt so damned good. "I told you as much," he said hoarsely, because he had to say . . . something.

She wagged an unsteady finger at him. "Now, now. Do not go and pretend you were trying toooo show me. You were trying to scaaare me into leaving." She curled her hands up into makeshift claws and raised them, in mock-menace, and then promptly dissolved into laughter, pitching forward.

Rafe caught her to him. "I think it is long past time for you to find your rooms."

"You're a killller of fun, Mr. Rafe Audddley. This is ever so much more funnn than I ever recalll. The people are sooooo nice," she slurred, as she held on to his waist, using him as a crutch.

"And that surprises you?"

Edwina hummed a jaunty tune under her breath as they walked. "Oh, yes."

The effects of the spirits made that admission casual . . . when it was anything but.

She'd been the recipient of unkindness. Knowing that she'd been subject to it, and also at his hands, left a tightness in his chest.

They made their way slowly and unsteadily across the taproom. The patrons lifted their glasses in greeting as they passed.

"Seee . . . how niiice." Leaning up on tiptoe, she pressed her mouth close to his ear, and her overconsumption of spirits turned a whisper into a shout. "People are not allllways kind, you know."

Yes, he did. "You said as much." And he expected coldness would meet him in London.

"Do you know what else is niiice?" she asked, as they made their way upstairs.

The feel of her pressed against his side. The taste of her lips. The bell-like quality of her laughter. "What is that, princess?"

They reached her rooms. "Those things you did to me the other night. Sooo nice."

He strangled on a groan. This was to be his punishment, then, for having been a bastard to her. "I am glad you found it so." Rafe guided her near the wall, so she had the support of it behind her. "Your key."

"My . . ." Her eyes went round. "Of course!" she exclaimed, and then as if he'd told the grandest of jests, she dissolved into laughter. "My keyyy," she slurred, when her merriment had faded to a giggle. She stared up at him with those doe-eyes. "Where is my keyyy?"

Rafe swiped a hand over his face, as a half groan, half laugh escaped him. He let his arm fall, and motioned to the bodice of her dress. "There, princess."

She followed that gesture, and promptly slapped two palms over her breasts and squeezed them together, those same gently rounded swells he'd been worshipping two days ago. His blood thickened . . . and then she reached inside the top of her gown, fishing around, feeling about.

Rafe briefly closed his eyes, and prayed for strength.

"It is . . . missing!" she cried out. "Gone. Absolutely

missing. What shall we *dooo*?" she wailed, her forlornness giving way to another bout of giggles. Edwina slid down, but managed to use the wall to stop herself from completely falling.

"It is there, Edwina." *For the love of all the saints in heaven, please, please find it*, he silently implored her. "Look again."

"It isn't." She thrust her bosom out, bringing his gaze there once more. "I've quite cheeeecked there, you knowww."

Yes, he knew. Lord, how he knew. He also knew that the absolute absence of that key meant more of this prolonged torture. Raising his eyes to the cracked plaster ceiling, he felt for that metal chain, and withdrew it.

Edwina clapped wildly. "Youuuu are a magician, Mr. Audley, do you know that?"

Rafe inserted the key into the lock. It gave with a little click, earning him another round of applause from the thoroughly foxed Edwina Dalrymple. "Come along, princess."

"And do you knowww, where they have magicians. Hmm? I shall tell you," she said, as he caught her by the waist, and guided her into the room. "In Londonnn!" she cried, and clasped her hands to her chest. That quick movement unsteadied the lady, and she toppled forward.

Rafe caught her, and kicking the door shut behind them, he led her onward to the cozy-looking bed she'd turned down earlier.

"And there's parlor tricks and museums and circuses, and you would love it soooo much," she prattled on.

The lady didn't miss a beat, selling him on a London visit even when she was deep in her cups.

Rafe set her down, and made to straighten up. Edwina caught his lapels, and dragged him down with her.

Cursing, he lost his balance, and fell atop her. He managed to catch himself on his elbows.

"I've decided you should stayyy." Edwina wrapped her arms about him and held tight.

"Have you?" he asked, perspiration beading his brow. *Think of something. Think of anything.* That was, anything other than the feel of her soft form under his, and her questing fingers moving purposefully under his jacket, and tugging his shirt free. He tried.

And failed.

Rafe intercepted her movements. "You don't want to do that, princess," he said gruffly, straightening to put some space between them.

"Oh, pooh." Edwina pushed herself up onto her elbows; her lush lips formed a perfect, and perfectly tempting pout. "I dooo." She flared her eyes. "That is a rhyme." She clapped wildly, and with a pained laugh, he used the opportunity to draw free.

"What am I going to do with you, princess?"

"I'll tell you," she spoke in a thick, sultry whisper, and with unsteady movements, Edwina got herself up onto her knees. "You're going to come with me. I want you here and there and everywhere." She again reached for him.

Cursing, Rafe caught her just as she would have pitched face-forward onto the floor. "I do want you, you knowww." With her face buried against his jacket, her words came muffled against him, but clear. Still so very clear. He stared over the top of her head, and prayed for strength and patience. "I want to do what we did again. I've thought about it all these days, and I'd like to do it again." Tossing her arms wide, she let herself flop onto her back.

He stared down at her where she lay, a silly smile on her crimson lips, and sighed. "Well, I cannot oblige this night," No matter how much he might want her. Which he did. Desperately.

She rolled onto her side and pouted. "Yes, you caaan."

"Not if I am a man of honor." Which he was. He didn't have legitimacy to his name, but he was also not one who'd ever take advantage of her, or any woman. Not in this way, and not in any way.

Edwina's lashes fluttered. "But I want it."

And with all his earlier insistences on his own honor, the devil was determined to tempt Rafe and taunt him, challenging him on that very thing.

She caught Rafe, and worked her hand under his jacket and up his shirt, stroking his chest. He groaned, and gently, but firmly, disentangled those searching fingers from his person. Edwina raised her mouth up to his, and he eyed that lush offering for a heartbeat. "How about I oblige you in a different way," he said hoarsely, taking a step back, to allow for some distance.

"What are you offfering, Rafe?"

"I'll join you in London." The sooner he did, the sooner he could be free of her, and return to a life without the distracting and delectable Edwina Dalrymple in it. "We can leave tomorrow at noon." The lady would need the morning to recover from her overindulgence.

She let out a squeal and then launched herself at him. "This is splendid," she said, pressing kisses against his cheek. "It's because of the magicians, isn't it?"

"N—"

"And you aren't allowed to change your mind, either. You are going to be ever so . . . glad you did." And then, her thick, dark lashes drifted down, and her frame went heavy in his arms.

He looked down.

A loud, bleating snore spilled from a slumbering Edwina Dalrymple.

Catching her, he guided her back down to the mattress; her curls lay spread about her lace-ruffled pillow. Rafe removed her slippers, and then drew the covers up to her chin.

In sleep, a little smile danced on her lips, as she snuggled deeper into that mattress.

Another endearing snore escaped her lips, and leaving her to her rest, Rafe left. Locking the door behind him, he took up a spot on the floor outside her rooms and stood guard.

Chapter 15

✐

The bad news was Edwina was dying.

The good news was that she'd managed to convince Rafe Audley to join her in London.

The very, very bad news was that she was going to have to begin a carriage ride while feeling like death was coming for her.

And it surely was.

Or, she thought he had agreed to accompany her. Everything about last evening was a blur. There'd been music. And ale. And even more ale. And her singing, too. She distantly and dimly recalled that.

Even thinking of the raucous crowd of the taproom sent pain shooting to her temples.

Edwina winced, and pressed her fingertips against them. If she weren't so miserable, she'd have been properly horrified and ashamed of her actions last evening.

Alas, the figure staring back at her in the cracked, dirty bevel mirror mocked her for her outrageousness.

Good, she deserved this reminder of what happened when a lady behaved as less than a lady. Wasn't she always telling her charges as much? That no good came from wickedness? Well, she'd learned that firsthand.

Except . . . a hazy memory slid in, of Edwina and Rafe in these rooms, with her on the bed, moving her hands under his shirt, and touching his naked skin.

She closed her eyes.

What . . . else had she done? There'd been no hint of blood on the sheets, but she also knew there didn't have to be.

A hard knock rent the quiet and split her skull.

She moaned, and when that slight sound spilling from her own lips nearly finished off the remainder of her head, she bit her lip, stifling the remainder of sound.

No. Sound.

Nothing. There could be no noise. None at—

"Edwina?" *Knock-knock-knock.*

Rafe.

He was here.

Just as he'd promised. And instead of the expected relief and sense of victory that should exist at what this day represented, dread churned low in her belly. A stomach already sick from her excess, now nauseated at the prospect of facing him.

Nay, that wasn't it.

At the prospect of facing what they had done. Or possibly done.

How could she face him?

"Edwina, did you survive last night?" *Knock-knock-knock.* That pounding grew more insistent, and it was a deserved punishment for the lack of restraint she'd shown.

Heading for the door as quick as she was able, given her current state, she unlocked the door and opened it, catching him mid-rap.

Rafe stood there with his fist in the air. He gave her an up and down. "You look like hell," he said, by way of greeting.

She winced again, and cradled her head between her fingers. "That is hardly something you wish to say to a woman. When we begin your lessons, we will address that."

"Is an appropriate amount of ale consumption to be included in our lessons, too?" he drawled.

"Oh, you lummox," she muttered, swatting at his arm, and then immediately regretted those efforts.

And, unlike in the past when mention of lessons came up, this time he grinned. Granted, it was more of a cynical half twist of his lips. But there was a hint of humor, which is more than she could have said for any other expression he'd worn when faced with the prospects of their working together.

Not bothering to wait for an invitation, Rafe stepped past her and into the room.

It wasn't the first he'd been in here . . . alone with her. But it would absolutely be the last. Joining him in his chambers in the duke's household would result in nothing other than her sacking, a loss of employment, an assurance that she'd never work again in any respectable role.

"You did this, in your current state?" he asked, taking in the packed trunks and valises that sat in the middle of the room, and the now completely undecorated room.

"I did. After all, there is nothing worse than wasted—"

"Time," he cut her off. "Yeah, yeah. I got all of that lesson the first time you gave it."

They were dancing around it. And coward that she was, Edwina found herself wanting to continue evading talk of what had happened just hours ago in this room. However, they needed to speak on it. She did.

Alas, a pair of the duke's footmen appeared at the front of the room, thus allowing her another brief reprieve.

Clasping her hands primly before her, she observed the young pair rushing about to gather up her things.

Before she'd met Rafe Audley, she would have been horrified at the mere thought of relinquishing her virtue. In her time here, however, she'd come to appreciate that there needn't necessarily be shame in letting herself, a grown woman, know and taste passion, but neither did she want it to be . . . with her inebriated, and unaware of . . . any of what should be special.

Her two trunks stacked atop the other, the young men balanced them, and carted them off.

When they'd left, and she and Rafe were alone once more, Edwina found her voice and the courage to continue. "What happened last evening should not have happened," she said bluntly. Every word uttered was a challenge to her throbbing head. "And I am embarrassed about my conduct and vow that you needn't worry about me . . . about us . . ." Doing what they'd done, and that which she couldn't remember.

And what deficit of her character existed that her failure to remember a night spent in his arms should inspire even more regret than what she'd done?

"Edwina," he murmured, lightly grazing her chin with his knuckles, and bringing her chin up to meet his. "Nothing happened."

Her heart stopped beating. "It d-didn't?" Edwina faltered over her own faintly spoken question.

He shook his head. "Nothing."

Of their own volition, her eyes slid closed, and she sent a prayer skyward. "Thank you. I don't know why . . . I just had the memory of something happening and—" Something appeared in his eyes, and then was gone. "Oh, God," She touched her fingers to her mouth.

Memories trickled in:

   . . . I want you here, there, and everywhere . . .

The feel of his flat, firm, and naked belly under her fingers. His removing her hands from his person. Her legs went weak, and she slid onto the edge of the bed. "I . . . was inappropriate, wasn't I?" she asked, her voice weak to her own ears. Except . . . she already knew.

"It is fine. The ale was strong. I should not have allowed you to . . . get that way."

Those were the most honorable and noble words he might have said in response to how she'd behaved . . . how she'd conducted herself. And yet—

Edwina looked up. "I am in control of my own actions and decisions, last evening and always. The fault lies with

me, Rafe." Never again. Never, ever would she be so careless. What was it about this man that made her forget
herself?

"We all have moments of imprudence. We should expect
the people around us to not take advantage if we do."

She drew in her breath. "Thank you. I don't know what
overcame me. I am always responsible and respectable and—"

"You let yourself freely live last night. Do not punish
yourself for it."

Tears stung her eyes. Why was he being so nice to her?

The footmen reappeared at the door, and she hurriedly
stood; her stomach turned at the sudden movement. One of
the boys collected the last of her valises and rushed off.

The other bowed deeply. "The carriages are packed. We
are ready, Mr. Audley."

We are ready . . . Mr. Audley.

"Thank you," he said gruffly, discomfort at that formality written on his features.

Everything from that proper bow to the words uttered
were, of course, directed at the duke's son. Which was as it
should be. The moment Rafe agreed to join his father, the
footman had ceased to answer to a mere servant, which was
what Edwina had always been. The walls were already beginning to go up. And it was for the best.

For the carriages might be ready, but she no longer knew
she was ready for this . . . any of it. Being in close quarters
with a man such as Rafe Audley. Letting her guard down,
as she had.

Returning to London, and beginning her assignment,
actually beginning, was what she needed to return to some
semblance of normality.

"Is there anything else you require, Mr. Audley?"

He looked to her. "Miss Dalrymple?"

He let the decision be hers. For some reason it made her
want to cry that he should include her in the final preparations for their travels. It was a small gesture, but a mighty
one, where she was granted some matter of say when she'd
never been before.

"There is not," she said, around the swell of emotion in her throat. "We are ready." And headed for the door, feeling Rafe following close behind.

Distance. That was what they needed. It was just that she had allowed herself to get too close and be too close to him. She'd been spending so much time trying to convince him, and not really working on the task at hand. That was why it was integral that she dive immediately into his edification.

The moment they reached the duke's carriage, Rafe handed her up, his fingers folding briefly over hers, sending warmth burning through her glove, and racing up her arm.

"Miss Dalrymple," Cailin cried happily, the moment Edwina took her place on the red upholstered bench.

"Miss Audley, it is so wonderful to see you." For so many reasons. Not just because her presence ensured Edwina and Rafe were not alone, that added level of defense against the pull he had over her, but also because she genuinely liked the other woman.

"Oh, no, you must call me Cailin."

"I am afraid that won't be permitted in London," she murmured.

The young woman frowned. "I have no intention of letting Polite Society dictate how I treat friends."

Edwina's heart lifted. *Friends?* It was the first time, really in the whole of her life, that she'd ever had anyone call her friend. And yet . . . "That is the way of this world, Cailin," she advised, managing to keep her own regret at bay.

Cailin snorted. "Well, I don't like that, at all."

Then she was going to like the constraints of Polite Society a lot less. However, there were so many more opportunities there for all the Audley siblings. As such, it was Edwina's responsibility to help them see the benefits outweighed the unfamiliar proprieties that would be expected of them.

Rafe entered, and took the place beside his sister. His tall, heavily muscled frame managed to shrink the immense space of the carriage, making it feel impossibly small under his herculean size.

The servant shut the door behind them, and a moment later . . . they were off.

Onward to London, as she'd been attempting for days now.

Onward to her future, working among the peerage.

And onward, to the end of her time with Rafe . . . and his family.

And with that came a wave of sadness . . . the likes of which she'd never felt upon the completion of any assignment she'd taken. Yes, she'd had friendly enough charges, some who'd even been kind to her, but Edwina had always known her time with each family was finite, and as a result, it had been ever-so-easy to end it.

But what if that hadn't really been the case? What if the reason she never felt bereft over a parting was because there'd not really been anyone worth being bereft over?

Stop it.

"What was that?" Rafe asked, and she blushed at having been caught speaking to herself.

"Starting," she amended, working through the misery of last night's overindulgence. "I thought starting your lessons would be a beneficial use of our travel time." As she collected her bag, she withdrew a small pink leather notebook and held it out.

Rafe stared blankly at it. "What the hell is that?"

She frowned. "Language, Mr. Audley. And I think it should be fairly clear . . . it is a notebook." When he still made no attempt to take it, she forced it into his hand, until he curled his fingers around the book. Edwina brandished a small, perfectly sharp charcoal pencil. "And your pencil!"

"My pencil."

Beside him, Cailin's shoulders shook with amusement, and the young woman made a poor show of staring out at the passing Staffordshire landscape.

"And just what am I to do with your pencil and notebook?" Rafe asked.

"They aren't mine. Well, they were. Not ones I've used, that is. They are for you. They are . . . gifts. To help you so that you might fill the pages with the most important details you learn in our time together."

There was a moment of silence and then—

He laughed.

Big, robust, and full, and in any other moment, that mirth would have been contagious . . . if it weren't very clearly directed at her.

"You want me to take notes, princess?"

"Do you find that very shocking?"

"Annoying. Ridiculous. A waste of time. Should I keep going?"

Edwina's frowned deepened. *He's just trying to get a rise out of you.* "Much can be learned from recording our thoughts, Rafe. And the more you come to do it, the more you will find it a rather impossible task to quit." Not allowing him a chance to get a word in, Edwina proceeded to withdrew her own writing materials, and began. "Now, the first detail I might mention is that you needn't thank servants." In fact, among the peerage, that familiarity was quite disdained.

With a scowl, Rafe set his book down hard on his knee. "That's utter shite. Why not?"

He sounded so genuinely outraged that she studied him a moment, confirming he wasn't making light of her. "And there's no swearing, Mr. Audley," she chided, as she set her bag down on the bench beside her. "You might wish to put that into your—" He'd already opened his notebook, and proceeded to write. "Oh, good, you're already recording it."

"No, I'm not," he said, hurriedly dashing off his notes.

She arched her head, but he angled the book away, finished whatever it was he'd been writing, and then snapped it shut, a smug, taunting grin that indicated he knew that she wanted to know what he'd written there instead. Though, if she were truly being honest, she rather thought it was best she not find out just what he'd put there.

Edwina tried a different approach. "Do you thank the miners at your coalfields for completing their work? It is no different."

He scoffed. "It's entirely different. Those people aren't at my beck and call. They're working on their own tasks, for the man who owns those fields. A servant catering to my whims and pleasures is expected to serve me, which I'm also not comfortable with," he added.

Cailin lifted her hand in agreement. "Neither am I."

Edwina glanced back and forth between the siblings. Her mouth moved, as she tried to form a counterargument to Rafe's position, only to struggle with a proper defense that challenged his viewpoint. "It is . . . just the way it is."

"It isn't my way."

"It has to be."

His expression darkened, and he leaned across the carriage, shrinking the space even more. "I agreed to go. I agreed to listen to what you have to say. But I'll be damned if I blindly follow along with things simply because it is," he flicked her notebook, "the way it is."

His eyes pierced hers, burning through her, the intensity of it robbing her of breath and any ability to form a response. And within those cobalt depths, there was that flash of disdain and annoyance that had been there from the beginning, and she hated it.

Cailin cleared her throat, and Edwina jerked her attention from the snarling man before her. "I must also say I believe being rude to people who are helping you is snobbery, and I'll not be part of it."

Yet again, her assignment proved it was going to be even more difficult than she'd anticipated.

"Very well. Starting with a different topic . . ." Snapping her notebook open, she shifted course. "Shall we begin?"

Chapter 16

Agreeing to accompany Edwina had been a mistake. There could be no doubt of it.

Him visiting London and attempting to mingle with Polite Society had all the makings of a disaster.

Rafe, however, had resolved to have some fun along the way.

Two days into the journey, with his sister sleeping soundly on the carriage bench and Edwina delivering a lesson to Rafe on propriety, it had proven even easier than he'd anticipated.

"No. No," Edwina was saying. "It is 'Your Grace' by inferiors, 'Duke' only by social equals, the first time in conversation, to then be followed by 'Sir,' and announced informally as 'the Duke of Bentley.'"

Furrowing his brow in feigned confusion, Rafe looked up from the ridiculously dainty notebook she'd given him. "So, all dukes are the Duke of Bentley, then?"

"No. No. No." Yes, it was entirely too easy. Rafe added several more items to his book, which, despite his original

192 CHRISTI CALDWELL

horror upon receiving it, he found himself to be enjoying rather more than he should.

"That is not at all—" Edwina stopped mid-lecture, and from over the top of *her* notes, narrowed her eyes on Rafe. "You are teasing." A little frown puckered the place between her eyebrows.

"Aye." And she was becoming more adept at identifying those instances. Finally.

"Hmph." She gave a little toss of her head. "Where were we?" she murmured, dropping her focus back to the book on her lap, and running her finger over the page written in her elegant scrawl.

Rafe propped an ankle across his opposite knee, and angled his writing away from her direct line of vision. "Finishing for the day?" he drawled. It wasn't entirely a jest. Since they'd departed the latest inn and boarded the duke's carriage some eight hours earlier, Edwina had been nonstop with her instructions.

She pursed her lips. "Of course we were not, Rafe. You know that is not possible. There is much to be done," she repeated that oft-uttered phrase aloud.

"Ah, there it is. You're predictable in your lessons, princess." He snapped his book shut.

Edwina followed suit, and rested hers upon her lap. "This is *serious*, Rafe."

"Oh, undoubtedly," he said with a mock seriousness that days ago would have likely flown up and over her very head. Now, however, she favored him with a frown. "Edwina, we've covered titles. We've gone over proper forms of address and appropriate topics of discussion between gentlemen and those between men and women."

"You are correct."

Well, that was not the admission he'd been expecting. "I—"

"It was a lot." She flipped her book back open, and sifted through the pages. "Perhaps we should go back and speak again about additional topics that are suitable in terms of discourse."

"We're not really speaking, though, are we?" He infused

a drollness into that query and waited until Edwina, at last, lifted her attention from her materials. A question furrowed her brow. "You're more lecturing and I'm more listening."

Edwina narrowed her eyes. "You are making jests again."

"Aye." He who'd never been the jest-making type couldn't seem to help himself where Edwina Dalrymple was concerned.

Sighing, Edwina snapped her book closed. "We do not have time for games."

She sounded endearingly close to stomping her foot on the carriage floor, and he found himself preferring this unrestrained side of her. In fact, he found himself very much missing the woman who had thrown herself so fully into living during her brief time in Staffordshire. Rafe resumed his writing. "I preferred you drinking ale," he said.

"Shh." She slapped a finger to her lips, and stole a frantic look over at his still soundly sleeping sister.

He chuckled and winked at her.

"Rafe, I have not only your education to see to, but now . . ." Her gaze slid once more over to the slumbering Cailin, curled up against the side of the conveyance. "Your sister's, as well. She must be prepared for her introduction to Polite Society."

And all his previous enjoyment at their exchange abruptly died. "My sister isn't taking part in the London Season," he said curtly, with a directness intended to end any discussion of it.

"She isn't?"

"No." The last place he wanted his sister mingling was in ballrooms where she'd be prey for men who had no honorable intentions were she was concerned.

"What? But she is also His Grace's child. A daughter of marriageable age. As such, she should also have the privilege of taking part—"

"Privilege?" he spat. That was what she would call it? "Privilege?" His voice rose a fraction, and on the bench beside him, Cailin stirred but then quieted, settling into a soft snore once more. Rafe waited, verifying she still slept,

and when he'd done so, he again spoke to Edwina in a quieter, more controlled voice. "What privilege is it you speak
of, Edwina?" Leaning across the bench, he shoved his face
close to hers, but she remained there, facing him down
squarely. "Finding herself at the heart of Polite Society's
gossip? Or is it so that she can find herself a victim of their
unkindness and prey to some bloody scoundrels? Or likely,
a combination of the two?" And despite how well he and
Edwina had gotten on these recent days, this gulf in their
opinions served as a reminder that they were of two different worlds, two people at odds, and he'd never, ever see eye
to eye with her on this.

"But . . . I thought you saw the benefits of bringing her
to London and away from Staffordshire," she said quietly,
sounding so thoroughly befuddled, he almost took pity
upon her.

Almost.

"Changing her scenery and forcing her to try and fit herself into a world she has no part of or place in are different
things, Edwina. Entirely."

Edwina shifted on the bench, matching his body's pos-
turing, leaning more closely toward him. "But she could,"
she said in entreating tones. "She could fit in. And she can
be happy there. And find respectability and a good, honorable gentleman who will see her for who she is."

God, she was tenacious. Fearless. And he wanted to resent her and not admire her for it, but for whatever reason
he was weak in ways where this woman was concerned.

"Your lives can only be improved by accepting what
your father has offered, Rafe."

"She's a bastard," he said bluntly, unapologetically.
"People will shun her and shame her for it. Do you find *that*
an improvement?"

Edwina winced.

Aye, because lofty as she was, talk of bastards would be
anathema to her ladylike proprieties. He latched on to that
truth, using it to hammer home his point.

"By whose standards, Edwina? Hmm?" Rafe didn't allow her a word in edgewise. "Do you truly believe she'll be treated with respect? As some fancy lady, simply because a duke acknowledged her as his child?"

He saw the indecision flash in her eyes. Because she knew, as well as he did, that illegitimate daughters were welcomed even less than bastard sons. "Yes," she said tentatively. "I . . . do believe it is *possible*."

"You're either a liar or as damned naïve and foolish"—*and innocent*—"as I took you for at our first meeting."

"The Duke of Clarence has ten bastard children. Ten of them," Edwina said with her usual enthusiasm when she spoke. "And they are treated well socially because it matters if one's parent rejects or accepts a child."

He clenched his jaw tight. God, she did not quit. "And what happens to those children who've been rejected for thirty-one years?" he asked bluntly. "Do you think the peerage is simply going to welcome strangers, found unworthy by our sire all the years prior to this, into their folds?"

As close as he was to her, Rafe caught the glimmer within her eyes that indicated she'd at last acknowledged his point . . . to herself, anyway.

"Let me ask you this." He shifted the topic. "Why does it matter so much to you whether or not I claim my, as you call it, 'rightful place'?" Rafe moved his eyes over her face, hating that his focus dipped to her mouth. "Why should it matter if Cailin does?"

She darted her tongue out, that delicate pink flesh, running a path over the seam of her lips, tempting him all the more, and tormenting him with this wanting of her. "It . . . just does. Because not everyone has the opportunity you are being presented with. And you deserve that." His lashes dipped, even as hers fluttered, and he angled his head. Edwina shifted hers, lifting her mouth a fraction. She spoke on a whisper. "I want . . ."

The carriage rocked to a halt, and the passion lifted from her gaze. "I want that for you, Rafe," she said, her voice now steadied. "And perhaps you respect Cailin enough to let her decide what she wants."

Cailin popped up on her bench and blinked back the sleep from her eyes. "We are here!" she exclaimed, yanking back the gold-velvet-trimmed curtains. His sister had her face pressed against the window.

They had . . . arrived.

With his sister chattering away as he'd never heard her do before, Rafe stared over the top of her head. There could be no doubting which of the townhouses belonged to the Duke of Bentley. The limestone soared above its neighboring counterparts, four times as wide with an ornate detail around the windows and trim that lent an extravagance to the point of garishness. The abode stood in stark contrast to the shorter, pink-and-brown stucco structures that had the distinction of anchoring the residence.

Why, even the bright afternoon sun cast a light upon the townhouse, the rays glistening off a gleaming golden lion's head knocker and all the other ornamental metal fixtures adorning the windows.

So this was the duke's household.

. . . oh, Rafe. I have heard it is ever so grand . . . someday, you shall see it. Someday we shall both see it . . .

His mother's words of long ago came whispering back, the same longing and wistfulness as clear as if she were still alive, speaking in his ear this day. For she had never seen it. She had never been good enough to marry. Not to the duke. She had been a shameful secret to hide away, left longing for more than she'd had with Bentley. Which hadn't been much. Which hadn't really been anything at all.

Outside, elegantly clad women, with their parasols perched upon their shoulders, went strolling past. Nursemaids and maids following at their heels, walking their equally fancy dogs and holding the hands of their children.

Disgust soured his mouth.

This was the world he was joining.

Temporarily. That was the only reminder that kept him sane as the driver drew the door open, and let the sunlight and stench of London's heavy air filter into the carriage.

The young man reached out, and helped Cailin down first.

As she made her descent, Rafe remained there, stone-faced. What in hell had he agreed to? And why?

And then, as if she had followed his silent thoughts, Edwina moved closer to him. "I saw your kerchief."

He stiffened, knowing what she was speaking about. Of course, a woman as clever as she was would have detected a detail such as that, the embroidered initials, the age of the fabric, the quality of it.

"You could have thrown it away. You could have burned it."

"And I should have," he rasped. He should have tossed it into a flame, and gleefully watched the fire consume it.

"Yes," she said gently. "But you did not. You kept it for a reason, Rafe. And I have to believe that reason also plays some part in why you are here with me now. I believe you truly want to have a relationship with your father."

"I'm here because you forced it," he said sharply.

A little smile danced on her lips. "No one can force you to do anything you do not want, Rafe Audley."

A servant appeared, and Rafe was saved from answering anything else, and presented squarely instead with the reality that waited for him outside these carriage walls.

All his muscles tensed. Sweat slicked his palms. What had he done?

"Just a moment," Edwina said to the footman, perfectly in control and able to issue directives. And calm in ways Rafe was unsteady.

Stop it. You are a damned foreman. You've climbed twenty feet underground and survived fires and cave-ins. This was nothing. Why, it was even less than nothing. Why then, even with all those assurances, did he struggle to believe it? Why didn't it lessen the growing panic threatening to drag him under and suffocate him in those ways the coalfields had failed.

The moment the servant stepped away, a light hand

brushed against his knee, lingering longer than was an accident. His gaze went to Edwina's.

"It is going to be fine," she said softly. "You are going to do well, and I truly believe you are going to be happy."

Rafe grunted. "That remains to be seen," he said gruffly.

She smiled, that beatific, cheerful one that had grown so very much on him. "I told you, I am invariably right. Trust me."

Trust her.

And interestingly, it was just that which accounted for his being here even now. For some unexplainable reason, he'd connected with her, the unlikeliest person for him *to* connect with. Knowing she would be here through this whole hellish experience made him somehow feel less alone.

She called out for the servant.

The young man reappeared at the door and reached for Edwina's hand. She paused, giving Rafe one last look. "It will be fine," she mouthed, one more time, in a continued display of support Rafe found himself so grateful for. Gathering up her books, she tucked them inside her bag and hung the strap over her shoulder. With a murmur of thanks, she swept off, her hips swaying as she went.

A veritable siren.

And perhaps that was the very reason he found himself able to climb out, and follow along so easily behind her.

It was time.

Notebook in hand, Rafe stepped out of the carriage, and prepared to face London . . . and his *father*.

Chapter 17

There was no rest for the weary.

There was even less for those of the working class.

It was why, upon being ushered to her rooms, Edwina was permitted just a short while to change out of her wrinkled garments and wash the dust from her person, before being summoned for a meeting with her employer . . . Rafe's father.

She found herself ushered through the maze of a household grander and finer than all the previous ones she'd entered combined. Her slippered feet were noiseless upon the checkered black-and-white marble floor. And as she walked alongside the young man escorting her to her meeting, Edwina took it all in. She'd never been one to be impressed by things. Her father had always sent the finest fripperies. There had been no shortage of dresses or bonnets or bows. There had been pretty necklaces and even prettier pins. And yet not any of that had ever really mattered because she had wanted something so much more desperately—respectability. Recognition.

Love.

Even so, even she was hard-pressed not to be absolutely awestruck of her surroundings.

Marble busts upon marble pedestals better suited for the finest museums in London lined the hallway. Heavy, ornate gold frames adorned the walls. The paintings within, vibrant, masterful masterpieces of floral arrangements, so vivid and so lush in the artists' rendering that it was as though they burst off the canvas.

It was an extravagant display of wealth, to which Rafe Audley now belonged.

Whether he liked it . . . or not.

"This way, miss," the servant murmured, bringing them to a stop outside a pair of gilt-framed double doors, painted ivory.

As she stepped inside the room for her meeting with the duke and duchess, the friendship she'd known with Rafe and Cailin slipped further away, as she became that which she'd always been to this family—a servant. That realization caused the oddest tightness in her chest. A divide now lay between her and Rafe. She'd already accepted her inferior status before this. Her knowledge of her place in the world had been as much a part of her as the oft-untamable auburn tresses atop her head. It was also the first time that she had ever wanted to cry over that realization.

"Miss Dalrymple," the duchess said with a smile.

Edwina sank into a deep, deferential curtsy. "Your Grace," she murmured to the regal pair at the center of the room.

The elegant woman swept forward with her hands outstretched, and then in the most unduchesslike gesture Edwina would have ever expected from one belonging to her vaunted status, the duchess gathered Edwina's palms in hers. "I know this has required extensive travel and efforts on your behalf, and we are ever so grateful to you for . . ." The woman's throat moved. "Managing to do what no one else was capable of."

Husband and wife shared a look, and again a wealth of

emotion passed between them, different from the reserve the nobility strove for.

"Yes," the duke said. He motioned to his desk and the chairs before them. The moment the duke and duchess and Edwina were seated, he spoke. "I cannot ever repay you for bringing my son and daughter to me, Miss Dalrymple. I confess, I despaired of ever meeting them." His features contorted in a paroxysm of pain she would have traded both arms to have seen on her own father's face.

Edwina inclined her head. "It has been my joy and honor." And it had. Initially this assignment had been solely about her future and the outcome of this assignment. Along the way, it had changed. In the time she'd spent with Rafe, she'd laughed more and been challenged more, in ways that she would one day miss. "Your son, Mr. Audley . . ." The duke fixed a gaze on her. "He is clever, and I believe it will take little for him to fit in effortlessly."

"Before he arrives, I would speak to you." He withdrew a page, and stretched an arm across the table.

With a word of thanks, Edwina accepted the sheet.

> *Dinner party*
> *Ball*
> *White's*

"That will be the extent to which your services are required."

The extent to which her services were required. How . . . formal. And why should it be any other way? "White's?" He'd have Rafe join that gentlemen's club. He would hate it. Everything about it. And yet, it was his place.

"Of course, I am not expecting you to advise him on White's. It is merely something I'd have him prepared to attend." The duke smiled, effortlessly, easily. Unlike Rafe, for whom every turn of his lips showed strain.

She cleared her throat, and lowered the page to her lap. "R—" *Rafe*. Except she no longer had leave to refer to him that way. Not by name. Not before this all-powerful gentleman . . . who was also her employer. Not before anyone, really. "Mr. Audley has proven most adept. We spent a good portion of the week in travels, reviewing and preparing some."

The duchess beamed. "Given the limited time we have to work, that was a splendid use of time."

Yes, splendid. There should be a rush of pride and relief at being that much closer to the end of this most distinguished of assignments, and references from the most elevated of peers. Except . . . it also meant, even sooner, she'd no longer be needed here. Soon, she would be free to begin expanding her business into the peerage. Why did that thought not bring with it the happiness it should?

The Duke removed his spectacles, folding the wire rims. "Yes, I must also say it is a rather pleasant surprise knowing he is that much closer to being able to enter Polite Society," he murmured.

Husband and wife shared a look, the depth of love that passed between them so intense and so very intimate, Edwina briefly glanced down at her lap so as to not intrude upon them.

"We understood you are quite accomplished and highly recommended by your previous employers," the duchess said quietly, and Edwina redirected her attention to the elegantly coiffed, stunning noblewoman before her. "However, we feared Mr. Audley's stubborn determination to reject the offer my husband extended him would prove too great for you or anyone to overcome." A sheen of tears filled the other woman's eyes, and she dabbed at them. "You are a wonder."

"The credit belongs to Mr. Audley," she demurred. "I am only as effective as my students are cooperative."

Student. Her heart clenched, for something also felt wrong in thinking of Rafe in those terms. For in their short time together, she'd become closer to him than . . . anyone in the whole of her life. He'd teased her and tended her injuries, and challenged her . . . and shown her passion, for the first time in her life.

And yet, none of that changed what he was—her student.

Another one of those private looks passed between the clearly devoted couple.

The duchess cleared her throat. "As we are on the topic of your next assignment," she segued. "We would ask that when you conclude with Rafe's edification, you then begin schooling Miss Audley, and preparing her for her entrance. I am thinking we might do a small entrance for her this year, and launch her completely next Season."

"Next Season makes sense, of course," the duke said with a nod. "Even as I would find it preferable that she be presented immediately, I would rather do so slowly, and permit her time to enjoy London and then . . ." Face the lion's den.

Next Season.

What the duchess assumed, that Edwina would take on the role, was a grand show of confidence in Edwina. It would also mean an additional client of the peerage for Edwina.

A lady, no less. That elusive and illustrious clientele that had until this moment escaped her.

It would also mean that Edwina remained with Rafe and his family beyond this short period. That she would stay with him . . . Her heart lifted.

Only to promptly plummet.

To stay through next year would mean she'd also be forced to face Rafe belonging here, and finding love here . . .

The duke and duchess continued to stare at her expectantly, with matching smiles, and it was abundantly clear that they'd already taken it as a fact that she would simply accept this next assignment.

Edwina clasped her shaking hands together. Before she could talk herself out of it, she spoke: "I am afraid I cannot do that."

Silence met her pronouncement.

The duke sat forward. "What was that?"

And it spoke volumes about Rafe's father that he did not

immediately turn her out, or call her out for rejecting that offer. "I said, I am afraid I cannot be the one to oversee Miss Audley's instruction beyond this Season." Never had she believed that she would or could reject a nobleman's request. She'd aspired to their ranks . . . to work among them. Something, however, in the time she had spent with Rafe had opened her eyes to how that drive had taken precedence over her morals . . . how she'd not previously thought of her clients as people with dreams and hopes and visions of their own, but rather of her own desires.

"I am afraid I do not understand, Miss Dalrymple," the duchess said, in those still unexpectedly gentle tones. "Is there a reason why? Is it the payment—"

"No!" she interrupted. "You have been most generous." Edwina took a breath and weighed her response, wishing to simultaneously speak freely and to protect Rafe and what he'd confided. "I . . ."

They continued to look at her.

The duchess broke the awkward impasse. "Perhaps you might reconsider."

"Though I am grateful for your offer, I must, however, decline," she said again, with greater insistence.

The duke's eyebrows came together. "I will pay you double."

That was the cost. She strangled, nearly choking on even the thought of that amount. What she could do with those funds. The security she might know. It would represent a bridge between clients, so that she might be more selective . . . unlike in the past, where no assignment had been safe to pass up. Edwina closed her eyes, fighting with herself. Debating. When it shouldn't be a debate. Not truly.

She was a woman bent on survival, and doing it respectably and respectfully. Never reliant upon a man for her comforts and security.

Oh, hell on Tuesday.

Edwina forced her eyes open. "I cannot," she said, before she had a chance to convince herself of the opposite. "I am grateful to you for wishing to employ my services for your daughter, but I cannot do so," and would not. "Not at this time."

The duke frowned, and she braced for dismissal.

The duchess leaned over and patted Edwina's hand. "There is no reason for any of us to make a decision now. Isn't that right?" She turned that question on her husband. He nodded once, and his wife resumed. "Now, let us focus instead on Rafe's lessons."

That was it? Edwina had asserted herself and not lost herself or her work in the process. Her spine grew under the dizzying power that came from that revelation. "Yes," she began. "As I was saying, we had already started some lessons on our journey here." Fishing a page out of her folio, she held it out. "I have established a schedule with . . ." *Rafe*. Except here he could not be that. Not to her. ". . . Mr. Audley." How foreign it felt forcing her tongue to wrap about those syllables when his Christian name had rolled so effortlessly forth.

"That will not be necessary. I have set a schedule based on the two events he'll require assistance preparing for." He handed over another, more officious page, and Edwina stared at it.

"Oh . . . Of course." One didn't tell a duke. She knew that, and yet, she'd just thought . . . she'd expected . . . what? *That your time with Rafe was so special and so intimate and so important that it would supersede the Duke of Bentley's intentions?*

Her nape prickling, that heightened sense a product of years of village scorn and scrutiny, she glanced up, and found the duchess looking at her.

"Is there a problem, Miss Dalrymple?" the gracious older woman asked still with that greater warmth and kindness than Edwina would have expected a duchess to demonstrate for a mere servant.

"None, Your Grace." Edwina dropped her gaze to the two sheets now in her care: the ones that recalled her to her place here and also rid her of that bit of control she'd been looking forward to, of shaping her and Rafe's time together. "None at all."

The Duchess of Bentley sailed to her feet and joined her husband around the desk. "I know you are ever so eager to begin readying Rafe for his entry into society, but Miss Dalrymple has traveled a good deal, and we should allow her the evening to rest and prepare for the morrow."

The just faintly graying duke captured his wife's hands and brought her fingers to his mouth. "Ever right, as you always are, love," he murmured, brushing a kiss upon his wife's hand. In a gesture so achingly intimate and sweet Edwina made herself look away.

Because contained within that tender moment was a closeness her mother had craved, with the man she'd loved, and a bond Edwina had never, ever even allowed herself to think of for herself.

But seeing this man, an older, slightly less muscled version of his son, Edwina saw within the exchange between husband and wife one of Rafe in the future. With a woman whom he loved and cherished and respected in that same way. Her chest hurt. All of her . . . ached. With envy. And a bitter, blinding jealousy for the woman who would one day have that which Edwina hadn't even realized she'd longed for . . . the devoted love of a man like Rafe Audley.

Her breath caught on a hiss, and instantly the duke and duchess glanced her way. She surged to her feet. "Thank you," she blurted out. "For everything." Edwina sank into a curtsy.

She'd just reached the middle of the room when the duke called out, "Miss Dalrymple." Edwina brought herself back around, facing Rafe's father. "I will be candid in saying, I had my doubts and reservations prior to hiring you, not because I did not believe you were capable but because I did not believe it was possible to sway my stubborn son." He smiled. "My wife insisted a female hand was what was needed, and my wife"—His Grace claimed the duchess's hand for another kiss—"was correct about you. You did it."

You did it . . .

Edwina tensed.

She had. It had seemed unlikely at times, and impossible

every other. Rafe had been adamant, fighting her along the way, and yet she had done it. She had succeeded where all the others who came before her had failed.

As such, she should feel only a keen sense of pride at that accomplishment.

Only, hearing His Grace speak as if she'd bagged a buck on a hunt made this . . . feel wrong. The time she'd spent with Rafe. The moments they'd shared.

"That is all," the duke said, nodding his head.

And she was dismissed.

Edwina made the remainder of the long walk across the Aubusson carpet, eager to leave.

Because . . . this confusion in her mind and in her heart, about her role and her relationship with Rafe . . . it did not make sense.

He was just a job. Assisting him in this endeavor was a means to rise up, and for her father to at last respect her and recognize her and for her to fit into this world that she'd been barred from since birth.

The servant stationed at the doorway, who'd remained invisible until just then, clasped the handle and opened the door, letting her out.

The moment she stepped into the hall, Edwina froze. Her gaze landed on him. *Rafe.* He made his way down the long corridor, headed for the very room she'd just vacated. Not, however, as someone in the duke's employ, but as a beloved son. Putting Rafe, as he'd always been—well beyond her reach.

And surely it was merely exhaustion accounting for the urge to curl up within a ball and just hold herself.

Get control of yourself.

Edwina forced herself to move, starting toward her rooms.

And Rafe.

At last, they reached one another. His shoulder-length dark hair, now wet, had been pulled back into a queue at the base of his neck, giving him . . . a more tamed look, and she . . . missed how he'd always worn it.

He moved his eyes over her face, his gaze inscrutable. "Edwina," he greeted her.

Bowing her head, she executed a curtsy. "Mr. Audley."

As little as Rafe had wanted to come to London, the decision to do so had not been as . . . difficult as he'd anticipated.

On the contrary, in fact.

When it had been framed with allowing his brother some space in which to grow and be independent of Rafe at the coalfields, and to get Cailin out and away from tragic memories, the decision had been surprisingly easy.

All of that had been true before this moment.

This one, right here: the long overdue, face-to-face meeting with the man his mother had so loved, and the one who'd fathered him and Cailin and Hunter and Wesley, and had remained ignorant of their existence.

That realization of what was to come had truly hit him the moment he'd entered this household, and been led down a different hall than Edwina.

Panic. Sheer, mind-numbing, all-consuming panic had swept over him.

And the only thing that had steadied him when thinking about this upcoming meeting . . . was her.

The person he'd sought so hard to send away, had become . . . something more. *Someone* more. Edwina now represented a lifeline in this hell as he braced for the first meeting with his father, and . . . the London Season.

And yet, she was curtsying. Nay, not just curtsying. This had been the manner of a reverent, deep, formal movement reserved for kings and queens.

Not . . . him. And certainly not from *this* woman. The woman who'd hiked her skirts up and danced merrily about the taproom, singing lustily?

And now she was *curtsying* to him?

"Don't do that," he said quietly. "You're not a damned servant."

She stared back at him, confusion in her hazel gaze. "I don't—"

"You do know," he interrupted, cutting her off. "You *do* know."

Edwina dampened her mouth, and for one infuriating moment he believed she intended to continue feigning puzzlement. She sighed.

Edwina stole a glance around at the closed panel and the footman staring straight ahead, his hands behind him, prepared for his next directive. When she looked back at Rafe, she spoke in a whisper. "You are my charge. As such, curtsies are . . . required, Mr. Audley."

Her charge?

Like a child with a tutor.

Like a lady with a governess.

He took two angry steps toward her, eliminating all the physical distance she'd erected, even as the intangible divide, which she and this place had put up between them, remained. "And enough with that," he said tightly. "I'll not be Mr. Audley to you, here."

"You have to be," she said simply, in nearly inaudible tones he strained to hear, and only the clear way she moved her lips, enunciating each one, confirmed that which she said.

"The hell I do," he snarled. Furious at her for insisting on it. Furious with society for making it so. And furious at the circumstances that had changed between them.

He tried again. "You agreed to call me Rafe."

She cast a sideways, pointed look at the servant.

"I don't give a damn about him," he snarled.

"You need to, Rafe," she said gently, in a concession that did little to calm the torrent of emotion simmering inside.

She was, aside from Cailin, the only friend he had in this place. Now, she'd attempt to take that away? She'd reduce the bond they'd shared to the original one of servant and charge that she'd first come to him with?

But isn't that really all she is, and all you are to one another? A voice jeered at him with that reminder. She had been. Something, however, had shifted. Changed. Just without his knowing, and to realize it, in this moment when she was determined to maintain nothing more than a professional relationship with him, left him shaken. Confused.

The door opened, and they looked over.

"His Grace is ready to see you."

All his muscles went taut.

His Grace is ready to see you . . . a damned summons for a *son*. Nothing had changed. Nor had he expected it, too. It was, however, a reminder of his place and it wasn't with this family.

"It is not because of you, Rafe." She lightly brushed her fingers against his in what could have been perceived by anyone around them as an accidental caress. "This is how all meetings play out between fathers and sons of the peerage."

Was that assurance coming from the unlikely friend he found in her? Or from the woman who was employed by his father? Either way, restless as he was, Rafe appreciated what she was doing.

The footman cleared his throat, and Rafe and Edwina glanced back toward the door.

"You will do wonderfully," she said softly.

All of his muscles coiled tight. "I don't give a damn about that." His mother would have. It would have been all that mattered to her: that Rafe proved himself to be capable of the etiquette and decorum a duke would expect.

"Of course you don't," she murmured, allowing him that lie. And with that, she left.

Rafe stared after her a moment, watching as she reached the end of the hall; she paused, looking back, and smiled.

Had he ever truly resented or disliked that smile? How, when it filled a person with such lightness, driving back all tension and unease? Even now it accounted for his ability to complete the walk to that door, and enter the room.

The duke and duchess stood in the middle of the office, their hands entwined.

The moment they spied him, they swiftly disentangled

their fingers. But it was too late. He'd already spied that tender touch.

The affection and warmth . . . and love between the pair. Rafe hardened his jaw. His mother would have sold her soul for a fraction of the affection known by the other woman.

The duchess must have seen something in his eyes, for she looked up at the duke and murmured something.

His Grace nodded.

She offered her husband a smile, not unlike the encouraging one Edwina had just bestowed upon Rafe in the hall, and he hated that parallel connection. Because whatever these two had was nothing like what he and Edwina shared.

And more, it was easier to not see the duke and duchess as real people, a couple capable of love and warmth. Because none of that fit with what he expected of them. Nay, what he knew of them.

Her Grace made a regal march across the office and stopped before Rafe, startling him. "I am so very happy you are here, Rafe," she said softly, warmly, and honestly.

Surely she couldn't want him here? He, the man whom her husband had sired on another woman. And yet, in her eyes there was none of the resentment that should be there.

Unnerved, he managed only to bow his head, grateful when she left.

And then he was alone with the duke.

Father and son eyed one another.

So this was him. The duke his mother had so loved. Similar in height to Rafe, His Grace was also of a like wiry strength. He possessed a thick head of black hair, barely dusted with gray, and then only along his temples. This man was certainly not what Rafe would have expected of a duke. Rafe had expected a paunch from age. Heavy jowls. A monocle as he studied Rafe.

"So you are him," the duke murmured. "My son."

My son.

Rafe's shoulders went taut. From the earliest years of Rafe's life, he had longed to have this man, a stranger, utter those words to him. But of course, he would have had to know Rafe. But he hadn't. In any way. And so for the next twenty-two years of his life, he'd resolved to never think of himself in the way this man now referred to him.

"*Another* one of your sons," Rafe said coolly.

Pain spasmed features that may as well have been a replica of his own thirty-one years into the future.

"One of my sons," the duke said sadly. "Yes. Yes. I met . . . Wesley."

He'd met Wesley. The resentment and bitterness at his brother having gone to this man in search of a favor and having it met soured his mouth.

"Please," the duke said, at last removing an arm from behind his back, and motioning to the winged leather chairs at the foot of his desk.

Rafe considered them for a moment. The bitter part of him wanted to tell Bentley to hell with that offer. However, he had agreed to come here, and as such, rejecting all that outreach would be emotionally driven, and not logical. And Rafe was nothing if not logical. Wordlessly making his way over, he claimed a seat.

The duke took the other.

Rafe quickly masked his surprise. When he'd also imagined this exchange playing out, there'd been an enormous desk, not unlike the one belonging to Bentley. The duke, however, had been seated behind it, and certainly had not given up that throne of authority in favor of the chair closest to Rafe.

The stretch of silence continued marching on between them.

Rafe had never been one to fill the quiet. He'd always been a man guarded and short with his words. And in this reunion, he found himself even more so. Nonetheless, Rafe cut to the heart of it. "I'm here for one reason and one reason only," he said, clearing up any potential confusion or hope on the older gentleman's part.

The duke sat up straighter.

"My sister wished to see London," Rafe spoke in deliberately cold tones, "and as such, she is here, free to do so."

"That is what I'd hoped," the duke said quickly. "That she could take part in—"

"In what? Polite Society?" Rafe rested his hands on his knees and leaned closer to his father. "Let us be clear," he said, cutting the other man off from speaking. "Whatever vision you have for her time here isn't what she has in mind, and it isn't what I intend to let happen. I'll attend your balls and dine at your dinner parties. But she'll not take part in your fancy affairs, where she'll be mocked and jeered for the bastard she is. Is that clear?" he clipped out that question.

His Grace winced, and then gave a slow, uneven nod. "Yes . . . I . . . understand. I had hoped—"

"Don't," Rafe snapped. "Because this is not about you or your hopes." Nor was it about Rafe. The sole reason he'd capitulated to the duke's demands had been because of the chance to see Cailin happy. And he'd no intention of sharing Cailin's wishes. They weren't for this man to know.

"You are right," the duke murmured. And then, Bentley just watched Rafe, the two of them engaging in a silent scrutiny of one another. After a long while, the duke sighed. "I have had so much time to prepare what to say to you. I've written pages with possible discussions and exact words I would speak to you. Only to find myself . . . lost as to what to say." Again, a heavy sadness wreathed the duke's features. "I am sorry. That seems like the most important place to begin."

"The funny thing about apologies is that they're really just empty words that change nothing and undo even less," Rafe said, frostily.

The duke flinched. "You are not incorrect. Deeds are evidence where words require proving. Which is why I've asked you to come. Only through my actions can I begin to attempt to make amends."

There was no making amends. There couldn't be forgiveness. Not truly. They were both over thirty years too late at having any kind of relationship. And pitting sibling against sibling as he'd done to get Rafe here? That was hardly any way to go about fostering any kind of connection. "Asked me to come?" he spat. "As if I'd really had a choice."

The duke had the good grace to at least blush with some modicum of shame. He coughed lightly into his fist. "It did require much effort, but you must understand, I do not want my children to struggle."

And yet, that was precisely what Rafe and his siblings had done. "I already have. We already have," he said quietly, matter-of-fact in that deliverance.

Bentley blanched. "Struggle anymore, then," he whispered.

And the truth of it was? He'd not trade a single one of those years. For he'd been built into the person he was by the work he'd done. "I am a coalfield foreman." Or he had been until the duke had manipulated his life. "And I enjoy what I do. Everything I've earned, I've earned with my hands." He lifted the callused, coal-stained palms and fingers for his father's view. "Nothing has been given to me just because of who my father was."

His Grace stared intently at Rafe's scarred hands. Aye, because what must he think, knowing these were the hands of the son he now sought to claim. Embarrassed and ashamed is what he would be.

"I am proud of you for having done what you've done in life," the duke said, his voice hoarse, that pronouncement knocking Rafe briefly off-balance for the unexpectedness of it. "I would have wished that you didn't have to know the difficulties you have. And . . . had I known about you, I promise you wouldn't have."

Had he . . . ? Rafe puzzled his brow; his mind registered those words, but he didn't process them. And then . . . "Are you claiming my existence was a secret to you?"

His father nodded, lifting his palms as if in supplication. "You've no reason to trust me, and yet, I give my word on this. Wesley was the one who . . . informed me of his existence, and yours. He came to London."

Rafe's mind raced with the words the duke now spoke,

and the last exchange he'd had with Wesley. Before his brother had left to battle Boney, before he had gone, he'd insisted Rafe listen to him about the duke. Rafe had been filled with too much rage and resentment that his brother had not only extended an olive branch to their sire, but that he'd accepted a commission Rafe wouldn't have ever been able to give him.

The duke rested a hand on Rafe's shoulder, jarring him back to the present. "I would have never willingly abandoned you or any of my children."

"I don't believe you," he said automatically, and yet that statement didn't ring with the same confidence he'd carried his whole life. For, how many times had his mother herself stated how important it was for her to keep her children a secret from the duke? Rafe had always assumed the duke had been a cold, ruthless nobleman and that had been the reason behind his mother's adamancy. Coming to know him, however, challenged everything Rafe knew. Or everything he thought he did. His temples suddenly throbbed, and he rubbed them. "But neither did you take care to ensure you didn't leave a litter of bastards upon my mother," he pointed out.

The duke winced. "That is . . . a very fair charge. In my indiscretion, I was careless."

Funny—were it not for that carelessness, Rafe and his siblings wouldn't be here now. It was . . . something hard to reconcile in his mind with the resentment he felt for the duke.

"I understand that you do not wish to be here, but it is also my hope that you will come to find that not only do you not mind this life so very much, but that you also see the good you are capable of doing with the wealth I will afford you—if you let me?"

That was what he wanted, then . . . what he thought to do? Pay Rafe and his siblings off. Just as he'd done with Wesley. And it brought stirring back to life resentment at the man who'd manipulated him. Rafe came to his feet. "I am here, but do not think for one moment that I intend to stay." He scraped a gaze over the gentleman as he hurriedly stood. "And do not ever dare pit me against my siblings, again, as you did with Wesley and Hunter, or I will destroy you." They were bold words directed at a man a step below a prince, and yet, where his siblings and their relationship were concerned, by God, he'd end up on the gallows and in hell to defend them.

Color flooded the duke's cheeks. "Wesley came to me, and I only sought to provide him with what he wished for."

A commission so he could go get his fool head killed? "That wasn't your place." And yet, Wesley had decided it was. "And then you had the bloody gall to interfere with Hunter, too?" Soon, it would be Cailin.

Confusion sparked to life in the duke's eyes. "Hunter? What . . . I don't . . . ?"

He scoffed. "Come, do not pretend anything different. You went to my employer and had him sack me and my assignment go to Hunter instead so you might get me here."

The duke sputtered, "I did not. Yes, I will admit to having coordinated Wesley's commission, but I have never . . ." And then understanding brought the duke's brows up. "You're re-ferring to Sparrow and the payment for your absence."

"My temporary absence," he bit out.

The duke shook his head. "That is . . . was not my doing or thinking. Though I stand in full support if it was needed to bring you here."

What . . . ? If not Bentley—

He stilled.

No. She wouldn't have. She—

. . . there is something else you should know about me . . . I'm a determined woman and I'll neither fail, nor take "no" for an answer where you are concerned . . .

Bloody hell.

He cursed as he recalled some of the first words she'd uttered to him.

"That idea was all Miss Dalrymple's," the duke said, confirming that ugly suspicion. "She wrote to me and ex-plained her intentions. I merely offered all my funds at her disposal, which she employed to coordinate a brief leave that your brother could fill. Why, she even had the idea to promote Hunter. Clever lady."

My God, the man was dicked in his nob. He actually thought Rafe would be . . . impressed by any of that?

Betrayal and hurt and fury all competed for supremacy within Rafe, the latter emotion, that safer one, proving triumphant. Not at his *father*. He would have expected as much from him. But Edwina? "Clever lady, indeed," he said between tight teeth.

"I have already met with Miss Dalrymple, and have allowed her the day to rest before you and she resume your lessons. I would encourage you to enjoy some rest as well, Rafe."

Enjoy his rest, indeed.

The duke appeared to wish to say more, but neither wanting nor needing a single word more from this man, in this moment, Rafe turned on his heel . . . and left.

And here he'd been all maudlin at the prospect of her resuming her role of emissary to the duke and he her charge.

Fury continued to wind a course through his veins, heating him up with a healthy and targeted anger.

And with his meeting concluded, Rafe set out . . . in search of that clever lady.

Chapter 18

Edwina had thought herself completely done with any aspect of the country life, only to have found upon her return to London . . . that she rather missed the crisp blue of the sky, and the lush blanket of grass covering the hillsides, or the random rivers or waters to be found in the most unexpected of places: a bend in the road. Under a small bridge.

It had been a revelation from her time in Staffordshire with Rafe . . . the discovery that she hadn't necessarily hated the country as much as she'd believed. That the resolve to leave and never return had less to do with all village people and village life, and more to do with the specific ones whom she'd had the unfortunate experience of knowing. The life she and her mother had lived in Leeds had soured her, and Edwina had come to associate that life outside London with misery and meanness.

Until Rafe had helped her appreciate that there were and could be kind people in the country.

And strangely, seated in the serene gardens of the duke's

Mayfair townhouse, she could almost believe she was back in the Staffordshire countryside.

Her knees drawn to her chest, and her arms folded around them, she stared at the placid lake that had been built into these grounds, transformed as if by magic from a London landscape into a bucolic sanctuary. It was a feat only a king of a man might manage, and as a duke whose connection to that title went back to William the Conqueror, he was very nearly of that most elevated of ranks.

And Rafe would now belong to that world, too. Nay, not would. He *did* belong to that world. It was what she wanted for him, too. At first, he'd only been a client . . . a means to an end. A way to achieve a success she'd fought desperately to know, teaching young ladies of the *ton*.

His meeting with the duke was likely concluded, and as she'd sat there, she'd sat with her worry, too. Wanting him to not only succeed in fully immersing himself in this world, but to be happy as well.

Along the way, however, so much had shifted and changed. He'd ceased being just another student. And instead, he'd gone from adversary to . . . friend.

Really, the first she'd ever known.

He had teased her, and had made her look at the smallish way in which she'd viewed country living, and demanded that she shift her thinking and immerse herself in a *different* world. And when she'd agreed to those terms, she'd expected him to be cold and mocking about it. She'd not anticipated that he'd sip ale beside her, confiding in her.

Letting her into his world.

And I want to be there . . .

Her body went numb, the air she breathed sticking in her chest, trapped, painfully caught there.

She didn't mean that. Not in the way it sounded.

She liked him. She enjoyed being with him. But it was still strictly and solely about their partnership, as fostered by the duke.

That was all it was.

Yes, they might be friendly toward one another. Even friends.

So why, with these assurances she gave herself, did she still fight to breathe evenly?

And then, as if she'd conjured him, he was there, a reflection in the water before her.

Edwina puzzled her brow. What . . . ?

"The princess at her moat," he drawled.

"Rafe," she gasped, jumping up, her heart racing as it always did when he was near. "How was your meeting?"

"Informative," he said in terse, sharp tones.

And then . . . she looked at him.

Really looked at him.

Oh, dear.

This was Rafe Audley as she'd first seen him.

Her stomach fell. "Your meeting did not go well."

"It went as I'd expected."

"You are upset," she said, when he offered nothing more. "With the duke." Oh, blast, and here she'd so desperately hoped that father and son would—

"Not the duke."

She paused. Not the duke? Oh, well, that was promising. Except . . . "The duchess, then." Now, that was even more unexpected.

"Try again, Edwina." He glared blackly at her, a piercing glint in those dark blue eyes that stabbed right through her.

Not the duke. Not the duchess.

Oh, dear.

Edwina touched a hesitant hand to her breast. "*Me*?" she ventured.

He clapped his hands in a slow, rhythmic beat, four times, giving sarcasm sound. "You."

She frowned. "Well, I cannot see what I have done—"

"You are the reason I'm without work."

"Oh," she said weakly. "That."

It had . . . been likely and inevitable that the matter of his role at the coalfields would have been discussed in some way with the duke. She had just thought there might be more time, and that when he did, he'd . . . *What? Be so thrilled at being here, he'd overlook your interference?*

Edwina forced a smile. "I prefer to think of it as I am the reason you are here in London."

He remained a stoic block of unmoving granite, his lips firm and hard.

Her heart fell.

He was taking this a good deal . . . worse than she'd hoped.

But should it really come as a surprise? Edwina sighed. She attempted a different approach. "I thought you had already agreed it was beneficial for Hunter to have the opportunity he now has. You saw—"

Rafe slammed a fist into his hand. "Goddamn it, Edwina. There is a difference between seeing the benefits and being denied a choice. And yet that is what you did to me." Had he bellowed his rage, it would have been preferable and easier and less painful than this quiet response, laced with a tangible disdain. He gave his head a disgusted shake, driving home those sentiments. "And what is worse, you lied."

Edwina immediately pounced. "Mm. Mm. No. I did not lie."

He stuck his face close to hers. "A lie by omission is still a lie."

She lifted her chin, holding his stare. "You were the one who assumed it was the duke because you didn't believe that I, a woman, was capable of achieving your cooperation." Edwina threw her arms up. "You were the one who declared war," she cried. "You said that. You set the terms, and now of a sudden, you should be so shocked and offended that I achieved what I never hid as my ends?" Why did that argument, though accurate and factual, sound hollow to her own ears?

His chest moved hard from that emotion within him; his eyes blazed fire.

Because of me . . .

Rafe hated her, and that realization left her bereft.

She tried again to make him see reason. "I told you all

along that I . . ." *needed* ". . . intended to secure your coop-eration. I never lied to you about . . . that."

Rafe peeled his lip back in a sneer. "Yes, because all you care about is your business and working for some fine, fancy lord."

That proof of how little he thought of her struck like an arrow to the breast. "That is not what it is about." Not really. Not in the way he thought.

Except he didn't hear her.

He took her lightly by the shoulders. "You don't just get to go manipulating people's lives because you somehow think you know things you don't."

"I was trying to help and—"

A sound of disgust spilled from his lips, drowning out the rest of her words, and he released her quickly. "You decided it was for the best. You did. Well, you got what you wanted, and I got what you think I *should* want."

Was this really what she'd wanted, however?

And when he put it that way . . . she understood his outrage . . . that seething, burning emotion he had directed at her.

Unable to meet the anger in his eyes, Edwina glanced down at the lush grass under their feet, studying it a mo-ment. "I did not think of it this way," she conceded. She forced her gaze up from the coward's path it had traveled, and of their volition, her fingers found a place on his sleeve. "I only sought to help." *Me. I was attempting to help my-self,* and just as he'd said, she'd done so without a thought of what he had been saying to her from the start.

But if you tell him . . . if you let him know you under-stand on a level he doesn't think you do—

That idea proved short-lived.

Rafe shrugged off her touch, and that rejection sent coldness sweeping over her. "No," he said tiredly. "You wouldn't think of that, would you? Because it would have required you to think of someone's wishes and desires above your own."

She bit the inside of her cheek hard, and it hurt less than

the accusations he now leveled at her. Coward that she was, Edwina moved, her legs carrying her away from him and this moment.

But he wasn't done with her.

He slid into her path, barring Edwina's retreat. "You created conflict between my brother and me," he whispered, hurt as she had never heard him. "My brother whom I've never before fought with—"

"But you said it was for the best," she cried. "You said—"

"You don't understand anything."

She turned her palms up beseechingly. "Then *help* me to."

*T*hen *help me to.*

    In that moment, in Edwina's shocked indignation and confusion, he alternated between the urge to shake her until she saw reason, and a hungering to kiss her.

And he hated himself for wanting her still. For caring as much as he did about this betrayal.

For betrayal was what it felt like.

Except, as she'd bluntly, if accurately pointed out—her determination had never been a surprise.

She had expressly stated her intentions from the start.

And it felt petty and bitter to resent her for things he'd already known.

Because you allowed yourself to forget who she was and whom she worked for, while all the while she'd never forgotten that . . . and her efforts were for him.

Not again. He'd not make that same error of mistaking her for anything or anyone more than she was.

"Do you enjoy what you do?" he asked, and her brow dipped.

"I . . ." She tipped her head, and that gesture sent the plait flopping over her shoulder.

"Grooming young women to be presented to Polite Society," he clarified when she still failed to respond.

And as her reply remained stalled . . . it occurred to him: she hadn't considered the question. There was no immediate assertion about the pleasure she found in her role, and the type of work she did. "You don't know," he said, with that dawning understanding.

Edwina bristled. "Of course I do," she said.

"You've never considered it, then. Either way . . . it is fairly simple: either you do"—he lifted one palm up—"or you don't." Rafe turned the other so his arms formed a scale of sorts.

A sound of frustration escaped her. "But that is it, with you. Everything exists in absolutes. I am either a terrible person or a friend. My work is either something I enjoy or don't. But that is not how life or decisions or anything really is, Rafe."

"Of course it is."

"Once again, because to you, it is a 'yes or no' or a 'black or white' world." She turned a question on him. "Why did you choose to be a coalfield worker?"

He folded his arms. "Because I live in a mining field—"

"And if you didn't," she interrupted. "If you were in London, what might you have done? What work might you have pursued? A stable-master. A steward. Yes, you slid into the role of foreman to a coalfield because of where you live, but even if you had been somewhere else? There would have been a different opportunity. *For you*." Her voice grew impassioned as she spoke. "I never had those same luxuries of choice that you did, Rafe. Nor do most women. We are either wives or whores or servants if we can find the work. And so do I *like* what I do? No, I hadn't really considered the question, because it is what enables me to survive without selling myself as"—she blanched, and he sharpened his eyes on her white-washed face—"as . . . so many other women are forced to do," she ultimately finished, leaving the echo of her charged words dancing on the air between them.

He'd stormed out here, anticipating the very debate, nay, fight they'd found themselves in. But he'd not expected . . . this. To be thrown off-balance by the truisms she'd leveled at him.

He'd not expected to be . . . humbled.

Humbled in that he'd not considered . . . what it must be

like for her, a woman surviving without the benefit of a brother or a husband or a father to rely upon. He clenched and unclenched his fists, balling them at his sides. This is what she wanted. *To weaken you, and make you feel guilty when she, with her deception, is the one entirely in the wrong.*

He took a step closer, and she eyed him warily.

"You've won, is that what you think?" he whispered against her ear, rosewater filling his senses, like a weapon she wielded to distract.

She didn't back away. She didn't retreat, and as he lowered his head, that cautiousness in her gaze gave way to desire, and he reveled in the truth that she was as hopeless as him in this desire they had for one another.

Rafe ran a finger along the curve of her jaw, and Edwina briefly closed her eyes; his touch seemed to prompt words. "I . . . have not thought of it in those terms for some time now, Rafe," she said softly, breathlessly, owning his name once more on her lips, as he'd requested a short while ago, and as he still foolishly craved to hear. "I-it is not about w-winning."

"No?" He cupped her nape, and she melted against him. But he froze, with his lips a hairsbreadth from hers, lingering there until her thick lashes drifted up, revealing the depths of her desire and confusion. "How did you think of them?"

"As both of us getting something we need." Edwina rested her palms against his chest, her long fingers curling in the fabric of his jacket. "We can help one another."

Another wave of passion assailed his senses and logic, as he tunneled in on only her words, and the double meaning there behind them.

"I don't need anything from you or anything you might bring," he taunted her, his voice coming out gravelly in the quiet around them. He moved his lips near the shell of her ear, whispering harshly, "I do, however, against all reason and good judgment, want you."

Edwina's breath caught on an intake, and he lowered his mouth to claim the sounds of her desire, even as she cupped his nape, leaning into him and their embrace, and kissed him with the same violent intensity with which he mated his mouth to hers.

"Let me in," he demanded against her mouth, leaving her to that decision, all the while knowing she was as hot for him as he for her.

She parted her lips, allowing him entry.

Rafe swept his tongue inside, and they made angry love with their mouths. All the while, he ran his hands over her, capturing the curves of her hips that continued to captivate him, and holding her close. He pressed his hard shaft against her soft, flat stomach.

Edwina moaned but one single syllable, his name, infused with so much passion that his manhood pulsed; he ached to lay her down, and at last claim her. Nay, there'd be no claiming a woman such as Edwina Dalrymple; she'd lay possession of him.

It was why, with each lash of her tongue against his, an embrace he'd intended as punishing, left him lost in an eddy of desire controlled in every way by this woman, while Rafe sank further and deeper into her snare. Lost.

With every moment, and every minute with her, and in her arms, he found himself lost in every way with her.

Wanting her.

In ways that were more dangerous than mere desire.

Rafe broke free of her hold, dragging his mouth from hers. "You thought . . . wrong. We cannot help one another, because there is nothing I want nor need your help with," he whispered harshly against her ear. He released her, and Edwina immediately sagged.

And with her noisy respirations echoing in his ears, he left.

Chapter 19

Since the volatile exchange between her and Rafe in the gardens, they had met daily, with her overseeing his and Cailin's lessons.

She'd been certain he would come 'round to the friendly way he'd been with her.

She had been so very convinced that she could get them back to the place they'd found themselves, as almost-friends.

A week later, she realized how wrong she'd been.

And though she and Cailin had maintained a warmth and friendship between them, when it came to Edwina and Rafe, well, the role of student and instructor was clear: and there'd never been a colder, more stubborn student than he. Oh, he met for their respective meetings during the agreed-upon time slots . . . but that was the extent of cooperation from Rafe Audley.

With a sigh, she collected her charcoal pencil, notebooks, the folio the duke had given her containing her schedule and the scheduled events, and made her way to the dining room for Rafe and Cailin's latest lesson.

This should be the easiest of all her other assignments.

This one, where she even had the details spelled out and planned for her by the duke. Every moment of her time with Rafe was crafted into a meticulous schedule that didn't require her to think beyond anything but preparing Rafe for his entry into Polite Society.

Only to find . . . it wasn't so very easy.

It didn't feel easy, at all.

Because he hated her. Even though he'd kissed her with all the passion he had during their first kiss, his resentment and disdain for her . . . of her, was so much worse.

And it hurt so much worse, too.

Edwina reached the dining room.

Two bewigged footmen in navy blue and gold uniforms flanked each side of the elaborately carved doorway; yet again, those less-than-subtle reminders of wealth all around. Along with the reminder that for all the work she had done preparing ladies for their time in Town, she'd not ever worked for or with families of the immense wealth and power possessed by the Duke of Bentley. And if she did not succeed in this assignment, it was unlikely she ever would again.

As such, taking Rafe's disdain as personally as she had was a distraction she could not afford.

Why, she was Miss Edwina Dalrymple, Transformer of Ladies, resolute in her work and her success. With that resolve strengthening her spine, Edwina lifted her chin, and entered the dining room to find Rafe seated, already helping himself to the meal she'd specifically had set out in preparation of his lesson, eating with one hand, while with the other, he scribbled away in that notebook he'd been using since they'd begun their lessons. And she knew she should, as an optimistic instructor, focus on that unexpected sign of his dedication. "You began without me," she needlessly stated. Edwina looked around the room, searching for the missing member of their group. "And without your sister? You really should have waited for Miss Audley's arrival."

Rafe continued adding notes to his book. "I decided that was at an end."

She waited for him to give some manner of clarification. "I do not follow, Mr. Audley," Edwina said slowly.

"I encouraged her to head on to Hatchard's, sparing her from"—not even deigning to look up, he gestured with his pencil between him and Edwina—"this tediousness."

"What?" Which meant she and Rafe were to be together alone? Which she'd not minded before. Not until he'd come to hate her.

At last, he looked up—briefly. "Come, Miss Dalrymple," he scoffed. "The only reason I'm here, and the only reason my sister wished to come here was so that she might experience the museums and culture of London. As such, she is done taking part in your societal experiment for us."

Her stomach fell. For coward that she was, she'd been welcoming the buffer the young woman would have presented between her and Rafe. "That is . . . certainly disappointing." Edwina perked up. "I'm certain the duke would—"

He leveled a flinty glare on her, icing the remainder of the words on her lips. "Do not even think about it. I've already spoken to the duke. He knows my being here and fulfilling his wishes are contingent upon his promise to not force Cailin to suffer through Polite Society."

"I wouldn't betray Cailin," she said softly, and promptly flinched. As she'd done just that to Rafe.

A cool grin formed on his lips.

Forcing her frustration on to a matter within her control, she met his smile with a frown. "I'll have you know, Mr. Audley, my lessons are—"

"Tardy? You were late," he interrupted, pausing long enough to carve himself a piece of his roast fowl. "And to your sessions?" A blush heated Edwina's cheeks. "Tsk. Tsk." Rafe popped the bite into his mouth.

Under any other circumstances, she would have been hopelessly captivated by a gentleman so determined to have his sister see London as she'd wished. But being called out? Even if it was deserved? Calling on a lifetime's worth of training, she swept forward with all the grace she could muster, and as she joined him, her mind raced. "My tardiness was . . . intentional." She lied. It was a blatant, shameful one, to salvage her pride. "There are some circumstances by which—"

"It is permissible?" He looked up again, a devastatingly distracting half grin on his lips, and she promptly missed a step, before correcting course. "Hmph," he said, making another note in his book.

Tardiness . . . permissible? Far from it? Edwina frowned and arched her neck, to peer at that page. "No! Do not write that." Only the most elevated arrived late, and when they did, their pride was called into question. *Think. Think.* She stopped before him. "I was merely illustrating just how valuable it is for a person to arrive promptly and punctually. Any disappointment you may have felt in this moment, you may be assured, the lords and ladies awaiting your company will too feel." Edwina couldn't help it. She smiled. Widely.

Suspicion glinted in his eyes, and for a moment she expected he'd call her out as the poor liar she was. "Tell me, is dinner at the noon hour permissible, too?"

Out of the corner of her eye, she caught the footmen stationed across the room glancing at one another and repressing smiles.

Hmph. Let them laugh and let Rafe be smug. The truth remained that, in knowing the specifics of when lords and ladies took their meals, he had learned something from her. "In order to prepare for the evening meal, it only makes sense that we have all those same courses laid out," she said in the tones she used for her most difficult charges.

He grunted.

"I should point out *once more* that it is impolite to grunt."

Rafe speared a pickle and popped it into his mouth. "Anything else, princess?" he asked around the rather large bite.

She sighed. "I need *also* remind you, speaking with your mouth full is *also* impolite."

He yanked a piece of bread off with his teeth, and proceeded to chew. "Who would have imagined that?" he drawled, and then swallowed.

And this time, it was her turn to sharpen her gaze upon

him. Why . . . why . . . he was making light of her. Refusing
to rise to his baiting, she helped herself to the chair next to his.
Edwina set down her things and looked to one of the footmen.
"If you would?" she asked, gesturing to Rafe's plate.

The young man came forward, hesitated a moment, eyeing the duke's son with a suitable level of wariness, before
clearing his dish.

"What the hell?" he groused, and the glare he favored
her with would have once terrified her. No more.

"This is a formal lesson, Mr. Audley, not a regular afternoon meal for you." The time for games with this man—with
this charge—she silently corrected—were at an end. He
could be annoyed with her. He might even dislike her immensely. Which he did. But those sentiments were not going
to interfere with the work she had to do—not anymore. She
had tiptoed enough around him in a bid to earn back his
friendship. It was time to focus upon their business together.
"As you know, His Grace intends to introduce you to an intimate gathering of his closest friends during a formal dinner
party this coming Saturday. It is time that we put your lectures into practice." Edwina snapped open her notebook, and
set it down above the empty plate in front of her. "As I have
with your previous assignments, I've taken the liberty of pro-
viding detailed notes for you to take with you after we've
finished so that you might read them at your leisure."

"Splendid," he drawled. Her heart fluttered at the hint of
teasing there. The first sign of it since their fight seven days
earlier. "I'll save it for kindling."

And just like that, her hopes were dashed. He would not
let go of his anger. *Do not give in to his baiting. Do not give
in to his baiting.*

Instead, she did that which she always did when he was
most cross—she smiled. "I expect you'll find the notes I've
shared entirely too helpful to burn."

"Oh, yes," he murmured. He leaned close, so his lips
nearly brushed her cheek. "It all sounds so very stimulating."

And she would have to be deaf to fail to hear the suggestive quality to those whispered words. Where in the past,

she'd received plenty of innuendos from plenty of employers, such whisperings were different with this man. With him, there had been shared passion, the like of which still kept her awake at night. And by the way he hooded his eyes, he well knew it, too.

She dampened her mouth, and his gaze followed that slight movement, settling there on her lips. "We should . . ." her words came breathless.

"Yes."

And everything was so twisted in this moment, she didn't know if his was a question or a statement, but it felt so very much like the latter.

Or . . . was that merely her yearning for it to be so?

"Begin." She managed to squeeze that husky syllable out.

"Yes, let's."

And then he sat back in his chair, ceding the lesson to her, and the moment was shattered.

Edwina exhaled quietly. *Dining. Dining. Focus on dining and not missing his embrace. Or his kindness.*

"Now, the first thing to be aware of is that there is an order to seating. The mistress of the household sits at the upper end, and then the seating falls, right to left, according to rank as to superiority and the next of rank following and so on and so on. The gentleman, in this case, being His Grace, shall take a seat up there." She pointed her pencil at the lower end of the table. "And there is no greater sign of ill-breeding than to alter this order or seat oneself in a place higher than one belongs."

"Oh, the scandal. The horror."

She ignored that heavy coating of sarcasm. "It is imperative that you do not shout across or even speak quietly across a table to another party. The parties seated to your right and left comprise the main individuals whom you should speak with."

"In this case, being you."

She nodded. "Precisely, in this—" She narrowed her eyes. "You're teasing again."

"I'm teasing again," he confirmed, unapologetically.

"Resuming your lesson," she said, not missing a beat. "We shall shift to the very important topic of . . . plates and silverware."

T his was hell.
  Or, it should be.

There'd been five courses thus far, to suffer through in an etiquette lesson on dining, doled out by a governess of fine ladies.

And yet, nearly two hours later, with Edwina still filling every spare space of quiet with her far-too-enthused-for-a topic-on-dining voice, just like all the days prior, Rafe found himself enjoying it all—immensely. Nor, for that matter, did it come from just teasing her . . . though that was of its own immense enjoyment. It was that her enthusiasm was contagious.

"This fork, then?" he asked, holding the wrong one aloft.

"No. No." Plucking the silver piece from his hand, she returned it to the legion of cutlery beside his plate. "Try again."

Rafe made a show of eyeing each fork and spoon. "Oh, dear, however will I choose? The decision seems veritably life-altering. Not unlike the mines in which if a person makes the wrong decision—"

She swatted his hand. "Oh, hush. I'm not saying it is the same matter of life and death as the work you do daily. But it is . . . important to your fitting in here, and successfully immersing yourself in society, Rafe."

Despite the footmen stationed at the front of the room, and her promise to the contrary, she'd used his Christian name.

That was, however, not what sent his earlier amusement fading. Rather . . . it had been what she'd said, as he fixed on not just the latest words driving her lecture, but on the solemnity to them and her, and the little tensing at the corners of her mouth.

"And you think that is so very important?" he murmured. "Fitting in?"

"Of course," she said instantly. "It is eminently more comfortable when one . . . belongs." She glanced down at her lap, and that slight dip of her gaze proved revealing in so many ways.

She spoke as one who knew what it was like to be excluded, and it also framed her efforts to transform her charges in a new light. Not ruthless, driven by prestige in her work . . . but rather, motivated because of her own understanding of what it was to be treated poorly.

And he didn't like it . . . this new way of viewing Edwina Dalrymple. Because it relaxed the guard he was so very determined to have up around her, a wall he'd firmly erected this past week that had brought them back to their respective roles as adversaries.

"One might argue that it isn't worth one's time exerting efforts to find oneself accepted by people who won't accept a person for who they are," he said quietly, careful to keep inflection from his voice.

A sound of frustration escaped her, and she spoke on a rush. "That is an idealistic way of viewing it. It is ever so easy to say one doesn't care, but when one is forced to live among people who deride you for not belonging?" Sadness filled her features, and she shook her head.

"Is that what happened to you?" he asked quietly. Despite all his resolve to not let himself be weak in any way around her, he couldn't keep that question back. "Is that why you are determined to transform women and now, me, into this paragon of propriety and society's rules?"

He tensed, anticipating that she would immediately default to the different standards she expected for them, one in which he was to share, while she kept her secrets close.

Then, Edwina nodded slowly, reluctantly. "People aren't kind, and perhaps you were spared in Staffordshire from the world's general meanness, but that isn't how it is usually and certainly not everywhere. And when it happens? It is awful," she finished on a whisper.

He'd been a bastard, but he'd been spared much of the cruelty that met illegitimate issue. The world had taken

Rafe's mother as the wife of a man who followed the drum; it was the lie she'd told to explain away the babes she often found herself carrying, and her husband's absence. There'd been suspicions raised by one of the boys who'd bullied Hunter, but none had hung too much on the wondering about their family. "I don't necessarily know what your experience was," he allowed, and waited until she lifted her eyes to his. "But those people?" People whom he had a violent hungering to hunt down and destroy for having hurt her. "Anyone who would expect you to change and be different, or who'd treat you poorly because of who you are? They aren't worthy of a moment of your time, Edwina."

Her lips trembled, and then parted, in a tender softening.

And despite every vow he'd taken not to feel anything but resentment and wariness for this woman, the anger in his chest . . . eased. Rafe resented how she'd betrayed him. But at least now, he understood *some* of what fueled her determination. She'd been treated poorly, and wished to spare him that same fate. "I'm not going to go about being someone other than I am to appease the duke or anyone else, Edwina," he said, his voice gruff.

"I'm not trying to change you, Rafe. I wouldn't *want* you to change who you are." When she spoke in those impassioned tones, he . . . could almost believe her. Her fingers crept toward his, and then she abruptly stopped with a breath of space between them, a divide that hadn't been there days ago. She lowered her hand to her lap, and he missed that touch. "I want you, however, to be prepared to be who you are in this world that is so very different."

For the first time, her motives made sense; they made sense in a way different than they had from the start. When he'd thought her a lofty lady trying to make him into something other than he was, to please a duke.

Goddamn it, why was he such a fool where this woman was concerned? Without thinking, he grabbed the correct fork. "This one is the dessert fork," he said between gritted teeth.

Edwina beamed, and he may as well have hefted the

globe on his back like Atlas himself. Then her smile froze, and she gasped.

"What?" he asked guardedly.

"Why . . . why . . ." Her gaze went from the doorway to the table, and then to Rafe himself. "You *know* these things."

He took a bite of the macaroon on his plate "'Things' is hardly precise." It was just that he was determined to make this as difficult as possible for her.

"You knew the rules of punctuality," she stated. "Just as you know that you are supposed to stand when a woman enters the room and not to grunt and which knife to use and which fork." She half sounded ready to cry.

At last, he took mercy. "Aye."

Edwina stared at him a long while. "That's it? That is all you'll say? *Ayyyyye*?"

That last deliverance was so identical to the graveled and gruff delivery of Rafe's response that he grinned. The moment she landed a sharp, disapproving look his way, he let his smile fall. "No," he murmured, and bowed his head in false contrition. "Aye, *Miss Dalrymple*."

She gasped and tossed her uneaten macaroon at him. The confectionery missile hit Rafe's arm and landed with a little forlorn thump on the floor.

And, in that moment, it was impossible to say who was more shocked: the pair of footmen who had been forced to attend this farcical lesson.

Edwina, with her horror-filled hazel eyes.

Or Rafe.

Picking up his napkin, he made a show of dusting the remnants of sugar from his sleeve. "Why . . . Miss Dalrymple, did you just hurl food at me?"

A crimson blush turned the lady's cheeks red. "No."

He lifted a brow. This one he really needed to hear.

"It was more like a little flick," and she demonstrated said gesture with a flex of her hands.

One of the young servants came forward to retrieve the discarded biscuit, but Rafe held up a hand. "A moment, please."

Taking their cue, the servants instantly filed out of the room, leaving Rafe and Edwina alone.

She opened her mouth.

"I know," he interrupted. "Our being together alone is improper."

"Yes." Edwina frowned. "You know that?"

He nodded.

Edwina narrowed her eyes. "What *don't* you know about proper etiquette, Mr. Audley?"

He opened his mouth to respond, but she beat him to it, peppering him with a rapid questioning. "What about proper forms of address?" she demanded.

"Before or after your recent lectures commenced?"

"They are lessons," she corrected. "And *when* did you master that particular topic?"

He lifted his head. "*Before.*"

With his every response, Edwina's brows dipped lower and lower. "What about the topic of acceptable discourse?"

"What of it?" he asked, furrowing his brow in fake confusion.

The young lady gnashed her teeth.

And it was wicked how very much he enjoyed himself. A better man might care. "What do you know of it?" she asked again.

"I know Commerce, Coin, and Shipping are generally the safest sources of conversation for a man to speak on." Rafe confirmed.

"You know *that*?" The lady looked unsure as to whether she wished to stamp her foot or cry, and Rafe, who'd been so determined to be coldly indifferent, couldn't resist the lure of teasing and tormenting her. "*How*?"

"Oh, from the seven-part history filled with topics suitable for discussion and *Rules of Good Deportment, or of Good Breeding* and *A Present for an Apprentice* by John Barnard." He nodded. "Yes. I'm extensively read on the matter, and as such, quite accomplished in *proper* discourse." He paused. "That is, according to Polite Society's standards."

Setting her book down hard, she leaned across the arm of her chair. "What of dancing?"

An image slipped in, of Edwina in his arms, her hands on his sleeves, his at her waist, while he waltzed her about an empty ballroom floor. And he was tempted to lie on this one. Alas, she'd no doubt already had a fine dance tutor lined up. "One might say I am . . . proficient," he settled for.

Edwina shoved her seat back so quickly, it scraped harshly over the hardwood floors. Hands upon her hips, the lady stood over him, an impressive dark scowl directed his way. "You . . . you . . . are . . . accomplished," she hissed. She may as well have called him out as an immoral cad, for all the wounded affront blazing back at him within her revealing eyes.

He sipped the claret she'd needlessly tutored him on how to properly pour.

If looks could smite a person, he'd have been laid dead at her feet.

With a sound of frustration, she stalked off.

Hurriedly setting aside his glass, he came to his feet and rushed after her, neatly sliding into her path before she could make her exit.

Edwina ground to a halt, and glared up at him. "What?" she bit out.

"Why are you so angry, princess?"

"You lied to me."

"It wasn't a lie. It was . . . merely an *omission* on my part. You were the one who assumed I was untutored in the ways of Polite Society, because I was raised in a mining town. I merely didn't bother to correct you."

Understanding filled her eyes, as he tossed those like words she'd used to defend her actions back at her. But instead of the fiery challenge he expected, her shoulders dipped slightly, rounding even more. "You are . . . right," she said softly, and he startled at the readiness with which she'd owned that. "I . . . was wrong in interfering with Mr. Sparrow."

No one he'd ever known would have so owned their mistake; it wasn't the Staffordshire way. It wasn't the human way. People dug in. And yet, Edwina had not, and it said far more about her character than the "lie of omission" she'd allowed.

His hand came up almost reflexively, and he ran his knuckles along her cheek. "One would think you'd be more grateful for not having to start at the most basic level of my refinement."

"I was grateful for the opportunity to do my work." Her features were ravaged, and the sight of it hit him harder than the unexpected fist he'd once taken to the gut from one of his miners who'd shown up to his shift drunk. "I did not want to take this assignment if I wasn't necessary, but so that I could actually do that which I was hired to do and prove myself capable."

That was something he could understand. For all the ways in which they were different, the sense of accomplishment and the need to succeed in their endeavors, without the help of anyone's interference, was a kindred connection shared between them. "It has been years since I had any of those lessons, Edwina," he said. "I didn't even think I recalled them until you came along." Nay, rather he'd shut out all those memories of everything his mother had cared so very much about.

"How?" she asked softly.

He glanced briefly over the top of her head; he'd not discussed his mother with anyone. Not even his siblings spoke of her. Cailin hadn't known her. Wesley had learned not to talk about *either* of their parents. Hunter had never *wanted* to speak of her. And it had been easier to let the sad memories of her go. "My mother was an actress. She had dreams of a different life, and that life always included the peerage. She was naïve. Foolish. Believing at first that a duke who'd been captivated by her could marry her. And then she settled . . . for less. She schooled my brothers and I on the ways of the peerage, because it was our"—he managed a wry grin—"birthright." He made himself look at Edwina, holding her eyes, and at last explained it to her. "So . . . I know the rules of this world. I know their ways. I've never *lived* them, but I know them. Just as I know that

I wouldn't want to be part of Polite Society. I've come for my sister and my brother. And so, I'll go along with what the duke wants and expects, but I'm also going to do that which I want, too . . . and that includes showing my sister something other than Staffordshire. We're visiting the British Museum tomorrow. You'll be joining us."

She nodded slowly. "I see." Bowing her head, Edwina turned to go.

He called out, staying her, "And I'd ask that you accompany us, not to instruct us, but . . . as a guest, Edwina."

"I . . ." Edwina eyed him warily, as if she thought there might be more to his request, as if she believed he put some manner of test before her. "I would like that very much," she finished softly, and this time, as she left, he let her go.

All the while, wanting her to stay . . .

His gaze fell to the table; where the notebook she'd given him, lay. Of their own volition, his fingers moved over the cover.

Footfalls echoed in the hall; and he immediately snatched his hand back lest she see him caressing the little volume. "E-*oh*," he blurted out.

Not Edwina.

The duke—Rafe's *father*—stared back. "Were you waiting for Miss Dalrymple?" he asked, without accusation. "I'd believed you had completed your lessons for the day."

"I . . . yes. No, we have. I . . . she'd forgotten her notebook," he lied. The duke glanced at the table where the notebook Edwina had given him rested, a perfect decoy. "I believed she returned . . ." He went and retrieved the article. "If you'll excuse me?" he said stiffly, letting the duke have the room.

"Please, don't go." His father lifted his palms, revealing a small leather book Rafe hadn't noted . . . until now. "I was told you were here."

"I take it you wish to discuss my progress?" he drawled. A large part of him wanted to tell the duke to shove off with that question, and taunt him, let him believe Rafe was the uncouth bastard the world took him for. To do so, however, would only have implications for Edwina and her future. "I assure you Miss Dalrymple is quite accomplished—"

"No," the duke interrupted. "No. That isn't what I intend to inquire after. I am confident in the young lady's capabilities . . . and yours, as well." His father paused, his eyes lingering on Rafe's face, and then he dropped his gaze to the book clenched tightly in his hand. "I . . . had the honor of accompanying Cailin to Hatchard's."

Of anything the duke might have said, that had certainly not been what Rafe had expected. "What?" he blurted out.

"I asked and she allowed me to join her."

Rafe drew back, incredulously. "She allowed *you*?"

"Yes. Imagine my surprise," the duke said dryly. A wistful smile stole over the duke's face, and when he again spoke, he did so as if he'd become lost in his own memory. "She is a clever young woman." She was, and yet for the duke to have ascertained as much, father and daughter would have had to engage in discussions in which Cailin had revealed as much to him. "Very self-possessed and unapologetic and proud. She has . . ." Their noble sire gave his head a rueful shake. ". . . a sharp sense of humor." The man's mouth pulled in a telling grimace.

Rafe tried to call forth an image of what that outing would have been like . . . between the father they'd spent their life speaking ill of and Cailin who thought nothing of telling a person precisely what she thought of him. "I trust you were a victim of that biting wit."

"Whew," the duke chuckled. "Like a masterful sword wielder she is."

And wonder of wonders, Rafe and the duke shared a smile.

"But," his father said softly, "Cailin was so good as to share her outing with me and we discussed some of her interests and beliefs, and I am grateful for that." The duke paused. "She was also good enough to make mention of . . . some of yours."

Rafe stiffened. "Oh." *Bloody hell.* Cailin had never been a prattler, and yet she'd chosen this time to begin speaking? What in blazes had she—?

"You . . . enjoy the kitchen," the duke murmured.

Bloody, bloody hell. Rafe fought the urge to wrestle with his cravat. So that was what this was about? Because, of course, a duke's son, even a bastard-born one, wasn't one to spend his time baking or cooking or overseeing any tasks set for servants. Neither, however, would he apologize for who he was. Rafe drew his lip back in a sneer meant to taunt. "I take it you've come here to lecture me."

Confusion creased the duke's face. "What?" he asked dumbly. "No . . . I . . . here," he blurted, holding out that small tome.

Rafe glanced down.

The Cooks and Confectioners Dictionary by John Nott.

Dumbstruck, he tried to speak, and failed. All words eluded him. That was what the duke had sought him out for this day? To give him this book . . . about cooking?

"Based on what Cailin shared, I thought you might enjoy it," the duke said into the silence. And when Rafe still made no move to accept the unexpected gift, his father let his arm fall to his side. "It is silly. Forgive me."

"No!" Rafe exclaimed, and at last reached for the cookbook. "I . . . thank you. I . . . thank you," he repeated, studying the etched gold lettering upon the cover, because it was easier to focus on those details than the man staring at him with a depth of emotion that bespoke far more than the indifference he'd believed the duke had held for Rafe and his siblings. Throughout his childhood, his mother would return with baubles and fineries from her time in London with the duke. While Rafe had been left behind to raise his siblings, looking after them. Being both parents the Audleys had never had. There'd been no gifts. Certainly not personal ones, such as this. And that didn't matter. Not truly. What did, however, what he'd never considered until this moment, was the burden that had been placed upon him as a boy. But that burden? It had come from his mother's refusal to share their existence with the duke, and his resentment hadn't been reserved just for the duke, but also for her, as well. He saw that now.

His father cleared his throat, bringing Rafe's gaze up from the book he'd been staring at.

Smoothing his hands along the front of his jacket, the duke shifted forward on his feet. "Yes, well, I am happy to know you do not hate it." A twinkle lit the older man's eyes. "Though, if I'm being fair and ascribing credit where credit is due, your sister may have encouraged me to choose this volume."

Unnerved by this new harmony between them, Rafe opened his mouth to again make his excuses, when his father spoke.

"I know it is early still, and that you are . . . angry with me. With reasons for it," his father rushed to add. "But I am also hoping in time you might come to find you could consider carving out a life here. That, perhaps, you might find a reason to stay."

Unlikely. Rafe opened his mouth to deliver that retort. But something held him back.

Unbidden, Rafe's gaze went first to the cookbook and then over to the notebook in hand . . . that gift from Edwina. "Perhaps," he allowed, and when he took leave of his father a short while later, he found himself thinking of Edwina here in London, and foolish as it was, the duke's words whispered around in Rafe's head long after he'd gone.

Chapter 20

All of her assignments and all of her roles had required Edwina to always be working.

Always be working had even come to be one of the mottos that drove her, and one that she used in interviews to sell her services to prospective clients.

Every moment of every day was to be filled.

This, however, proved to be the first time that her day was filled . . . in a different way. In a way that wasn't work.

As such, the following morn, just arrived at the British Museum with Rafe and his sister, it was still nigh impossible for Edwina to separate herself from her assignment.

"The building is known as Montagu House," she said as she followed close behind Rafe, Cailin, and the young woman's maid up the wide marble stairs that led to the main floor. "There are three main floors. The first and lower floor is where you might find the library of printed books. Then there is the Gallery." That had forever been her favorite, and yet, not a single one of her charges had ever wished to explore, and as such, she'd never had the opportunity to do so herself. "It features Greek and Roman sculptures. Egyptian antiquities, as well as Sir William Hamilton's collection, which features both engravings and drawings."

While she spoke, Cailin chatted excitedly up at her brother. And Edwina briefly paused in her recitation and simply watched the pair. They chatted amicably, with Rafe periodically saying something that brought Cailin to laughter. Never, in all the households Edwina had worked within, had there been any brother who'd even acknowledged his sister in a conversation, let alone taken her on outings to museums. Those were *chores* left to maids and governesses and companions.

And . . . here was this man. Forsaking a vow to subvert his father's will and never journey to London . . . for his sister. Despite his resentment of the duke, and his hatred of everything London and Polite Society represented, he'd been willing to immerse himself in that which he abhorred because of his siblings.

And at the realization of that loving devotion, a piece of her heart was forever lost to Rafe Audley.

Her breath caught on a quick intake.

What was she thinking? Thoughts of . . . losing her heart to him?

She wasn't. It had been merely rhetorical. An appreciation—

Rafe reached the top landing, and looked back to where Edwina still stood. "Is everything all right, Miss Dalrymple?"

Is everything all right? No, everything was absolutely wrong. Completely upside down. Particularly where her nonsensical musings were concerned. "Everything is fine," she called up, her voice inordinately loud, carrying through the soaring museum. Gathering up her skirts, she rushed on ahead. Remembering what Cailin had shared when they'd been baking in Staffordshire, Edwina told them, "This floor, I believe, will be of particular interest to you. It features fossils, minerals, snakes, lizards, herbals."

"Oh, that sounds splendid!" Cailin exclaimed, resting a hand on her brother's shoulder. "We are going there first, brother." Before he could respond, the younger woman looked at Edwina. "You, Edwina, are free to have some time for yourself. Isn't that right, Rafe?"

Did Edwina merely imagine the regret in his eyes, because she wished to see that emotion there?

"Of course," he said, so fluidly, she likely had. "Miss Dalrymple is deserving of time of her own."

"Thank you," she said softly. It was the first time she'd been permitted time of her own. Time being a gift that she didn't even know what to do with, when it existed outside of her work. As such, she should be more grateful than . . . downhearted.

He lingered a moment before following after his sister.

When the brother-sister pair had gone, Edwina found her way back to the Gallery. As she went, she trailed a leisurely path around, winding her way through the Greek statues, glorious masterpieces carved of white marble, so very real and lifelike.

All around her, lords and ladies strolled past exhibits, barely pausing to look at the ancient artifacts around them, more engrossed in discussions with their companions than in the art they'd come to *observe*.

And yet, in this moment, she found herself not unlike those unappreciative patrons . . . because she should only be focusing on the fact that she was at last granted time for herself to take in the works of the ancient Greeks and Romans. Instead, she found herself . . . regretting that.

It was silly.

It had been kind and considerate. Far more so than any previous employer who'd barely seen her, beyond the work she did for their daughters.

Rafe had given her the gift of her own time here.

And all she could focus on was the fact that he'd sent her away, and how desperately she wished to be with—

"Oh, bloody *hellll*, Miss Dalrymple, not again."

She froze at that familiar voice from behind her, his tones a study in beleaguerment and annoyance. Edwina briefly closed her eyes, all the while cringing inside.

I've done nothing wrong.

Not this time. Not the last either.

Even as she reminded herself of that over and over, as she squared her shoulders and made herself face the gentleman, shame knotted at her insides. It had been years since she had seen him. He who'd stood in for her—their—father, and made it clear in no uncertain terms that she was not to pay their household another visit.

But this was different. She was no longer the bereft young woman whose mother had just died, and who'd gone in search of her father. Not as proud as her mother in asking to be part of his life. Not as smart as her mother in having failed to realize he didn't want her in it.

"*My lord,*" she murmured, dropping the requisite curtsy, because damn him. Because he thought her less than him. Because he likely thought she didn't know better. But she had as much of their father's blood in her veins, and she'd not be shamed for being here.

"I told you not to return," he said quietly, in those gentle, pitying tones more grating than any hateful, hurtful words he could have hurled at her.

"And I didn't." Edwina prided herself on her calm reply, when inside her heart was knocking sickeningly against her ribcage. This was horrid. She hated it. Still, she'd not back down. "I haven't returned to you or your household. Surely you weren't thinking to bar me from all of London?"

A flush splotched his cheeks. "Am I to believe your being here doesn't in some way have something to do with my father?"

"Our father?" she corrected on a question, winging a brow high.

"Shh!" His color grew heightened, and he stole a frantic look about. "I've told you, it is essential my mother is not hurt, and your mere presence threatens her well-being. Your mere presence endangers that."

"No, my saying something, or your saying something does. I've no intention of outing myself as your father's bastard." How was she so calm? How when inside she was trembling? At having to defend herself . . . at the feeling of being somehow less, a shameful secret to be hidden away. "As I see it, you've sought *me* out this time."

"You pledged to leave my family alone."

"And I maintain still, that I've not forced myself in any way upon your family." *No, but you had thought that if your father saw the success you had, that he would accept you.*

Only to find . . . in this moment, facing down the half-brother so very ashamed of her, that she didn't need their approval. She . . . had left that household, built a career and future, and found security all without the support or acknowledgment of the man who'd sired her. Rafe had helped her to see that, and it was that which gave her the courage to bring her shoulders back and cross over to Lord Blakeney. "I owe you no apologies. I've done nothing you can or should take fault with. As I see it, your seeking me out, interfering in my leisure, puts you in the wrong."

His jaw tensed. "Why are you here then?"

"I owe you nothing, and certainly not answers to any questions you might put to me," she said evenly, adrenaline pumping, her heart racing, and somehow all the more strengthened for it. "I have every right to be in London. I have work here."

He eyed her suspiciously. "What manner of *work*?"

By the slight emphasis he placed on that word, she well knew what opinion he'd already reached. "Do you fear I intend to make a scandal of myself and drag you into public shame?" she taunted him with that ask.

A vein at the corner of his eye bulged. "Yes, that is precisely my worry. I have a mother and a sister whose sensibilities and reputations I seek to protect above all else."

Hearing those words and witnessing the fear that marched across his features should not hurt her. And yet it did. She hated him. This man with his dark hair and hazel eyes, so very much like her own. As such, she shouldn't care even now that his opinion of her was as low as . . . *this*.

And she would be well within her right to drag out his panic, to torment him with the possibility of some hidden purpose to her being here. But . . . she could not. "It is respectable work," she murmured. Why, why was it so very important that he know that? "Work among the peerage." The color bled from his cheeks. She left him to his worry, a deliberate moment born of resentment. "Work that requires I be respectable, and as such, you needn't worry about me revealing the truth of my birthright and upsetting your mother. I have even more reason to not reveal the truth about my . . . existence." She'd thought she'd found peace with living a life in secret . . . only to find herself exhausted by it . . . and just then, she not only understood but admired and appreciated Rafe who'd never made any secret about his bastardy.

Lord Blakeney moved a searching gaze over her face. "Do you want money?"

"No!" the exclamation burst from her. "I don't want his money. I don't want yours. I told you that." He'd offered her funds then. And he'd do so again. To make her go away? Because his father felt guilty? Obligation? Whatever it was, she didn't care. And neither did she intend to take a pence from these people.

"What have we here?" a booming voice called out, and as one, they looked to the approaching gentleman. Attired in puce trousers and a waterfall cravat of brown silk, with his hair arranged in the Brutus cut, he'd all the makings of a dandy.

The earl cursed, and made to step in front of Edwina. "Nothing, Frimount. If we can—"

The other man, undeterred by those attempts, stopped before them. "And here, you insisted you wished to see my father's collection here for a potential purchase, and all the while . . ." The gentleman settled a leering gaze upon her mouth. Men always liked her mouth. "You had intentions of meeting this lovely number."

Revulsion scraped over her skin, and she made herself absolutely still, kept her features even under that repulsive scrutiny as all her previous encounters with lecherous pigs came rushing back. No matter how many improper looks or innuendos she'd had directed her way, they always grated. They always left a woman alternately wanting to slap the

smug face of the gentleman and slink away in shame. With
Rafe, however, it had never been that way. With him, she'd
only felt . . . beautiful.

"We were just remarking upon the . . ."

Edwina stole a glance at the little placard before them.
"Artemision Bronze," she supplied for a still-tongue-twisted
Lord Blakeney.

Good, let him be equally miserable. Had he not sought
her out, then neither of them would be in this discomfiting
situation.

And yet, his friend proved undeterred. "Oh, indeed." He
smirked. "I expect I might know what has attracted your
interest." He gestured less than subtly to the statue's gen-
itals.

Her cheeks flamed hot. The part of her that wished to
send him on to the devil was also cognizant of the fact that
any scandal attached to her name would also be calamitous
to her reputation working among the peerage. "If you'll
excuse me," she said stiffly, and turned to go.

Lord Blakeney's friend slid into her path . . . ending her
attempt at extricating herself. Her heart knocked against
her chest.

"That is enough, Frimount," Lord Blakeney said sharply,
that challenge of his friend, on her behalf, unexpected. Or
mayhap it was just that he wanted to avoid further questions
as to her identity. "It is we who should leave. The young
woman is a stranger, and I would allow her to her examination." He took the other man by the arm, and attempted to
steer him away.

His partner, however, proved tenacious.

"A young woman, unattended, in the naughty section of
a museum," Lord Frimount shot back. High color splotched
the man's clean-shaven cheeks, as he shrugged off Blakeney's hold. She shivered, inherently knowing the matter
wasn't at an end. It couldn't be. Because wounded pride in
a man was a dangerous thing. "Seems to me you duped me
into coming to this miserable place, under false pretenses.
Visit my father's collection so you might make a purchase,

you said. All the while, you're interested in a different sort of fun." In a shocking display of forwardness, he brushed a hand along her exposed right shoulder.

Then, it came . . . more ominous growl than shout; it rumbled off the walls of the Gallery: "You there!"

Oh, hell.

Edwina's heart sank for altogether different reasons. She looked on at the tall, dark, and avenging figure now striding towards her. She briefly closed her eyes. She didn't want to see him now. Not like this. Not confused and weak and just trapped with her *brother*.

And with that, Rafe's appearance managed that which the earl's had previously failed at: the cad released her.

R afe had left Cailin with her maid, and gone off in search of Edwina . . . to be sure she was well. Even as he'd known that reasoning was ridiculous in his own mind. Perils in a museum were likely few, and the real truth compelling him to seek her out being—the moment she'd gone off her own way—that he'd missed her.

Only to find . . . he'd been wrong.

She hadn't been so very safe, after all.

All Rafe's energy, all his attention was tunneled on the man who'd dared touch her.

Rage had clouded out reason within Rafe's head, so that he knew only one thing in that moment: he was going to sever the arm of the man who'd grabbed Edwina.

And he was going to do so viciously. Bloodily. And more so, happily.

And then when he was done with the blighter, he was going to beat his lifeless body with that bloody appendage.

At Rafe's approach, the shorter, stockier fellow who'd dared to put a hand upon Edwina's shoulder sputtered, "Wh-what is the meaning of this?"

Rafe didn't break his momentum; he came forward and let his fist fly, felling the dandified fop with one blow. The young man cried out, and crumpled into a cowering heap.

Edwina buried a gasp in her hands. "No!" she pleaded softly, as Rafe reached for the cowering, blubbering mess at their feet. "Please, do not."

". . . I'm bleeeeeding," the gent sobbed.

Bypassing the fellow with his fractured nose, Rafe turned his attention on the other nob. "Has *this one* hurt you, as well?" he asked her, hungry to destroy his next target. "Has he offended you in any way?"

Edwina and the gentleman exclaimed at the same time. "No!"

She turned to the gentleman, standing over his friend. "Please, take him out of here."

And yet, it did not escape Rafe's notice that there was a sense of familiarity with which she spoke to that particular gentleman. Jealousy, impotent, stark, and biting, coursed through his veins.

Nodding quickly, the young man helped the still-sobbing scoundrel to his feet, and steadying him with an arm about his shoulder, led him off. All the while, the gent continued to steal uneasy looks over his shoulder at Rafe.

So the cad wasn't completely empty in the head.

Rafe narrowed his eyes all the more on him. "You are certain he did not hurt you?" *Say the word, so I can destroy him . . .*

Because Rafe wanted to. Desperately . . . and violently.

"He . . ."

At that tangible hesitation, he whipped his attention Edwina's way.

Tension continued to whip through Rafe, his muscles coiled tight, braced for the fight he so desperately craved with the pair slinking off like the cowards they were. And yet, this was not about how he felt and his need to have his bloodlust slaked. This was about . . . Edwina. He forced himself to reign in that volatile emotion, and looked at her. Truly looked at her.

Edwina, who'd always been ready with a smile, now unsmiling, as he'd never seen her . . . and he wanted to bloody the bounders responsible for her upset, all over again.

"Rafe." She touched his arm, staying him, and then as if she recalled what she did and where they were, removed her hand. "You cannot simply go about reacting this way when someone offends me."

That is what she'd say? "Are you mad?" he whispered. "Do you truly believe I will stand by and allow you to be treated so?"

Her lips softened, parting a fraction. "Rafe, I have a reputation to maintain, and your responding as you did, only jeopardizes it."

"You believe *I* am the one who placed you in jeopardy on this day?" He gnashed his teeth and railed in silence that she should care so about her reputation and less for her actual well-being.

"Neither of them hurt me. It was . . . nothing."

"Nothing?" he snapped. "That one put his hand on you." That skin Rafe had worshipped with his mouth, sullied by the unworthy hands of a pale, dough-faced fellow who wasn't worthy of kissing her heels.

"That is . . . just the way it is sometimes, Rafe," she said simply, lifting her shoulders in a shrug.

A shrug?

As if it were entirely normal for a stranger to put their hands on her. Or commonplace for her to be accosted while . . . The air stuck in his chest, as the truth slammed into him like a ton of coal dropped upon him. She was . . . not shocked by that earlier treatment because she was . . . *accustomed* to it. It offered a deeper glimpse than anything she'd said prior about the manner of abuses she had put up with in her work.

Still, he made himself say it anyway . . . ask it. Even as he didn't want the answer. Not the real one, because he was a coward, and her confirmation would ravage him. "Has this happened to you before?"

"I am fine," she said with such an insistence, he almost believed her.

He did not doubt it. She was stronger than any of the hardened coalfield workers he knew, and yet, neither had she answered his question. And that evasion did not escape his notice. "Has this happened to you before?" he repeated, quieter, forcing a gentleness that went against all the volatile emotion pounding in his chest.

She nodded.

He closed his eyes. This was why, when he'd made to inspect her injured ankle, she'd beat him over the head with her silly parasol, transformed into a makeshift cudgel.

"I'm fine. Really," she said with a slight emphasis there, meant to calm him. "I'm quite capable, you know. I do fend them off. Eventually." She was attempting to reassure him? "I just have to be . . . *careful* about how I do it, you know . . . because . . . because . . ."

"Because of your work," he murmured. "And the need for maintaining your reputation."

She smiled. "Yes. That is it exactly."

Except, this smile she wore was strained with all the resentment—the deserved resentment she carried for a life where women were at the mercy of men, bounders, the lot of them. Rafe himself not excluded from their ranks.

He wasn't naïve. He knew the way of the world. And yet, neither had he allowed himself to think about Edwina out there in the world, on her own. Truly on her own. Perhaps then, if he had, it would have been harder to resent her for the determination with which she'd approached her job for the duke.

And this time, when his fury spiked, it was not only with those two strangers, but with himself, as well. It was, however, easier and safer to have a target for his rage. Rafe seethed. "How many have there been?"

"Too many to name. Even more whose names I don't know," she said. "It is how women are treated, and as such, we become adept at . . . navigating such situations."

His eye twitched. "I'll kill them. I'll kill them all."

"No, you won't," she said quietly and composed in ways that he wasn't . . . and felt he'd never again be. "There is a way to conduct yourself in society, and this isn't it, Rafe," she said quietly.

By God . . . was she lecturing him? Doling out another lesson about propriety and properness in the wake of that offense committed against her?

"That doesn't make it acceptable," he said between his teeth.

"No," she said. "But neither does it mean you should go about beating a man down."

"He deserved it." And he'd beat the cad again, happily and harder.

"Yes, however, you can't be the one . . . going about thrashing people who offend you or do something you take exception with."

Rafe stared incredulously at her. That was how she'd liken what that fop had done? Taking her lightly by the arm, he steered her behind the enormous Greek statue, stealing them that privacy. "He put his hands on you," he repeated.

"I am aware of that," she spoke with a calm that contradicted all the violent energy simmering inside him.

A moment later, with her staring expectantly at him, it became apparent that she intended to say nothing more. "That is it?"

"What would you have me say? I know what this world is. It isn't the first time it has happened." And it would not be her last. That unfinished thought hung there. Edwina angled her head back to meet his gaze; it was a warrioress's stare that enthralled him. "I handled those situations myself and I'll continue to do so . . ."

She'd do so when he and Edwina parted ways. And he despised that with all he was. Both the idea of her leaving, which left him achingly and strangely bereft. That, coupled with the idea that she'd fought all those battles on her own, and it suddenly became a chore to get air into his lungs.

"I don't want you to be in a position where you have to defend yourself," he said quietly. A wrong that she'd faced time and time again to the point it had become a common occurrence she expected, and had to learn how to deal with. "I wouldn't want it for you, or my sister, or any woman."

"Then, how fortunate that as a duke's son, with his influence behind you now, you are in a position to challenge how society allows women to be treated."

He stiffened. She'd steered him into that trap. "I see what you've done there."

Edwina smiled, the first real one he'd seen her wear since he'd come upon her and those two strangers. "Always be working."

Some of the tension went out of him, and he shook his head wryly. "You are . . . something, Edwina Dalrymple."

She winked. "I shall take that as a compliment from you, Mr. Audley."

And it was one. Because there wasn't a suitable compliment to capture his appreciation and awe of her will and dedication to that which she believed to be of import—him and his joining Polite Society, being one of them. That admiration could only be what accounted for his next question: "I'm not saying I intend to stay, but what . . . manner of change could I bring?"

"Well," she explained, "there are charities and institutions dedicated to the betterment of causes that you feel matter. Anything you choose to put your weight and name behind allows you the power to exact change . . . and to give strength and support to those who might benefit." People like his mother, who'd survived without the assistance of a husband.

"Who was the other gent?" he asked quietly, diverting her back to that which he cared most about in that instant—her.

It had been too much to hope that he'd have let the matter rest as to the identity of the two gentlemen.

Not that with her suggestion she'd set out to deliberately distract him. She truly yearned for Rafe to see that there was no shame in claiming a rightful place among this world he was so determined to shun. To show him that with power and money came influence with which to make change.

And that change included a better future not only for

him and his siblings, but others to whom he extended his support.

Nor could there be any doubting that he was one who'd not sit idly, an indolent son of a duke, while people suffered and struggled around him. His background wouldn't allow it. And the fact that he'd come to her defense as he had, more offended than she herself, was testament to who he was as a person.

"This isn't the place to have this discussion, Rafe," she whispered. But then, was there really any appropriate place for her to discuss with him, or anyone, the circumstances of her birth and the secret she carried?

"So you *did* know him."

God, he missed nothing. "I didn't say that," she said evenly.

"Yes, you did. It was another one of those omissions you use to either lie or conceal."

Touché.

In fairness, this one had been unintended. Edwina troubled the inside of her cheek, biting at that flesh. And how was it possible that this man who'd been a stranger to her until just recently should know her so well? "I've already assured you, neither gentleman hurt me." Wasn't that enough?

"That isn't what I asked."

Apparently, it wasn't enough. And no, he was correct. That hadn't been the question he'd put to her. God, he was tenacious. She released a sigh. "Yes, I . . . know him." She winced. "In a way. I do not even really know-him, know-him."

His eyes narrowed, and she gasped.

"Not in that way. I haven't known any man like . . . that. Other than you." She slapped a hand over her mouth. Except . . . "Not that you and I . . . did . . ." *Stop it, Edwina.* "Do you know, as I said, this isn't really suitable conversation for the museum? Or anywhere." She made herself stop talking.

Tension poured from his body. "Tell me, Edwina." There was a slight pause. "Please."

Please.

Edwina closed her eyes.

Why must he do that? It was easier to stand firm when he was gruff and demanding, but time and time again, he revealed himself to be a man both gentle and tender.

Her whole career had been predicated on a lie about her very life, her birthright. She'd clung to those secrets, knowing they were all that kept her from ruin, and the same scandalous fate her mother had known. As such, she wrestled with herself, warring . . . and ultimately sharing. "He is the Earl of Blakeney." She paused. "He is . . . my brother."

And yet, as Rafe's jaw went slack, and more questions rose in his gaze, there was something so very freeing in Edwina having, at last, made that admission. "Your . . ."

"Brother," she said. "He is my brother." And yet, they weren't really siblings. Not in any sense of the word. Not as Rafe was with Cailin and Hunter and Wesley.

"You are the daughter of an earl," he said slowly, in the way of one who'd been handed the pieces of a puzzle and then tasked with the assignment of putting them into their proper place.

"No." Because that wasn't quite right. "I am the daughter of a marquess." She scrabbled with her skirts before she realized the distracted actions her fingers had taken on. And before her courage deserted her, she spoke her truth. "The *illegitimate* daughter." And yet, even that was the prettiest way of dressing up what she was . . . when he had only ever been blunt and honest. "I am a bastard," she said softly. At last, saying it to another person.

Rafe's jaw slackened. "What?"

"My mother made the mistake of falling in love with a man who was married. She gave up her place in society so that she could be with him, in any way." Accepting meager scraps of a man, in a way that Edwina had never been able to understand.

And she braced for dread and terror to come crashing down with that revelation. It had been the greatest fear she'd carried, that after having left Leeds to create her own life that someone would discover who she was. *What* she was.

Only, that fear . . . did not come. But . . . then perhaps it was because this wasn't just *any* person. Along the way, somewhere, Rafe Audley had come to mean so very much to her.

Instead, there was a buoyant lightness that suffused her breast, and lifted her up, and brought her lips curling at the corners. And with Rafe stunned into silence, she left him there . . . alone with her secret. At last, she'd shared the truth about her birthright.

Edwina was no longer a lie. Her life wasn't. And she'd been forthright with Rafe.

She was free.

Chapter 21

As a boy working in the coalfields, Rafe would return home, hang up his cap, and head to the kitchen. Ofttimes he'd worked beside his mother. Most of the time he'd work in the kitchen alone. When the coalfields represented uncertainty and peril at every turn, baking and cooking in the kitchen had offered a calm predictability that he'd craved. His sister hadn't understood his fascination. His brothers had just welcomed anything other than Cailin's cooking.

But in the kitchen, everything made sense. If a man followed a recipe, there were no mistakes. Everything went precisely to plan, and that constancy was a luxury no miner who risked his life in the fields was afforded.

In time, the kitchen had come to be a refuge of sorts.

This particular evening, however, with the duke's household abed, and turbulent emotion haunting Rafe still, calm proved elusive.

Frantically stirring the flour and yeast, he slogged through the slightly too-thick mixture. Any other time, he'd be able to focus on just what the recipe required. And how to adjust the ingredients from sight and feel alone.

Quitting his efforts, Rafe stared vacantly into the bowl.
She was illegitimate.

A bastard like him.

And when that admission from Edwina should have
united them, somehow it had driven a wedge between them.

She had *let* it become a wedge between them. He drove
the bottom of his spoon into the thick mixture several times,
splattering bits of dough onto the table, and onto his face.

Leaning his cheek into his shoulder, he wiped those remnants from his cheek.

Since her revelation in the British Museum gallery that
afternoon, Edwina had gone out of her way to avoid him.
And he hated it. He hated that she hadn't shared that with
him, when she knew so much about him and his life. But
more? He hated this divide. And that it had come . . . from
this? From her sharing the truth about her birthright? A
birthright that was no different than his. And for the regret
that had held him in its grip since she'd thrown up this barrier, there was . . . resentment, too. That she, who'd been bold
and unapologetic at every turn, should hide from him. He—

Once again, Rafe stilled. He felt her presence, before he
saw her.

Of course she'd be here. They were alike, even in this.
Where they found their peace. How they sought their calm.

He glanced up.

Edwina hovered at the doorway.

Hovered, when she'd only ever been bold with her forward steps.

Still attired in the same bright garments she'd worn at
the museum, the violet hue of her dress was a juxtaposition
of cheer in the shadowed kitchen.

She dampened her mouth, those lips he'd kissed, and
longed to kiss again.

For a moment, he expected she'd leave.

But then, she entered the room, joining him at the table,
taking up a place directly beside him.

*Say something . . . Speak like the glorious magpie you
are.* Only, as Rafe resumed stirring his dough, she kept si-

lent. From the moment she'd come hurtling across the coal-fields, waving her silly parasol to gain his attention, he'd lamented her endless chattering. Only to learn too late, with her now terse and laconic, just how very much he'd enjoyed her endless stream of talking.

Had he ever truly been annoyed with her prattling? What a damned fool he'd been, finding out now, too late, just how damned much he loved it, and now missed it.

Wordlessly, Edwina picked up a wooden spoon, and dipping it into the bowl of water, she sprinkled some drops into the mixture.

Rafe and Edwina continued that way, working silently. Even with no words flowing between them, they remained lockstep in harmony, with Edwina adding the remaining ingredients he'd set out.

All the while, from the corner of his eye, he continued to steal glances her way.

Look at me. He willed her to do so. And yet, since they'd returned, she'd continued to evade Rafe, even when with him.

She added a pinch of salt, and Rafe mixed it into the dough.

Very well, the roles had shifted, and he found himself in the unlikely role of the talkative one of their pair. "It is an impressive oven, is it not?"

And just like that, they found their way again.

Her eyes lit upon the stove. "I've visited many kitchens, and in all the households, I've never seen a Rumford one before."

No, neither Rafe nor Edwina would have. Cleverly designed, but enormous in their size, only the finest kitchens would have been capable of holding one.

"And I trust, incredibly efficient."

She scoffed. "Oh, undoubtedly."

Rafe and Edwina shared a smile, and some of the tension he'd carried that day left him. Adding the dough to the individual pans, he collected two, with Edwina grabbing the others, and carrying them over to the stove, they slid them inside.

They set to work tidying the table, with Rafe stacking the mixing bowls, while Edwina ran a wet rag over the surface of the table, cleaning up around him. "You weren't at dinner," he remarked.

Edwina paused. "No." She resumed scrubbing the table, this time harder.

"And is there a reason you didn't come?" he pressed, when she still didn't speak, urging her on to dialogue. "After all, I thought you would welcome that final preparation before the duke's formal gathering," he added, tossing her way the one thing she'd never been able to resist, the opportunity to discuss his lessons.

"You proved yourself capable on the topic of formal dining." Edwina didn't so much as lift her head from the now nearly immaculately cleaned table. "As such, I didn't feel I could offer any further tutelage that might benefit you."

She'd not thought she could offer him anything? How could she be . . . so casual? With her actions in this moment, and in her words?

Well, he'd wanted her there. And he'd wanted her to want to be there. And not because of her assignment, either. Which was preposterous, as she'd indicated at every turn that was the most important thing between them.

Perhaps that was why what she'd shared today . . . hurt in ways it shouldn't. That she'd kept that detail about her past from him. Something that had been a bond she'd known of, but kept to herself. And it was petty and small to be resentful. Or, for that matter, to even care.

But he did.

Rafe rested a hand on Edwina's long fingers, staying her distracted efforts.

She stiffened.

"You thought we wouldn't speak more of it?" he asked gently. That he would simply let go of all talk of her parentage?

With a ragged sigh, she sank onto the long, narrow bench. "I didn't really think anything else needed to be said." She twisted the damp rag in her fingers, her white-knuckled grip betraying the sense of calm she evinced.

And his heart ached at this new side of Edwina, vulnerable in ways he'd never before known her to be.

Slowly, Rafe sat beside her, their knees and shoulders kissing, and because of that nearness he felt it all, the tension that went through her lithe frame, the rigidity of her arm against his, the tightening of her leg.

Rafe angled his head so he might see her. "Why didn't you tell me?" he asked finally, getting to the heart of what she still wouldn't speak freely about.

Edwina's features pulled, and she shook her head. "It . . . didn't seem worth mentioning?" She directed that answer at the rag in her hands.

"It didn't seem worth mentioning?" he asked incredulously. And he couldn't hold back the resentment that she'd not trusted him enough.

A sound of frustration escaped her, and she stormed to her feet, forcing him to crane his head back to meet her gaze. "If I had told you, Rafe, you would have simply thought I was using my past as a way to a false bond between us."

It wouldn't have been false.

But was she wrong in thinking he would have been cynical in questioning why she'd shared what she had? Instead, she'd kept her secret close.

"I thought we'd become friends, enough that you trusted me more than that."

"What would you have me say?" she demanded on a harsh whisper. Edwina bit at her lower lip, but not before he caught the slight tremble of that flesh. "You thought I should . . . tell you that how after my mother died, I went to my father and asked to be part of his life, and he rejected me?"

He winced. "No."

"How I arrived from Leeds where I was taunted for being a bastard, every day of my life, and thought that he could offer me a new beginning?"

Oh, God. Every word was a lash. For as cruel as the world had been, he'd never been the object of shame. *And mayhap that was why you were so afraid to give in and come here? Perhaps you feared that after a lifetime being respected, you'd be reduced to someone who was scorned.* "I didn't know . . ." he said dumbly, his words empty. Because of course he'd not known.

"Or should I have told you how when I arrived in London, he wouldn't even meet me but instead sent his son to offer me money to never come back?" Tears filled her eyes, but she gave them an angry swipe, refusing them purchase on her cheeks. "Of how I refused it and demanded references from him instead, about my suitability as a governess, so that I might fashion myself a respectable life."

His admiration only swelled, and yet, she'd been forced to build a future based on her family's rejection. "Oh, Edwina," he said hoarsely; her words, and the hurt behind them, left him splayed open and aching for her. God, how he wanted to destroy the man who'd sired her, who'd left her at the mercy of a merciless world. He immediately stood, reaching for her.

She backed away, and angled her chin up. Proud as the princess he'd called her from the start. "I do *not* want your pity or scorn," she said, fire burning from her eyes. "I did what I had to do."

Pity? Scorn? That was what she believed he could feel after everything she'd shared? "I would never pity you," he said slowly, more than half-afraid if he moved too quickly, she'd flee . . . and this time would keep running until she was gone, and he was left only with the memory of her. "Admire you. Appreciate your resourcefulness. But never pity." Not for her. It was an impossibility.

She eyed him warily.

"How could you think I would not keep your secret." He fisted his hands at his side, hating that she'd never felt she could trust him. "That I would somehow use it *against* you?" he asked in a whisper laced with as much hurt as anger.

And what was worse than any answer was the confirmation he detected in her revealing eyes even before she spoke. "I coerced you into coming, which was wrong." She added that latter part on a rush. "And I do trust you. I respect you.

I l—" his ears pricked up at that lone syllable she immediately cut herself off from speaking. "Like to think that you would not have," she finished, his chest deflating oddly when those words were not the ones he'd . . . thought she intended. "But neither could I be certain that revealing . . . my secret would be safe, because there is no certainty with anything, and I don't have the luxury of trusting in anything."

How optimistic and sunny and cheerful he'd always found her, only to find, deep inside, she was as scarred and as scared as he was.

Thrumming with a volatile energy, he slid his focus over the top of her head. She really didn't know him. That she could have believed him capable of destroying her with the circumstances of her birth, a situation beyond her control and one that he knew firsthand? *But then, what reasons have you given her to trust you?* That voice taunted him with the reminder. He'd been uncouth from the start, and contentious the whole way, only peppering in moments of kindness between. Why, her rooms had even been destroyed because of him. "I'm sorry I didn't give you reason enough to trust me," he said quietly, and truthfully.

"Oh, Rafe. It isn't just that. Wasn't just that," she amended. "It wasn't really about you." Edwina hugged her arms close in a sad-looking, lonely little embrace. "I do not have the ability to . . . to . . . talk of those things"—her bastardy—"the same as you. Not in the ways you can. You have support and you have protection should you so wish to take it from your father. And then, if you don't? If you'd allow pride to come before all? You'll still have a future in Staffordshire that is safe and secure. It doesn't matter if people judge you." It mattered if people, however, judged her. She brought her gaze back to meet his. "I would be ruined, and I'd never recover."

Nay, she'd be on the streets, some wealthy man's mistress, and hatred ate him up alive in that moment even thinking of the imagined man who'd use her so.

He cupped her shoulders and ran his thumbs over the

satiny soft skin of her upper arms, in a smoothing, soothing little circle. "Your secret is mine, and it always would have been safe."

"Now you know," Edwina said softly. She lifted her chin a notch. "I *am* a bastard, and so I can now be free in telling you this: I know the gift you've been given, Rafe," she said, her voice creeping up a pitch. "I know because it was the one I wanted." She pressed a fist hard against her breast. "And one I will never, ever, ever have and to see you throw it away, and choose a life of toil and strife for you and your siblings is not something I can ever, ever understand, because I would do anything," her voice broke on a little sob that ravaged him, her pain was his, in that moment, the intensity of it stabbing like a thousand knives as she looked away in a bid to maintain her pride. "I would do anything to have my father acknowledge me."

And now, so much made sense. She made so much sense. Why it had been so important that Rafe accepted the olive branch his father had offered. Not because of rank or power, but because he'd been given that which she'd been searching for.

He brought a palm up, cupping her cheek, and it was though his touch calmed her, for the frantic rush of words falling from her lips ended on a shuddering little sigh as she pressed her eyes closed.

"Your father never deserved a daughter such as you. You are better without one such as him in your life."

"Perhaps." A sad, watery smile trembled on her lips, and he stroked that flesh with his finger. "But not safer."

No. Not safer. And it was why she'd been so resolute in her goal to succeed in the duke's mission for her and Rafe. Because her future had always been dependent upon Rafe coming to London, but also upon succeeding at the task— an impossible one at that—the duke had thrown her way.

He knew that now. At last, he understood.

Rafe continued to move his finger in a light stroke over her generous lower lip . . . when something shifted in this moment, the energy, everything around them.

Her lashes fluttered, but not before he caught the blaze of passion spark to life in her hazel irises.

"You should go," he said gruffly. *Release her. Stop touching her.* Because this, his hunger for her, was not what this moment was about.

Edwina caught his hand, trapping him there, holding him close. "I don't want to leave," she whispered.

He swallowed hard. "You don't know what you're saying." She didn't know what he wanted to do to her . . . with her in this moment.

"I do. I'm a woman who knows my mind, and what I'm saying, and what I want. And what I want, Rafe, is you."

Edwina's heart hammered, under the enormity of the words she'd uttered.

And more, the weight behind them. The truth *of* them.

In this moment, having shared the most secret parts of herself with Rafe Audley, she wanted to share every part of herself with him. She wanted to give herself to him, and take from him. Soon she would go, and he would remain here, part of this new world, and she would have this piece of him to take with her.

His thick, dark lashes swept down, and he swept his hooded gaze over her face.

And tiring of his restraint and honor, she wrapped her arms about his neck, and drawing herself up, she kissed him.

He stilled; the corded muscles of his chest and arms rippled.

And then his mouth met hers with a wild, wicked intensity that matched her own, and she moaned, welcoming this kiss she had so craved.

His tongue lashed against hers, a hot brand that she teased and tasted. Dueling with him.

Catching her thigh, he drew her leg up around his waist, so her gown climbed high, and the night air slapped at her skin, the cool a balm upon her heated skin. And moaning, she rubbed herself against him, her actions and those naughty sounds spilling from her mouth and into his adding a heightened layer to her desire.

"You want this again," he rasped.

His wasn't a question, and yet, neither was he correct. Not in his entirety. "I want more than that." She lifted her eyes to his. "I want all of you."

His eyes darkened, and then he smashed his mouth over hers again, as he was consuming her, once more. His kiss raw. Primal. Gathering both of her legs, he guided them up about his waist, and she wrapped them about him. Their bodies flush as they were, with his trousers and her flimsy dress the only barrier between them, she felt his rigid shaft against her center, and moaned desperately, pushing herself against him.

How very good he felt.

So very good.

The table met the backs of her legs, and she gave silent thanks for that sturdy oak that kept her up. That, and Rafe, whose mouth never lost contact with hers. She lifted her hips, rocking them forward in a bid to ease that aching need for him.

And yet, with each thrust of her hips, that hungering only grew, more desperate, more acute.

Then, he reached down, and finding the opening in her chemise, he cupped her mound.

She keened his name over and over again into his mouth. Sweat beaded on her brow, and slipped down her cheeks, as he rubbed her in a wicked caress that taunted as much as it tempted.

"You deserve more than a cold kitchen for your first time," he rasped, honor warring with desire.

"Don't presume to tell me what I should want, Rafe Audley," Edwina panted, undulating her hips. "I need more," she begged, biting her lower lip. She wanted more. That taste of passion he'd gifted her in Staffordshire, she hungered to taste again.

And then he answered her pleas. God, how he listened. Rafe slipped a finger inside her channel, and a hiss ex-

ploded from her teeth; her legs moved convulsively as he
stroked her. Each glide of that long digit, within her shamefully wet, tight channel a piece of magic. He rubbed her,
teasing her nub. Caressing that little pleasure button.

"Do you like that, love?" he rasped in that harsh, demanding baritone, against her neck.

He bit at her flesh, suckling, and she squeezed her eyes
shut. "I love it," she panted, her profession ending on a long
moan as he increased his movements within her. *I love you.*
I love you. It was a litany within her head, made all the more
powerful by being in his arms, and being loved by him now.

He removed his hand, and she wept at that loss, pushing
her hips up, silently begging him to fill that void once more.

But he was only lowering her onto the table, and then
grabbing his jacket, he set it down beside them. Lifting her
up slightly, Rafe guided her onto the makeshift bed offered
by that wool garment. Then, as he came down over her,
Rafe freed himself from his trousers, and the glow cast by
the hearth and lent support by the moon's light flickering
through the lead windowpanes allowed her to drink in the
sight of him. Long and thick and possessed of a ridged
crown, his shaft jutted out almost angrily, amid a patch of
black curls, reaching for her.

And she curved her hand about him, feeling him as
she'd longed to for so long.

Silk that had been set afire; it burned her skin, and drew
a long groan from Rafe's lips that contained her name:
"Edwina."

"Do you like that?" she teased, as he had her. For she
already knew with Eve's intuition. She continued to stroke
him, the glide of her hand growing bolder and smoother,
and he surged, pulsing and throbbing within her palm.

With a growl, he adjusted himself over her, shifting so
that he lay between her legs, and the head of his shaft
probed her entry. With a desperate little whimper, she
wrapped her legs about him, and followed where he led,
undulating wildly, begging him with her body, as words
had failed her, to give her this. All of this.

Just this once.

Except, as he slid himself inside her, slowly, inch by agonizing inch, stretching her walls, until all she wanted was for him to fill her fully, she knew that this would never be enough. That she wanted— "More," she pleaded.

Sweat beaded his brow, and he clenched his eyes tight, as if that slow glide was even more pleasurable for him, which was impossible. Nothing could be better than this. Than this moment. Than they two together.

Then, he reached that slight barrier, and stopped.

No!

She moaned her outrage. "Make love to me," she whispered harshly against his ear, and then opening his eyes, Rafe scraped a harsh, passion-filled gaze over her face.

"Forgive me," he whispered, and taking her mouth under his, he thrust.

There came a slight pressure, uncomfortable but insignificant next to the hungering inside her. Wrapping her arms about him, she tangled her tongue with his and moved, urging him with both her mouth and the undulation of her hips to continue.

And then he was. Withdrawing slowly, he teased her as he drew himself from her drenched channel and then entered her. Again and again. Grunting, she lifted her hips to take his every thrust. To meet it. Demanding more, and more. "Raaaafe," she moaned, squeezing endless syllables into his name, as her body pulsed and thrummed, and the pressure built. That wicked, wonderful pressure that bordered on pleasure and excruciating pain, the one she knew.

She knew because of this man. Because he'd shown her that bliss.

And she wanted that, and so much more with him.

Edwina's movements became more frenzied, so that she had no control over the jerky flex of her hips, and then she froze, and went hurtling over that magnificent precipice; an explosion of light burst behind her eyes, pure and white and blinding, as she screamed her release to the high ceiling overhead.

His movements grew frantic, less coordinated, and his breathing dissolved to ragged, primitive gasps and groans, and then with a shout he withdrew, letting his seed fall in a shimmery, translucent arc on the floor beside them.

All the while he came, she stroked the tight, tense lines of his face.

And then he collapsed atop her, just catching himself on his elbows.

Edwina wrapped her arms about him; his breath came fast and quick, like her own. And she held him. A dazed, contented smile played on her lips. This would be enough.

It had to be.

Chapter 22

The following evening, Edwina found herself living in a moment she'd never thought to know—at last, she moved among the peerage: in a grand, golden drawing room, of a duke and duchess, and marquess and marchioness, no less.

Granted, she was not an equal member. Not truly. She'd not, however, ever really thought to be included that way. Working among the peerage, however? That had been the most she had hoped for, in what had come to seem like an impossible dream.

Only to find how little she'd ever really known about dreams. The slight discomfort between her legs as she moved, however, proved a wicked and wanton reminder of that stolen moment she'd known with him.

With Rafe.

Her heart danced and fluttered as it always did from the mere thought of him. As the companion on the fringe of the festivities, not really part of the event beyond the role of an elevated servant, she was free to watch him.

And since he'd entered the drawing room a quarter of an hour earlier, she'd done just that.

Moving comfortably among the guests, he may as well have been born to this life. And the lightness that came in watching him wasn't pride at any accomplishment she was responsible for, but rather . . . joy. It came from the happiness in witnessing Rafe so at ease, so comfortable in the presence of his father, and the duke's wife, and the marquess, the marchioness, and their three daughters and son, who rounded out the esteemed company for the night.

Of course, she hadn't had so very much to do with it. None at all. Yes, she'd managed to get him to come here, but that had really been the extent of her assistance. His late mother had fully prepared him for just this moment, and she knew he'd never needed her.

Nay, Edwina's happiness came in knowing . . . he was going to be just fine, that he would succeed, and because of that, he'd be spared from the unkindness that was such a part of Polite Society. That was such a part of any society, really.

Standing beside the duke's esteemed guest, the Marquess of Tweeddale and his son, Rafe proved taller, noticeably more muscular, and a king among lesser men. And last night, he had been hers. Her mouth went dry, and she knew propriety said she was supposed to feel shamed and embarrassed for it, but she was incapable of feeling anything than the ache that formed between her legs at the memory of what they had shared last evening.

As if he felt her stare, Rafe glanced across the room, and his eyes found hers.

Edwina's heart jumped as it always did when he looked her way. They shared a smile, and she sighed softly. How very different that smile was, how much less strained and tense and how very natural and—

A tall, distinguished figure slid into her path, shattering the moment, and she gasped. "Your Grace!" She promptly sank into a curtsy, lowering her head in a bid to conceal the fact that she'd been just then, and really all night, openly ogling the gentleman's son.

And yet, by the warm smile he wore, he appeared obliv-

ious to Edwina's singular focus on Rafe this evening. Because surely he wouldn't be smiling so if he knew just how
head over heels she'd fallen for his son. But then a solemn
mask fell over his face, driving his lips back down at the
corner, and her stomach muscles clenched. "Miss Dalrymple."

"Your Grace," she repeated and then bit the inside of her
cheek, as she'd already greeted him by his title. As she
rambled when she was uneasy, and always revealed more
than she ought.

"Miss Dalrymple, I had the opportunity to observe you
working with my son," Oh, God. He had. Her mouth went
dry. She'd not known. Because she'd been so focused on
Rafe, and only Rafe, that the whole world melted away when
they were together.

"Did you, Your Grace?" she said with a calm she didn't
know how she found within herself.

"Indeed."

Just that: *indeed*.

She tried to make herself breathe evenly, as her mind
raced to recall every detail of that particular lesson. Had she
been overly familiar? Likely so. As she was always overly
familiar with Rafe. They had been from the start.

Edwina stole a sideways peek at Rafe's father. The duke
had his gaze directed out on Rafe, who was conversing still
with the marquess and the older gentleman's son. She
searched for some hint that he knew the level of intimacy
that had formed between her and Rafe, and yet could see . . .
nothing. He was a duke, in perfect control of his emotions
and thoughts.

"I was . . . concerned some," he murmured, and Edwina's stomach roiled.

Oh, God, what had he seen?

"My son was . . ."

What? She silently screamed, alternately wanting with
an urgency the remainder of his response, and never wanting to know the remainder of that unfinished sentence.

". . . not entirely cooperative."

Edwina blinked slowly. *Cooperative?* And a giddy laugh built in her chest that she just managed to suppress. This is what he wished to speak with her about?

"In fact, he appeared quite difficult." He slanted a look her way. "I trust you have met much of that resistance from him along the way."

She tensed. To respond felt like a betrayal of her time with Rafe, and yet, her time with Rafe had only been a product of the duke who'd hired her, and therefore, the gentleman, as her employer, expected and was entitled to answers.

A small smile formed on the duke's lips. "You needn't answer that. That was more of a statement based on my own interactions with Rafe, and observations of you and he together."

"I trust a man as proud as Mr. Audley would never appreciate outside interference in his life. We are both guilty of that," she murmured, and there would have been a time when she'd have never dared utter such a bold challenge to an employer, let alone a duke. But in her time with Rafe, she'd come to appreciate she was entitled to a voice.

"No, you are correct on that score," the duke said, still watching his son, appearing so very comfortable as he spoke to Lord Tweeddale. "And yet . . ." At last, he moved his focus to Edwina, and she stiffened. ". . . he is not rude or discourteous now. He is . . . very much at home here."

Very much at home. How she wished that for Rafe. Whether he would ever feel that way about this place, she did not know, but she knew the duke was correct . . . his son moved with an effortless grace among the *ton*.

"That is a credit to you, Miss Dalrymple," the duke said quietly, cutting into her musings.

"Oh, no," she said, quickly shaking her head. Perhaps at another time she would have been so disingenuous as to accept that credit from such a lofty patron, and yet it wouldn't be honest, and it wouldn't be fair to the one truly responsible. "Though appreciative of your praise, I . . . cannot in good conscience claim it. Ra . . ." No, that was not who he was to her. At least not outside the privacy of their own interactions. "Mr. Audley was already in possession of most of the skills you tasked me with seeing to. His mother properly instructed him. As such—"

"You do not do yourself enough credit, Miss Dalrymple."

"It would not be genuine to let you assume I'm responsible for something I'm not."

"How very admirable."

Or stupid.

"Tell me, you claim he . . . came to you prepared. Do you believe him ready to face a ballroom, filled with guests?"

"Yes," she said automatically. "I do not doubt it. In addition to his being a proficient dancer, he is also . . . comfortable with anyone, able to converse on all topics, and well aware of that which is suitable, and not, in discourse." There was nothing Rafe could not do.

"Yes, he is . . . very comfortable here. Isn't he?" the duke murmured, and there was such raw emotion in the gaze he had trained on his son, a display of sentimentality and pride she'd have never expected a duke to reveal to anyone, let alone her, a servant in his employ.

"Indeed," she added, even though she didn't believe he truly expected an answer. Rafe moved with an ease that students she'd instructed for years hadn't managed. There was a natural grace and confidence to all he did. As if to illustrate that very point, laughter went up across the room at something that Rafe had said. Lord Tweeddale patted an also-laughing Rafe on the back. And her breath hitched at the sight of him, so comfortable. Fully immersed.

He belonged . . .

The evidence of that should only fill her with the same that she'd found when she'd arrived to the drawing room. Instead, there was this overwhelming urge . . . to cry. Because it was apparent and clear that she was no longer needed. She'd known as much. Now, however, the duke did, too.

And yet, mayhap that was for the best? Because the longer she stayed here with Rafe, the more lost she became, and the more her heart beat for him.

And then, it was as though fate sought to taunt her for those yearnings as the duchess escorted one of the marquess's daughters over to Rafe.

Edwina's body went absolutely stock-still, the muscles of her face frozen to the point of pain, as she stood on the side, an observer to that introduction. The young woman, with her thick blonde curls and perfect, pale pallor, epitomized English gentility. And where Edwina was tall and gangly, there was a delicate lushness to the lady's frame that was all voluptuous beauty, and it was a physical effort Edwina exerted to not give in to the tears, once more, threatening. For, as Rafe bowed over her hand, gracing the lady's gloved knuckles with a kiss, there could be no doubting the intentions Rafe's family had for him. Or the ones the nameless lady's family had for her. Oh, God.

Just then, mid-conversation, Rafe looked across the room and his gaze landed on Edwina. He smiled, wholly oblivious to his father standing beside her, just as her heart was oblivious to that presence, too; instead, that organ in her chest was aware only of the effects Rafe Audley had on her. Then he returned his attention to whatever it was the duchess just then said to him.

"He . . . likes you," the duke remarked, without inflection.

Not this. "Your Grace?" she ventured hesitantly.

"My son will barely speak to me, and certainly won't take advice from me. Not that I expect him to. But I see that he listens to you."

"Oh, you are mistaken. Mr. Audley is a man who knows his own mind, and I am just . . . just . . ." She floundered, searching about for some explanation of what exactly her relationship was with Rafe.

"And you are *just* underestimating your role and influence," he said gently, and it was those kindly tones that served as proof that he still had no idea that she was hopelessly and helplessly in love with his son. For if he was, he'd not be speaking to Edwina so. For that matter, he would have had her belongings packed up for her, and loaded her in his carriage away from this place, and his cherished son. "He is . . . better for you."

Better for her?

No. She, because of him. But she'd only brought him around to doing something that went against his moral grain. Who Rafe was, was entirely because of him.

She was saved from having to talk any further about the man she loved, with the man who employed her, by the appearance of the butler and the summons to dinner.

Following a five-course meal, with the duke and duchess's esteemed guests, Rafe found himself with the shocking discovery . . . that the engagement hadn't been so very awful at all. He'd expected the cut direct. But the men whom he'd spoken to were not only lords, but gentlemen who possessed business ventures.

And yet, as surprisingly well as the evening had gone, there was one particular aspect that he'd despised with every fiber of his being—the placements based on rank and title that saw him at the head, nearer his father, and Edwina somewhere at the lower middle, removed from him, and relegated to the bottom of the guests.

Even so, throughout it, he had watched her unabashedly, unable to look away; she sat like a queen. Perfectly at ease, and comfortable as she conversed with Lord Tweeddales's youngest son and daughter. And the resentment he'd felt that night came from Rafe's inability to be there.

Until the ladies and gentlemen separated after the evening meal, and came together once more, in the parlor.

She tensed at his approach. "You should not be here," she murmured, her lips barely moving, her gaze on Lady Elizabeth at the pianoforte.

"That's rot. Of course I can." And Rafe rested a shoulder against the wall, indicating he'd no plans to leave.

"No. No, you cannot. I'm not company, Mr. Audley."

He narrowed his eyes. "Don't 'Mr. Audley' me, Edwina."

"And don't put me in the position of being caught speaking to you, using one another's Christian names in front of company." There was something slightly desperate and pleading there that, coupled with the worry in her eyes, indicated the depth of her unease.

"I don't care what they say."

"Well, I have to care."

He started, as that matter-of-fact deliverance lodged an arrow steeped in logic through the place that had been so consumed with his need to see her. "You spoke to the duke, the marquess, and as you are my," he placed his lips nearer her ear, "instructor, I trust it is not unexpected that we might speak."

Her lips formed a tight line. She wanted him gone. And . . . he hated that she did, as much as he hated the hurt that caused.

"How have I done?" he asked, as the chords of Lady Elizabeth's playing filled the room, mingling with the quiet discussions also taking place.

And this time, Edwina's features softened, and she looked at him. "You have done splendidly, and it is, as I said to your father, no credit to me."

"You're wrong," he murmured. "If it weren't for you, I wouldn't even be here."

"And . . . have you given more thought to whether you might stay?"

He tensed. Would he stay? "Is that my father asking?" he asked, unable to keep his lip from pulling.

"No," she said gently. "That is I, wondering as your friend."

A friend. "Is that what we are?" he murmured, working his gaze over her face. "Friends."

Edwina glanced briefly down at her slippers. "Are we not?"

Friends . . . and lovers.

And what of more . . . ?

His mind balked and screeched at the question whispering around there. "Yes," he allowed himself to say, owning the truth in that. "I rather think we are." Rafe winked.

He and Edwina shared a smile, and just like that, he

broke through her guard, and she was restored to the cheerful young woman always at ease around him.

"Will you play?"

"Regale them with more of my bawdy tavern songs?" Edwina waggled her eyebrows. "Oh, they'd be quite scandalized. I fear I'd never work again," she said, recalling her as she'd been, wildly dancing and singing before the coalfield miners at the inn, startled a laugh from him.

A number of stares came their way, and then returned to Lady Elizabeth.

Biting back laughter, Rafe and Edwina stole a secretive glance at one another, that intimate moment they shared adding to the sense of connection.

"You are going to find me in trouble, Mr. Audley."

"Hardly," he scoffed. "Why, imagine what would be said about you if you were. Everyone would take you for an inattentive companion who failed to place sufficient effort into her errant charge's tutelage."

"Oh, undoubtedly," she said with mock solemnity, before giving in to another laugh, this one quiet and controlled, and as he looked at her, her cheeks entrancingly flushed and her eyes bright, Rafe's breath lodged in his chest as he stared, captivated. And he didn't want her to have to hide her amusement. Or them to shield their enjoyment together, as if it was a tawdry secret to be kept close and protected. He wanted . . . His chest tightened.

"What?" she whispered, her smile fading. "Why are you looking at me like that?"

"I don't . . . know." He wasn't really certain of anything in that moment.

"There you are, Rafe!"

They looked up as the duchess approached with the marquess's eldest daughter, Lady Elizabeth, on her arm.

Rafe swallowed a curse.

Edwina, however, was polite, and perfectly composed as she sank into a deep curtsy. "Your Grace," she murmured, melting into the shadows.

"Miss Dalrymple, a pleasure," the duchess returned.

Edwina dropped one more curtsy before slipping off . . . leaving Rafe, the duchess, and Lady Elizabeth alone. Rafe's mouth tensed, and he stared after her, wanting to call her back, not because he feared the duchess's company, but because he wanted Edwina there, still. Since the museum, since she'd shared everything she had, they'd forged a bond that he didn't want to break. Now, he watched as she moved along, hugging the perimeter of the room, part of the evening's festivities . . . but not really. Ever careful not to step too close.

Even as she deserved to be there.

Even as he wanted her to be fully part of it . . . with him.

Chapter 23

The following evening, seated at the mahogany secretaire in her guest chambers, Edwina closed her notes on Rafe Audley.

Her work here was nearly done.

Tonight, Rafe had entered the duke's ballrooms, presented before all of society as the Duke of Bentley's son . . . and Edwina had not been there for the moment. She'd not be there for any of it.

Because that had never been her place.

Everything had just become confused where she'd felt closer to Rafe, and it had felt right to be with him, at his side . . . as his friend. And lover.

But that had never really been her place. Not truly. She'd always been a servant to his rank of cherished son—even if he hadn't believed himself valued by the duke. He was. And she, as a mere servant, had no place wanting . . . that which she desperately wanted.

Him.

I want him.

Tears filled her eyes, and with a groan, she picked her

notebook up and hit herself lightly across the forehead. What had she done? She'd gone and lost herself completely to the last man she ought.

A knock sounded at her door, and she instantly lowered her book to her lap. Puzzling her brow, she stared at the doorway, almost believing she'd imagined that soft rapping. Because who would be there for her?

There was no one who would seek her out . . .

Rap-rap-rap.

This knock came harder, firmer, more decisive.

Her heart knocking furiously against her ribcage, Edwina hurried to her feet, the chair scraping the floor, as she hurried across the room.

No one would be looking for her. She grabbed the panel and drew the door open. Except—

"Oh." Rafe's sister stared back. Not Rafe.

Cailin blinked slowly. "Forgive me. I did not mean to be a bother."

Edwina immediately found herself. "No, forgive me. I was . . . not expecting you." Which suggested she'd been expecting another. She grimaced. "Won't you come in?" She urged the other woman inside.

Cailin hesitated, and then ventured into the guest chambers. Edwina shut the door behind them and motioned to the delicate gilded and caned *canapé* sofa near the fireplace. Rafe's sister claimed a seat and drew her legs up close to her chest and folded her arms around her knees.

Edwina claimed the Rococo-style gilt armchair near Rafe's sister.

There was a time when Edwina would have filled this moment with a lesson on the proper way to sit and not sit. Every moment of every day was filled with lessons. Only to find that when one filled one's day with one's work, then the most important parts of life were lost: how another person was feeling. What they were thinking.

Until Rafe, Edwina had not thought of people in terms beyond "charges" and "employers" because, well, there'd never been anyone in her life beyond her mother. And after her mother had died quickly of a wasting illness, there'd been only people whom she worked with and for in Edwina's life. Until this family that had become so very important to her . . . for reasons entirely divorced from her assignment.

Now, she took in, not the manner in which the lady held herself, but what the lady said, along with how she did: her troubled gaze directed toward the lit fire, as she rubbed her chin back and forth in a distracted pattern.

Edwina gave the young woman several moments of that silence she clearly needed, before encouraging her to speak. "What is it, Cailin?"

"My brother insists I would never want a London Season. Both of them," she clarified, and fell quiet once more.

"Yes, that does sound like the both of them," Edwina said dryly, diffusing the tension. They shared a smile. Edwina drew her chair closer to Cailin's. "What about what you want?"

Rafe's sister wrinkled her nose. "Well, I was so very certain that a Season was the last thing I wanted. I did, however, wish to come to London and enjoy anonymity as I did at the museum. Seeing anything outside of Staffordshire was enough." The young lady's cheeks colored. "Not that I believe I am in any way better than Staffordshire."

"Of course not," Edwina rushed to assure her.

"But I wanted to see museums and visit parks, and escape . . ."

"Escape?" she murmured.

"My sweetheart was grievously injured in the coalfields, and whenever I am there, that is what I see." Cailin averted her face, but before she did, Edwina caught the way it buckled in grief. This was why Rafe had agreed to come to London, against all his wishes . . . not only for Hunter, but for the woman before him. And Edwina fell in love with him all over again for that sacrifice, even as her heart simultaneously broke at the sight of Cailin's suffering. "But what I found . . . is that it doesn't go away," Cailin said, when she'd composed herself, and looked once more at Edwina. "He is still there. I still see him. And I will never forget him or what happened . . . no matter how the scene may change or where I live . . . but perhaps . . ." Cailin stopped herself.

"Perhaps," Edwina gently urged the other woman to complete that thought.

"Perhaps I too might experience . . . all of London, as my brother is. I know it won't be the same, as I'm a woman," she hurried to add, "and even as bastards, women are not afforded the same treatment as men."

It was an unfairness Edwina had always known.

"But mayhap because the pleasures in London are mindless, it would be wrong if I wished to take part?"

There was a question there from the younger woman, one that suggested she was hoping Edwina would confirm that opinion so Cailin might, in turn, lay to rest the wonderings she had about remaining in Town.

"No woman, nor man, should be made to apologize for wanting to experience life, and one certainly shouldn't make apologies for whatever pleasure one finds in it."

In that moment, it was hard to say whether Edwina's quietly spoken words were for the young woman before her . . . or for Edwina herself.

Cailin smiled. "Thank you. I thought I might . . . steal a glimpse of the evening's festivities. Will you join me?"

The proper governess within her said absolutely not, and strengthened that declination with a lengthy list of all the reasons it would be wrong to do so. The new person she'd become wanted to go. She wanted to see what Cailin saw . . . but for altogether different reasons.

Rafe.

To see how he fared, and what this world looked like with him in it, when she could not actually be there.

Edwina's heart knocked hard against her chest.

She nodded.

Smiling widely, Cailin swung her feet to the floor and jumped up. "Come!" Taking Edwina by the hand, she tugged her to standing.

Still, Edwina made an attempt to talk herself and the other woman out of it. "This is inappropriate."

"Then we shall take care not to be discovered."

And so it was, some ten minutes or so later of winding their way through the sprawling household, they reached one of the alcoves that overlooked the dance floor, and Edwina's mouth dropped at the sight of it. For she had attended events before, always as a companion. But never had she set foot inside an event . . . such as this.

In fairness, she wasn't really setting a foot inside.

But that was neither here nor there.

"*My goodness.*"

Whether those words belonged to Cailin or Edwina, or to the both of them, remained unclear. The two women, however, remained united in their awe.

Crystal chandeliers crisscrossed the length of the ceiling, resplendent in long white-tapered candles; at the center, a golden one hung larger than the rest, an extravagant, elaborate piece that fair hurt the eye to look at for the gleam of the metal.

Edwina and Cailin sank to the floor, like the naughty children of her employers used to do at the country balls their parents had attended. Except, as Edwina lowered herself onto her belly, and stared between the marble slats at the swirl of vibrantly clad dancers below, she realized for the first time: mayhap they'd not been naughty. Mayhap they'd simply wished a taste of the grandeur and revelry playing out, even now.

"It doesn't . . . look so very terrible."

"No," Edwina murmured. "It doesn't." It was the insidious gossip taking place that was the real source of badness of this place.

But from up here, to a spectator above, there was only a kaleidoscope of color from the dancers sweeping across the floor, and the swell of the orchestra's chords rising above the laughter. It was a world her mother had wished to be part of . . .

Edwina cocked her head.

And me, too . . .

She'd wished to know a hint of the excitement below. Only to find she didn't want that, really. Not alone. She wanted to experience it with Rafe.

What had she thought?

More than that, what had she been thinking?

She didn't love him. She liked being with him. She liked how he challenged her and made her see the world and her role as a governess in ways she'd never before thought, but love? Surely not. Surely—

Cailin pointed. "And my brother doesn't seem to mind it so very terribly, either."

Edwina followed the young woman's gesture and froze.

He'd proven to be . . . a liar. He'd called himself proficient, and yet, even hovering above the crowd, unnoticed, unobserved, as she was, there could be no doubting or disputing that Rafe was pure magic upon his feet, confident, graceful, in possession of the intricate movements of everything from a country reel to a Viennese waltz.

As his instructor, she should be beaming with the greatest pride at his accomplishments.

"Will you stay?"

"Hmm?" she murmured distractedly; it took a moment to register the spoken question beside her. Edwina whipped her head sideways.

"I believe I shall request that London Season, after all, and I would have you there with me."

Edwina fought for a proper breath, wanting to give Cailin the confirmation she sought, and deserved. And yet . . . Tears pricked at her lashes. "I am honored." *But I cannot.*

Just as she could not bring herself to decline that offer, and steal this newfound eagerness and excitement from Rafe's sister.

Cailin's face lit up. "Splendid."

And Edwina, if possible, felt all the worse.

The young woman popped up, and then as it became apparent Edwina wasn't joining her, she wrinkled her brow.

"I'm just . . . going to stay on a bit longer. See . . ." *Your brother with another woman in his arms.* "That my instructions proved . . . helpful," she finished lamely.

Oh, God.

"You have done wonderfully by him, Edwina," the other woman said softly, her voice quietly melding with the strains of the haunting waltz below. "He is a different man because of you. You encouraged him to stretch his wings and leave a world he never would have. He smiles more." *Stop. Please, stop.* "He listens more, because of."

Because of me.

Edwina bit hard on the inside of her cheek. Despite what his sister might believe, Edwina had not really changed Rafe. He'd done everything himself. He'd never needed her here, and he'd certainly not need her when she was gone.

When Cailin had gone, Edwina made herself look out once more, searching frantically over the crowded floor and easily finding him. Taller, broader, more everything than the lords around him, he was a king among lesser men, twirling Lady Elizabeth about.

They'd never danced together, Edwina and Rafe. That was a gift this other woman now had, that Edwina never would.

Petty and small, and loving him as she did, she found herself incapable of laying mastery over the insidious jealousy eating away at her at the sight of him dancing that flawless English beauty across his father, the Duke of Bentley's gleaming Italian marble floor.

Oh, God. Edwina gave thanks for already being flat on her belly.

And this . . . watching as he waltzed and wooed and captivated as desperately and deeply as he had Edwina? She'd always known he would ultimately choose to join this world. She knew it because she knew that he'd come to see the good he was capable of with the money and power afforded him by his parentage. Long before he'd revealed he wasn't so very ignorant of Town life, she'd known he'd take to this world. Because a man such as him commanded any place or lot that he might meet. There would be a lofty lady to be his wife, a woman perfectly suited to him, and who complimented him in every way.

What she'd not imagined was that she'd be around to see it. Edwina had anticipated being long gone.

Except, mayhap that had been her own naïveté. The wish that she'd not have to witness any of it.

Just then, whatever he said to his dancing partner, the lady with perfect gold ringlets and a ready smile, brought her to laughter. Lady Elizabeth, born to her elevated rank, Edwina wanted to hate and find exception with and to, when the only thing remotely offensive about the woman was her name, and that a woman who had the name Dalrymple had even less reason to take exception with.

It marked Edwina as selfish and self-centered and petty and terrible. For loving him as she did, and wanting the best for him, she should only be overjoyed at Rafe's success and the fact that he'd met a woman who was kind and wonderful.

Only to discover, Edwina resented the woman not because she belonged to a world Edwina had thought she wished to be part of . . . but because she had the opportunity to have a life with Rafe.

And Edwina wanted to cry because of it.

And to taunt her with her misery, fate sent that pair waltzing past, the lady's gold skirts dancing wildly at her ankles, as Rafe twirled her about the ballroom floor.

A pressure squeezed at her heart.

It was too much.

Coming to her feet, she crept from the alcove. And the moment the curtains fluttered shut behind her, she broke. The music and the laughter all jumbled with her heartbeat clamoring away in her ears, in a sickening, dizzying cacophony that she needed to escape.

Edwina rushed along long corridors and continued onward, until the music faded and her heart raced, and the serenity of the duke's gardens met her.

Gasping and out of breath, she crashed through the glass double doors leading out, and drawing them shut fast behind her, she kept running and didn't stop until there was no place left to run; the marble goddess playing her lyre, guarding that ivy-covered brick wall, blocked her escape.

Edwina collapsed against it, and catching herself on the garden statue's shoulder, fought to drag air into her lungs. All these years, she'd pitied her mother. She'd not ever worried about becoming her, because Edwina had always known she was too sensible to ever do anything as foolish as fall in love . . . with anyone.

She'd been so very convinced.

And she'd also been so very wrong.

Edwina pressed her face against the cold, unforgiving marble back of the statue. "What have I *done*?" she whispered. She remained there, unable to move. And time became as jumbled as her thoughts inside.

She froze, feeling him. Sensing his presence even before he spoke.

She looked around the shoulder of the marble Greek goddess now offering Edwina her protection.

At some point, he'd found his way outside . . . to her. He was . . . magnificent. Attired in elegantly cut midnight trousers and jacket; but for the snow-white of his cravat and the slip of lawn shirt revealed, he was sin and temptation that she'd tasted of and had hungered for since. And yet, unlike her, he was completely composed, even breathed, and in full control. "R . . . Rafe." There was a slight accusation so subtle she could have easily feigned an inability to hear it. Instead, she chose the safer, more cowardly course of redirection. "Forgive me," she said straightening, still breathless. "I didn't hear you." And then came the realization . . . he was here. Not with his Lady Elizabeth. "You shouldn't be out here," she said softly, rubbing at her shoulders.

He stopped just on the other side of the statue, so close.

His hooded gaze moved over her. "I don't want to be in there."

Odd, how that was the one place she wished to be . . . and yet, there with *him*. *Not* the collection of women who were his potential brides. She drew in a breath through constricted lungs and made herself stop with what she wanted, and focused her attention and concern on where it should be—on him. "Is something wrong?"

"Yes."

She frowned. "What is it?"

"You weren't there," he said gruffly. "I want you."

Edwina's breath hitched at the possessiveness and power of that declaration. And propriety and good sense said to reject that . . . to deny him.

Soon, very soon, she would leave, and they would part ways. He'd already fit himself perfectly into this world, and would remain. She'd seen that. Just as she'd seen that there would be a lovely wife there. And Edwina could not be there when that happened, but she could take this last moment, and keep it with her forever.

"I want you," he repeated, on a harsh growl.

Her breath hitched, as desire pooled between her legs, from just those three words spoken in that guttural, harsh way. "And I want you."

They were in one another's arms, and it was impossible to say who had reached for whom first. Or mayhap it was just that they moved in tandem in this . . . and in so many ways. With a wanton moan, she melted against him, and kissed him back. She kissed him as she'd longed to.

And like all the times before, passion burned strong, and in their desire, they didn't bother with gentleness. But then, they never had. The fire between them was too great. And yet, as they ran their hands over one another, stroking and caressing, there was an even greater raw vitality to this meeting.

Her panting melded with his grunts, as he seated himself on the wrought iron bench and pulled her down atop him. Edwina's skirts rucked up in a noisy, hedonistic rustle about them, and he edged them up even higher, exposing her skin to the crisp night air, and that kiss of coolness was a balm upon her.

Never breaking contact with his mouth, she stroked her tongue against his, and he met each thrust, lightly nipping the tip of hers. Rafe reached between them, freed himself from his trousers, and then guided his length to her moist curls. She clenched her thighs as he slid inside, filling her, and unlike the first time, when there'd been a moment of pain and tension, now there was only bliss. Her eyes slid shut as she took all of him inside her, sinking all the way until he filled her, deeply. Completely.

Edwina and Rafe each caught their breath on a quick intake, and she forced her heavy lashes open.

They held one another's eyes, and she tangled her fingers through the dark strands of his hair, as he guided her hips, and she began to move. Rising and falling over him. Taking him and releasing him, again and again, their flesh slapping against one another, Edwina rode him. Harder and faster. He kneaded her hips, urging her on. The pleasure he drew from her with every stroke brought her higher and higher. She panted. It was too much. This pleasure was even more sharp, more consuming than the time before. "Rafffe," she pleaded. Burying her face against his neck, she bit his shoulder hard; the bergamot scent clinging to that fine wool filled her senses.

"That's it, love," he urged, his voice harsh, his breathing labored.

Love. Her heart stuttered. And then she gave herself over to surrender, crying out, the sound muffled in the folds of his jacket, as she moved over him, her undulations jerky and frantic, and she came, in long, glorious waves so sweet and so sharp, she wept.

He tightened his hold around her, and she knew from the way his body stiffened that he was joining her.

Crying out just one word, he slid her off him, and gave in to his release.

And even as she reveled in the way his face clenched and rippled as he found his pleasure, and she knew he protected her in ways her mother and his mother hadn't, she mourned that severed connection. Wanted to know what it was to take all of him.

But you don't have that right. He is . . .

"Rafe?"

Her body jerked, passion receding quickly, as that familiar voice called out from the front of the gardens.

"Oh, hell," she whispered, Rafe's heavy breathing, mixed with her own, damning.

She scrambled frantically to her feet, pushing her skirts down, even as Rafe stood, and positioned himself in front of her.

It was too late.

"R . . . *Raafe*?" the duke's question came again, this time hesitant, horrified, and so very near.

The duchess gasped, pressing a hand to her mouth.

Oh, God. Edwina's entire body recoiled from shame, and an even greater horror, and she wanted to hide, wanted the earth to open up and feast on her, so she didn't have to confront . . . the audience standing before them. All in like, silent shock, but for the triumph of a younger gentleman with a crooked nose . . . the lord Rafe had beat down, who'd now had the ultimate triumph. Because . . . the *ton*, of course.

At his side was her brother . . .

And she jerked her gaze away from him, past the gentleman whom her future depended upon, over to the older gentleman before them, a man who was older and grayer but still familiar. She jerked as a different shock knocked the air from her lungs, as she stared slack-jawed—at the man whose carelessness had consigned her to that uncertain future.

Her father.

And Edwina ran . . . past the group who'd born witness to her fall from grace, and continued running, her slippers slick on the grass, until she reached the path, and sent gravel up as she went. Grateful that no one stopped her or called out. Because then there would have to be words exchanged, and more of those looks. The horror-filled ones belonging to Rafe's father and the duchess, and Edwina's own brother . . . and father.

She reached her rooms, panting and out of breath, shoved the door shut behind her, and just stood there. The noisy inhalation and exhalation as she tried to suck in her breath, loud in her ears, mingling with the steady beat of her pulse, both racing, a product more of horror than even the pace she'd set for herself.

She had let her greed destroy her, because once in Rafe's arms hadn't been enough. She'd wanted to steal one more moment, and one more embrace . . . even, as, all the while, she had lied to herself, ultimately knowing in her heart that it would have never been enough. That she wanted . . . forever with him. And in the end, Edwina had done precisely as her mother had done . . . she had thrown away a life of respectability, one that in Edwina's case she had dedicated years to building so that she would not become her mother. Failing to see, until this night, that she had been destined to be her mother, because when she'd found someone such as Rafe, Edwina would have loved as wholly and completely . . . and foolishly, thinking of only him.

She pressed her shaking hands over her face, and worked at the chore that was breathing, taking slow, deep breaths, and counting them as she did.

She'd ruined her future, and she'd ruined Rafe's entrance into the *ton*. As he'd pointed out from the beginning, Polite Society had been destined to question his place among them, to disdain him for his illegitimacy. And what she'd done, this night, was ensure there would only be gossip and scandal.

Edwina choked on a sob.

Yes, they had both come together in that moment of passion, but she had known more than he what was at stake.

Just as she knew she had to leave. There would be no references. There would be nothing but a late-night, hasty flight for a disgraced governess whom all of London would now be speaking about. Letting her arms fall, she gave her head a clearing shake, and proceeded to fetch her trunk. Dragging it over to the painted armoire, Edwina opened the doors, and dedicated all her attention to carefully drawing out each dress. The task proved steadying and distracting. Because when she was focused on neatly stacking each garment, and each pair of slippers, it was time she wasn't thinking about what came next. Concentrating only on the now allowed her control over the immediacy of her life.

Rap-rap-rap.

Her heart hammering, Edwina clutched the mud-stained parasol she'd used in Staffordshire when she'd first met Rafe.

And there had never been a door she had more dreaded opening than this one.

Because there wasn't anyone she wanted to face in this instance. And that included Rafe.

Edwina forced herself to walk the remaining way, and then she brought her shoulders back, and opened the door.

The parasol slipped from her fingers, and tumbled with a quiet *thwack*.

The dark-haired gentleman there bent to retrieve it, but he made no attempt to turn it over. Instead, he studied the forlorn, once-beautiful article a moment.

Edwina's lips moved, but no words were forthcoming. Dumbstruck, she looked at the duchess.

"Lord Rochester explained he was your father, and asked to speak with you," Her Grace explained. "Would that be . . . permissible, Miss Dalrymple?"

Her father.

He'd identified himself as her father? And to a duchess, no less? It didn't make sense. He had gone out of his way to avoid her, and avoid all acknowledgment of his connection to her.

It took a moment to realize the duchess had put a question to her. Asking whether Edwina wished to see the gentleman. Unable to speak, Edwina managed a nod.

The duchess hesitated a moment, and then nodded. "I shall be in the hall."

It was an unexpected offer of . . . support, from a woman who should have greeted Edwina with fury and horror.

The moment she'd gone, and Edwina found herself alone with the marquess, she looked at him.

How long it had been since she'd seen him. He'd visited monthly, for the first years of her life . . . and when he did, he showered Edwina and mother with gifts and baubles. Then, one day, he'd ended it with her mother and proceeded to send on only his financial support. Time had been kind to him. Still dashing, still handsome, his features not-at-all wrinkled, his hair not even showing a hint of gray or white. He was, in short, a likeness of the man who'd said goodbye one last time, and disappeared forever from her life.

Since he'd gone for good, she'd dreamed of this day. She'd longed for it. To see him again. To be reunited. Only to find there wasn't joy in his being here. In seeing him. She'd been so starved for family and friendship that he'd been that link. And what a weak link it had been.

When she'd come to find in Rafe a friend, a lover, one to challenge her and make her look at herself and be better. And to demand better . . . *for* herself.

Her father continued to hold her parasol, eyeing it distractedly, that parasol he had purchased and gifted her. Did he even recall as much? Or had it been simply something a servant had picked out and purchased that he'd come to her with? Those were the questions that had haunted her when he'd gone, and she'd been left with the pretty knickknacks around her and Mama's cottage.

At last, he looked up. "My son indicated that you and he happened upon one another at the museum." A wistful glimmer lit his eyes. "He also has a fascination with ancient—"

"I was working," she said bluntly, cutting him off. The gall of him, finding a tender connection in that moment. "That is all it was." This is what he should come for? To chastise her for being here in London? "He came and sought me out. I did not approach him. I don't—"

"No! You misunderstand. I'm not . . . upset at your being here." He paused. "I have missed you, Edwina," he spoke quietly. He always had. He'd been more serious where her mother had been a burst of sunshine who'd managed to make him laugh, and Edwina along with them.

She flinched. Of everything he might have said, that had certainly not been what she wanted to hear. "Yes, well, pardon me if I do not necessarily believe you." And a lifetime of bitterness she'd not even realized she'd carried inside brought her words out sharply.

His features twisted. "I am deserving of that."

Yes, he was. That and more.

"I didn't know your mother died."

"You should have. She loved you." She'd loved him more than he'd ever deserved.

"And I loved her—"

Edwina made a sound of protest, and covered her ears to stamp out his lies. "Don't do that. You did not love her. You didn't love either of us."

"I did," he entreated her.

She glared at him. "Then not enough."

All along, she'd been searching for this man's approval, wanting his praise. Wanting him to accept her. To love her. Rafe had helped her to see that the marquess had never been deserving of any of that.

"Did you know I came to you upon her death?" she demanded. "When you sent your son to meet me?" *My brother.* "More money. You always were free with your funds." And that would have been enough for many. All most bastards would ask for. But she'd wanted more. She'd deserved more. She'd deserved to be cared for and loved.

He scraped a hand through his hair, tousling those black strands. "My wife was sick. I was . . ."

"Riddled with grief?" she supplied, taunting him. "Unlike when my mother died?"

"I carried guilt. Much of it." He took a step toward her, and she automatically retreated. The marquess stopped. "It is no excuse, Edwina. My love was first and always to your mother. My guilt came from marrying where I shouldn't have, marrying a woman who always knew my love belonged to another. When she fell ill, it led me to end my arrangement with your mother."

Arrangement.

He'd come to a cottage and bedded her and played a

devoted lover for a handful of days each month, before going on his way to his real life.

She hugged her arms around her middle.

"I vowed to be loyal to my wife, Edwina, and care for you still. That was the best I could offer all of you."

Loyal to his wife. "How admirable of you. Thank you for the . . . funds."

His features crumpled. He dropped his gaze to the parasol once more, and he passed the article back and forth between his gloved hands. At last, he looked up. "I know forgiveness will not come easy, but I wish to make amends. I want to have you in my life. I want to claim you outright as my daughter, as I should have done, long ago. You shouldn't have had to work as you have."

"I've enjoyed what I've done. I did it myself," she said, lifting her chin up in defiance.

"I am proud of that." He turned a palm up, as if willing her to believe the sincerity of that admission. "But you shouldn't know struggle and you certainly shouldn't . . . shouldn't . . ." Color flooded his cheeks.

Edwina scrunched her toes up tight as she was presented with the closest thing to words of what she'd done . . . what she'd been caught doing. And her father had been witness to her scandal.

"Come home with me, Edwina," her father murmured. "Please."

There it was.

It was all she'd ever wished for.

Acceptance.

And following her scandal, and the end of her career . . . he offered something more: security.

He might have failed her in the past, but he was offering to save her now.

And yet, staring back at him, she found herself thinking of what she truly wanted now—Rafe.

Chapter 24

For almost thirty-one years of his life, Rafe had gone without knowing his father.

When he'd been a boy, however, he'd dreamed of having a relationship with him . . . that unknown duke his mother had simultaneously sung the praises of and wept from the pain of missing. In those earliest years, even hating the Duke of Bentley as he had, Rafe had imagined a world in which he was a son in every sense of the word. In those wonderings, there would have been a father to laugh with, and learn from . . . and he'd been so desperate to know all of that intangible relationship that he'd even welcomed and fancied the idea of a father whose disapproval he'd earned, and the lectures that would come.

Only to find out a lifetime later, in his father's office, faced with the duke's damning silence, just how miserable the moment in fact was.

Not that Bentley's or any man's shame and disappointment could be any greater than that which knifed at Rafe now.

Standing in the middle of the duke's office, with his

hands clasped behind him, Rafe directed his gaze at his father. Or in this case, his father's back.

The duke considered the tray of bottles on his sideboard, hovering briefly over a decanter of brandy, before ultimately bypassing it for the stronger whiskey.

It was the choice Rafe himself would have made, if he'd been in a frame of mind to consume spirits. Because the situation certainly called for it.

She'd been ruined. And he well knew the future and fate that awaited a ruined woman. His mother had been one.

It was what Edwina had feared above all else, and had sought to protect herself against. Only to find herself destroyed, because of Rafe.

And the truth of that ravaged him.

Setting down the bottle, and with two whiskeys in hand, his father came forward.

"I'm not looking to have a discussion," Rafe said tightly. "I want to see Edwina." Nay, he needed to see her.

The moment he'd caught her stricken expression, and watched as she'd taken flight, he'd wanted to set out after her.

"Sit, Rafe."

Rafe flexed his jaw. "I don't have time to talk to you about this."

"I said, 'sit down,' Rafe," his father said again, when Rafe made to leave. "No good will come from you flying after her, to her rooms, without talking this through, and thinking this through."

Talking this through? Thinking this through?

What was there to think through? He'd ruined Edwina. And he would be damned if Edwina suffered that same existence.

"Please," his father said quietly, and this time, Rafe crossed over, jerked the chair out, and sat.

Bentley joined him, offering one of the whiskeys.

Rafe ignored that offering. "I don't need a lecture," he cut in, before the other man could speak, and lecture or scold or sway Rafe.

"Well, that is fortunate, as I don't have a lecture to give." The ghost of a smile hovered on the duke's lips. "I'm hardly the one to be lecturing anyone, particularly you, on just why it was wrong for you to be meeting Miss Dalrymple, alone, and engaging . . . as you were."

Rafe winced. "Yes, well, you managed to get that in, anyway."

"Yes, I thought I might attempt to have a"—Bentley held an index finger and thumb, a bare fraction of a hair apart—"very small piece said."

Rafe sat back, and dropping an elbow on the arm of the chair, he rested his forehead in his hand, and rubbed at a swift-developing headache. What a damned mess.

"When I met your mother," the duke began quietly, and startlingly, "I was . . . captivated. I was young. I'd just suffered a broken heart, and desperately needed a distraction. But . . . she was a friend, one whom I confided in, and who eventually became . . . more. I told her it was a terrible idea for us to alter our relationship. I told her I couldn't give her more because I'd loved another and was incapable of feeling that depth of emotion again. She insisted she didn't want more. And I . . . allowed myself to believe that mayhap she meant it. Because it was easier. Because I cared for her. And . . . I lost a lifetime of happiness for it . . . just as I undoubtedly cost your mother much happiness."

It didn't escape Rafe's notice that love was not mentioned. Not in terms of Rafe's mother, and given what the duke shared just then, it also served as a revelation as to why she'd not confided in him about her children. Why she'd gone to London, and accepted the carefree entanglement he sought, before returning to Rafe and, eventually, the siblings he had. "I don't see how this has anything to do with . . ."

"What has passed between you and Miss Dalrymple . . . ?"

"I'm going to marry her," Rafe said bluntly.

He braced for the outrage.

That didn't come. Instead, his pronouncement was met with a calm curiosity. "Why?"

Why . . . ?

Rafe paused.

"I don't have much advice to impart, but what I will tell you is this. I always did that which was expected of me by society. My best friend fell in love with the same woman I did . . . first. And I thought honor dictated that I let her go. I could have been happy with your mother, and yet I didn't marry her because of the expectations imposed by society." Setting down his drink, the duke leaned forward. "Instead, in my first marriage, I wed where there was no love and no affection and I was . . . miserable for it."

"You would be an immoral cad to urge me to leave her to her own mercy." Rafe peeled his lip in a sneer. "I am not you. I would never abandon her. I . . ." *Love her too much for that.*

Rafe froze. His heart knocked around in his chest.

I love her.

Of course he did. It was . . . all that really made sense. He suspected he'd fallen head over heels for her the moment she came sauntering into his coalfield, waving that silly parasol.

"Rafe?" He stared blankly at his father. "Rafe?"

He gave his head a clearing shake. He felt as if he'd been flipped and then turned upside down. "I'm sorry, what?"

"I'm not encouraging you to abandon her. Quite the opposite. I have seen the way you and Miss Dalrymple are with one another, and I'm encouraging you, if you care for her, as I suspect you do, to not be the stubborn man I was."

No, he was a better man than his father. And he knew his heart, and he knew his mind. Rafe stood.

"There is something I should mention."

"What?" he asked when the duke didn't immediately speak.

"The elder gentleman who served as witness to the . . . to the . . . scandal in the gardens tonight, the same one Lydia escorted off"—Rafe didn't give a damn about any of the people who'd been present beyond one—Edwina—"he is an acquaintance."

And yet Rafe's ears pricked up, as he intuitively heard more there. "What?" Rafe demanded.

"He is . . . also Miss Dalrymple's father."

Rafe stiffened, as silence rolled over the room.

That person . . . did matter. To Edwina. The man who'd failed her. Whose love and admiration she'd sought, when she'd always been too good for him. And yet, even as Rafe had known as much, Edwina had cared so very much for the man's approval . . . and she'd wished to live the life that had been denied her. "What?" he asked dumbly, sinking back into the seat.

A knock sounded at the door, and Rafe was grateful for that interruption as he tried to put his disordered thoughts back together.

He dimly registered his father calling out a greeting to the duchess.

She came over and claimed the chair beside Rafe. "Lord Rochester asked to speak in private with Edwina," she said quietly, without preamble, with a directness that normally would have made sense to him, but now he struggled to keep up.

"For what end?" Rafe managed to make himself ask.

"He has asked Edwina to leave with him, so that she might have a life here in London . . . as part of his family," the duchess explained.

There it was.

It was all Edwina had ever wanted, that recognition. Acknowledgment from her father. And it didn't matter what Rafe thought of the heartless cad; it was about what Edwina wished for.

"And he invited her to go with him this evening."

"What?" he blurted out.

The duke and duchess exchanged a look.

"Now?" Rafe demanded, when neither of them spoke.

"Given the circumstances, he thought it best for Miss Dalrymple's reputation if she—"

Rafe was already out of his chair. "To hell with the circumstances," he hissed.

"—return with him. And he'd not have you feel obligated—"

Rafe saw red. "*Obligated*?" he echoed. It wasn't about obligation. Yes, there was of course the sense of wanting to do right by her. But that was not what had driven him to her this night. That was the need to be with her. And see her. And— "Where is she?" he demanded.

"She accompanied the marquess to his carriage . . ."

The man was a stranger, and yet, he was also the one whom she'd wanted a life with. She'd wished for the man's acknowledgment. And now, she'd been invited to reside there with that marquess. It was everything she wanted. And therefore, he should be relieved: one, that she had what she wished for. And two . . .

No, there was no "two."

With a curse, Rafe took off running.

The duke laughed. "And that, son," he called after him, "is why you marry her."

His heart pounding, Rafe sprinted from his father's office and bolted down the hall for the front doors. Needing to stop her.

To stop this.

To tell her he loved her. To tell her that he wanted her happy above all else, and if that meant her leaving to live a respectable life with her father, and having the life she'd dreamed, then he'd let her to it. Even as it would destroy him.

The butler stood in wait, opening the doors as if it were the most normal thing in the world for people to go flying out that exit. "Rochester—"

The servant pointed to the pink-lacquered carriage.

It would be a damned pink carriage, too. Rafe had to compete with that. An older gentleman stood beside Edwina. Edwina . . . with her back to him, and her foot in that damned pink carriage, and—

Rafe bolted down the steps, his gaze on that pair preparing to leave. *When Satan sits with God himself for tea.* "Yoo-hoo!" he shouted, that greeting she'd called out to him in Staffordshire once-upon-a-lifetime-ago. "Miss Dalrymple." Edwina's back tensed, and then ever so slowly she turned.

Surprise rounded her features.

Surprise? How could it be such a shock to her that he'd come after her?

Perhaps, because you never gave her any indication of how you truly felt.

Because he'd been so damned bad at emotions and laughter and . . . all of it. Until her.

She said something to the marquess. Edwina's father hesitated. Then, with a nod, he entered the carriage.

When he'd gone, Edwina faced Rafe once more. "Are you looking for me?" she asked softly, her words an echo of his own at their first meeting.

Was he looking for her? All along, she'd been everything he'd never known he needed. "You just . . . *left.*"

She bit at her lip, troubling that flesh, and briefly studying the pavement. "It seemed . . . for the best."

Rafe searched each cherished plain of her heart-shaped face. How could she ever think that was for the best? Except . . . what if it was the best of what she wanted? "I know you have waited for this moment, and I want that for you . . . if that is what you truly want." Even as it would destroy him to lose her completely. "And I cannot . . . compete with . . ." He waved a hand at the carriage. "This. This, what you have wanted your whole life." Rafe reached inside his jacket; Edwina's eyes following his every movement, and he withdrew the small pink notebook he kept there.

She shook her head in confusion. "What is that?"

"It is called a notebook," he said in another echo of her words to him from the day they left Staffordshire. "*My* notebook." Rafe licked the tip of his finger and turned to the first page. "Fortunately, I once had a wise instructor."

"Did you?" she whispered.

"Oh, yes." He paused; he held her eyes with his, hers red with tears that she'd shed at some point, ravaging him inside. "You see, she advised me to fill the pages with the most important details of our time together." He held the book in one hand. "And I did . . . and the thing of it is, Edwina, all those pages . . . came to be about you."

"About me?"

"You see, it was as you said. I learned from recording my thoughts, Edwina. I recorded every thought of you, everything I loved, everything that made me laugh and smile and frustrated me and intrigued me."

She sucked in a quavering little breath.

Rafe stared over the top of the page, the words there, long memorized. "'I have never known a person more clever and witty, who makes me think more, and about things I've never before thought of.'"

Her lower lip trembled.

"I learned there are more than a hundred different smiles, because you showed them to me—the ones that light your eyes and dimple your cheeks when you're truly happy, or the ones that hide upon your lips, as if you have the grandest secret, that makes a man yearn to know."

"You have many smiles, t-too." Her voice caught.

Emotion filled his throat, and he swallowed past it, looking at her squarely. "That is because of you. That is one more lesson you gave; you taught me to smile, too. When I didn't realize I needed to or wanted to."

Tears gleamed in her eyes.

Rafe continued, "I learned you are a woman of strength and resilience, unafraid and unwilling to take no for an answer."

"But you said you resented th-that," she said, brushing back a lone tear that found a winding path down her cheek.

"Ah," Rafe lifted a finger, and then quickly turned the page. "'She is a remarkable teacher, filling every moment of every day with some teaching. I'm a fool. That message was delivered and received many times.'"

She made a sound of protest.

"Uh-uh," he wagged a finger. "Do not go lying to me now, princess."

Another watery smile formed on her lips.

"You taught me what a fool I was and have been . . . about

so much." He let his arm fall to his side. "About so damned much," he said hoarsely. "All of it, where you were concerned. I have been a fool, fighting you along the entire way, but I love you, Edwina Dalrymple." Rafe continued over her gasp, "I love everything about you, from how you sing bawdy tavern songs to the way you make a flawless bed."

A half laugh, half sob burst from her lips, and she pressed her hands to her face; that joyous sound left him buoyant inside. "I even love the way you slice a damned strawberry, Edwina." He held the book out to Edwina, and she accepted it almost reverently, drawing it close to her chest. "You can take this and go, reading through all the ways in which I love you and appreciate you." Tears stung his eyes. "However, I would dearly love it if you remain by my side and marry me so that I can spend the rest of my days *showing* you all the ways I love you, and—"

On a sob, Edwina threw herself against him, clutching the pink notebook in one hand, while the other she wrapped about his nape, and drew his mouth to hers for a kiss.

Edwina drew back. "Are you asking me to marry you, Rafe Audley?" she whispered.

Rafe touched his brow to hers. "I was going to before you went and kissed me, Miss Dalrymple."

She smoothed her features, her face a study in mock solemnity. "My apologies. As you were, Mr. Audley."

He caressed her satin-soft cheek with his palm, and she leaned into his touch. "Spend forever with me?" he asked, his voice hoarse from the hungering that came at the mere thought of that dream.

Edwina nodded, her tears falling once more. "Forever," she vowed, and Rafe swept her into his arms, their laughter mingling.

Forever.

ACKNOWLEDGMENTS

All the Duke's Sins was a series I'd dreamed of telling . . . for years.

To my agent, Kim Witherspoon, who encouraged me to pursue the dream I'd always carried, of seeing Rafe and Edwina in print, and to my wonderful editors, Sarah Blumenstock and Cindy Hwang, for making it come true . . . I am so very grateful to each of you!

Ready to find
your next great read?

Let us help.

Visit prh.com/nextread

Penguin
Random
House